NEW YORK REVIEW BOOKS

CLASSICS

THE STORIES OF
J. F. POWERS

J. F. POWERS (1917–1999) was born in Jacksonville, Illinois, and studied at Northwestern University while holding a variety of jobs in Chicago and working on his writing. He published his first stories in *The Catholic Worker* and, as a pacifist, spent thirteen months in prison during World War II. Powers was the author of three collections of short stories and two novels—*Morte D'Urban*, which won the National Book Award, and *Wheat That Springeth Green*—all of which have been reissued by New York Review Books. He lived in Ireland and the United States and taught for many years at St John's University in Collegeville, Minnesota.

DENIS DONOGHUE is University Professor at New York University, where he holds the Henry James Chair of English and American Letters. He is the author of many books, including *Connoisseurs of Chaos*, *Reading America*, *We Irish*, and *Walter Pater: Lover of Strange Souls.*

THE STORIES OF
J. F. POWERS

■

Introduction by

DENIS DONOGHUE

NEW YORK REVIEW BOOKS

New York

THIS IS A NEW YORK REVIEW BOOK
PUBLISHED BY THE NEW YORK REVIEW OF BOOKS

This edition published in 2000 in the United States of America by
The New York Review of Books
435 Hudson Street
New York, NY 10014
www.nyrb.com

5 7 9 10 8 6 4

Library of Congress Cataloging-in-Publication Data

Powers, J. F. (James Farl), 1917–
    [Short Stories]
    Collected Stories / by J. F. Powers ; introduction by Denis Donoghue
        p.   cm.
    ISBN 0-940322-22-6 (acid-free paper)
    1. Catholic Church—Middle West—Clergy—Fiction. 2. Middle West
—Religious life and customs—Fiction. 3. Middle West—Social life and
customs—Fiction. 4. United States—Social life and customs—20th
century —Fiction. I. Donoghue, Denis. II. Title.
    PS3566.O84 A6 2000
    813'.54—dc 21   99-047885

ISBN 978-0-940322-22-6

Printed in the United States of America on acid-free paper.

CONTENTS

INTRODUCTION

H E W A S James Farl Powers on his birth certificate and Jim Powers to his friends. In the history of modern fiction J. F. Powers (1917–1999) was a distinctive figure, a loner, emerging from quietness every few years when he published a book or won a prize, but otherwise content to mind his own professional business. He is sometimes described as a writer's writer, meaning that he was an artist too good to gratify the most casual reader, but he was also a reader's writer, if we assume a reader who thinks of fiction as intelligent art rather than low entertainment. Such writers tend not to be abundant, they work hard on their sentences. Powers published only a few books—three collections of short stories, *Prince of Darkness, and Other Stories* (1947), *The Presence of Grace* (1956), and *Look How the Fish Live* (1975), the contents of which have been gathered in this volume, and two novels, *Morte D'Urban* (1962) and *Wheat that Springeth Green* (1988). But these are treasured, guarded with jealousy by those who know of them. News of their quality is passed from one adept to another, like word of an idyllic village in an unfashionable part of France, not to be disclosed to the ordinary camera-flashing tourist. Now that Powers is dead, he has become his admirers, as W. H. Auden said of the poet Yeats.

I met Powers only once. He and his wife and children lived for several years in Ireland, in a small seaside town about seventeen miles south of Dublin called Greystones. (It is clearly the Ballydoo of his short story "Tinkers.") He rarely left the town, even to sample the joys of Dublin. But he became friends with the Irish novelist and short-story writer Sean O'Faolain, who lived a few miles away in an even more salubrious place, Killiney. I lived in Mount Merrion, a suburb on the south side of Dublin. My social life was meager, so I accepted with enthusiasm an invitation from O'Faolain to come to lunch in Killiney. Jim Powers would be there.

I reached Killiney rather early. Before Powers arrived, O'Faolain passed the time making mild fun of him. Did I know that Powers spent the morning putting in a comma and the afternoon wondering whether or not he should replace it with a semicolon? O'Faolain's teasing didn't stop when Powers rang the doorbell. "I've been telling Donoghue about your attentiveness to commas and semicolons." Powers smiled and indicated by his silence that he was not inclined to argue the question. O'Faolain was an amiable host, and a good writer when he cared to be, but I'm sure he never worried about the relative merits of a comma and a semicolon. It was said that he wrote two thousand words a day whether he felt well or ill. I recall nothing of the conversation at lunch, beyond an impression that O'Faolain, his wife Eileen, and I talked a lot and to no memorable purpose. Powers nodded his head from time to time, either in agreement on the point being made or to indicate the degree of his indifference to the issue.

Morte D'Urban won the National Book Award in 1963 and gained for Powers recognition as a novelist. But he seems to me by native gift a short-story writer. I recall getting a letter from the poet William Carlos Williams in which he said that writers have each their own natural breath. Some take short breaths, others long. Whitman took long breaths, Emily Dickinson short ones. It required talent to judge what your natural form of breathing was. I think Powers knew that his native breath was that of the short story. He tried for the longer breath of the novel twice because, I assume, he wanted to deal with a bigger cast of characters and a wider screen. But I think his talent was happiest in the concentration, the focus, of the short story. It was as if he thought life most clearly disclosed in the telling anecdote.

In one of the prefaces to the New York edition of his fiction, Henry James spoke of his experience in writing short stories. He recalled that his "struggle to keep compression rich, if not, better still, to keep accretions compressed, betrayed for me such community with the anxious effort of some warden of the insane engaged at a critical moment in making fast a victim's straitjacket." James was exhilarated by the restriction. He was stirred by the necessity of "treating a theme that 'gave' much in a form that, at the best, would give little." He was inclined to follow the anecdote from which the little story arose "as much as possible from its outer edge in, rather than from its center outward." He accepted the anecdote for what it was, trying always to keep the possible accretions compressed.

Powers observed the same formal policy. The outer edge was for him the everyday visible world, full of rectories, priests, housekeepers, cars, cats, parishioners. The center, however, bristled with little disclosures, nuances of personality, prejudice, and mood. In "The Valiant Woman" Father Firman wants to get rid of his housekeeper, Mrs Stoner. She is a holy terror, a predictable aggravation, runs his life for him, gives him minor hell. But he knows that he can't get rid of her. The oppressive thought occurs to him that she treats him as if she were his wife; except that she sleeps in the guest room. Every evening, before going to bed, they play cards: "the final murderous hour in which all they wanted to say—all he wouldn't and all she couldn't—came out in the cards." Mrs Stoner always wins. "Skunked you! . . . Had enough, huh!" From the outside in: all the possibilities are contained in the scene as given, including the rage with which Father Firman, in his bedroom last thing one night, tries to swat a mosquito, misses, and smashes the statue of St Joseph on the bookcase. Powers compresses the embarrassments of a lifetime into a few episodes. The story he tells is not just short; it delights in its brevity.

The tragicomedy of these stories about priests arises from a further constraint that Powers imposes on himself. The priests are shown in the world, quarreling with their colleagues and pastors, grubbing for money, angling for promotion, playing golf, drinking beer, passing the time. If they have an intense spiritual life, we are not shown it. We are not told what it means that as young men they responded to a vocation, a calling. We don't see them in their relation to God. Might they just as well have become insurance agents? Not quite. French fiction on similar themes—that of Mauriac, Bernanos's *Diary of a Country Priest*—is deeply preoccupied with the inner life, with consciences, temptations, and doubts, with religious and moral scruples. But in Powers's stories and novels the spiritual atmosphere is entirely different; it is not expressed but implied. His priests are small people in a big world, and he never forgets the spaciousness of that world, so strongly felt in the Midwest where many of the stories are set, in his concentration upon them. But they are not little in the eyes of God. Powers impresses upon us that no matter how commonplace or compromised the priest there is still a relation between him and the Christian vision he has acknowledged.

In "One of Them" the curate, Father Simpson, has long tried to extract from the pastor a spare key for the front door of the rectory. The pastor is going away for a few days, and the question of a key arises again over the dinner table. As usual, the pastor has left an edifying pamphlet on Father Simpson's plate, without comment:

> "Father," said Simpson, coming to dessert, and remembering how he'd phrased the question before ("Father, how long will you be gone?") rephrased it, "will you be gone long?"
>
> "Not long," said the pastor, as before.
>
> "Father," said Simpson when he'd eaten his peaches, "while you're away, if I have to go out at night—hospital or something—and the church is locked, I can knock or ring, I know, but I'd hate to disturb Ms Burke, if you know what I mean, Father?"
>
> The pastor nodded, as if he did know, but bowed his head in silent grace.
>
> So did Simpson then, and, when they rose from the table, did not forget the pamphlet by his plate. "So I should knock or ring, Father?"
>
> "Ring," said the pastor.

It is the priests' pretense that every constituent of their lives is transparent that gives this exchange its comic poignancy: "... but bowed his head in silent grace." Look how the fish live: look how the priests live. What has happened to the impulses and the spiritual visitations, the qualms and scruples, that must have directed curate and pastor in earlier years toward the priesthood? And now they are embroiled in a little play of power about a key. Was it for this that Christ was crucified and Paul set up a church? James, in writing "The Turn of the Screw," determined that instead of supplying instances of the evil deeds of Peter Quint and Miss Jessel, he would "make the reader *think* the evil." "Make him think it for himself, and you are released from weak specifications." Similarly, Powers—precisely by keeping everything he shows visible, external, and conventional—makes the reader think the forces that are not on show, the spiritual experiences that started out so compellingly and have issued in these penuries.

Not all of these stories are about priests. My favorite story, "Renner," is entirely secular: we are shown an eating house in a Midwestern city. There are seven characters: the narrator, his colleague Renner, the waiter Emil, a patron named Ross, a not-entirely-sober Irishman, a German, and "the fat one." Nothing much happens, there is no plot, there are no dramatic climaxes or crises. Some of the characters are merely playing cards at a table. They are nearly anonymous. But they, and the lives they lead, are revealed by small gestures and silences, minute changes of tone. It is not a typical story of Powers's. His talent may have been startled to find itself taking this form. But the story is, in its quiet way, thrilling. The first time I read it, I knew I was reading the work of a master. A work of literature is a book you'd be happy to read again and again—like the book in your hand.

—DENIS DONOGHUE

THE STORIES
OF
J. F. POWERS

THE LORD'S DAY

THE TREES HAD the bad luck to be born mulberry and to attract bees. It was not the first time, Father said, and so you could not say he was being unfair. It was, in fact, the second time that a bee had come up and stung him on the front porch. What if it had been a wasp? How did he know it was one of the mulberry bees? He knew. That was all. And now, Sister, if you'll just take the others into the house with you, we'll get down to work. She had ordered the others into the convent, but had stayed to plead privately for the trees. The three big ones must go. He would spare the small one until such time as it grew up and became a menace.

Adjusting the shade, which let the sun through in withered cracks like the rivers on a map, she peeked out at the baking schoolyard, at the three trees. Waves of heat wandered thirstily over the pebbles, led around by the uncertain wind. She could see the figure of Father walking the heat waves, a fat vision in black returning to the scene of the crime, grabbing the axe away from the janitor . . . Here, John, let me give her the first lick! . . . And so, possibly fancying himself a hundred years back, the most notable person at the birth of a canal or railroad, and with the children for his amazed audience, he had dealt the first blow. Incredible priest!

She left the room and went downstairs. They were waiting in the parlor. She knew at a glance that one was missing. Besides herself, they were twelve—the apostles. It was the kind of joke they could appreciate, but not to be carried too far, for then one of them must be Judas, which was not funny. In the same way she, as the leader of the apostles, feared the implication as blasphemous. It was not a very good joke for the convent, but it was fine to tell lay people, to let them know there was life there.

She entered the little chapel off the parlor. Here the rug was thicker and the same wide-board floor made to shine. She knelt for a moment and then, genuflecting in the easy, jointless way that comes from years of it, she left. Sister Eleanor, the one missing, followed her into the parlor.

"All right, Sisters, let's go." She led them through the sagging house, which daily surpassed itself in gloominess and was only too clean and crowded not to seem haunted, and over the splintery floor rising and sinking underfoot like a raft. She opened the back door and waited for them to pass. She thought of herself as a turnkey releasing them briefly to the sun and then to their common, sudden doom. They proceeded silently across the schoolyard, past the stumps bleeding sap, the bright chips dirtying in the gravel, a few twigs folded in death.

Going under the basketball standards she thought they needed only a raven or two to become gibbets in the burning sun. A pebble lit in the lacings of her shoe. She stopped to free it. She believed she preferred honest dust to manufactured pebbles. Dust lent itself to philosophizing and was easier on the children's knees.

They climbed the cement steps, parting the dish towels on

the porch as portieres, and entered the rectory. The towels were dry and the housekeeper would be gone. She sensed a little longing circulate among the sisters as they filed into the kitchen. It was all modern, the *after* for the *before* they would always have at the convent. She did not care for it, however. It hurt the eyes, like a field of sunny snow. A cockroach turned around and ran the other way on the sink. At least he was not modern.

The dining room was still groggy from Sunday dinner. They drew chairs up to the table in which the housekeeper had inserted extra leaves before taking the afternoon off. The table was covered with the soiled cloth that two of them would be washing tomorrow. They sighed. There, in the middle of the table, in canvas sacks the size of mailbags, were the day's three collections, the ledgers and index cards for recording individual contributions. They sat down to count.

With them all sitting around the table, it seemed the time for her to pray, "Bless us, O Lord, and these Thy gifts . . ."

Sister Antonia, her assistant, seized one of the sacks and emptied it out on the table. "Come on, you money-changers, dig in!" Sister Antonia rammed her red hands into the pile and leveled it off. "Money, money, money."

"Shall we do what we did last week?" asked Sister Florence. She looked hopefully at Sister Antonia.

"Cubs and White Sox?" said Sister Antonia. "O.K., if it'll make you happy." Sister Antonia dumped out the other sack. The winner would be the one counting the most money. They chose up sides and changed seats accordingly, leaving Sister Antonia and herself to do the envelopes.

Sister Louise and Sister Paula, who could remember several regimes before hers and might have been mothers superior themselves, constituted a resistance movement, each in her fashion. Sister Louise went to sleep in a nice, unobtrusive way, chin in wimple. But Sister Paula—Sister Cigar Box to the children, with whom she was *not* a great favorite—stayed awake to grumble and would touch only the coins that appeared old, foreign, or very new to her. She stared long and hard at them while Sister Louise dozed with a handful of sweaty nickels.

It was their way of informing everyone of their disapproval, of letting her know it had not been like this in former times, that Sunday had been a day of rest under other leadership. They were right, she knew too well, and was ashamed that she could not bring herself to make a stand against Father. Fortunately, the two old sisters could not carry the resistance beyond themselves. She left them to Sister Antonia. The others, to make the contest even, divided the dead weight between them. The Cubs got Sister Louise and Sister Paula went with the White Sox.

A horn tooted out in front of the rectory, and from his room upstairs young Father shouted, "*Cominnggg!* Tell him I'm coming!" The shout sailed down the stairway and out to Father on the porch.

"He's coming," Father called to the car. "How's your health?"

She could not catch the reply for the noise young Father made running around upstairs. He had on his shower clogs and was such a heavy man.

Finally the ceiling settled, and young Father came clattering down the front stairs, dragging his golf clubs behind him. He spoke to Father on the porch.

"Want me home for Devotions, Father?"

"Oh hell, Bill, have a good time. Won't anybody come in weather like this but the nuns. I'll handle it."

"Well—thanks, Boss."

"Look out for that nineteenth hole; that's all I got to say. Have a good time."

"You talked me into it."

Sister Cigar Box dropped a half dollar from an unnecessary height and listened to the ring. "Lead! And I suppose that was that Father O'Mammon in his new machine out waking the dead! I'm on to him. I had him in school."

"O'Hannon, Sister," corrected Sister Antonia.

"Of St Judas's parish. I know."

"Of St Jude's, Sister."

"Crazy!"

Father's radio woke up with a roar.

"The symphony!" breathed Sister Charlotte, who gave piano lessons to beginners six days a week.

"It's nice," Sister Cigar Box rasped when Father dialed away from it. "Wasn't it?"

Now Father was getting the news and disputing with the commentator. "Like hell you say!" Father had the last word and strode into the dining room with his collar off, bristling.

"Good afternoon, Father!" they all sang out.

"We'll have to fight Russia," he said, plunging into the kitchen. She heard him in the refrigerator and could tell that, rather than move things, he squeezed them out. He passed through the dining room, carrying a bottle of beer and a glass.

"Hot," he said to nobody.

The radio came on again. Father listened to an inning of the ball game. "Cubs are still in second place!" he shouted back to them.

"Thank you, Father," said Sister Florence involuntarily.

Sister Cigar Box said, "Humph!"

Now she could tell from the scraping noises that Father was playing himself a game of checkers. Periodically the moves became more rapid, frenzied, then triumphant. He was winning every game.

She asked Sister Eleanor how the map was coming.

"All in except Rhode Island and Tennessee. I don't know what's keeping them." They all knew Sister Eleanor was putting together a map from free road maps she got from the oil companies. She had been unable to get an appropriation from

Father for a new one. He said they had a map already and that he had seen it a few years back. She had tried to tell him it was too old and blurry, that Arizona and Oklahoma, for instance, had now been admitted to the Union. Who cares about them? said Father. Give the kids a general idea—that's all you can do in the grades. Same as you give them catechism. You'd have them all studying Saint Thomas in the Latin.

"How big's it now?" asked Sister Antonia.

"Enormous. We'll have to put it up in sections, I guess. Like the Eastern states, the Middle Atlantic, and so on."

"You could hang it in the gym."

"If Father moved out his workshop."

"Some of the maps don't dovetail when they come from different companies. But you get detail you wouldn't get in a regular map. It's just awkward this way."

Father appeared in the door of the dining room. "How's she look?"

"More envelopes this week, Father," said Sister Antonia.

"Guess that last blast got them. How's the hardware department?"

Three sisters saw each other about to speak, gulped, and said nothing. "It's better, isn't it, Sister?" inquired Sister Antonia.

"Yes, Sister."

Father came over to the table. "What's this?" He picked up a Chinese coin with a hole in it that Sister Cigar Box had been glad to see earlier. "Well, we don't get so many buttons nowadays, do we?" Father's fingers prowled the money pile sensitively.

"No, Father," said Sister Florence. "One last week, one today." She looked like a small girl who's just spoken her piece.

"One again, huh? Have to tell the ushers to bear down. Here, Sister, you keep this." Father gave the Chinese coin to Sister Cigar Box. "For when you go on the missions."

Sister Cigar Box took the coin from him and said nothing—

about the only one not smiling—and put it down a trifle hard on the table.

Father went over to the buffet. "Like apples? Who wants an apple?" He apparently expected them to raise their hands but did not seem disappointed when no one did. He placed the bowl on the table for them. Three apples on top were real, but the ones underneath were wax and appeared more edible. No one took an apple.

"Don't be bashful," Father said, straying into the kitchen.

She heard him in the refrigerator again.

In a moment he came out of the kitchen with a bottle of beer and a fresh glass, passed quickly through the room, and, hesitating at the door, turned toward them. "Hot weather," he said. "Makes you sleepy. That's all I got to say." He left them for the porch.

The radio went on again. He had the Catholic Hour for about a minute. "Bum speaker," he explained while dialing. "Else I'd keep it on. I'll try to get it for you next week. They're starting a new series."

"Yes, Father," said Sister Florence, not loud enough to be heard beyond the table.

Sister Cigar Box said, "Humph!"

Father could be heard pouring the beer.

Next he got "The Adventures of Phobe Smith, the Phantom Psychiatrist." It was better than the ball game and news.

But Phobe, if Muller wasn't killed in the plane crash and Mex was really working for British Intelligence, tell me how the heck could Colonel Barnett be a Jap spy and still look like —uh—the real Colonel Barnett? Plastic surgery. Plastic surgery —well, I never! Plus faricasalicasuki. Plus farica—what! Faricasalicasuki—a concentrate, something like our penicillin. And you knew all the time—! That Colonel Barnett's wife, Darlene, was not . . . unfaithful? Yes! I'm afraid so. Whew!

An organ intervened and Father turned off the radio.

She recorded the last contribution on the last index card. The money was all counted and wrapped in rolls for the bank. The White Sox had won. She told them to wait for her and ventured out on the porch, determined to make up for the afternoon, to show them that she knew, perhaps, what she was doing.

"Father"—he was resting in an orange-and-green deck chair —"I wonder if you could come and look at our stove."

Father pried his legs sideways, sat up, and rubbed his eyes. "Today? *Now?*"

She nodded dumbly and forced herself to go through with it. "It's smoking so we can't use it at all." She was ready, if necessary, to mention the old sisters who were used to hot tea.

Father massaged his bald head to rouse himself. He wrinkled the mottled scalp between his hands and it seemed to make a nasty face at her. "Let's go," he said. Evidently he had decided to be peppy—an example to her in time of adversity. He scooped his collar off the radio and let it snap to around his neck. He left it that way, unfastened.

"Father is going to look at the stove," she told them in the dining room. They murmured with pleasure.

Father went first, a little unsteady on stiff legs, not waiting for them. He passed the stumps in the yard with satisfaction, she thought. "Whyn't you ask John to look at it yesterday?" he demanded over his shoulder.

She tried to gain a step on him, but he was going too fast, wobbling in a straight line like a runaway trolley. "I thought you'd know more about it, Father," she lied, ashamed that the others could hear. John, looking at it, had shaken his head.

"Do we need a new one, John?"

"If you need a stove, Sister, you need a new one."

Father broke into their kitchen as into a roomful of assassins, and confronted the glowering hulk of iron that was their stove. "Is it dirty or does it just look that way?"

She swallowed her temper, but with such bad grace there was no merit in it, only design. She gave the others such a terrible frown they all disappeared, even Sister Antonia.

Father squinted to read the name on the stove. "That stove cost a lot of money," he said. "They don't make them like that anymore." He slapped the pipe going up and through the side of the wall. He gave the draft regulator a twist.

He went to the window and peered out. When he turned around he had the print of the screen on his nose. She would not say anything to distract him. He seemed to be thinking. Then he considered the stove again and appeared to have his mind made up. He faced her.

"The stove's all right, Sister. It won't draw properly, is all."

"I know, Father, but—"

"That tree," he said, pointing through the wall at the small tree which had been spared, "is blocking the draft. If you want your stove to work properly, it'll have to come down. That's all I got to say."

He squinted to read the name on the stove again.

She felt the blood assembling in patches on her cheeks. "Thank you, Father," she said, and went quickly out of the kitchen, only wanting to get upstairs and wash the money off her hands.

THE TROUBLE

*Neither the slavers' whip nor the lynchers' rope nor the
bayonet could kill our black belief.*

—MARGARET WALKER, *FOR MY PEOPLE*

WE WATCHED AT the window all that afternoon. Old
Gramma came out of her room and said, "Now you kids get
away from there this minute." And we would until she went
back to her room. We could hear her old rocking chair creak
when she got up or sat down, and so we always ran away from
the window before she came into the room to see if we were
minding her good or looking out. Except once she went back
to her room and didn't sit down, or maybe she did and got up
easy so the chair didn't creak, or maybe we got our signals
mixed, because she caught us all there and shooed us away and
pulled down the green shade. The next time we were real sure
she wasn't foxing us before we went to the window and lifted
the shade just enough to peek out.

It was like waiting for rats as big as cats to run out from under a tenement so you could pick them off with a .22. Rats are about the biggest live game you can find in ordinary times and you see more of them than white folks in our neighborhood—in ordinary times. But the rats we waited for today were white ones, and they were doing most of the shooting themselves. Sometimes some coloreds would come by with guns, but not often; they mostly had clubs. This morning we'd seen the whites catch up with a shot-in-the-leg colored and throw bricks and stones at his black head till it got all red and he was dead. I could still see the wet places in the alley. That's why we kept looking out the window. We wanted to see some whites get killed for a change, but we didn't much think we would, and I guess what we really expected to see was nothing, or maybe them killing another colored.

There was a rumpus downstairs in front, and I could hear a mess of people tramping up the stairs. They kept on coming after the second floor and my sister Carrie, my twin, said maybe they were whites come to get *us* because we saw what they did to the shot-in-the-leg colored in the alley. I was scared for a minute, I admit, but when I heard their voices plainer I knew they were coloreds and it was all right, only I didn't see why there were so many of them.

Then I got scared again, only different now, empty scared all over, when they came down the hall on our floor, not stopping at anybody else's door. And then there they were, banging on our door, of all the doors in the building. They tried to come right on in, but the door was locked.

Old Gramma was the one locked it and she said she'd clean house if one of us kids so much as looked at the knob even, and she threw the key down her neck somewhere. I went and told her that was our door the people were pounding on and where was the key. She reached down her neck and there was the key all right. But she didn't act much like she intended to open the door. She just stood there staring at it like it was somebody alive, saying the litany to the Blessed Virgin: *Mère du Christ, priez pour nous, Secours des chrétiens, priez...* Then all of a sudden she was crying; tears were blurry in her old yellow eyes, and she put the key in the lock, her veiny hands shaking, and unlocked the door.

They had Mama in their arms. I forgot all about Old Gramma, but I guess she passed out. Anyway, she was on the floor and a couple of men were picking her up and a couple of women were saying, "Put her here, put her there." I wasn't worried as much about Old Gramma as I was about Mama.

A bone—God, it made me sick—had poked through the flesh of Mama's arm, all bloody like a sharp stick, and something terrible was wrong with her chest. I couldn't look anymore and Carrie was screaming. That started me crying. Tears got in the way, but still I could see the baby, one and a half, and brother George, four and a half, and they had their eyes wide-open at what they saw and weren't crying a bit, too young to know what the hell.

They put Old Gramma in her room on the cot and closed the door on her and some old woman friend of hers that kept dipping a handkerchief in cold water and laying it on Old Gramma's head. They put Mama on the bed in the room where everybody was standing around and talking lower and lower until pretty soon they were just whispering.

Somebody came in with a doctor, a colored one, and he had a little black bag like they have in the movies. I don't think our family ever had a doctor come to see us before. Maybe before I was born Mama and Daddy did. I heard the doctor tell Mr Purvine, that works in the same mill Daddy does, only the night shift, that he ought to set the bone, but honest to God he thought he might as well wait, as he didn't want to hurt Mama if it wasn't going to make any difference.

He wasn't nearly as brisk now with his little black bag as

he had been when he came in. He touched Mama's forehead a couple of times and it didn't feel good to him, I guess, because he looked tired after he did it. He held his hand on the wrist of her good arm, but I couldn't tell what this meant from his face. It mustn't have been any worse than the forehead, or maybe his face had nothing to do with what he thought, and I was imagining all this from seeing the shape Mama was in. Finally he said, "I'll try," and he began calling for hot water and other things, and pretty soon Mama was all bandaged up white.

The doctor stepped away from Mama and over to some men and women, six or seven of them now—a lot more had gone —and asked them what had happened. He didn't ask all the questions I wanted to ask—I guess he already knew some of the answers—but I did find out Mama was on a streetcar coming home from the plant—Mama works now and we're saving for a cranberry farm—when the riot broke out in that section. Mr Purvine said he called the mill and told Daddy to come home. But Mr Purvine said he wasn't going to work tonight himself, the way the riot was spreading and the way the coloreds were getting the worst of it.

"As usual," said a man with glasses on. "The Negroes ought to organize and fight the thing to a finish." The doctor frowned at that. Mr Purvine said he didn't know. But one woman and another man said that was the right idea.

"If we must die," said the man with glasses on, "let it not be like hogs hunted and penned in an inglorious spot!"

The doctor said, "Yes, we all know that."

But the man with glasses on went on, because the others were listening to him, and I was glad he did, because I was listening to him too. "We must meet the common foe; though far outnumbered, let us still be brave, and for their thousand blows deal one deathblow! What, though before us lies the open grave? Like men we'll face the murderous, cowardly pack, pressed to the wall, dying, but—fighting back!"

They all thought it was fine, and a woman said that it was poetry, and I thought if that is what it is I know what I want to be now—a poetryman. I asked the man with glasses on if that was his poetry, though I did not think it was for some reason, and the men and women all looked at me like they were surprised to see me there and like I ought not hear such things —except the man with glasses on, and he said, No, son, it was not his poetry; he wished it was, but it was Claude McKay's, a Negro, and I could find it in the public library. I decided I would go to the public library when the riot was over, and it was the first time in my life I ever thought of the public library the way I did then.

They all left about this time, except the doctor and the old woman friend of Old Gramma's. She came out of Old Gramma's room, and when the door opened I saw Old Gramma lying on the cot with her eyes closed. The old woman asked me if I could work a can opener, and I said, "Yes, I can," and she handed me a can of vegetable soup from the shelf. She got a meal together and us kids sat down to eat. Not Carrie, though. She sat in our good chair with her legs under her and her eyes closed. Mama was sleeping and the doctor rolled up the shade at the window and looked out while we ate. I mean brother George and the baby. I couldn't eat. I just drank my glass of water. The old woman said, Here, here, I hadn't ought to let good food go to waste and was that any way to act at the table and I wasn't the first boy in the world to lose his mother.

I wondered was she crazy and I yelled I wasn't going to lose my mother and I looked to see and I was right. Mama was just sleeping and the doctor was there in case she needed him and everything was taken care of and . . . everything. The doctor didn't even turn away from the window when I yelled at the old woman, and I thought at least he'd say I'd wake my mother up shouting that way, or maybe that I was right and the old woman was wrong. I got up from the table and stood by the doctor at the window. He only stayed there a minute more then and went over to feel Mama's wrist again. He did not touch her forehead this time.

Old Gramma came out of her room and said to me, "Was that you raising so much cain in here, boy?"

I said, "Yes, it was," and just when I was going to tell her what the old woman said about losing Mama I couldn't. I didn't want to hear it out loud again. I didn't even want to think it in my mind.

Old Gramma went over and gazed down at Mama. She turned away quickly and told the old woman, "Please, I'll just have a cup of hot water, that's all, I'm so upset." Then she went over to the doctor by the window and whispered something to him and he whispered something back and it must've been only one or two words, because he was looking out the window the next moment.

Old Gramma said she'd be back in a minute and went out the door, slipslapping down the hall. I went to the window, the evening sun was going down, and I saw Old Gramma come out the back entrance of our building. She crossed the alley and went in the back door of the grocery store.

A lot of racket cut loose about a block up the alley. It was still empty, though. Old Gramma came out of the grocery store with something in a brown bag. She stopped in the middle of the alley and seemed to be watching the orange evening sun going down behind the buildings. The sun got in her hair and somehow under her skin, kind of, and it did a wonderful thing to her. She looked so young for a moment that I saw Mama in her, both of them beautiful New Orleans ladies.

The racket cut loose again, nearer now, and a pack of men came running down the alley, about three dozen whites chasing two coloreds. One of the whites was blowing a bugle—*tan tivvy, tan tivvy, tan tivvy*—like the white folks do when they go fox hunting in the movies or Virginia. I looked down, quick, to see if Old Gramma had enough sense to come inside, and I guess she did because she wasn't there. The two coloreds ran between two buildings, the whites ran after them, and then the alley was quiet again. Old Gramma stepped out, and I watched her stoop and pick up the brown bag that she had dropped before.

Another big noise made her drop it again. A whole smear of men swarmed out of the used-car lot and came galloping down the alley like wild buffaloes. Old Gramma scooted inside our building and the brown bag stayed there in the alley. This time I couldn't believe my eyes; I saw what I thought I'd never see; I saw what us kids had been waiting to see ever since the riot broke out—a white man that was fixing to get himself nice and killed. A white man running—running, God Almighty, from about a million coloreds. And he was the one with the tan-tivvy bugle, too. I hoped the coloreds would do the job up right.

The closer the white man came the worse it got for him, because the alley comes to a dead end when it hits our building. All at once—I don't know why—I was praying for that fool white man with the bugle to get away. But I didn't think he had a Chinaman's chance, the way he was going now, and maybe that's what made me pray for him.

Then he did a smart thing. He whipped the bugle over his shoulder, like you do with a horseshoe for good luck, and it hit the first colored behind him smack in the head, knocking him out, and that slowed up the others. The white man turned into the junk yard behind the furniture warehouse and the Victory Ballroom. Another smart thing, if he used his head. The space between the warehouse and the Victory is just wide enough for a man to run through. It's a long piece to the street, but if he made it there, he'd be safe probably.

The long passageway must've looked too narrow to him, though, because the fool came rushing around the garage next to our building. For a moment he was the only one in the alley. The coloreds had followed him through the junk yard and probably got themselves all tangled up in garbage cans and rusty bed springs and ashpiles. But the white man was a goner just the same. In a minute they'd be coming for him for real. He'd have to run the length of the alley again to get away and the coloreds have got the best legs.

Then Old Gramma opened our back door and saved him.

I was very glad for the white man, until suddenly I remembered poor Mama all broken to pieces on the bed, and then I was sorry Old Gramma did it. The next moment I was glad again that she did. I understood now I did not care one way or the other about the white man. Now I was thinking of Mama —not of myself. I did not see what difference it could make to Mama if the white man lived or died. It only had something to do with us and him.

Then I got hold of a funny idea. I told myself the trouble is somebody gets cheated or insulted or killed and everybody else tries to make it come out even by cheating and insulting and killing the cheaters and insulters and killers. Only they never do. I did not think they ever would. I told myself that I had a very big idea there, and when the riot was over I would go to the public library and sit in the reading room and think about it. Or I would speak to Old Gramma about it, because it seemed like she had the same big idea and like she had had it a long time, too.

The doctor was standing by me at the window all the time. He said nothing about what Old Gramma did, and now he stepped away from the window and so did I. I guess he felt the same way I did about the white man and that's why he stepped away from the window. The big idea again. He was afraid the coloreds down below would yell up at us, did we see the white man pass by. The coloreds were crazy mad all right. One of them had the white man's bugle and he banged on our door with it. I was worried Old Gramma had forgot to lock it and they might walk right in, and that would be the end of the white man and the big idea.

But Old Gramma pulled another fast one. She ran out into the alley and pointed her old yellow finger in about three wrong directions. In a second the alley was quiet and empty, except for Old Gramma. She walked slowly over against our building, where somebody had kicked the brown bag, and picked it up.

Old Gramma brought the white man right into our room, told him to sit down, and poured herself a cup of hot water. She sipped it and said the white man could leave whenever he wanted to, but it might be better to wait a bit. The white man said he was much obliged, he hated to give us any trouble, and, "Oh, oh, is somebody sick over there?" when he saw Mama, and that he'd just been passing by when a hundred nig—when he was attacked.

Old Gramma sipped her hot water. The doctor turned away from the window and said, "Here they come again," took another look, and said, "No, they're going back." He went over to Mama and held her wrist. I couldn't tell anything about her from his face. She was sleeping just the same. The doctor asked the white man, still standing, to sit down. Carrie only opened her eyes once and closed them. She hadn't changed her position in the good chair. Brother George and the baby stood in a corner with their eyes on the white man. The baby's legs buckled then—she'd only been walking about a week—and she collapsed softly to the floor. She worked her way up again without taking her eyes off the white man. He even looked funny and out of place to me in our room. I guess the man for the rent and Father Egan were the only white people come to see us since I could remember; and now it was only the man for the rent since Father Egan died.

The doctor asked the white man did he work or own a business in this neighborhood. The white man said, No, glancing down at his feet, no, he just happened to be passing by when he was suddenly attacked like he said before. The doctor told Old Gramma she might wash Mama's face and neck again with warm water.

There was noise again in the alley—windows breaking and fences being pushed over. The doctor said to the white man, "You could leave now; it's a white mob this time; you'd be safe."

"No," the white man said, "I should say not; I wouldn't be seen with them; they're as bad as the others almost."

"It is quite possible," the doctor said.

Old Gramma asked the white man if he would like a cup of tea.

"Tea? No," he said, "I don't drink tea; I didn't know you drank it."

"I didn't know you knew her," the doctor said, looking at Old Gramma and the white man.

"You colored folks, I mean," the white man said, "Americans, I mean. Me, I don't drink tea—always considered it an English drink and bad for the kidneys."

The doctor did not answer. Old Gramma brought him a cup of tea.

And then Daddy came in. He ran over to Mama and fell down on his knees like he was dead—like seeing Mama with her arm broke and her chest so pushed in killed him on the spot. He lifted his face from the bed and kissed Mama on the lips; and then, Daddy, I could see, was crying—the strongest man in the world was crying with tears in his big dark eyes and coming down the side of his big hard face. Mama called him her John Henry sometimes and there he was, her John Henry, the strongest man, black or white, in the whole damn world, crying.

He put his head down on the bed again. Nobody in the room moved until the baby toddled over to Daddy and patted him on the ear like she wanted to play the games those two make up with her little hands and his big ears and eyes and nose. But Daddy didn't move or say anything, if he even knew she was there, and the baby got a blank look in her eyes and walked away from Daddy and sat down, *plump*, on the floor across the room, staring at Daddy and the white man, back and forth, Daddy and the white man.

Daddy got up after a while and walked very slowly across the room and got himself a drink of water at the sink. For the first time he noticed the white man in the room. "Who's he?" he said. "Who's he?" None of us said anything. "Who the hell's he?" Daddy wanted to know, thunder in his throat like there always is when he's extra mad or happy.

The doctor said the white man was Mr Gorman, and went over to Daddy and told him something in a low voice.

"Innocent! What's he doing in this neighborhood then?" Daddy said, loud as before. "What's an *innocent* white man doing in this neighborhood now? Answer me that!" He looked at all of us in the room and none of us that knew what the white man was doing in this neighborhood wanted to explain to Daddy. Old Gramma and the doctor and me—none of us that knew—would tell.

"I was just passing by," the white man said, "as they can tell you."

The scared way he said it almost made me laugh. Was this a white *man*, I asked myself. Alongside Daddy's voice the white man's sounded plain foolish and weak—a little old tug squeaking at a big ocean liner about the right of way. Daddy seemed to forget all about him and began asking the doctor a lot of questions about Mama in a hoarse whisper I couldn't hear very well. Daddy's face got harder and harder and it didn't look like he'd ever crack a smile or shed a tear or anything soft again. Just hard, it got, hard as four spikes.

Old Gramma came and stood by Daddy's side and said she had called the priest when she was downstairs a while ago getting some candles. She was worried that the candles weren't blessed ones. She opened the brown bag then, and that's what was inside—two white candles. I didn't know grocery stores carried them.

Old Gramma went to her room and took down the picture of the Sacred Heart all bleeding and put it on the little table by Mama's bed and set the candles in sticks on each side of it. She lit the candles and it made the Sacred Heart, punctured by the wreath of thorns, look bloodier than ever, and made me think of that song, "To Jesus' Heart All Burning," the kids sing at Our Saviour's on Sundays.

The white man went up to the doctor and said, "I'm a Catholic, too." But the doctor didn't say anything back, only nodded. He probably wasn't one himself, I thought; not many of the race are. Our family wouldn't be if Old Gramma and Mama didn't come from New Orleans, where Catholics are thicker than flies or Baptists.

Daddy got up from the table and said to the white man. "So help me God, mister, I'll kill you in this room if my wife dies!" The baby started crying and the doctor went to Daddy's side and turned him away from the white man, and it wasn't hard to do because now Daddy was kind of limp and didn't look like he remembered anything about the white man or what he said he'd do to him if Mama . . . or anything.

"I'll bet the priest won't show up," Daddy said.

"The priest will come," Old Gramma said. "The priest will always come when you need him; just wait." Her old lips were praying in French.

I hoped he would come like Old Gramma said, but I wasn't so sure. Some of the priests weren't much different from anybody else. They knew how to keep their necks in. Daddy said to Mama once if you only wanted to hear about social justice you could turn on the radio or go to the nearest stadium on the Fourth of July, and there'd be an old white man in a new black suit saying it was a good thing and everybody ought to get some, and if they'd just kick in more they might and, anyway, they'd be saved. One came to Our Saviour's last year, and Father Egan said this is our new assistant and the next Sunday our new assistant was gone—poor health. But Daddy said he was transferred to a church in a white neighborhood because he couldn't stand to save black souls. Father Egan would've come a-flying, riot or no riot, but he was dead now and we didn't know much about the one that took his place.

Then he came, by God; the priest from Our Saviour's came to our room while the riot was going on. Old Gramma got all excited and said over and over she knew the priest would come. He was kind of young and skinny and pale, even for a white man, and he said, "I'm Father Crowe," to everybody in the room and looked around to see who was who.

The doctor introduced himself and said Old Gramma was Old Gramma, Daddy was Daddy, we were the children, that was Mr Gorman, who was just passing by, and over there was poor Mama. He missed Old Gramma's old woman friend; I guess he didn't know what to call her. The priest went over and took a look at Mama and nodded to the doctor and they went into Old Gramma's room together. The priest had a little black bag, too, and he took it with him. I suppose he was getting ready to give Mama Extreme Unction. I didn't think they would wake her up for Confession or Holy Communion; she was so weak and needed the rest.

Daddy got up from the table mad as a bull and said to the white man, "Remember what I said, mister."

"But why me?" the white man asked. "Just because I'm white?"

Daddy looked over at Mama on the bed and said, "Yeah, just because you're white; yeah, that's why . . ." Old Gramma took Daddy by the arm and steered him over to the table again and he sat down.

J. F. POWERS

The priest and the doctor came out of Old Gramma's room, and right away the priest faced the white man, like they'd been talking about him in Old Gramma's room, and asked him why he didn't go home. The white man said he'd heard some shouting in the alley a while ago that didn't sound so good to him and he didn't think it was safe yet and that was why.

"I see," the priest said.

"I'm a Catholic too, Father," the white man said.

"That's the trouble," the priest said.

The priest took some cotton from his little black bag, dipped his fingers in holy oil, and made the sign of the cross on Mama's eyes, nose, ears, mouth, and hands, rubbing the oil off with the cotton, and said prayers in Latin all the time he was doing it.

"I want you all to kneel down now," the priest said, "and we'll say a rosary. But we mustn't say it too loud because she is sleeping."

We all knelt down except the baby and Carrie. Carrie said she'd never kneel down to God again. "Now Carrie," Old Gramma said, almost crying. She told Carrie it was for poor Mama and wouldn't Carrie kneel down if it was for poor Mama?

"No!" Carrie said. "It must be a white God too!" Then she began crying and she did kneel down after all.

Even the white man knelt down and the doctor and the old woman friend of Old Gramma's, a solid Baptist if I ever saw one, and we all said the rosary of the five sorrowful mysteries.

Afterwards the white man said to the priest, "Do you mind if I leave when you do, Father?" The priest didn't answer, and the white man said, "I think I'll be leaving now, Father. I wonder if you'd be going my way?"

The priest finally said, "All right, all right, come along. You won't be the first one to hide behind a Roman collar."

The white man said, "I'm sure I don't know what you mean

by that, Father." The priest didn't hear him, I guess, or want to explain, because he went over to Mama's bed.

The priest knelt once more by Mama and said a prayer in Latin out loud and made the sign of the cross over Mama: *In nomine Patris et Filii et Spiritus Sancti.* He looked closer at Mama and motioned to the doctor. The doctor stepped over to the bed, felt Mama's wrist, put his head to her chest, where it wasn't pushed in, and stood up slowly.

Daddy and all of us had been watching the doctor when the priest motioned him over, and now Daddy got up from the table, kicking the chair over he got up so fast, and ran to the bed. Shaking all over, he sank to his knees, and I believe he must've been crying again, although I thought he never would again and his head was down and I couldn't see for sure.

I began to get an awful bulging pain in my stomach. The doctor left the bed and grabbed the white man by the arm and was taking him to the door when Daddy jumped up, like he knew where they were going, and said, "Wait a minute, mister!"

The doctor and the white man stopped at the door. Daddy walked draggily over to them and stood in front of the white man, took a deep breath, and said in the stillest kind of whisper, "I wouldn't touch you." That was all. He moved slowly back to Mama's bed and his big shoulders were sagged down like I never saw them before.

Old Gramma said, "*Jésus!*" and stumbled down on her knees by Mama. Then the awful bulging pain in my stomach exploded, and I knew that Mama wasn't just sleeping now, and I couldn't breathe for a long while, and then when I finally could I was crying like the baby and brother George, and so was Carrie.

LIONS, HARTS, LEAPING DOES

"'THIRTY-NINTH POPE. Anastasius, a Roman, appointed that while the Gospel was reading they should stand and not sit. He exempted from the ministry those that were lame, impotent, or diseased persons, and slept with his forefathers in peace, being a confessor.'"

"Anno?"

"'Anno 404.'"

They sat there in the late afternoon, the two old men grown gray in the brown robes of the Order. Angular winter daylight forsook the small room, almost a cell in the primitive sense, and passed through the window into the outside world. The distant horizon, which it sought to join, was still bright and strong against approaching night. The old Franciscans, one priest, one brother, were left among the shadows in the room.

"Can you see to read one more, Titus?" the priest Didymus asked. "Number fourteen." He did not cease staring out the window at day becoming night on the horizon. The thirty-ninth pope said Titus might not be a priest. Did Titus, reading, understand? He could never really tell about Titus, who said nothing now. There was only silence, then a dry whispering of pages turning. "Number fourteen," Didymus said. "That's Zephyrinus. I always like the old heretic on that one, Titus."

According to one bibliographer, Bishop Bale's *Pageant of Popes Contayninge the Lyves of all the Bishops of Rome, from the Beginninge of them to the Year of Grace 1555* was a denunciation of every pope from Peter to Paul IV. However inviting to readers that might sound, it was in sober fact a lie. The first popes, persecuted and mostly martyred, wholly escaped the author's remarkable spleen and even enjoyed his crusty approbation. Father Didymus, his aged appetite for biography jaded by the orthodox lives, found the work fascinating. He usually referred to it as "Bishop Bale's funny book" and to the Bishop as a heretic.

Titus squinted at the yellowed page. He snapped a glance at the light hovering at the window. Then he closed his eyes and with great feeling recited:

" 'O how joyous and how delectable is it to see religious men devout and fervent in the love of God, well-mannered—' "

"Titus," Didymus interrupted softly.

" '—and well taught in ghostly learning.' "

"Titus, read." Didymus placed the words in their context. The First Book of *The Imitation* and Chapter, if he was not mistaken, XXV. The trick was no longer in finding the source of Titus's quotations; it was putting them in their exact context. It had become an unconfessed contest between them, and it gratified Didymus to think he had been able to place the fragment. Titus knew two books by heart, *The Imitation* and *The Little Flowers of St Francis*. Lately, unfortunately, he had begun to learn another. He was more and more quoting from Bishop Bale. Didymus reminded himself he must not let Titus read past the point where the martyred popes left off.

What Bale had to say about Peter's later successors sounded incongruous—"unmete" in the old heretic's own phrase— coming from a Franciscan brother. Two fathers had already inquired of Didymus concerning Titus. One had noted the antique style of his words and had ventured to wonder if Brother Titus, Christ preserve us, might be slightly possessed. He cited the case of the illiterate Missouri farmer who cursed the Church in a forgotten Aramaic tongue.

"Read, Titus."

Titus squinted at the page once more and read in his fine dead voice.

" 'Fourteenth pope, Zephyrinus. Zephyrinus was a Roman born, a man as writers do testify, more addicted with all endeavor to the service of God than to the cure of any worldly affairs. Whereas before his time the wine in the celebrating the communion was ministered in a cup of wood, he first did alter that, and instead thereof brought in cups or chalices of glass. And yet he did not this upon any superstition, as thinking wood to be unlawful, or glass to be more holy for that use, but because the one is more comely and seemly, as by experience it appeareth than the other. And yet some wooden dolts do dream that the wooden cups were changed by him because that part of the wine, or as they thought, the royal blood of Christ, did soak into the wood, and so it can not be in glass. Surely sooner may wine soak into any wood than any wit into those winey heads that thus both deceive themselves and slander this Godly martyr.' "

"Anno?"

Titus squinted at the page again. " 'Anno 222,' " he read.

They were quiet for a moment which ended with the clock in the tower booming once for the half hour. Didymus got up and stood so close to the window his breath became visible. Noticing it, he inhaled deeply and then, exhaling, he sent a gust of smoke churning against the freezing pane, clouding it.

Some old unmelted snow in tree crotches lay dirty and white in the gathering dark.

"It's cold out today," Didymus said.

He stepped away from the window and over to Titus, whose face was relaxed in open-eyed sleep. He took Bishop Bale's funny book unnoticed from Titus's hands.

"Thank you, Titus," he said.

Titus blinked his eyes slowly once, then several times quickly. His body gave a shudder, as if coming to life.

"Yes, Father?" he was asking.

"I said thanks for reading. You are a great friend to me."

"Yes, Father."

"I know you'd rather read other authors." Didymus moved to the window, stood there gazing through the tops of trees, their limbs black and bleak against the sky. He rubbed his hands. "I'm going for a walk before vespers. Is it too cold for you, Titus?"

" 'A good religious man that is fervent in his religion taketh all things well, and doth gladly all that he is commanded to do.' "

Didymus, walking across the room, stopped and looked at Titus just in time to see him open his eyes. He was quoting again: *The Imitation* and still in Chapter XXV. Why had he said that? To himself Didymus repeated the words and decided Titus, his mind moving intelligently but so pathetically largo, was documenting the act of reading Bishop Bale when there were other books he preferred.

"I'm going out for a walk," Didymus said.

Titus rose and pulled down the full sleeves of his brown robe in anticipation of the cold.

"I think it is too cold for you, Titus," Didymus said.

Titus faced him undaunted, arms folded and hands muffled in his sleeves, eyes twinkling incredulously. He was ready to go. Didymus got the idea Titus knew himself to be the healthier of the two. Didymus was vaguely annoyed at this manifestation of the truth. *Vanitas.*

"Won't they need you in the kitchen now?" he inquired.

Immediately he regretted having said that. And the way he had said it, with some malice, as though labor *per se* were important and the intention not so. *Vanitas* in a friar, and at his age too. Confronting Titus with a distinction his simple mind could never master and which, if it could, his great soul would never recognize. Titus only knew all that was necessary, that a friar did what he was best at in the community. And no matter the nature of his toil, the variety of the means at hand, the end was the same for all friars. Or indeed for all men, if they cared to know. Titus worked in the kitchen and garden. Was Didymus wrong in teaching geometry out of personal preference and perhaps—if this was so he was—out of pride? Had the spiritual worth of his labor been vitiated because of that? He did not think so, no. No, he taught geometry because it was useful and eternally true, like his theology, and though of a lower order of truth it escaped the common fate of theology and the humanities, perverted through the ages in the mouths of dunderheads and fools. From that point of view, his work came to the same thing as Titus's. The vineyard was everywhere; they were in it, and that was essential.

Didymus, consciously humble, held open the door for Titus. Sandals scraping familiarly, they passed through dark corridors until they came to the stairway. Lights from floors above and below spangled through the carven apertures of the winding stair and fell in confusion upon the worn oaken steps.

At the outside door they were ambushed. An old friar stepped out of the shadows to intercept them. Standing with Didymus and Titus, however, made him appear younger. Or possibly it was the tenseness of him.

"Good evening, Father," he said to Didymus. "And Titus."

Didymus nodded in salutation and Titus said deliberately,

as though he were the first one ever to put words in such conjunction:

"Good evening, Father Rector."

The Rector watched Didymus expectantly. Didymus studied the man's face. It told him nothing but curiosity—a luxury which could verge on vice in the cloister. Didymus frowned his incomprehension. He was about to speak. He decided against it, turning to Titus:

"Come on, Titus, we've got a walk to take before vespers."

The Rector was left standing.

They began to circle the monastery grounds. Away from the buildings it was brighter. With a sudden shudder, Didymus felt the freezing air bite into his body all over. Instinctively he drew up his cowl. That was a little better. Not much. It was too cold for him to relax, breathe deeply, and stride freely. It had not looked this cold from his window. He fell into Titus's gait. The steps were longer, but there was an illusion of warmth about moving in unison. Bit by bit he found himself duplicating every aspect of Titus in motion. Heads down, eyes just ahead of the next step, undeviating, they seemed peripatetic figures in a Gothic frieze. The stones of the walk were trampled over with frozen footsteps. Titus's feet were gray and bare in their open sandals. Pieces of ice, the thin edges of ruts, cracked off under foot, skittering sharply away. A crystal fragment lit between Titus's toes and did not melt there. He did not seem to notice it. This made Didymus lift his eyes.

A fine Franciscan! Didymus snorted, causing a flurry of vapors. He had the despicable caution of the comfortable who move mountains, if need be, to stay that way. Here he was, cowl up and heavy woolen socks on, and regretting the weather because it exceeded his anticipations. Painfully he stubbed his toe on purpose and at once accused himself of exhibitionism. Then he damned the expression for its modernity. He asked himself wherein lay the renunciation of the world, the flesh and the devil, the whole point of following after St Francis today. Poverty, Chastity, Obedience—the three vows. There was nothing of suffering in the poverty of the friar nowadays: he was penniless, but materially rich compared to—what was the phrase he used to hear?—"one third of the nation." A beggar, a homeless mendicant by very definition, he knew nothing—except as it affected others "less fortunate"—of the miseries of begging in the streets. Verily, it was no heavy cross, this vow of Poverty, so construed and practiced, in the modern world. Begging had become unfashionable. Somewhere along the line the meaning had been lost; they had become too "fortunate." Official agencies, to whom it was a nasty but necessary business, dispensed Charity without mercy or grace. He recalled with wry amusement Frederick Barbarossa's appeal to fellow princes when opposed by the might of the medieval Church: "We have a clean conscience, and it tells us that God is with us. Ever have we striven to bring back priests and, in especial, those of the topmost rank, to the condition of the first Christian Church. In those days the clergy raised their eyes to the angels, shone through miracles, made whole the sick, raised the dead, made Kings and Princes subject to them, not with arms but with their holiness. But now they are smothered in delights. To withdraw from them the harmful riches which burden them to their own undoing is a labor of love in which all Princes should eagerly participate."

And Chastity, what of that? Well, that was all over for him—a battle he had fought and won many years ago. A sin whose temptations had prevailed undiminished through the centuries, but withal for him, an old man, a dead issue, a young man's trial. Only Obedience remained, and that, too, was no longer difficult for him. There was something—much as he disliked the term—to be said for "conditioning." He had to smile at himself: why should he bristle so at using the word? It was only contemporary slang for a theory the Church had always known. "Psychiatry," so called, and all the ghastly superstition that attended its practice, the deification of its high priests in the secular schools, made him ill. But it would pass. Just look how alchemy had flourished, and where was it today?

Clearly an abecedarian observance of the vows did not promise perfection. Stemmed in divine wisdom, they were branches meant to flower forth, but requiring of the friar the water and sunlight of sacrifice. The letter led nowhere. It was the spirit of the vows which opened the way and revealed to the soul, no matter the flux of circumstance, the means of salvation.

He had picked his way through the welter of familiar factors again—again to the same bitter conclusion. He had come to the key and core of his trouble anew. When he received the letter from Seraphin asking him to come to St Louis, saying his years prohibited unnecessary travel and endowed his request with a certain prerogative—No, he had written back, it's simply impossible, not saying why. God help him, as a natural man, he had the desire, perhaps the inordinate desire, to see his brother again. He should not have to prove that. One of them must die soon. But as a friar, he remembered: "Unless a man be clearly delivered from the love of all creatures, he may not fully tend to his Creator." Therein, he thought, the keeping of the vows having become an easy habit for him, was his opportunity—he thought! It was plain and there was sacrifice and it would be hard. So he had not gone.

Now it was plain that he had been all wrong. Seraphin was an old man with little left to warm him in the world. Didymus asked himself—recoiling at the answer before the question was out—if his had been the only sacrifice. Rather, had he not been too intent on denying himself at the time to notice that he was denying Seraphin also? Harshly Didymus told himself he had used his brother for a hair shirt. This must be the truth, he thought; it hurts so.

The flesh just above his knees felt frozen. They were drawing near the entrance again. His face, too, felt the same way, like a slab of pasteboard, stiffest at the tip of his nose. When he wrinkled his brow and puffed out his cheeks to blow hot air up to his nose, his skin seemed to crackle like old parchment. His eyes watered from the wind. He pressed a hand, warm from his sleeve, to his exposed neck. Frozen, like his face. It would be chapped tomorrow.

Titus, white hair awry in the wind, looked just the same.

They entered the monastery door. The Rector stopped them. It was almost as before, except that Didymus was occupied with feeling his face and patting it back to life.

"Ah, Didymus! It must be cold indeed!" The Rector smiled at Titus and returned his gaze to Didymus. He made it appear that they were allied in being amused at Didymus's face. Didymus touched his nose tenderly. Assured it would stand the operation, he blew it lustily. He stuffed the handkerchief up his sleeve. The Rector, misinterpreting all this ceremony, obviously was afraid of being ignored.

"The telegram, Didymus. I'm sorry; I thought it might have been important."

"I received no telegram."

They faced each other, waiting, experiencing a hanging moment of uneasiness.

Then, having employed the deductive method, they both looked at Titus. Although he had not been listening, rather had been studying the naked toes in his sandals, he sensed their eyes questioning him.

"Yes, Father Rector?" he answered.

"The telegram for Father Didymus, Titus?" the Rector demanded. "Where is it?" Titus started momentarily out of willingness to be of service, but ended, his mind refusing to click, impassive before them. The Rector shook his head in faint exasperation and reached his hand down into the folds of Titus's cowl. He brought forth two envelopes. One, the telegram, he gave to Didymus. The other, a letter, he handed back to Titus.

"I gave you this letter this morning, Titus. It's for Father Anthony." Intently Titus stared unremembering at he letter. "I wish you would see that Father Anthony gets it right away, Titus. I think it's a bill."

Titus held the envelope tightly to his breast and said, "Father Anthony."

Then his eyes were attracted by the sound of Didymus tearing open the telegram. While Didymus read the telegram, Titus's expression showed he at last understood his failure to deliver it. He was perturbed, mounting inner distress moving his lips silently.

Didymus looked up from the telegram. He saw the grief in Titus's face and said, astonished, "How did you know, Titus?"

Titus's eyes were both fixed and lowered in sorrow. It seemed to Didymus that Titus knew the meaning of the telegram. Didymus was suddenly weak, as before a miracle. His eyes went to the Rector to see how he was taking it. Then it occurred to him the Rector could not know what had happened.

As though nothing much had, the Rector laid an absolving hand lightly upon Titus's shoulder.

"Didymus, he can't forgive himself for not delivering the telegram now that he remembers it. That's all."

Didymus was relieved. Seeing the telegram in his hand, he folded it quickly and stuffed it back in the envelope. He handed it to the Rector. calmly, in a voice quite drained of feeling, he said, "My brother, Father Seraphin, died last night in St Louis."

"Father Seraphin *from Rome*?"

"Yes," Didymus said, "in St Louis. He was my brother. Appointed a confessor in Rome, a privilege for a foreigner. He was ninety-two."

"I know that, Didymus, an honor for the Order. I had no idea he was in this country. Ninety-two! God rest his soul!"

"I had a letter from him only recently."

"You did?"

"He wanted me to come to St Louis. I hadn't seen him for twenty-five years at least."

"Twenty-five years?"

"It was impossible for me to visit him."

"But if he was in this country, Didymus . . ."

The Rector waited for Didymus to explain.

Didymus opened his mouth to speak, heard the clock in the tower sound the quarter hour, and said nothing, listening, lips parted, to the last of the strokes die away.

"Why, Didymus, it could easily have been arranged," the Rector persisted.

Didymus turned abruptly to Titus, who, standing in a dream, had been inattentive since the clock struck.

"Come, Titus, we'll be late."

He hastened down the corridor with Titus. "No," he said in agitation, causing Titus to look at him in surprise. "I told him no. It was simply impossible." He was conscious of Titus's attention. "To visit him, Seraphin, who is dead." That had come naturally enough, for being the first time in his thoughts that Seraphin was dead. Was there not some merit in his dispassionate acceptance of the fact?

They entered the chapel for vespers and knelt down.

The clock struck. One, two . . . two. Two? No, there must have been one or two strokes before. He had gone to sleep. It was three. At least three, probably four. Or five. He waited. It could not be two: he remembered the brothers filing darkly into the chapel at that hour. Disturbing the shadows for matins and lauds. If it was five—he listened for faint noises in the building—it would only be a few minutes. They would come in, the earliest birds, to say their Masses. There were no noises. He looked toward the windows on the St Joseph side of the chapel.

He might be able to see a light from a room across the court. That was not certain even if it was five. It would have to come through the stained glass. Was that possible? It was still night. Was there a moon? He looked round the chapel. If there was, it might shine on a window. There was no moon. Or it was overhead. Or powerless against the glass. He yawned. It could not be five. His knees were numb from kneeling. He shifted on them. His back ached. Straightening it, he gasped for breath. He saw the sanctuary light. The only light, red. Then it came back to him. Seraphin was dead. He tried to pray. No words. Why words? Meditation in the Presence. The perfect prayer. He fell asleep . . .

. . . Spiraling brown coil on coil under the golden sun the river slithered across the blue and flower-flecked land. On an eminence they held identical hands over their eyes for visors and mistook it with pleasure for an endless murmuring serpent. They considered unafraid the prospect of its turning in its course and standing on tail to swallow them gurgling alive. They sensed it was in them to command this also by a wish. Their visor hands vanished before their eyes and became instead the symbol of brotherhood clasped between them. This they wished. Smiling the same smile back and forth they began laughing: "Jonah!" And were walking murkily up and down the brown belly of the river in mock distress. Above them, foolishly triumphant, rippling in contentment, mewed the waves. Below swam an occasional large fish, absorbed in ignoring them, and the mass of crustacea, eagerly seething, too numerous on the bottom to pretend exclusiveness. "Jonah indeed!" the brothers said, surprised to see the bubbles they birthed. They strolled then for hours this way. The novelty wearing off (without regret, else they would have wished themselves elsewhere), they began to talk and say ordinary things. Their mother had died, their father too, and how old did that make them? It was the afternoon of the funerals, which they had managed, transcending time, to have held jointly. She had seemed older and for some reason he otherwise. How, they wondered, should it be with them, *memento mori* clicking simultaneously within them, lackaday. The sound of dirt descending six feet to clatter on the coffins was memorable but unmentionable. Their own lives, well...only half curious (something to do) they halted to kick testingly a waterlogged rowboat resting on the bottom, the crustacea complaining and olive-green silt rising to speckle the surface with dark stars... well, what *had* they been doing? A crayfish pursued them, clad in sable armor, dearly desiring to do battle, brandishing hinged swords. Well, for one thing, working for the canonization of Fra Bartolomeo, had got two cardinals interested, was hot after those remaining who were at all possible, a slow business. Yes, one would judge so in the light of past canonizations, though being stationed in Rome had its advantages. Me, the same old grind, teaching, pounding away, giving Pythagoras no rest in his grave... They made an irresolute pass at the crayfish, who had caught up with them. More about Fra Bartolomeo, what else is there? Except, you will laugh or have me excommunicated for wanton presumption, though it's only faith in a faithless age, making a vow not to die until he's made a saint, recognized rather—he is one, convinced of it, Didymus (never can get used to calling you that), a saint sure as I'm alive, having known him, no doubt of it, something wrong with your knee? Knees then! The crayfish, he's got hold of you there, another at your back. If you like, we'll leave—only I do like it here. Well, go ahead then, you never did like St Louis, isn't that what you used to say? Alone, in pain, he rose to the surface, parting the silt stars. The sun like molten gold squirted him in the eye. Numb now, unable to remember, and too blind to refurnish his memory by observation, he waited for this limbo to clear away...

Awake now, he was face to face with a flame, blinding him.

He avoided it. A dead weight bore him down, his aching back. Slowly, like ink in a blotter, his consciousness spread. The supports beneath him were kneeling limbs, his, the veined hands, bracing him, pressing flat, his own. His body, it seemed, left off there; the rest was something else, floor. He raised his head to the flame again and tried to determine what kept it suspended even with his face. He shook his head, blinking dumbly, a four-legged beast. He could see nothing, only his knees and hands, which he felt rather, and the flame floating unaccountably in the darkness. That part alone was a mystery. And then there came a pressure and pull on his shoulders, urging him up. Fingers, a hand, a rustling related to its action, then the rustling in rhythm with the folds of a brown curtain, a robe naturally, ergo a friar, holding a candle, trying to raise him up, Titus. The clock began striking.

"Put out the candle," Didymus said.

Titus closed his palm slowly around the flame, unflinching, snuffing it. The odor of burning string. Titus pinched the wick deliberately. He waited a moment, the clock falling silent, and said, "Father Rector expects you will say a Mass for the Dead at five o'clock."

"Yes, I know." He yawned deliciously. "I told him *that*." He bit his lips at the memory of the disgusting yawn. Titus had found him asleep. Shame overwhelmed him, and he searched his mind for justification. He found none.

"It is five now," Titus said.

It was maddening. "I don't see anyone else if it's five," he snapped. Immediately he was aware of a light burning in the sacristy. He blushed and grew pale. Had someone besides Titus seen him sleeping? But, listening, he heard nothing. No one else was up yet. He was no longer pale and was only blushing now. He saw it all hopefully. He was saved. Titus had gone to the sacristy to prepare for Mass. He must have come out to light the candles on the main altar. Then he had seen the bereaved keeping vigil on all fours, asleep, snoring even. What did Titus think of that? It withered him to remember, but he was comforted some that the only witness had been Titus. Had the sleeping apostles in Gethsemane been glad it was Christ?

Wrong! Hopelessly wrong! For there had come a noise after all. Someone else was in the sacristy. He stiffened and walked palely toward it. He must go there and get ready to say his Mass. A few steps he took only, his back buckling out, humping, his knees sinking to the floor, his hands last. The floor, with fingers smelling of dust and genesis, reached up and held him. The fingers were really spikes and they were dusty from holding him this way all his life. For a radiant instant, which had something of eternity about it, he saw the justice of his position. Then there was nothing.

A little snow had fallen in the night, enough to powder the dead grass and soften the impression the leafless trees etched in the sky. Grayly the sky promised more snow, but now, at the end of the day following his collapse in the chapel, it was melting. Didymus, bundled around by blankets, sat in a wheelchair at the window, unsleepy. Only the landscape wearied him. Dead and unmoving though it must be—of that he was sure—it conspired to make him see everything in it as living, moving, something to be watched, each visible tuft of grass, each cluster of snow. The influence of the snow perhaps? For the ground, ordinarily uniform in texture and drabness, had split up into individual patches. They appeared to be involved in a struggle of some kind, possibly to overlap each other, constantly shifting. But whether it was equally one against one, or one against all, he could not make out. He reminded himself he did not believe it was actually happening. It was confusing and he closed his eyes. After a time this confused and tired him in the same way. The background of darkness became a field of varicolored factions, warring, and, worse than the landscape, things like worms and comets wriggled and exploded before his closed eyes. Finally, as though to orchestrate their motions, they carried with them a bewildering noise or music which grew louder and cacophonous. The effect was cumulative, inevitably unbearable, and Didymus would have to open his eyes again. The intervals of peace became gradually rarer on the landscape. Likewise when he shut his eyes to it the restful darkness dissolved sooner than before into riot.

The door of his room opened, mercifully dispelling his illusions, and that, because there had been no knock, could only be Titus. Unable to move in his chair, Didymus listened to Titus moving about the room at his back. The tinkle of a glass once, the squeak of the bookcase indicating a book taken out or replaced—they were sounds Didymus could recognize. But that first tap-tap and the consequent click of metal on metal, irregular and scarcely audible, was disconcertingly unfamiliar. His curiosity, centering on it, raised it to a delicious mystery. He kept down the urge to shout at Titus. But he attempted to fish from memory the precise character of the corner from which the sound came with harrowing repetition. The sound stopped then, as though to thwart him on the brink of revelation. Titus's footsteps scraped across the room. The door opened and closed. For a few steps, Didymus heard Titus going down the corridor. He asked himself not to be moved by idle curiosity, a thing of the senses. He would not be tempted now.

A moment later the keystone of his good intention crumbled, and the whole edifice of his detachment with it. More shakily than quickly, Didymus moved his hands to the wheels of the chair. He would roll over to the corner and investigate the sound . . . He would? His hands lay limply on the wheels, ready to propel him to his mind's destination, but, weak, white, powerless to grip the wheels or anything. He regarded them with contempt. He had known they would fail him; he had been foolish to give them another chance. Disdainful of his hands, he looked out the window. He could still do that, couldn't he? It was raining some now. The landscape started to move, rearing and reeling crazily, as though drunken with the rain. In horror, Didymus damned his eyes. He realized this trouble was probably going to be chronic. He turned his gaze in despair to the trees, to the branches level with his eyes and nearer than the insane ground. Hesitating warily, fearful the gentle boughs under scrutiny would turn into hideous waving tentacles, he looked. With a thrill, he knew he was seeing clearly.

Gauzily rain descended in a fine spray, hanging in fat berries from the wet black branches where leaves had been and buds would be, cold crystal drops. They fell now and then ripely of their own weight, or shaken by the intermittent wind they spilled before their time. Promptly they appeared again, pendulous.

Watching the raindrops prove gravity, he was grateful for nature's, rather than his, return to reason. Still, though he professed faith in his faculties, he would not look away from the trees and down at the ground, nor close his eyes. Gratefully he savored the cosmic truth in the falling drops and the mildly trembling branches. There was order, he thought, which in justice and science ought to include the treacherous landscape. Risking all, he ventured a glance at the ground. All was still there. He smiled. He was going to close his eyes (to make it universal and conclusive), when the door opened again.

Didymus strained to catch the meaning of Titus's movements. Would the clicking sound begin? Titus did go to that corner of the room again. Then it came, louder than before, but only once this time.

Titus came behind his chair, turned it, and wheeled him over to the corner.

On a hook which Titus had screwed into the wall hung a bird cage covered with black cloth.

"What's all this?" Didymus asked.

Titus tapped the covered cage expectantly.

A bird chirped once.

"The bird," Titus explained in excitement, "is inside."

Didymus almost laughed. He sensed in time, however, the necessity of seeming befuddled and severe. Titus expected it.

"I don't believe it," Didymus snapped.

Titus smiled wisely and tapped the cage again.

"There!" he exclaimed when the bird chirped.

Didymus shook his head in mock anger. "You made that beastly noise, Titus, you mountebank!"

Titus, profoundly amused by such skepticism, removed the black cover.

The bird, a canary, flicked its head sidewise in interest, looking them up and down. Then it turned its darting attention to the room. It chirped once in curt acceptance of the new surroundings. Didymus and Titus came under its black dot of an eye once more, this time for closer analysis. The canary chirped twice, perhaps that they were welcome, even pleasing, and stood on one leg to show them what a gay bird it was. It then returned to the business of pecking a piece of apple.

"I see you've given him something to eat," Didymus said, and felt that Titus, though he seemed content to watch the canary, waited for him to say something more. "I am very happy, Titus, to have this canary," he went on. "I suppose he will come in handy now that I must spend my days in this infernal chair."

Titus did not look at him while he said, "He is a good bird, Father. He is one of the Saint's own good birds."

Through the window Didymus watched the days and nights come and go. For the first time, though his life as a friar had been copiously annotated with significant references, he got a good idea of eternity. Monotony, of course, was one word for it, but like all the others, as well as the allegories worked up by imaginative retreat masters, it was empty beside the experience itself, untranslatable. He would doze and wonder if by some quirk he had been cast out of the world into eternity, but since it was neither heaven nor exactly purgatory or hell, as he understood them, he concluded it must be an uncharted isle subscribing to the mother forms only in the matter of time. And having thought this, he was faintly annoyed at his ponderous whimsy. Titus, like certain of the hours, came periodically. He would read or simply sit with him in silence. The canary was there always, but except as it showed signs of sleepiness at twilight and spirit at dawn, Didymus regarded it as a subtle device, like the days and nights and bells, to give the lie to the vulgar error that time flies. The cage was small and the canary would not sing. Time, hanging in the room like a jealous fog, possessed him and voided everything except it. It seemed impossible each time Titus came that he should be able to escape the room.

" 'After him,' " Titus read from Bishop Bale one day, " 'came Fabius, a Roman born, who (as Eusebius witnesseth) as he was returning home out of the field, and with his countrymen present to elect a new bishop, there was a pigeon seen standing on his head and suddenly he was created pastor of the Church, which he looked not for.' "

They smiled at having the same thought and both looked up at the canary. Since Didymus sat by the window most of the day now, he had asked Titus to put a hook there for the cage. He had to admit to himself he did this to let Titus know he appreciated the canary. Also, as a secondary motive, he reasoned, it enabled the canary to look out the window. What a little yellow bird could see to interest it in the frozen scene was a mystery, but that, Didymus sighed, was a two-edged sword. And he took to watching the canary more.

So far as he was able to detect the moods of the canary he

participated in them. In the morning the canary, bright and clownish, flitted back and forth between the two perches in the cage, hanging from the sides and cocking its little tufted head at Didymus querulously. During these acrobatics Didymus would twitch his hands in quick imitation of the canary's stunts. He asked Titus to construct a tiny swing, such as he had seen, which the canary might learn to use, since it appeared to be an intelligent and daring sort. Titus got the swing, the canary did master it, but there seemed to be nothing Didymus could do with his hands that was like swinging. In fact, after he had been watching awhile, it was as though the canary were fixed to a pendulum, inanimate, a piece of machinery, a yellow blur—ticking, for the swing made a little sound, and Didymus went to sleep, and often when he woke the canary was still going, like a clock. Didymus had no idea how long he slept at these times, maybe a minute, maybe hours. Gradually the canary got bored with the swing and used it less and less. In the same way, Didymus suspected, he himself had wearied of looking out the window. The first meager satisfaction had worn off. The dead trees, the sleeping snow, like the swing for the canary, were sources of diversion which soon grew stale. They were captives, he and the canary, and the only thing they craved was escape. Didymus slowly considered the problem. There was nothing, obviously, for him to do. He could pray, which he did, but he was not sure the only thing wrong with him was the fact he could not walk and that to devote his prayer to that end was justifiable. Inevitably it occurred to him his plight might well be an act of God. Why this punishment, though, he asked himself, and immediately supplied the answer. He had, for one thing, gloried too much in having it in him to turn down Seraphin's request to come to St Louis. The intention—that was all important, and he, he feared, had done the right thing for the wrong reason. He had noticed something of the faker in himself before. But it was not clear if he had erred. There was a certain consolation, at bottom dismal, in this doubt. It was true there appeared to be a nice justice in being stricken a cripple if he had been wrong in refusing to travel to see Seraphin, if human love was all he was fitted for, if he was incapable of renunciation for the right reason, if the mystic counsels were too strong for him, if he was still too pedestrian after all these years of prayer and contemplation, if . . .

The canary was swinging, the first time in several days.

The reality of his position was insupportable. There were two ways of regarding it and he could not make up his mind. Humbly he wished to get well and to be able to walk. But if this was a punishment, was not prayer to lift it declining to see the divine point? He did wish to get well; that would settle it. Otherwise his predicament could only be resolved through means more serious than he dared cope with. It would be like refusing to see Seraphin all over again. By some mistake, he protested, he had at last been placed in a position vital with meaning and precedents inescapably Christian. But was he the man for it? Unsure of himself, he was afraid to go on trial. It would be no minor trial, so construed, but one in which the greatest values were involved—a human soul and the means of its salvation or damnation. Not watered-down suburban precautions and routine pious exercises, but Faith such as saints and martyrs had, and Despair such as only they had been tempted by. No, he was not the man for it. He was unworthy. He simply desired to walk and in a few years to die a normal, uninspired death. He did not wish to see (what was apparent) the greatest significance in his affliction. He preferred to think in terms of physical betterment. He was so sure he was not a saint that he did not consider this easier road beneath him, though attracted by the higher one. That was the rub. Humbly, then, he wanted to be able to walk, but he wondered if there was not presumption in such humility.

Thus he decided to pray for health and count the divine hand not there. Decided. A clean decision—not distinction— no mean feat in the light of all the moral theology he had swallowed. The canary, all its rocking come to naught once more, slept motionless in the swing. Despite the manifest prudence of the course he had settled upon, Didymus dozed off ill at ease in his wheelchair by the window. Distastefully, the last thing he remembered was that prudence" is a virtue more celebrated in the modern Church.

At his request in the days following a doctor visited him. The Rector came along, too. When Didymus tried to find out the nature of his illness, the doctor looked solemn and pronounced it to be one of those things. Didymus received this with a look of mystification. So the doctor went on to say there was no telling about it. Time alone would tell. Didymus asked the doctor to recommend some books dealing with cases like his. They might have one of them in the monastery library. Titus could read to him in the meantime. For, though he disliked being troublesome, "one of those things" as a diagnosis meant very little to an unscientific beggar like him. The phrase had a philosophic ring to it, but to his knowledge neither the Early Fathers nor the Scholastics seemed to have dealt with it. The Rector smiled. The doctor, annoyed, replied drily:

"Is that a fact?"

Impatiently Didymus said, "I know how old I am, if that's it."

Nothing was lost of the communion he kept with the canary. He still watched its antics and his fingers in his lap followed them clumsily. He did not forget about himself, that he must pray for health, that it was best that way—"prudence" dictated it—but he did think more of the canary's share of their captivity. A canary in a cage, he reasoned, is like a bud which never blooms.

He asked Titus to get a book on canaries, but nothing came of it and he did not mention it again.

Some days later Titus read:

" 'Twenty-ninth pope, Marcellus, a Roman, was pastor of the Church, feeding it with wisdom and doctrine. And (as I may say with the Prophet) a man according to God's heart and full of Christian works. This man admonished Maximianus the Emperor and endeavored to remove him from persecuting the saints—' "

"Stop a moment, Titus," Didymus interrupted.

Steadily, since Titus began to read, the canary had been jumping from the swing to the bottom of the cage and back again. Now it was quietly standing on one foot in the swing. Suddenly it flew at the side of the cage nearest them and hung there, its ugly little claws, like bent wire, hooked to the slender bars. It observed them intently, first Titus and then Didymus, at whom it continued to stare. Didymus's hands were tense in his lap.

"Go ahead, read," Didymus said, relaxing his hands.

" 'But the Emperor being more hardened, commanded Marcellus to be beaten with cudgels and to be driven out of the city, wherefore he entered into the house of one Lucina, a widow, and there kept the congregation secretly, which the tyrant hearing, made a stable for cattle of the same house and committed the keeping of it to the bishop Marcellus. After that he governed the Church by writing Epistles, without any other kind of teaching, being condemned to such a vile service. And being thus daily tormented with strife and noisomeness, at length gave up the ghost. Anno 308.' "

"Very good, Titus. I wonder how we missed that one before."

The canary, still hanging on the side of the cage, had not moved, its head turned sidewise, its eye as before fixed on Didymus.

"Would you bring me a glass of water, Titus?"

Titus got up and looked in the cage. The canary hung there, as though waiting, not a feather stirring.

"The bird has water here," Titus said, pointing to the small cup fastened to the cage.

"For me, Titus, the water's for me. Don't you think I know you look after the canary? You don't forget us, though I don't see why you don't."

Titus left the room with a glass.

Didymus's hands were tense again. Eyes on the canary's eye, he got up from his wheelchair, his face strained and white with the impossible effort, and, his fingers somehow managing it, he opened the cage. The canary darted out and circled the room chirping. Before it lit, though it seemed about to make its perch triumphantly the top of the cage, Didymus fell over on his face and lay prone on the floor.

In bed that night, unsuffering and barely alive, he saw at will everything revealed in his past. Events long forgotten happened again before his eyes. Clearly, sensitively, he saw Seraphin and himself, just as they had always been—himself, never quite sure. He heard all that he had ever said, and that anyone had said to him. He had talked too much, too. The past mingled with the present. In the same moment and scene he made his first Communion, was ordained, and confessed his sins for the last time.

The canary perched in the dark atop the cage, head warm under wing, already, it seemed to Didymus, without memory of its captivity, dreaming of a former freedom, an ancestral summer day with flowers and trees. Outside it was snowing.

The Rector, followed by others, came into the room and administered the last sacrament. Didymus heard them all gathered prayerfully around his bed thinking (they thought) secretly: this sacrament often strengthens the dying, tip-of-the-tongue wisdom indigenous to the priesthood, Henry the Eighth had six wives. He saw the same hackneyed smile, designed to cheer, pass bravely among them, and marveled at the crudity of it. They went away then, all except Titus, their individual foot-steps sounding (for him) the character of each friar. He might have been Francis himself for what he knew then of the little brothers and the cure of souls. He heard them thinking their expectation to be called from bed before daybreak to return to his room and say the office of the dead over his body, become the body, and whispering hopefully to the contrary. Death was now an unwelcome guest in the cloister.

He wanted nothing in the world for himself at last. This may have been the first time he found his will amenable to the Divine. He had never been less himself and more the saint. Yet now, so close to sublimity, or perhaps only tempted to believe so (the Devil is most wily at the death-bed), he was beset by the grossest distractions. They were to be expected, he knew, as indelible in the order of things: the bingo game going on un-der the Cross for the seamless garment of the Son of Man: everywhere the sign of the contradiction, and always. When would he cease to be surprised by it? Incidents repeated them-selves, twined, parted, faded away, came back clear, and would not be prayed out of mind. He watched himself mounting the pulpit of a metropolitan church, heralded by the pastor as the renowned Franciscan father sent by God in His goodness to preach this novena—like to say a little prayer to test the mi-crophone, Father?—and later reading through the petitions to Our Blessed Mother, cynically tabulating the pleas for a Cath-olic boyfriend, drunkenness banished, the sale of real estate and coming furiously upon one: "that I'm not pregnant." And at the same church on Good Friday carrying the crucifix along the communion rail for the people to kiss, giving them the in-dulgence, and afterwards in the sacristy wiping the lipstick of the faithful from the image of Christ crucified.

"Take down a book, any book, Titus, and read. Begin anywhere."

Roused by his voice, the canary fluttered, looked sharply about and buried its head once more in the warmth of its wing.

" 'By the lions,' " Titus read, " 'are understood the acrimonies and impetuosities of the irascible faculty, which faculty is as bold and daring in its acts as are the lions. By the harts and the leaping does is understood the other faculty of the soul, which is the concupiscible—that is—' "

"Skip the exegesis," Didymus broke in weakly. "I can do without that now. Read the verse."

Titus read: " 'Birds of swift wing, lions, harts, leaping does, mountains, valleys, banks, waters, breezes, heats and terrors that keep watch by night, by the pleasant lyres and by the siren's song, I conjure you, cease your wrath and touch not the wall . . .' "

"Turn off the light, Titus."

Titus went over to the switch. There was a brief period of darkness during which Didymus's eyes became accustomed to a different shade, a glow rather, which possessed the room slowly. Then he saw the full moon had let down a ladder of light through the window. He could see the snow, strangely blue, falling outside. So sensitive was his mind and eye (because his body, now faint, no longer blurred his vision?) he could count the snowflakes, all of them separately, before they drifted, winding, below the sill.

With the same wonderful clarity, he saw what he had made of his life. He saw himself tied down, caged, stunted in his apostolate, seeking the crumbs, the little pleasure, neglecting the source, always knowing death changes nothing, only immortalizes . . . and still ever lukewarm. In trivial attachments, in love of things, was death, no matter the appearance of life. In the highest attachment only, no matter the appearance of death, was life. He had always known this truth, but now he was feeling it. Unable to move his hand, only his lips, and hardly breathing, was it too late to act?

"Open the window, Titus," he whispered.

And suddenly he could pray. *Hail Mary . . . Holy Mary, Mother of God, pray for us sinners now and at the hour of our death . . .* finally the time to say, *pray for* me *now—the hour of my death, amen.* Lest he deceive himself at the very end that this was the answer to a lifetime of praying for a happy death, happy because painless, he tried to turn his thoughts from himself, to join them to God, thinking how at last he did— didn't he *now*?—prefer God above all else. But ashamedly not sure he did, perhaps only fearing hell, with an uneasy sense of justice he put himself foremost among the wise in their own generation, the perennials seeking after God when doctor, law- yer, and bank fail. If he wronged himself, he did so out of hu- mility—a holy error. He ended, to make certain he had not fallen under the same old presumption disguised as the face of humility, by flooding his mind with maledictions. He suffered the piercing white voice of the Apocalypse to echo in his soul: *But because thou art lukewarm, and neither cold, nor hot, I will begin to vomit thee out of my mouth.* And St Bernard, fiery-eyed in a white habit, thundered at him from the twelfth century: "Hell is paved with the bald pates of priests!"

There was a soft flutter, the canary flew to the window sill, paused, and tilted into the snow. Titus stepped too late to the window and stood gazing dumbly after it. He raised a trem- bling old hand, fingers bent in awe and sorrow, to his forehead, and turned stealthily to Didymus.

Didymus closed his eyes. He let a long moment pass before he opened them. Titus, seeing him awake then, fussed with the window latch and held a hand down to feel the draft, nodding anxiously as though it were the only evil abroad in the world, all the time straining his old eyes for a glimpse of the canary somewhere in the trees.

Didymus said nothing, letting Titus keep his secret. With his whole will he tried to lose himself in the sight of God, and failed. He was not in the least transported. Even now he could find no divine sign within himself. He knew he still had to look outside, to Titus. God still chose to manifest Himself most in sanctity.

Titus, nervous under his stare, and to account for staying at the window so long, felt for the draft again, frowned, and kept his eye hunting among the trees.

The thought of being the cause of such elaborate dissimulation in so simple a soul made Didymus want to smile—or cry, he did not know which . . . and could do neither. Titus persisted. How long would it be, Didymus wondered faintly, before Titus ungrievingly gave the canary up for lost in the snowy arms of God? The snowflakes whirled at the window, for a moment for all their bright blue beauty as though struck still by lightning, and Didymus closed his eyes, only to find them there also, but darkly falling.

JAMESIE

THERE IT WAS, all about Lefty, in Ding Bell's Dope Box.

"We don't want to add coals to the fire, but it's common knowledge that the Local Pitcher Most Likely To Succeed is fed up with the home town. Well, well, the boy's good, which nobody can deny, and the scouts are on his trail, but it doesn't say a lot for his team spirit, not to mention his civic spirit, this high-hat attitude of his. And that fine record of his—has it been all a case of him and him alone? How about the team? The boys have backed him up, they've given him the runs, and that's what wins ball games. They don't pay off on strike-outs. There's one kind of player every scribe knows—and wishes he didn't—the lad who gets four for four with the willow, and yet, somehow, his team goes down to defeat—but does that worry this gent? Not a bit of it. He's too busy celebrating his own personal success, figuring his batting average, or, if he's a pitcher, his earned run average and strike-outs. The percentage player. We hope we aren't talking about Lefty. If we are, it's too bad, it is, and no matter where he goes from here, especially if it's up

to the majors, it won't remain a secret very long, nor will he
... See you at the game Sunday. Ding Bell."

"Here's a new one, Jamesie," his father said across the
porch, holding up the rotogravure section.

With his father on Sunday it could be one of three things—a
visit to the office, fixing up his mother's grave in Calvary, or
just sitting on the porch with all the Chicago papers, as today.

Jamesie put down the *Courier* and went over to his father
without curiosity. It was always Lindy or the *Spirit of St Louis*,
and now without understanding how this could so suddenly
be, he was tired of them. His father, who seemed to feel that a
growing boy could take an endless interest in these things, appeared to know the truth at last. He gave a page to the floor—
that way he knew what he'd read and how far he had to go—
and pulled the newspaper around his ears again. Before he went
to dinner he would put the paper in order and wish out loud
that other people would have the decency to do the same.

Jamesie, back in his chair, granted himself one more chapter
of *Baseball Bill in the World Series*. The chapters were running out again, as they had so many times before, and he knew,
with the despair of a narcotic, that his need had no end.

Baseball Bill, at fifty cents a volume and unavailable at the
library, kept him nearly broke, and Francis Murgatroyd, his best
friend ... too stingy to go halves, confident he'd get to read
them all as Jamesie bought them, and each time offering to exchange the old Tom Swifts and Don Sturdys he had got for
Christmas—as though that were the same thing!

Jamesie owned all the Baseball Bills to be had for love or
money in the world, and there was nothing in the back of this
one about new titles being in preparation. Had the author died,
as some of them did, and left his readers in the lurch? Or had
the series been discontinued—for where, after *Fighting for the
Pennant* and *In the World Series*, could Baseball Bill go? *Baseball Bill, Manager*, perhaps. But then what?

"A plot to *fix* the World Series! So that was it! Bill began to see it all ... The mysterious call in the night! The diamond necklace in the dressing room! The scribbled note under the door! With slow fury Bill realized that the peculiar odor on the note paper was the odor in his room now! It was the odor of strong drink and cigar smoke! And it came from his midnight visitor! The same! Did he represent the powerful gambling syndicate? Was *he* Blackie Humphrey himself? Bill held his towering rage in check and smiled at his visitor in his friendly, boyish fashion. His visitor must get no inkling of his true thoughts. Bill must play the game—play the very fool they took him for! Soon enough they would discover for themselves, but to their everlasting sorrow, the courage and daring of Baseball Bill ..."

Jamesie put the book aside, consulted the batting averages in the *Courier*, and reread Ding Bell. Then, not waiting for dinner and certain to hear about it at supper, he ate a peanut butter sandwich with catsup on it, and left by the back door. He went down the alley calling for Francis Murgatroyd. He got up on the Murgatroyd gate and swung—the death-defying trapeze act at the circus—until Francis came down the walk.

"Hello, Blackie Humphrey," Jamesie said tantalizingly.

"Who's Blackie Humphrey?"

"You know who Blackie Humphrey is all right."

"Aw, Jamesie, cut it out."

"And you want me to throw the World Series!"

"Baseball Bill!"

"In the World Series. It came yesterday."

"Can I read it?"

Jamesie spoke in a hushed voice. "So you're Blackie Humphrey?"

"All right. But I get to read it next."

"So you want me to throw the World Series, Blackie. Is that it? Say you do."

"Yes, I do."

"Ask me again. Call me Bill."

"Bill, I want you to throw the World Series. Will you, Bill?"

"I might." But that was just to fool Blackie. Bill tried to keep his towering rage in check while feigning an interest in the nefarious plot. "Why do you want me to throw it, Blackie?"

"I don't know."

"Sure you know. You're a dirty crook and you've got a lot of dough bet on the other team."

"Uh, huh."

"Go ahead. Tell me that."

While Blackie unfolded the criminal plan Bill smiled at him in his friendly, boyish fashion.

"And who's behind this, Blackie?"

"I don't know."

"Say it's the powerful gambling syndicate."

"It's them."

"Ah, ha! Knock the ash off your cigar."

"Have I got one?"

"Yes, and you've got strong drink on your breath, too."

"Whew!"

Blackie should have fixed him with his small, piglike eyes.

"Fix me with your small, piglike eyes."

"Wait a minute, Jamesie!"

"Bill. Go ahead. Fix me."

"O.K. But you don't get to be Bill all the time."

"Now blow your foul breath in my face."

"There!"

"Now ask me to have a cigar. Go ahead."

Blackie was offering Bill a cigar, but Bill knew it was to get him to break training and refused it.

"I see through you, Blackie." No, that was wrong. He had to conceal his true thoughts and let Blackie play him for a fool. Soon enough his time would come and... "Thanks for the cigar, Blackie," he said. "I thought it was a cheap one. Thanks, I'll smoke it later."

"I paid a quarter for it."

"Hey, that's too much, Francis!"

"Well, if I'm the head of the powerful—"

Mr Murgatroyd came to the back door and told Francis to get ready.

"I can't go to the game, Jamesie," Francis said. "I have to caddy for him."

Jamesie got a ride with the calliope when it had to stop at the corner for the light. The calliope was not playing now, but yesterday it had roamed the streets, all red and gold and glittering like a hussy among the pious, black Fords parked on the Square, blaring and showing off, with a sign, Jayville vs. Beardstown.

The ball park fence was painted a swampy green except for an occasional new board. Over the single ticket window cut in the fence hung a sign done in the severe black and white railroad manner, "Home of the Jayville Independents," but everybody called them the "Indees."

Jamesie bought a bottle of Green River out of his savings and made the most of it, swallowing it in sips, calling upon his willpower under the sun. He returned the bottle and stood for a while by the ticket window making designs in the dust with the corrugated soles of his new tennis shoes. Ding Bell, with a pretty lady on his arm and carrying the black official scorebook, passed inside without paying, and joked about it.

The Beardstown players arrived from sixty miles away with threatening cheers. Their chartered bus stood steaming and dusty from the trip. The players wore gray suits with "Barons" written across their chests and had the names of sponsors on their backs—Palms Café, Rusty's Wrecking, Coca-Cola.

Jamesie recognized some of the Barons but put down a desire to speak to them.

The last man to leave the bus, Jamesie thought, must be Guez, the new pitcher imported from East St Louis for the game. Ding Bell had it in the Dope Box that "Saliva Joe" was one of the few spitters left in the business, had been up in the Three Eye a few years, was a full-blooded Cuban, and ate a bottle of aspirins a game, just like candy.

The dark pitcher's fame was too much for Jamesie. He walked alongside Guez. He smelled the salt and pepper of the gray uniform, saw the scarred plate on the right toe, saw the tears in the striped stockings—the marks of bravery or moths— heard the distant chomp of tobacco being chewed, felt—almost —the iron drape of the flannel, and was reduced to friendliness with the pitcher, the enemy.

"Are you a real Cuban?"

Guez looked down, rebuking Jamesie with a brief stare, and growled, "Go away."

Jamesie gazed after the pitcher. He told himself that he hated Guez—that's what he did, hated him! But it didn't do much good. He looked around to see if anybody had been watching, but nobody had, and he wanted somebody his size to vanquish —somebody who might think Guez was as good as Lefty. He wanted to bet a million dollars on Lefty against Guez, but there was nobody to take him up on it.

The Indees began to arrive in ones and twos, already in uniform but carrying their spikes in their hands. Jamesie spoke to all of them except J. G. Nickerson, the manager. J. G. always glared at kids. He thought they were stealing his baseballs and laughing about it behind his back. He was a great one for signaling with a score card from the bench, like Connie Mack, and Ding Bell had ventured to say that managers didn't come any brainier than Jayville's own J. G. Nickerson, even in the big time. But if there should be a foul ball, no matter how tight the game or crucial the situation, J. G. would leap up, straining like a bird dog, and try to place it, waving the bat boy on without taking his eyes off the spot where it disappeared over the fence or in the weeds. That was why they called him the Foul Ball.

The Petersons—the old man at the wheel, a red handkerchief tied tight enough around his neck to keep his head on, and the sons, all players, Big Pete, Little Pete, Middle Pete, and Extra Pete—roared up with their legs hanging out of the doorless Model T and the brass radiator boiling over.

The old man ran the Model T around in circles, damning it for a runaway horse, and finally got it parked by the gate.

"Hold 'er, Knute!" he cackled.

The boys dug him in the ribs, tickling him, and were like puppies that had been born bigger than their father, jollying him through the gate, calling him Barney Oldfield.

Lefty came.

"Hi, Lefty," Jamesie said.

"Hi, kid," Lefty said. He put his arm around Jamesie and took him past the ticket taker.

"It's all right, Mac," he said.

"Today's the day, Lefty," Mac said. "You can do it, Lefty."

Jamesie and Lefty passed behind the grandstand. Jamesie saw Lefty's father, a skinny, brown-faced man in a yellow straw katy.

"There's your dad, Lefty."

Lefty said, "Where?" but looked the wrong way and walked a little faster.

At the end of the grandstand Lefty stopped Jamesie. "My old man is out of town, kid. Got that?"

Jamesie did not see how this could be. He knew Lefty's father. Lefty's father had a brown face and orange gums. But Lefty ought to know his own father. "I guess it just looked like him, Lefty," Jamesie said.

Lefty took his hand off Jamesie's arm and smiled. "Yeah, that's right, kid. It just looked like him on account of he's out of town—in Peoria."

Jamesie could still feel the pressure of Lefty's fingers on his arm. They came out on the diamond at the Indees bench near first base. The talk quieted down when Lefty appeared. Everybody thought he had a big head, but nobody could say a thing against his pitching record, it was that good. The scout for the New York Yankees had invited him only last Sunday to train with them next spring. The idea haunted the others. J. G. had shut up about the beauties of teamwork.

J. G. was counting the balls when Jamesie went to the suitcase to get one for Lefty. J. G. snapped the lid down.

"It's for Lefty!"

"Huh!"

"He wants it for warm up."

"Did you tell this kid to get you a ball, Left?"

"Should I bring my own?" Lefty said.

J. G. dug into the suitcase for a ball, grunting, "I only asked him." He looked to Jamesie for sympathy. He considered the collection of balls and finally picked out a fairly new one.

"Lefty, he likes 'em brand new," Jamesie said.

"Who's running this club?" J. G. bawled. But he threw the ball back and broke a brand new one out of its box and tissue paper. He ignored Jamesie's ready hand and yelled to Lefty going out to the bull pen, "Coming at you, Left," and threw it wild.

Lefty let the ball bounce through his legs, not trying for it. "Nice throw," he said.

Jamesie retrieved the ball for Lefty. They tossed it back and forth, limbering up, and Jamesie aped Lefty's professional indolence.

When Bugs Bidwell, Lefty's battery mate, appeared with his big mitt, Jamesie stood aside and buttoned his glove back on his belt. Lefty shed his red blanket coat with the leathersleeves and gave it to Jamesie for safekeeping. Jamesie folded it gently over his arm, with the white chenille "J" showing out. He took his stand behind Bugs to get a good look at Lefty's stuff.

Lefty had all his usual stuff—the fast one with the two little hops in it, no bigger than a pea; his slow knuckler that looked like a basketball, all the stitches standing still and staring you in the face; his sinker that started out high like a wild pitch, then dipped a good eight inches and straightened out for a called strike. But something was wrong—Lefty with nothing to say, no jokes, no sudden whoops, was not himself. Only once did he smile at a girl in the bleachers and say she was plenty... and sent a fast one smacking into Bugs's mitt for what he meant.

That, for a moment, was the Lefty that Jamesie's older cousins knew about. They said a nice kid like Jamesie ought to be kept away from him, even at the ball park. Jamesie was always afraid it would get back to Lefty that the cousins thought he was poor white trash, or that he would know it in some other way, as when the cousins passed him on the street and looked the other way. He was worried, too, about what Lefty might think of his Sunday clothes, the snow-white blouse, the floppy sailor tie, the soft linen pants, the sissy clothes. His tennis shoes—sneakers, he ought to say—were all right, but not the golf stockings that left his knees bare, like a rich kid's. The tough guys, because they were tough or poor—he didn't know which—wore socks, not stockings, and they wore them rolled down slick to their ankles.

Bugs stuck his mitt with the ball in it under his arm and got out his Beechnut. He winked at Jamesie and said, "Chew?"

Jamesie giggled. He liked Bugs. Bugs, on loan from the crack State Hospital team, was all right—nothing crazy about him; he just liked it at the asylum, he said, the big grounds and lots of cool shade, and he was not required to work or take walks like the regular patients. He was the only Indee on speaking terms with Lefty.

Turning to Lefty, Bugs said, "Ever seen this Cuban work?"

"Naw."

"I guess he's got it when he's right."

"That so?" Lefty caught the ball with his bare hand and spun it back to Bugs. "Well, all I can promise you is a no-hit game. It's up to you clowns to get the runs."

"And me hitting a lousy .211."

"All you got to do is hold me. Anyhow what's the Foul Ball want for his five bucks—Mickey Cochrane?"

"Yeah, Left."

"I ought to quit him."

"Ain't you getting your regular fifteen?"

"Yeah, but I ought to quit. The Yankees want me. Is my curve breaking too soon?"

"It's right in there, Left."

It was a pitchers' battle until the seventh inning. Then the Indees pushed a run across.

The Barons got to Lefty for their first hit in the seventh, and when the next man bunted, Lefty tried to field it instead of letting Middle Pete at third have it, which put two on with none out. Little Pete threw the next man out at first, the only play possible, and the runners advanced to second and third. The next hitter hammered a line drive to Big Pete at first, and Big Pete tried to make it two by throwing to second, where the runner was off, but it was too late and the runner on third scored on the play. J. G. from the bench condemned Big Pete for a dumb Swede. The next man popped to short center.

Jamesie ran out with Lefty's jacket. "Don't let your arm get cold, Lefty."

"Some support I got," Lefty said.

"Whyn't you leave me have that bunt, Lefty?" Middle Pete said, and everybody knew he was right.

"Two of them pitches was hit solid," Big Pete said. "Good anywhere."

"Now, boys," J. G. said.

"Aw, dry up," Lefty said, grabbing a blade of grass to chew. "I ought to quit you bums."

Pid Kirby struck out for the Indees, but Little Pete walked, and Middle Pete advanced him to second on a long fly to left. Then Big Pete tripled to the weed patch in center, clear up against the Chevrolet sign, driving in Little Pete. Guez whiffed Kelly Larkin, retiring the side, and the Indees were leading the Barons 2 to 1.

The first Baron to bat in the eighth had J. G. frantic with fouls. The umpire was down to his last ball and calling for more. With trembling fingers J. G. unwrapped new balls. He had the bat boy and the bat boy's assistant hunting for them behind the grandstand. When one fell among the automobiles parked near first, he started to go and look for himself, but thought of Jamesie and sent him instead. "If anybody tries to hold out on you, come and tell me."

After Jamesie found the ball he crept up behind a familiar blue Hupmobile, dropping to his knees when he was right under Uncle Pat's elbow, and then popping up to scare him.

"Look who's here," his cousin said. It had not been Uncle Pat's elbow at all, but Gabriel's. Uncle Pat, who had never learned to drive, sat on the other side to be two feet closer to the game.

Jamesie stepped up on the running board, and Gabriel offered him some popcorn.

"So you're at the game, Jamesie," Uncle Pat said, grinning as though it were funny. "Gabriel said he thought that was you out there."

"Where'd you get the cap, Jamesie?" Gabriel said.

"Lefty. The whole team got new ones. And if they win today J. G. says they're getting whole new uniforms."

"Not from me," Uncle Pat said, looking out on the field. "Who the thunder's wearing my suit today?"

"Lee Coles, see?" Gabriel said, pointing to the player. Lee's back—Mallon's Grocery—was to them.

Uncle Pat, satisfied, slipped a bottle of near beer up from the floor to his lips and tipped it up straight, which explained to Jamesie the foam on his mustache.

"You went and missed me again this week," Uncle Pat said broodingly. "You know what I'm going to do, Jamesie?"

"What?"

"I'm going to stop taking your old *Liberty* magazine if you don't bring me one first thing tomorrow morning."

"I will." He would have to bring Uncle Pat his own free copy and erase the crossword puzzle. He never should have sold out on the street. That was how you lost your regular customers.

Uncle Pat said, "This makes the second time I started in to read a serial and had this happen to me."

"Is it all right if the one I bring you tomorrow has got 'Sample Copy' stamped on it?"

"That's all right with me, Jamesie, but I ought to get it for nothing." Uncle Pat swirled the last inch of beer in the bottle until it was all suds.

"I like the *Post*," Gabriel said. "Why don't you handle the *Post*?"

"They don't need anybody now."

"What he ought to handle," Uncle Pat said, "is the *Country Gentleman*."

"How's the Rosebud coming, Jamesie?" Gabriel asked. "But I don't want to buy any."

Uncle Pat and Gabriel laughed at him.

Why was that funny? He'd had to return eighteen boxes and tell them he guessed he was all through being the local representative. But why was that so funny?

"Did you sell enough to get the bicycle, Jamesie?"

"No." He had sold all the Rosebud salve he could, but not

nearly enough to get the Ranger bicycle. He had to be satisfied with the Eveready flashlight.

"Well, I got enough of that Rosebud salve now to grease the Hup," Gabriel said. "Or to smear all over me the next time I swim the English Channel—with Gertrude Ederle. It ought to keep the fishes away."

"It smells nice," Uncle Pat said. "But I got plenty."

Jamesie felt that they were protecting themselves against him.

"I sent it all back anyway," he said, but that was not true; there were six boxes at home in his room that he had to keep in order to get the flashlight. Why was that the way it always worked out? Same way with the flower seeds. Why was it that whenever he got a new suit at Meyer Brothers they weren't giving out ball bats or compasses? Why was it he only won a half pound of bacon at he carnival, never a Kewpie doll or an electric fan? Why did he always get tin whistles and crickets in the Cracker Jack, never a puzzle, a ring, or a badge? And one time he had got nothing! Why was it that the five-dollar bill he found on South Diamond Street belonged to Mrs Hutchinson? But he *had* found a quarter in the dust at the circus that nobody claimed.

"Get your aunt Kate to take that cap up in the back," Uncle Pat said, smiling.

Vaguely embarrassed, Jamesie said, "Well, I got to get back."

"If that's Lefty's cap," Gabriel called after him, "you'd better send it to the cleaners."

When he got back to the bench and handed the ball over, J. G. seemed to forget all about the bases being crowded.

"Thank God," he said. "I thought you went home with it."

The Barons were all on Lefty now. Shorty Parker, their manager, coaching at third, chanted, "Take him out . . . Take him out . . . Take him out."

The Barons had started off the ninth with two clean blows.

Then Bugs took a foul ball off the chicken wire in front of the grandstand for one out, and Big Pete speared a drive on the rise for another. Two down and runners on first and third. Lefty wound up—bad baseball—and the man on first started for second, the batter stepping into the pitch, not to hit it but to spoil the peg to second. The runner was safe; the man on third, threatening to come home after a false start, slid yelling back into the sack. It was close and J. G. flew off the bench to protest a little.

After getting two strikes on the next batter, Lefty threw four balls, so wide it looked like a deliberate pitchout, and that loaded the bases.

J. G. called time. He went out to the mound to talk it over with Lefty, but Lefty waved him away. So J. G. consulted Bugs behind the plate. Jamesie, lying on the grass a few feet away, could hear them.

"That's the first windup I ever seen a pitcher take with a runner on first."

"It was pretty bad," Bugs said.

"And then walking that last one. He don't look wild to me, neither."

"He ain't wild, J. G.; I'll tell you that."

"I want your honest opinion, Bugs."

"I don't know what to say, J. G."

"Think I better jerk him?"

Bugs was silent, chewing it over.

"Guess I better leave him in, huh?"

"You're the boss, J. G. I don't know nothing for sure."

"I only got Extra Pete to put in. They'd murder him. I guess I got to leave Lefty in and take a chance."

"I guess so."

When J. G. had gone Bugs walked halfway out to the mound and spoke to Lefty. "You all right?"

"I had a little twinge before."

"A little what?"

Lefty touched his left shoulder.

"You mean your arm's gone sore?"

"Naw. I guess it's nothing."

Bugs took his place behind the plate again. He crouched, and Jamesie, from where he was lying, saw two fingers appear below the mitt—the signal. Lefty nodded, wound up, and tried to slip a medium-fast one down the middle. Guez, the batter, poled a long ball into left—foul by a few feet. Bugs shook his head in the mask, took a new ball from the umpire, and slammed it hard at Lefty.

Jamesie saw two fingers below the mitt again. What was Bugs doing? It wasn't smart baseball to give Guez another like the last one!

Guez swung and the ball fell against the left-field fence—fair. Lee Coles, the left fielder, was having trouble locating it in the weeds. Kelly Larkin came over from center to help him hunt. When they found the ball, Guez had completed the circuit and the score was 5 to 2 in favor of the Barons.

Big Pete came running over to Lefty from first base, Little Pete from second, Pid Kirby from short, Middle Pete from third. J. G., calling time again, walked out to them.

"C'mere, Bugs," he said.

Bugs came slowly.

"What'd you call for on that last pitch?"

"Curve ball."

"And the one before that?"

"Same."

"And what'd Lefty give you?"

"It wasn't no curve. It wasn't much of anything."

"No," J. G. said. "It sure wasn't no curve ball. It was right in there, not too fast, not too slow, just right—for batting practice."

"It slipped," Lefty said.

"Slipped, huh!" Big Pete said. "How about the other one?"

"They both slipped. Ain't that never happened before?"

"Well, it ain't never going to happen again—not to me, it ain't," J. G. said. "I'm taking you out!"

He shouted to Extra Pete on the bench, "Warm up! You're going in!" He turned to Lefty.

"And I'm firing you. I just found out your old man was making bets under the grandstand—and they wasn't on us! I can put you in jail for this!"

"Try it," Lefty said, starting to walk away.

"If you knew it, J. G.," Big Pete said, "whyn't you let us know?"

"I just now found it out, is why."

"Then I'm going to make up for lost time," Big Pete said, following Lefty, "and punch this guy's nose."

Old man Peterson appeared among them—somebody must have told him what it was all about. "Give it to him, son!" he cackled.

Jamesie missed the fight. He was not tall enough to see over all the heads, and Gabriel, sent by Uncle Pat, was dragging him away from it all.

"I always knew that Lefty was a bad one," Gabriel said on the way home. "I knew it from the time he used to hunch in marbles."

"It reminds me of the Black Sox scandal of 1919," Uncle Pat said. "I wonder if they'll hold the old man, too."

Jamesie, in tears, said, "Lefty hurt his arm and you don't like him just because he don't work, and his father owes you at the store! Let me out! I'd rather walk by myself than ride in the Hupmobile—with you!"

He stayed up in his room, feigning a combination stomach-ache and headache, and would not come down for supper. Uncle Pat and Gabriel were down there eating. His room was over the dining room, and the windows were open upstairs and down, but he could not quite hear what they said. Uncle Pat was laughing a lot—that was all for sure—but then he always did that. Pretty soon he heard no more from the dining room and he knew they had gone to sit on the front porch.

Somebody was coming up the stairs. Aunt Kate. He knew the wavering step at the top of the stairs to be hers, and the long pause she used to catch her breath—something wrong with her lungs? Now, as she began to move, he heard ice tinkling in a glass. Lemonade. She was bringing him some supper. She knocked. He lay heavier on the bed and with his head at a painful angle to make her think he was suffering. She knocked again. If he pinched his forehead it would look red and feverish. He did. Now.

"Come in," he said weakly.

She came in, gliding across the room in the twilight, tall and white as a sail in her organdy, serene before her patient. Not quite opening his eyes, he saw her through the lashes. She thought he was sick all right, but even if she didn't, she would never take advantage of him to make a joke, like Uncle Pat, prescribing, "A good dose of salts! That's the ticket!" Or Gabriel, who was even meaner, "An enema!"

He had Aunt Kate fooled completely. He could fool her every time. On Halloween she was the kind of person who went to the door every time the bell rang. She was the only grownup he knew with whom it was not always the teetertotter game. She did not raise herself by lowering him. She did not say back to him the things he said, slightly changed, accented with a grin, so that they were funny. Uncle Pat did. Gabriel did. Sometimes, if there was company, his father did.

"Don't you want the shades up, Jamesie?"

She raised the shades, catching the last of that day's sun, bringing the ballplayers on the wall out of the shadows and into action. She put the tray on the table by his bed.

Jamesie sat up and began to eat. Aunt Kate was the best

one. Even if she noticed it, she would say nothing about his sudden turn for the better.

She sat across from him in the rocker, the little red one he had been given three years ago, when he was just a kid in the first grade, but she did not look too big for it. She ran her hand over the front of his books, frowning at Baseball Bill, Don Sturdy, Tom Swift, Horatio Alger, Jr, and the *Sporting News*. They had come between him and her.

"Where are the books we used to read, Jamesie?"

"On the bottom shelf."

She bent to see them. There they were, his old friends and hers—hers still. Perseus. Theseus. All those old Greeks. Sir Lancelot. Merlin. Sir Tristram. King Arthur. Oliver Twist. Pinocchio. Gulliver. He wondered how he ever could have liked them, and why Aunt Kate still did. Perhaps he still did, a little. But they turned out wrong, most of them, with all the good guys dying or turning into fairies and the bad guys becoming dwarfs. The books he read now turned out right, if not until the very last page, and the bad guys died or got what was coming to them.

"Were they talking about the game, Aunt Kate?"

"Your uncle was, and Gabriel."

Jamesie waited a moment. "Did they say anything about Lefty?"

"I don't know. Is he the one who lost the game on purpose?"

"That's a lie, Aunt Kate! That's just what Uncle Pat and Gabriel say!"

"Well, I'm sure I don't know—"

"You *are* on their side!"

Aunt Kate reached for his hand, but he drew it back.

"Jamesie, I'm sure I'm not on anyone's side. How can I be? I don't know about baseball—and I don't care about it!"

"Well, I *do*! And I'm not one bit sick—and you thought I was!"

Jamesie rolled out of bed, ran to the door, turned, and said, "Why don't you get out of my room and go and be with them! You're on their side! And Uncle Pat drinks *near beer*!"

He could not be sure, but he thought he had her crying, and if he did it served her right. He went softly down the stairs, past the living room, out the back door, and crept along the house until he reached the front porch. He huddled under the spiraea bushes and listened to them talk. But it was not about the game. It was about President Coolidge. His father was for him. Uncle Pat was against him.

Jamesie crept back along the house until it was safe to stand up and walk. He went down the alley. He called for Francis.

But Francis was not home—still with his father, Mrs Murgatroyd said.

Jamesie went downtown, taking his own special way, through alleys, across lots, so that he arrived on the Square without using a single street or walking on a single sidewalk. He weighed himself on the scales in front of Kresge's. He weighed eighty-three pounds, and the little card said, "You are the strong, silent type, and silence is golden." He weighed himself in front of Grant's. He weighed eighty-four pounds, and the card said, "Cultivate your good tastes and make the most of your business connections."

He bought a ball of gum from the machine in front of the Owl Drugstore. It looked like it was time for a black one to come out, and black was his favorite flavor, but it was a green one. Anyway he was glad it had not been white.

He coveted the Louisville Sluggers in the window of the D. & M. Hardware. He knew how much they cost. They were autographed by Paul Waner, Ty Cobb, Rogers Hornsby, all the big league stars, and if Lefty ever cracked his, a Paul Waner, he was going to give it to Jamesie, he said.

When Lefty was up with the Yankees—though they had not talked about it yet—he would send for Jamesie. He would make Jamesie the bat boy for the Yankees. He would say to Jake Ruppert, the owner of the Yankees, "Either you hire my friend, Jamesie, as bat boy or I quit." Jake Ruppert would want his own nephew or somebody to have the job, but what could he do? Jamesie would have a uniform like the regular players, and get to travel around the country with them, living in hotels, eating in restaurants, taking taxicabs, and would be known to everybody as Lefty's best friend, and they would both be Babe Ruth's best friends, the three of them going everywhere together. He would get all the Yankees to write their names on an Official American League ball and then send it home to Francis Murgatroyd, who would still be going to school back in Jayville—poor old Francis; and he would write to him on hotel stationery with his own fourteen-dollar fountain pen.

And then he was standing across the street from the jail. He wondered if they had Lefty locked up over there, if Uncle Pat and Gabriel had been right—not about Lefty throwing a game —that was a lie!—but about him being locked up. A policeman came out of the jail. Jamesie waited for him to cross the street. He was Officer Burkey. He was Phil Burkey's father, and Phil had shown Jamesie his father's gun and holster one time when he was sleeping. Around the house Mr Burkey looked like anybody else, not a policeman.

"Mr Burkey, is Lefty in there?"

Mr Burkey, through for the day, did not stop to talk, only saying, "Ah, that he is, boy, and there's where he deserves to be."

Jamesie said "Oh yeah!" to himself and went around to the back side of the jail. It was a brick building, painted gray, and the windows were open, but not so you could see inside, and they had bars over them.

Jamesie decided he could do nothing if Mr Burkey was off duty. The street lights came on; it was night. He began to wonder, too, if his father would miss him. Aunt Kate would not tell. But he would have to come in the back way and sneak up to his room. If it rained tomorrow he would stay in and make up with Aunt Kate. He hurried home, and did not remember that he had meant to stay out all night, maybe even run away forever.

The next morning Jamesie came to the jail early. Mr Burkey, on duty, said he might see Lefty for three minutes, but it was a mystery to him why anyone, especially a nice boy like Jamesie, should want to see the bum. "And don't tell your father you was here."

Jamesie found Lefty lying on a narrow iron bed that was all springs and no covers or pillow.

"Lefty," he said, "I came to see you."

Lefty sat up. He blinked at Jamesie and had trouble getting his eyes to see.

Jamesie went closer. Lefty stood up. They faced each other. Jamesie could have put his hand through the bars and touched Lefty.

"Glad to see you, kid."

"Lefty," Jamesie said, "I brought you some reading." He handed Lefty Uncle Pat's copy of *Liberty* magazine.

"Thanks, kid."

He got the box of Rosebud salve out of his pocket for Lefty.

"Well, thanks, kid. But what do I do with it?"

"For your arm, Lefty. It says 'recommended for aches and pains.'"

"I'll try it."

"Do you like oranges, Lefty?"

"I can eat 'em."

He gave Lefty his breakfast orange.

A funny, sweet smell came off Lefty's breath, like perfume, only sour. Burnt matches and cigar butts lay on the cell floor. Did Lefty smoke? Did he? Didn't he realize what it would do to him?

"Lefty, how do you throw your sinker?"

Lefty held the orange and showed Jamesie how he gripped the ball along the seams, how he snapped his wrist before he let it fly.

"But be sure you don't telegraph it, kid. Throw 'em all the same—your fast one, your floater, your curve. Then they don't know where they're at."

Lefty tossed the orange through the bars to Jamesie.

"Try it."

Jamesie tried it, but he had it wrong at first, and Lefty had to reach through the bars and show him again. After that they were silent, and Jamesie thought Lefty did not seem very glad to see him after all, and remembered the last gift.

"And I brought you this, Lefty."

It was *Baseball Bill in the World Series*.

"Yeah?" Lefty said, momentarily angry, as though he thought Jamesie was trying to kid him. He accepted the book reluctantly.

"He's a pitcher, Lefty," Jamesie said. "Like you, only he's a right-hander."

The sour perfume on Lefty's breath came through the bars again, a little stronger on a sigh.

Wasn't that the odor of strong drink and cigar smoke—the odor of Blackie Humphrey? Jamesie talked fast to keep himself from thinking. "This book's all about Baseball Bill and the World Series," he gulped, "and Blackie Humphrey and some dirty crooks that try to get Bill to throw it, but . . ." He gave up; he knew now. And Lefty had turned his back.

After a moment, during which nothing happened inside him to explain what he knew now, Jamesie got his legs to take him away, out of the jail, around the corner, down the street—away. He did not go through alleys, across lots, between buildings, over fences. No. He used the streets and sidewalks, like anyone else, to get where he was going—away—and was not quite himself.

HE DON'T PLANT COTTON

SPRING ENTERED THE black belt in ashes, dust, and drabness, without benefit of the saving green. The seasons were known only by the thermometer and the clothing of the people. There were only a few nights in the whole year when the air itself told you. Perhaps a night in April or May might escape the plague of smells, achieve a little of the enchantment, be the diminished echo of spring happening ardently in the suburbs, but it was all over in a night and the streets were filled with summer, as a hollow mouth with bad breath, and even the rain could not wash it away. And winter...

The beginning snow swirled in from the lake, dusting the streets with white. Baby squinted down the lonesome tracks. The wind twisted snow into his eyes, the flakes as sharp as sand, grinding, and his eyeballs were coated with cold tears. Baby worked his hands in his overcoat pockets to make heat. He saw a woman cross the street to catch the Big Red, which was coming now, but the woman refused stiffly to run for it. The wind went off hooting down the tracks ahead. Baby got on.

The conductor held out one hand for the fare and yanked a cord twice with the other, prodding the red monster into motion.

Baby sat down inside. A cold breeze swept the floor, rattling old transfers and gum wrappers. Baby placed his feet uneasily on the heater to make the meager warmth funnel up his pants' legs. The dark flesh beneath the tuxedo was chilled to chalky gray at the joints. He listened to the wheels bump over the breaks in the track, and the warmth from the heater rose higher on his legs. He became warm and forgetful of the weather, except as scenery. The streets were paved evenly with snow twinkling soft and clean and white under the lights, and velvet red and green from the neon signs.

New York may be all right, he hummed to himself, but Beale Street's paved with gold. That's a lie, he thought; I been down on Beale. And Chicago, same way. All my life playing jobs in Chicago, and I still got to ride the Big Red. And that's no lie. Jobs were getting harder and harder to find. What they wanted was Mickey Mouse sound effects, singing strings, electric guitars, neon violins, even organs and accordions and harmonica teams. Hard to find a spot to play in, and when you did it was always a white place with drunken advertising men wanting to hear "a old song"—"My Wild Irish Rose" or "I Love You Truly." So you played it, of course, and plenty of schmaltz. And the college kids who wanted swing—any slick popular song. So you played that, too. And always you wanted to play the music you were born to, blue or fast, music that had no name. You managed somehow to play that, too, when there was a lull or the place was empty and you had to stay until 4 A.M. anyway.

Baby got off the streetcar and walked the same two blocks he saw every night except Tuesday. The wind had died down almost entirely and the snow whirled in big flakes end over end. Padding along, Baby told himself he liked winter better than summer. Then he came to the place, said, "How's it,

Chief?" to the doorman, an Indian passing for Negro, went down three steps, and forgot all about winter and summer. It was always the same here. It was not so much a place of temperatures as a place of lights and shades and chromium, pastel mirrors, the smell of beer, rum, whisky, smoke—a stale blend of odors and shadows, darkness and music. It was a place of only one climate and that was it.

Baby's overcoat, hat, and scarf went into a closet and settled familiarly on hooks. His old tuxedo walked over to the traps. Its black hands rubbed together briskly, driving out the chill. One hand fumbled in the dark at the base of the big drum, and a second later a watery blue light winked on dully and flooded the drumhead, staring like a blind blue eye. Immediately the tuxedo sat down and worked its feet with a slight rasping noise into the floor. The fingers thumped testingly on the hide, tightened the snare. They knew, like the ears, when it was right. Gingerly, as always, the right foot sought the big drum's pedal. The tuxedo was not ready yet. It had to fidget and massage its seat around on the chair, stretch out its arms, and hug the whole outfit a fraction of an inch this way and that. Then the eyes glanced at the piano player, signaling ready. The drumsticks paused a moment tensely, slid into the beat, barely heard, accenting perfectly the shower of piano notes. Everything worked together for two choruses. Then the piano player tapered his solo gently, so that at a certain point Baby knew it was his. He brought the number to a lifeless close, run down. Too early in the evening.

"Dodo," Baby said to the piano player, "Libby come in yet?"

Dodo sent a black hand up, slow as smoke, toward the ceiling. "Upstairs," he said, letting the hand fall to the keyboard with a faint, far-off chord. It stirred there, gently worming music from the battered upright. Notes drew nearer, riding on ships and camels through a world of sand and water, till they came forthright from the piano, taking on patterns, as the other black hand came to life on the bass keys, dear to Dodo. Baby picked up his sticks, recognizing the number. He called it "Dodo's Blues," though he knew Dodo called it nothing. Every night about this time, when there was no crowd and Dodo hadn't yet put on the white coat he wore servicing the bar, they would play it. Baby half closed his eyes. With pleasure he watched Dodo through the clouds of rhythm he felt shimmering up like heat from his drums. Baby's eyes were open only enough to frame Dodo like a picture; everything else was out. It was a picture of many dimensions; music was only one of them.

Here was a man, midgety, hunchbacked, black, and proud—mostly all back and music. A little man who, when he was fixing to play, had to look around for a couple of three-inch telephone directories. Piling them on top of the piano bench, he sat down, with all their names and streets and numbers and exchanges under him. He had very little of thighs and stomach—mostly just back, which threw a round shadow on the wall. When he leaned farther away from the piano, so the light slanted through his hands, his shadow revealed him walking on his hands down the keyboard, dancing on the tips of fingery toes. Sometimes it seemed to Baby through half-closed eyes, when Dodo's body was bobbing on the wall and his hands were feet dancing on the keyboard, as though the dim light shaped him into a gigantic, happy spider. When he became a spider you could forget he was a man, hunchbacked, runtish, black; and he, too, could forget perhaps that he had to be careful and proud. Perhaps he could be happy always if his back and size and color and pride were not always standing in the way. The piano made him whole. The piano taught him to find himself and jump clean over the moon. When he played, his feet never touched the pedals.

People were beginning to fill the place. They finished off the number, Baby smiling his admiration, Dodo scrupulously expressionless.

"For a young man . . ." Baby said.

Dodo got down off the telephone directories and threw them under the piano at the bass end, beyond the blue glow of the big drum. He had seen Libby come down the steps from the dressing room—a red dress, a gardenia. Dodo went behind the bar and put on his white service coat. Libby sat down at the piano.

Helplessly attracted, several men came over from the bar and leaned on the piano. They stared, burdening Libby's body with calculations. Singly at first and then, gathering unity, together. Libby sang a popular song. The men went back to the bar to get their drinks, which they brought over and set on top of the upright. Libby sang the words about lost love, and the men licked their lips vacantly. At the end of the song they clapped fiercely. Libby ignored them with a smile.

"Say, that was just fine," one man said. "Where you from anyhow?"

With a little grin Libby acknowledged Baby. Baby, beaming his veteran admiration of a fine young woman, nodded.

"Where you from? Huh?"

"New Orleans."

"Well, you don't say!" the man blurted out joyfully. "We're from down South, too . . . Mississippi, matter of fact!"

Icily, Libby smiled her appreciation of this coincidence. She looked at Baby, who was also registering appropriately. Just think of that! Small world! And welcome to our city!

"Well, what do you know!" crowed the gentleman from Mississippi. "So you're from down South!" He was greatly pleased and already very drunk. He eyed his friends, four or five of them, distributing his discovery equally among them.

"You never know," he explained. Then he appeared to suffer a pang of doubt. He turned quickly to Libby again, as though to make sure she was still there. His eyes jellied blearily and in them an idea was born.

"I know," he said. "Sing . . . sing—sing 'Ol' Man River' for the boys. They all'd sure like that."

Without responding, Libby looked down at her hands, smiling. She measured chords between her thumbs and little fingers, working her amusement into the keys. Baby stared at the mottled hide of his snare drum, at the big one's rim worn down from playing "Dixieland." The gentleman from Mississippi got worried.

"Aw, sing it," he pleaded. So Libby sang a chorus. The gentlemen from Mississippi were overwhelmed. They loved the song, they loved the South, the dear old Southland. Land of cotton, cinnamon seed, and sandy bottom. Look away! Look away! They loved themselves. Look away! Look away! There was the tiniest touch of satire in Libby's voice, a slightly overripe fervor. Baby caught it and behind the bar Dodo caught it, but the gentlemen did not. Dodo had put down the martini glass he was polishing and look away! look away!— good.

At the bridge of the second chorus, Libby nodded "Take it!" to Baby. He stood up, staggering from the heat of the fields, clenching his black, toilworn fists. In profound anguish, he hollered, giving the white folks his all, really knocking himself out.

> "Tote dat barge
> Lift dat bale
> Git a little drunk—"

Baby grimaced in torment and did his best to look like ol' Uncle Tom out snatchin' cotton.

Behind the bar, unnoticed, Dodo's sad black face had turned beatific. "—And you land in jail!" Dodo could not see the other faces, the big white ones, but he could imagine them, the heads fixed and tilted. It was too dark in the place, and he could make out only blurrily the outlines of the necks. Ordinarily he was capable only of hating them. Now he had risen to great unfamiliar heights and was actually enjoying them. Surprised at this capacity in himself, yet proud he could feel this way, he was confused. He went further and started to pity them. But his memory stood up outraged at his forgetfulness and said, Kill that pity dead. Then he remembered he was really alone in the place. It was different with Libby and Baby, though they were black, too. He did not understand why. Say their skin was thicker—only that was not why. Probably this was not the first time they had jived white folks to death and them none the wiser. Dodo was not like that; he had to wait a long time for his kicks. From his heart no pity went out for the white men. He kept it all to himself, where it was needed. But he had to smile inside of him with Libby and Baby. Only more. Look at that fool Baby! Jam up!

> "Bend yo' knees
> An' bow yo' head
> An' pull dat rope
> Until yo're dead."

Baby sat down with a thud, exhausted. The gentlemen from Mississippi brayed their pleasure. My, it was good to see that black boy all sweatin' and perspirin' that way. They clapped furiously, called for drinks, gobbled . . .

"And bring some for the darkies!"

Baby swallowed some of his drink. He looked at the beaten rim of the big drum, then at the sticks. He took out his pocketknife and scraped the rough, splintery places smooth. He glanced at Libby and ventured the kind of smile he felt and knew she did. He finished his drink. The gentlemen from Mississippi hung around the piano, getting drunker, shouting in one another's faces. Nervously Libby lighted a cigarette. A college boy tried to make conversation with her while his honey-haired girl assumed an attitude of genuine concern.

"Can you play 'Hot Lips'?" He was the real American Boy.

"Don't know it," Libby lied. She wished she didn't.

"Can you play 'Sugar Blues'?" Right back.

"Don't know it."

One of the Mississippi gentlemen, who had been hanging back, crowded up to the piano, making his move. He drained his drink and pushed closer to the piano so as to brush Libby's left hand with the front of his trousers. Libby moved her hand, sounding a chord that Baby caught. The gentleman, grinning lewdly, tried to follow her hand up the keyboard.

"That's all right," he snickered. "Play lots of bass, honey."

The first gentleman from Mississippi, drink in hand, stumbled over from the bar. He told Libby to play that "Ol' Man River" song some more. Libby hesitated. Then she lit into it, improvising all around it, and it was a pleasure for Baby, but the first gentleman from Mississippi was not happy. He said if that was the best she could do she had better try singing. Libby sang only one chorus. The gentlemen from Mississippi, though they applauded, were not gratified. There was an air of petulance among them. They remembered another time they heard the song, but it was not clear now what had made it different and better. They saw Baby all right, but they did not remember that he was the one who had sung before, the good one that toted their bars, lifted their bales, and landed drunk in their jails. Something was wrong, but they saw no remedy. Each gentleman suspected the fault was personal, what with him drinking so heavy and all.

Dodo, behind the bar, had not enjoyed the song the last time, hating the coercion the white men worked on Libby and Baby, and feared his advantage was slipping away. In a minute he would be hating them to pieces again.

"Can you play 'Tiger Rag'?" The American Boy was back.

"No." Libby made a face and then managed to turn it into a smile for him. He held his drink up for the world to see on the night before the big game.

The honey-haired girl wrenched her face into a winning smile and hit the jackpot. "Can you play 'St Louis Blues'?"

"How you want it?" Libby said. She put out her cigarette. "Blues, rhumba . . . what kind a way?"

"Oh, play it low down. The way *you people* play it." So Libby would understand, she executed a ponderous wink, narrowed her eyes, and made them glitter wantonly behind the lashes. "*You* know," she said.

Libby knew. She played "St Louis," losing herself in it with Baby. She left the college boy and the honey-haired girl behind. She forgot she knew. She gazed at Baby with her eyes dreamy, unseeing, blind with the blue drum, her head nodding in that wonderful, graceful way. Baby saw his old tuxedo in the mirror, its body shimmying on the chair, and he was pleased. The drums, beating figures, rocked with a steady roll. They were playing "Little Rock Getaway" now, the fine, young-woman music.

And Libby was pleased, watching Baby. And then, somehow, he vanished for her into the blue drum. The sticks still danced at an oblique angle on the snare, but there were no hands to them and Libby could not see Baby on the chair. She could only feel him somewhere in the blue glow. Abandoning herself, she lost herself in the piano. Now, still without seeing him, she could feel him with a clarity and warmth beyond vision. Miniature bell notes, mostly blue, blossomed ecstatically, perished *affettuoso*, weaving themselves down into the dark beauty of the lower keys, because it was closer to the drum, and multiplied. They came back to "St Louis" again.

"Stop." The first gentleman from Mississippi touched Libby on the arm. "When I do that to you, that means 'Stop,'" he said. Libby chorded easily. "Some of the boys like to hear that

'Ol' Man River' some more." He straightened up, turning to the other gentlemen, his smile assuring them it would not be long now.

"Kick off," Baby sighed.

But Libby broke into "St Louis" again. Baby, with a little whoop, came clambering after, his sticks slicing into the drum rim, a staccato "Dixieland."

The first gentleman frowned, touching Libby's arm, "Remember what that means? Means 'Ol' Man River,' " he said calmly, as though correcting a slight error. "Toot sweet. Know what that means? That's French. Means right now." No harm done, however. Just that his friends here, a bunch of boys from down South, were dying to hear that song again—up to him to see that they got satisfaction—knew there would be no trouble about it.

"We'll play it for you later on," Libby said quickly. "We got some other requests besides yours. How many you got now, Baby?"

Baby held up eight fingers, very prompt.

"Coming up," he said.

The first gentleman was undecided. "Well . . ." he drawled. Libby began a popular song. The first gentleman faced his friends. His eyes more or less met theirs and found no agreement. The boys looked kind of impatient, like a bunch of boys out for a little fun and not doing so well. He turned to Libby again.

"We just gotta have that 'Ol' Man River' some more. Boys all got their hearts set on it," he said. "Right away! Toot sweet! Toot—away!" There he'd gone and made a joke, and the boys all laughed and repeated it to each other. Libby played on, as though she had not heard. The first gentleman took hold of her arm. She gazed steadily up into his bleary eyes.

"Not now. Later."

"No, you don't. You gotta play it right now. For a bunch of

boys from down South. They all got a hankerin' to hear that
'Ol' Man River' some more."

"So you best play it," another gentleman said, leaning down
hard on the old upright piano. "On account of I'm gonna take
and give ear. We kinda like how that old song sounds up
North. Whatcha all need. The drummer will sing," he said,
and looked at Baby. Baby looked back, unsmiling.

Libby chorded lightly, waiting for the gentlemen from
Mississippi to get tired. They could not see how it was with
her and Baby—never.

"You ain't gonna play?"

Baby's eyes strained hard in their sockets.

"We ain't comin'," Libby said.

Baby's eyes relaxed and he knew the worst part was over.
They felt the same way about it. They had made up their
minds. The rest was easy. Baby was even a little glad it had
happened. A feeling was growing within him that he had
wanted to do this for a long time—for years and years, in a
hundred different places he had played.

Secretly majestic, Baby sat at his drums, the goal of count-
less uplifted eyes—beseeching him. For it seemed that hordes
of white people were far below him, making their little com-
motions and noises, asking favors of him, like Lord, please
bring the rain, or Lord, please take it away. Lord Baby. Waves of
warm exhilaration washed into him, endearing him to himself.
No, he smiled, I am sorry, no favors today. Yes, Lord, they all
said, if that's the way it is, so be it.

But somebody objected. The manager's voice barked, far below, scarcely audible to Baby in his new eminence. ". . . honoring requests," he heard, and ". . . trouble with the local," and
". . . wanting to get a sweet-swing trio in this place a long time
now." And the manager, strangely small, an excited, pale pygmy,
explaining to the gentlemen from Mississippi, also small, how
it was, "That's all I can do in the circumstances," and them

saying, "Well, I guess so; well, I guess so all right; don't pay to pamper 'em, to give 'em an inch."

Baby noticed Libby had got up from the piano and put on her coat, the long dress hanging out at the bottom, red.

"I won't change," she said, and handed Baby the canvas cover for the snare drum.

"Huh?" Baby said foggily. He set about taking his traps apart. Dodo, not wearing his white service coat, came over to help.

"You don't have to," Baby said.

Chief, freezing outside in his long, fancy maroon coat, opened the door for them. "You all through, Baby?"

"Yeah, Chief. You told that right."

They walked down the street toward the car line. Baby, going first, plowed a path for Libby and Dodo in the snow. Window sills, parked cars, and trees were padded with it. The wind was dead and buried. Baby bore the big drum on his shoulder and felt the sticks pressing tight and upright in his vest pockets, two on each side. Libby had her purse and street clothes rolled up under her arm. Dodo carried the snare drum.

Softly as snow, Libby laughed, "That's all I can do in the circumstances," she said.

"I got your old circumstances," Baby said.

Then they were silent, tramping in the snow.

At the corner they waited in a store entrance for a southbound streetcar. Libby raised a foot now and then, shuddering with cold. Dead still, Dodo breathed down inside the collar of his overcoat, retarding his breath, frowning at the little smoke trickling out, as though it were the only thing left in the world to remind him he was alive. Baby talked of taking a cab and finally did go out into the street to hail one approaching. It slowed up, pulled over to the curb, hesitated . . . and lurched away, with Baby's hand reaching for the door. Baby watched the cab speed down the snowy street, following it for a few steps, speechless. There was nothing to do. Without looking, he saw Libby and Dodo shivering in the store entrance. They had seen the cab come and go. They had not moved an inch. They waited unfooled, as before, for the Big Red.

"What's wrong with you, Baby?" Libby called out. A tiny moment of silence, and she was laughing, gradually louder, mellow octaves of it, mounting, pluming . . .

Like her piano, it seemed to Baby—that fine, young-woman laughter.

"Why you laugh so much, woman?" he inquired plaintively from the street. Then he moved to join them, a few steps only, dallying at the curb to temper the abruptness of his retreat. Like her piano on "Little Rock"—that fine, young-woman laughter.

THE FORKS

THAT SUMMER WHEN Father Eudex got back from saying Mass at the orphanage in the morning, he would park Monsignor's car, which was long and black and new like a politician's, and sit down in the cool of the porch to read his office. If Monsignor was not already standing in the door, he would immediately appear there, seeing that his car had safely returned, and inquire:

"Did you have any trouble with her?"

Father Eudex knew too well the question meant, Did you mistreat my car?

"No trouble, Monsignor."

"Good," Monsignor said, with imperfect faith in his curate, who was not a car owner. For a moment Monsignor stood framed in the screen door, fumbling his watch fob as for a full-length portrait, and then he was suddenly not there.

"Monsignor," Father Eudex said, rising nervously, "I've got a chance to pick up a car."

At the door Monsignor slid into his frame again. His face expressed what was for him intense interest.

"Yes? Go on."

"I don't want to have to use yours every morning."

"It's all right."

"And there are other times." Father Eudex decided not to be maudlin and mention sick calls, nor be entirely honest and admit he was tired of busses and bumming rides from parishioners. "And now I've got a chance to get one—cheap."

Monsignor, smiling, came alert at *cheap*.

"New?"

"No, I wouldn't say it's new."

Monsignor was openly suspicious now. "What kind?"

"It's a Ford."

"And not new?"

"Not new, Monsignor—but in good condition. It was owned by a retired farmer and had good care."

Monsignor sniffed. He *knew* cars. "V-Eight, Father?"

"No," Father Eudex confessed. "It's a Model A."

Monsignor chuckled as though this were indeed the damnedest thing he had ever heard.

"But in very good condition, Monsignor."

"You said that."

"Yes. And I could take it apart if anything went wrong. My uncle had one."

"No doubt." Monsignor uttered a laugh at Father Eudex's rural origins. Then he delivered the final word, long delayed out of amusement. "It wouldn't be prudent, Father. After all, this isn't a country parish. You know the class of people we get here."

Monsignor put on his Panama hat. Then, apparently mistaking the obstinacy in his curate's face for plain ignorance, he shed a little more light. "People watch a priest, Father. *Damnant quod non intelligunt*. It would never do. You'll have to watch your tendencies."

Monsignor's eyes tripped and fell hard on the morning paper lying on the swing where he had finished it.

"Another flattering piece about that crazy fellow . . . There's a man who might have gone places if it weren't for his mouth! A bishop doesn't have to get mixed up in all that stuff!"

Monsignor, as Father Eudex knew, meant unions, strikes, race riots—all that stuff.

"A parishioner was saying to me only yesterday it's getting so you can't tell the Catholics from the Communists, with the priests as bad as any. Yes, and this fellow is the worst. He reminds me of that bishop a few years back—at least he called himself a bishop, a Protestant—that was advocating companionate marriages. It's not that bad, maybe, but if you listened to some of them you'd think that Catholicity and capitalism were incompatible!"

"The Holy Father—"

"The Holy Father's in Europe, Father. Mr Memmers lives in this parish. I'm his priest. What can I tell him?"

"Is it Mr Memmers of the First National, Monsignor?"

"It is, Father. And there's damned little cheer I can give a man like Memmers. Catholics, priests, and laity alike—yes, and princes of the Church, all talking atheistic communism!"

This was the substance of their conversation, always, the deadly routine in which Father Eudex played straight man. Each time it happened he seemed to participate, and though he should have known better he justified his participation by hoping that it would not happen again, or in quite the same way. But it did, it always did, the same way, and Monsignor, for all his alarms, had nothing to say really and meant one thing only, the thing he never said—that he dearly wanted to be, and was not, a bishop.

Father Eudex could imagine just what kind of bishop Monsignor would be. His reign would be a wise one, excessively so. His mind was made up on everything, excessively so. He would know how to avoid the snares set in the path of the just man, avoid them, too, in good taste and good conscience. He would not be trapped as so many good shepherds before him had been trapped, poor souls—caught in fair-seeming dilemmas of justice that were best left alone, like the first apple. It grieved him, he said, to think of those great hearts broken in silence and solitude. It was the worst kind of exile, alas! But just give him the chance and he would know what to do, what to say, and, more important, what not to do, not to say—neither yea nor nay for him. He had not gone to Rome for nothing. For him the dark forest of decisions would not exist; for him, thanks to hours spent in prayer and meditation, the forest would vanish as dry grass before fire, his fire. He knew the mask of evil already—birth control, indecent movies, salacious books—and would call these things by their right names and dare to deal with them for what they were, these new occasions for the old sins of the cities of the plains.

But in the meantime—oh, to have a particle of the faith that God had in humanity! Dear, trusting God forever trying them beyond their feeble powers, ordering terrible tests, fatal trials by nonsense (the crazy bishop). And keeping Monsignor steadily warming up on the sidelines, ready to rush in, primed for the day that would perhaps never dawn.

At one time, so the talk went, there had been reason to think that Monsignor was headed for a bishopric. Now it was too late; Monsignor's intercessors were all dead; the cupboard was bare; he knew it at heart, and it galled him to see another man, this *crazy* man, given the opportunity, and making such a mess of it.

Father Eudex searched for and found a little salt for Monsignor's wound. "The word's going around he'll be the next archbishop," he said.

"I won't believe it," Monsignor countered hoarsely. He glanced at the newspaper on the swing and renewed his horror.

"If that fellow's right, Father, I'm"—his voice cracked at the idea—"*wrong!*"

Father Eudex waited until Monsignor had started down the steps to the car before he said, "It could be."

"I'll be back for lunch, Father. I'm taking her for a little spin."

Monsignor stopped in admiration a few feet from the car—her. He was as helpless before her beauty as a boy with a birthday bicycle. He could not leave her alone. He had her out every morning and afternoon and evening. He was indiscriminate about picking people up for a ride in her. He kept her on a special diet—only the best of gas and oil and grease, with daily rubdowns. He would run her only on the smoothest roads and at so many miles an hour. That was to have stopped at the first five hundred, but only now, nearing the thousand mark, was he able to bring himself to increase her speed, and it seemed to hurt him more than it did her.

Now he was walking around behind her to inspect the tires. Apparently O.K. He gave the left rear fender an amorous chuck and eased into the front seat. Then they drove off, the car and he, to see the world, to explore each other further on the honeymoon.

Father Eudex watched the car slide into the traffic, and waited, on edge. The corner cop, fulfilling Father Eudex's fears, blew his whistle and waved his arms up in all four directions, bringing traffic to a standstill. Monsignor pulled expertly out of line and drove down Clover Boulevard in a one-car parade; all others stalled respectfully. The cop, as Monsignor passed, tipped his cap, showing a bald head. Monsignor, in the circumstances, could not acknowledge him, though he knew the man well—a parishioner. He was occupied with keeping his countenance kindly, grim, and exalted, that the cop's faith remain whole, for it was evidently inconceivable to him that Monsignor should ever venture abroad unless to bear the Holy Viaticum, always racing with death.

Father Eudex, eyes baleful but following the progress of the big black car, saw a hand dart out of the driver's window in a wave. Monsignor would combine a lot of business with pleasure that morning, creating what he called "good will for the Church"—all morning in the driver's seat toasting passersby with a wave that was better than a blessing. How he loved waving to people!

Father Eudex overcame his inclination to sit and stew about things by going down the steps to meet the mailman. He got the usual handful for the Monsignor—advertisements and amazing offers, the unfailing crop of chaff from dealers in church goods, organs, collection schemes, insurance, and sacramental wines. There were two envelopes addressed to Father Eudex, one a mimeographed plea from a missionary society which he might or might not acknowledge with a contribution, depending upon what he thought of the cause—if it was really lost enough to justify a levy on his poverty—and the other a check for a hundred dollars.

The check came in an eggshell envelope with no explanation except a tiny card, "Compliments of the Rival Tractor Company," but even that was needless. All over town clergymen had known for days that the checks were on the way again. Some, rejoicing, could hardly wait. Father Eudex, however, was one of those who could.

With the passing of hard times and the coming of the fruitful war years, the Rival Company, which was a great one for public relations, had found the best solution to the excess-profits problem to be giving. Ministers and even rabbis shared in the annual jackpot, but Rival employees were largely Catholic and it was the checks to the priests that paid off. Again, some thought it was a wonderful idea, and others thought that Rival, plagued by strikes and justly so, had put their alms to work.

There was another eggshell envelope, Father Eudex saw,

among the letters for Monsignor, and knew his check would be for two hundred, the premium for pastors.

Father Eudex left Monsignor's mail on the porch table by his cigars. His own he stuck in his back pocket, wanting to forget it, and went down the steps into the yard. Walking back and forth on the shady side of the rectory where the lilies of the valley grew and reading his office, he gradually drifted into the backyard, lured by a noise. He came upon Whalen, the janitor, pounding pegs into the ground.

Father Eudex closed the breviary on a finger. "What's it all about, Joe?"

Joe Whalen snatched a piece of paper from his shirt and handed it to Father Eudex. "He gave it to me this morning."

He—it was the word for Monsignor among them. A docile pronoun only, and yet when it meant the Monsignor it said, and concealed, nameless things.

The paper was a plan for a garden drawn up by the Monsignor in his fine hand. It called for a huge fleur-de-lis bounded by smaller crosses—and these Maltese—a fountain, a sundial, and a cloister walk running from the rectory to the garage. Later there would be birdhouses and a ten-foot wall of thick gray stones, acting as a moat against the eyes of the world. The whole scheme struck Father Eudex as expensive and, in this country, Presbyterian.

When Monsignor drew the plan, however, he must have been in his medieval mood. A spouting whale jostled with Neptune in the choppy waters of the fountain. North was indicated in the legend by a winged cherub huffing and puffing.

Father Eudex held the plan up against the sun to see the watermark. The stationery was new to him, heavy, simulated parchment, with the Church of the Holy Redeemer and Monsignor's name embossed, three initials, W. F. X., William Francis Xavier. With all those initials the man could pass for a radio station, a chancery wit had observed, or if his last name had not been Sweeney, Father Eudex added now, for high Anglican.

Father Eudex returned the plan to Whalen, feeling sorry for him and to an extent guilty before him—if only because he was a priest like Monsignor (now turned architect) whose dream of a monastery garden included the overworked janitor under the head of "labor."

Father Eudex asked Whalen to bring another shovel. Together, almost without words, they worked all morning spading up crosses, leaving the big fleur-de-lis to the last. Father Eudex removed his coat first, then his collar, and finally was down to his undershirt.

Toward noon Monsignor rolled into the driveway.

He stayed in the car, getting red in the face, recovering from the pleasure of seeing so much accomplished as he slowly recognized his curate in Whalen's helper. In a still, appalled voice he called across the lawn, "Father," and waited as for a beast that might or might not have sense enough to come.

Father Eudex dropped his shovel and went over to the car, shirtless.

Monsignor waited a moment before he spoke, as though annoyed by the everlasting necessity, where this person was concerned, to explain. "Father," he said quietly at last, "I wouldn't do anymore of that—if I were you. Rather, in any event, I wouldn't."

"All right, Monsignor."

"To say the least, it's not prudent. If necessary"—he paused as Whalen came over to dig a cross within earshot—"I'll explain later. It's time for lunch now."

The car, black, beautiful, fierce with chromium, was quiet as Monsignor dismounted, knowing her master. Monsignor went around to the rear, felt a tire, and probed a nasty cinder in the tread.

"Look at that," he said, removing the cinder.

Father Eudex thought he saw the car lift a hoof, gaze around, and thank Monsignor with her headlights.

Monsignor proceeded at a precise pace to the back door of the rectory. There he held the screen open momentarily, as if remembering something or reluctant to enter before himself—such was his humility—but then called to Whalen with an intimacy that could never exist between them.

"Better knock off now, Joe."

Whalen turned in on himself. "*Joe*—is it!"

Father Eudex removed his clothes from the grass. His hands were all blisters, but in them he found a little absolution. He apologized to Joe for having to take the afternoon off. "I can't make it, Joe. Something turned up."

"Sure, Father."

Father Eudex could hear Joe telling his wife about it that night—yeah, the young one got in wrong with the old one again. Yeah, the old one, he don't believe in it, work, for them.

Father Eudex paused in the kitchen to remember he knew not what. It was in his head, asking to be let in, but he did not place it until he heard Monsignor in the next room complaining about the salad to the housekeeper. It was the voice of dear, dead Aunt Hazel, coming from the summer he was ten. He translated the past into the present: I can't come out and play this afternoon, Joe, on account of my monsignor won't let me.

In the dining room Father Eudex sat down at the table and said grace. He helped himself to a chop, creamed new potatoes, pickled beets, jelly, and bread. He liked jelly. Monsignor passed the butter.

"That's supposed to be a tutti-frutti salad," Monsignor said, grimacing at his. "But she used green olives."

Father Eudex said nothing.

"I said she used green olives."

"I like green olives all right."

"*I* like green olives, but *not* in tutti-frutti salad."

Father Eudex replied by eating a green olive, but he knew it could not end there.

"Father," Monsignor said in a new tone. "How would you like to go away and study for a year?"

"Don't think I'd care for it, Monsignor. I'm not the type."

"You're no canonist, you mean?"

"That's one thing."

"Yes. Well, there are other things it might not hurt you to know. To be quite frank with you, Father, I think you need broadening."

"I guess so," Father Eudex said thickly.

"And still, with your tendencies . . . and with the universities honeycombed with Communists. No, that would never do. I think I meant seasoning, not broadening."

"Oh."

"No offense?"

"No offense."

Who would have thought a little thing like an olive could lead to all this, Father Eudex mused—who but himself, that is, for his association with Monsignor had shown him that anything could lead to everything. Monsignor was a master at making points. Nothing had changed since the day Father Eudex walked into the rectory saying he was the new assistant. Monsignor had evaded Father Eudex's hand in greeting, and a few days later, after he began to get the range, he delivered a lecture on the whole subject of handshaking. It was Middle West to shake hands, or South West, or West in any case, and it was not done where he came from, and—why had he ever come from where he came from? Not to be reduced to shaking hands, you could bet! Handshaking was worse than foot washing and unlike that pious practice there was nothing to support it. And from handshaking Monsignor might go into a general discussion of Father Eudex's failings. He used the open forum method, but he was the only speaker and there was never time enough for questions from the audience. Monsignor seized his examples at random from life. He saw Father Eudex coming out of his bedroom in pajama bottoms only and so told him about the dressing gown, its purpose, something of its history. He advised Father Eudex to barber his armpits, for it was being done all over now. He let Father Eudex see his bottle of cologne, "Steeple," special for clergymen, and said he should not be afraid of it. He suggested that Father Eudex shave his face oftener, too. He loaned him his Rogers Peet catalogue, which had sketches of clerical blades togged out in the latest, and prayed that he would stop going around looking like a rabbinical student.

He found Father Eudex reading *The Catholic Worker* one day and had not trusted him since. Father Eudex's conception of the priesthood was evangelical in the worst sense, barbaric, gross, foreign to the mind of the Church, which was one of two terms he used as sticks to beat him with. The other was taste. The air of the rectory was often heavy with The Mind of the Church and Taste.

Another thing. Father Eudex could not conduct a civil conversation. Monsignor doubted that Father Eudex could even think to himself with anything like agreement. Certainly any discussion with Father Eudex ended inevitably in argument or sighing. Sighing! Why didn't people talk up if they had anything to say? No, they'd rather sigh! Father, don't ever, ever sigh at me again!

Finally, Monsignor did not like Father Eudex's table manners. This came to a head one night when Monsignor, seeing his curate's plate empty and all the silverware at his place unused except for a single knife, fork, and spoon, exploded altogether, saying it had been on his mind for weeks, and then descending into the vernacular he declared that Father Eudex did not know the forks—now perhaps he could understand that! Meals, unless Monsignor had guests or other things to struggle with, were always occasions of instruction for Father Eudex, and sometimes of chastisement.

And now he knew the worst—if Monsignor was thinking of recommending him for a year of study, in a Sulpician seminary probably, to learn the forks. So this was what it meant to be a priest. *Come, follow me. Going forth, teach ye all nations. Heal the sick, raise the dead, cleanse the lepers, cast out devils.* Teach the class of people we get here? Teach Mr Memmers? Teach Communists? Teach Monsignors? And where were the poor? The lepers of old? The lepers were in their colonies with nuns to nurse them. The poor were in their holes and would not come out. Mr Memmers was in his bank, without cheer. The Communists were in their universities, awaiting a sign. And he was at table with Monsignor, and it was enough for the disciple to be as his master, but the housekeeper had used green olives.

Monsignor inquired, "Did you get your check today?"

Father Eudex, looking up, considered. "I got *a* check," he said.

"From the Rival people, I mean?"

"Yes."

"Good. Well, I think you might apply it on the car you're wanting. A decent car. That's a worthy cause." Monsignor noticed that he was not taking it well. "Not that I mean to dictate what you shall do with your little windfall, Father. It's just that I don't like to see you mortifying yourself with a Model A—and disgracing the Church."

"Yes," Father Eudex said, suffering.

"Yes. I dare say you don't see the danger, just as you didn't a while ago when I found you making a spectacle of yourself with Whalen. You just don't see the danger because you just don't think. Not to dwell on it, but I seem to remember some overshoes."

The overshoes! Monsignor referred to them as to the Fall.

Last winter Father Eudex had given his overshoes to a freezing picket. It had got back to Monsignor and—good Lord, a man could have his sympathies, but he had no right clad in the cloth to endanger the prestige of the Church by siding in these wretched squabbles. Monsignor said he hated to think of all the evil done by people doing good! Had Father Eudex ever heard of the Albigensian heresy, or didn't the seminary teach that anymore?

Father Eudex declined dessert. It was strawberry mousse.

"Delicious," Monsignor said. "I think I'll let her stay."

At that moment Father Eudex decided that he had nothing to lose. He placed his knife next to his fork on the plate, adjusted them this way and that until they seemed to work a combination in his mind, to spring a lock which in turn enabled him to speak out.

"Monsignor," he said. "I think I ought to tell you I don't intend to make use of that money. In fact—to show you how my mind works—I have even considered endorsing the check to the strikers' relief fund."

"So," Monsignor said calmly—years in the confessional had prepared him for anything.

"I'll admit I don't know whether I can in justice. And even if I could I don't know that I would. I don't know why . . . I guess hush money, no matter what you do with it, is lousy."

Monsignor regarded him with piercing baby blue eyes. "You'd find it pretty hard to prove, Father, that *any* money *in se* is . . . what you say it is. I would quarrel further with the definition 'hush money.' It seems to me nothing if not rash that you would presume to impugn the motive of the Rival Company in sending out these checks. You would seem to challenge the whole concept of good works—not that I am ignorant of the misuses to which money can be put." Monsignor, changing tack, tucked it all into a sigh. "Perhaps I'm just a simple soul, and it's enough for me to know personally some of the people in the Rival Company and to know them good people. Many of them Catholic . . ." A throb had crept into Monsignor's voice. He shut it off.

"I don't mean anything that subtle, Monsignor," Father Eudex said. "I'm just telling you, as my pastor, what I'm going to do with the check. Or what I'm not going to do with it. I don't know what I'm going to do with it. Maybe send it back."

Monsignor rose from the table, slightly smiling. "Very well, Father. But there's always the poor."

Monsignor took leave of Father Eudex with a laugh. Father Eudex felt it was supposed to fool him into thinking that nothing he had said would be used against him. It showed, rather, that Monsignor was not winded, that he had broken wild curates before, plenty of them, and that he would ride again.

Father Eudex sought the shade of the porch. He tried to read his office, but was drowsy. He got up for a glass of water. The saints in Ireland used to stand up to their necks in cold water, but not for drowsiness. When he came back to the porch a woman was ringing the doorbell. She looked like a customer for rosary beads.

"Hello," he said.

"I'm Mrs Klein, Father, and I was wondering if you could help me out."

Father Eudex straightened a porch chair for her. "Please sit down."

"It's a German name, Father. Klein was German descent," she said, and added with a silly grin, "It ain't what you think, Father."

"I beg your pardon."

"Klein. Some think it's a Jew name. But they stole it from Klein."

Father Eudex decided to come back to that later. "You were wondering if I could help you?"

"Yes, Father. It's personal."

"Is it matter for confession?"

"Oh no, Father." He had made her blush.

"Then go ahead."

Mrs Klein peered into the honeysuckle vines on either side of the porch for alien ears.

"No one can hear you, Mrs Klein."

"Father—I'm just a poor widow," she said, and continued as though Father Eudex had just slandered the man. "Klein was awful good to me, Father."

"I'm sure he was."

"So good . . . and he went and left me all he had." She had begun to cry a little.

Father Eudex nodded gently. She was after something, probably not money, always the best bet—either that or a drunk in the family—but this one was not Irish. Perhaps just sympathy.

"I come to get your advice, Father. Klein always said, 'If you got a problem, Freda, see the priest.' "

"Do you need money?"

"I got more than I can use from the bakery."

"You have a bakery?"

Mrs Klein nodded down the street. "That's my bakery. It was Klein's. The Purity."

"I go by there all the time," Father Eudex said, abandoning himself to her. He must stop trying to shape the conversation and let her work it out.

"Will you give me your advice, Father?" He felt that she sensed his indifference and interpreted it as his way of rejecting her. She either had no idea how little sense she made or else supreme faith in him, as a priest, to see into her heart.

"Just what is it you're after, Mrs Klein?"

"He left me all he had, Father, but it's just laying in the bank."

"And you want me to tell you what to do with it?"

"Yes, Father."

Father Eudex thought this might be interesting, certainly a change. He went back in his mind to the seminary and the class in which they had considered the problem of inheritances. Do we have any unfulfilled obligations? Are we sure? ... Are there any impedimenta? ...

"Do you have any dependents, Mrs Klein—any children?"

"One boy, Father. I got him running the bakery. I pay him good—too much, Father."

"Is 'too much' a living wage?"

"Yes, Father. He ain't got a family."

"A living wage is not too much," Father Eudex handed down, sailing into the encyclical style without knowing it.

Mrs Klein was smiling over having done something good without knowing precisely what it was.

"How old is your son?"

"He's thirty-six, Father."

"Not married?"

"No, Father, but he's got him a girl." She giggled, and Father Eudex, embarrassed, retied his shoe.

"But you don't care to make a will and leave this money to your son in the usual way?"

"I guess I'll have to ... if I die." Mrs Klein was suddenly crushed and haunted, but whether by death or charity, Father Eudex did not know.

"You don't have to, Mrs Klein. There are many worthy causes. And the worthiest is the cause of the poor. My advice to you, if I understand your problem, is to give what you have to someone who needs it."

Mrs Klein just stared at him.

"You could even leave it to the archdiocese," he said, completing the sentence to himself: but I don't recommend it in your case ... with your tendencies. You look like an Indian giver to me.

But Mrs Klein had got enough. "Huh!" she said, rising. "Well! You *are* a funny one!"

And then Father Eudex realized that she had come to him for a broker's tip. It was in the eyes. The hat. The dress. The shoes. "If you'd like to speak to the pastor," he said, "come back in the evening."

"You're a nice young man," Mrs Klein said, rather bitter now and bent on getting away from him. "But I got to say this—you ain't much of a priest. And Klein said if I got a problem, see the priest—huh! You ain't much of a priest! What time's your boss come in?"

"In the evening," Father Eudex said. "Come any time in the evening."

Mrs Klein was already down the steps and making for the street.

"You might try Mr Memmers at the First National," Father Eudex called, actually trying to help her, but she must have thought it was just some more of his nonsense and did not reply.

After Mrs Klein had disappeared Father Eudex went to his room. In the hallway upstairs Monsignor's voice, coming from the depths of the clerical nap, halted him.

"Who was it?"

"A woman," Father Eudex said. "A woman seeking good counsel."

He waited a moment to be questioned, but Monsignor was not awake enough to see anything wrong with that, and there came only a sigh and a shifting of weight that told Father Eudex he was simply turning over in bed.

Father Eudex walked into the bathroom. He took the Rival check from his pocket. He tore it into little squares. He let them flutter into the toilet. He pulled the chain—hard.

He went to his room and stood looking out the window at nothing. He could hear the others already giving an account of their stewardship, but could not judge them. I bought baseball uniforms for the school. I bought the nuns a new washing machine. I purchased a Mass kit for a Chinese missionary. I bought a set of matched irons. Mine helped pay for keeping my mother in a rest home upstate. I gave mine to the poor.

And you, Father?

RENNER

EXCEPT FOR A contemporary placard or two, the place conspired to set me dreaming of the good old days I had never known. The furniture did it—the cloudy mirrors, the grandiose mahogany bar, the tables and chairs ornate with spools and scrollwork, the burnished brass coat hooks and cuspidors, all as shiny-ugly as the day they were made, and swillish brown paintings, inevitable subjects, fat tippling friars in cellars, velvet cavaliers elegantly eying sherry, the deadliest of still-life fruit, but no fishes on platters.

At a table across the room, Emil, the waiter, and two patrons finished a hand, talked about it, scraped the cards into a muddy deck. They spoke an aromatic mixture of English and German. Emil, a little spaniel of a man, fussed with his flapping sleeves and consoled the fat man whose king had not been good enough.

Renner, using both hands, elevated a glass of beer in momentary exposition, raised his eyes to heaven, and drank deeply. I wondered if, despite everything, he might still be fascinated by the Germans. I could think of no other reason for coming here.

I signaled Emil. He smiled too graciously, put down his cards, and came over to pick up our glasses, saying "Gentlemen." One of the cardplayers frowned at me for interrupting the game. He was the one we called the Entrepreneur. Renner had acquired his English abroad and reporters to him were journalists; the cardplayer, who might possibly be a salesman, had become an Entrepreneur.

When Emil brought our glasses back, quivering and amber, I became preoccupied with a button on my coat, escaping the gelatinous impact of his smile. I could sense Renner undergoing it. When Emil withdrew, Renner said, "He's not as simple as he pretends to be." This struck me as off-key to the point of being funny. And still it may have been that I had already recognized, without consciously acknowledging, something dimly sinister about Emil.

Renner dipped his glass at a bowl of fruit rotting on the wall. "It's too bad *der Fuehrer* couldn't paint a little. Another bad painter, we could have stood that." He began to speak in what I had come to know as his autobiographical tone. He appeared to listen to himself, skeptical, though he was accenting words and ideas, of the meaning in what he said, trying to account for himself on earth. "Anyway, my mother hired a sergeant major to discipline me when I was eight years old. The Austrian army was not the most formidable in the world, except of course at regimental balls, but she hoped he could do the job. He couldn't. I was not to have many such victories."

The idea of Renner the child died away when I looked at the man across the table from me. Renner had rusty hair, bristling abundantly, tufted eyebrows, an oddly handsome face with the depth and decision of a wood carving about it. When I looked again Renner the man was lost in our surroundings. I saw an album world: exaggerated bicycles and good-old-summertime girls, picnics and family reunions, mustachioed quartets, polished horses galloping through Budweiser advertisements, the heroes and adventures of Horatio Alger, the royal commerce of the day. The furniture reached boldly into the past and yanked these visions into being. I had only to step out the door to find everything changed back fifty years. Meanwhile the green walls, waiting to be smoked black, stood patiently around us.

"Because he could paint like that," Renner said, "my uncle became president of the Vienna Academy." I glanced needlessly at the pictures. Renner laughed shortly. "He had a patriarchal beard, however, which he used to clean his brushes on. His only attempt at eccentricity and it failed. In fact, it killed him— lead poisoning."

There was a fictitious feeling about sitting so casually with a man whose uncle had been president of an art academy. Renner himself had taught at the University of Vienna, had perhaps come into a little eminence of his own, but compared to his uncle he was small fry indeed. Achievement through violence or succession or cunning or even merit is common enough. But president of an academy of art—now there was an inscrutable honor, beyond accounting for, like being an archbishop (except in Italy), only more so.

A dark man in tweeds came in. Emil threw down his cards, rushed to meet him, and the two left at the table turned slowly to see. First disappointed, then a little disgusted, they turned up Emil's cards on the table.

"My good friend, Mr Ross," Emil purred. Mr Ross extended his hand and they stood there shaking, smiling at each other. Mr Ross finally got around to saying he came in for a glass. Emil went behind the bar and took down a bottle of brandy. Emil was still oppressing Mr Ross with his smile, but Mr Ross seemed to think it no more than right or less than real.

"Well, Renner," I said. Renner, who had been watching them,

began talking again—against his will, I thought, but anxious to get Emil and Mr Ross out of our minds.

"At the beginning of the last war—this was in Innsbruck—we had a geometry teacher, very droll. He'd get furious and throw the squares and triangles at the pupils. He also rode a horse, as if in battle, to school. He would say, 'Miller, what color should I make this line?'—some line in geometry; he'd be standing at the blackboard. 'Red,' Miller would answer. 'Why red, Miller?' You see the pupils knew what to say, I among them. 'Red for the blood of the Serbs, Herr Professor.' 'Very good, Miller! And this line, Scheutzer?' 'Yellow—for the enemy.' 'Very good!' You know," Renner said, "the man of action," and was silent.

"I know."

"Delightful task," as one of the cheery English poets says, "to rear the tender thought, to teach the young idea how to shoot."

I almost added that the geometry teacher, if living, must be cherished by the Fatherland today, but I thought better of it: such men are everywhere, never without a country.

Emil was begging Mr Ross to stay for a bite to eat. At first Mr Ross refused and then, overcome by the fervor of Emil's invitation, he said he would look at the menu.

"You won't need to look today, Mr Ross." Emil rubbed his hands in polite ecstasy, became intent, his eyes glazed, as though savoring some impossible dream. "The pike," he said, "is delicious." But rare Mr Ross was reluctant to have pike. "Well, then!" Emil said, pretending outrage; he handed Mr Ross his fate in the menu. He folded his arms and waited scornfully.

Immediately Mr Ross proclaimed: "Chicken livers and mushrooms."

Emil showed a suffering cheerfulness, shaking his head, the good loser. Plainly Mr Ross had divined chicken livers and mushrooms against all Emil's efforts to keep them in the kitchen for himself. "Ah, they're very excellent today, Mr Ross."

All this playing at old world *délicatesse* seemed to annoy Renner too much. Slowly he began to ramble, his eyes fixed on Emil, as though it were all there to be read in his face. "You wouldn't think a little stenographer would remember what you said for ten years back and write it down every night—and the day they sent for you (bring two suits of underclothes and a roll of toilet paper; we'll do the rest) you'd hear it all then, also recordings they'd made of your telephone conversations . . . because there were little telephone operators like the little stenographer . . ." Renner stopped speaking when Emil went into the kitchen, as if the inspiration to continue were gone with Emil.

"Is Mr Ross Jewish?" I asked.

Renner nodded indistinctly.

On occasion I had wondered whether Renner was Jewish, always halfheartedly, so that I forgot what I was wondering about, and it would be a while before I wondered again. His being a refugee proved nothing so specific or simple as that: his species, spiritually speaking, tends to make itself at home in exile.

Emil came out of the kitchen with bread, butter, and a dish of beets.

"I don't want those," Mr Ross said—cruelly, it seemed to me, for Emil dearly wanted him to have them. Then it occurred to me that it was part of Mr Ross's grand manner. He had considered the saving to Emil and his own loss in waving aside the bread, butter, and beets. It had been a telling act and there could be no turning back. Emil propitiated him with a devout and carefully uncomprehending look, such as he must have fancied appropriate to menials like himself and soothing to men of business like Mr Ross.

The Entrepreneur leaned forward and spoke passionately in German to the fat one, who agreed with him, nodding and grunting.

"Now what?" I asked Renner.

Renner listened further before venturing a translation.

"Well," he said finally, as though I would not be getting the whole story. "A certain man is a good bookkeeper, but not a good businessman."

"But the Entrepreneur is?"

"He is." Renner began to deliberate in a familiar voice, not his own. "It's all right, this tobacco. But I"—a very capital I— "I would never pay twenty-five cents. *I* would pay, say, twenty." He struck a match, touched the flame to his pipe, looked shrewd, and blew out a mouthful of smoke to close the deal. It was the voice of the superintendent where we both worked, and it was Renner's theory, to which I subscribed, that the super haggled about everything because secretly he yearned to be a purchasing agent.

Renner watched the cardplayers. "The Entrepreneur has a very expressive head, too." I could see what Renner meant. Seen, as now, from the rear, the Entrepreneur's head was most expressive. I had noticed his face before; it was gross and uninteresting.

"In fact," Renner said, "they are almost identical."

"What?"

"Their heads *par derrière*, the Entrepreneur's and the super's. I think it's mostly in the ears. They both have histrionic ears. Seismographic instruments. See. The Entrepreneur needs no face or voice or hands. His ears tell all."

The back of the Entrepreneur's head grimaced, his ears blushed, and his hand slapped a losing card on the table. He snarled something in German.

"You see!" Renner said. "Just like the super—*dynamic!*" When Renner used a word like "dynamic" he thought he was very American.

I took out my pipe. Renner shoved the package of tobacco across the table. "Stalin imports tobacco from this country, did you know? No one else in Russia may." A revealing sidelight, it seemed to me, and I hoped Renner's source was obscure, if not reliable. "Edgeworth," Renner said. "Stalin smokes only Edgeworth."

"Think of the dilemma Stalin's endorsement must constitute for the Edgeworth company," I reflected. "One faction wants to launch the product as the choice of dictators."

Renner took up the idea. "Another faction doggedly holds out for the common man."

"Finally," I said, slightly excited, "a futile attempt (by visionaries in the advertising department) to square the circle."

"We can't all be dictators," Renner broke in like a radio announcer, "but we can all—"

"Exactly."

A stocky man plodded out of the washroom. The cardplayers hardly noticed him. I could not help thinking of him in terms of *deus ex machina*, for we had not seen him before and we had been in the place too long. He stood in the middle of the floor, a crumpled, somewhat parliamentary figure, and said:

"If I was sober . . ."

Then, accounting for his long exile in the washroom, he dislodged from his coat pocket a newspaper, folded editorial page out, and threw it with a sigh across the mahogany bar. He sat down in the empty fourth chair at the card table. This, too, seemed to be foreordained. The fat one dealt him in without comment. Emil laid down his cards, disappeared into the kitchen, and returned with a cup of something, probably black coffee. The stocky man received it silently, his just due, and drank. He put the cup, wobbling, down and said:

"If I was sober . . ."

"Irish," I said.

"An age-old alliance," Renner said. "The Irish and the Germans."

There was, in fact, a rough unity about them. The fat one and the Entrepreneur thrust themselves in and seemed to maintain their positions with a forcefulness suggesting fear.

Emil, with whom cordiality was a method, never granted a more confidential glance to one than to another, and by the very falsity of his servility distinguished himself as a strong character. The stocky Irishman, who had pleasant puffy eyes and vigorous wattles, loomed up as a most accomplished fact. He was closer to the furniture than the others, a druid. While the fat one and the Entrepreneur experienced mortal joy and sorrow, according to their luck at cards, and Emil dealt nervously in camaraderie, the Irishman was satisfied to be present and one with the universe. One thing was sure: they all *belonged*.

Emil sacrificed his place at the card table and plied efficiently among his patrons. He brought us beer, the cardplayers drinks and matches, and Mr Ross delicacies and homage. When Emil came by the cardplayers' table, I heard them urge him to get through with the carriage trade. That could mean only Mr Ross, for he was being smiled and grunted at among them. They could tell that he had a romantic concept of the place. It was celebrated now and then by broken book reviewers as the erstwhile hearth of the nation's literary great. Perhaps poor, tweedy Mr Ross was drunk with longing for a renaissance in letters and took the cardplayers for poets. They, I suspected, were all worried about how Mr Ross made his money where he'd just come from and aggravated to think (the Jews got all the money!) he'd be going back to make more when he left. It seemed to pain Renner that Mr Ross could confide in Emil and permit him clucking around his table.

Renner breathed over his empty glass and resumed his autobiography. Some middle chapters seemed to be missing, for we were in New York in 1939. "Some employment agencies had signs saying sixteen or seventeen dishwashers wanted. I just stood in the doorway and the agent waved his hand—No! Others, too; one look at me and—No! They're very good, they know their business, the agents."

"What about teaching?"

Renner

"*Ja*, sure. That was interesting, too. 'Of course you've taught for years at the University of Vienna' "—Renner reproduced a stilted voice and I knew we were at an interview he must have had—" 'but surely you must know that what counts in this country is a degree from Columbia, Harvard, or here, the *only* schools for political science. I thought *everyone* knew that. I suggest you try one of the smaller schools.'

"So I tried one of the smaller plants. I went to a teachers' agency and eventually entered into correspondence with a Midwestern college. 'It is true' "—here was another, more nasal voice—" 'that there is an opening on our staff for a qualified man in your field, but it is true also that it will remain vacant till doomsday before we appoint a tobacco addict, especially one constrained to advertise that sorry fact.' A veiled reference," Renner laughed, "to the pipe in the snapshot I sent."

"American Gothic," I said.

"Just as well," he said. "I was through with teaching when I left Europe. Too much guilt connected with it. Although clergymen and educators are not so influential as might be supposed from pulpits and commencement addresses, and the real influences are the grocer, the alderman, the radio comedian (and of course the men who pay them), still that's pretty shabby exoneration . . ."

I noticed that Renner had become angry and disheveled. Poor Renner! It was his wife's lament that nothing roused him. She had made herself an enemy to the Heimwehr in Vienna and been forced to leave Austria long before the Nazis arrived, bringing their own brand of fascism to the extermination of the local product. Renner had stayed on, however, reading in the cafés (he'd lost out at the University through his wife's activities) and thinking nothing could happen to him—until everything did. His wife, in judging him lethargic, was wrong in the way such vigilant people can never detect. Renner, I believe, was only insensitive to political events, to the eternal

119

traffic jams of empires, and felt it was hardly his fault that he lived when and where he did in time and space. If he had been a boy, he would not have believed he might someday be President, nor even have wished it.

I could understand from this what he meant when he said, in one of his extravagant statements, that he loved horses and foxes and could not forgive the English for what they do to both. Those were the symbols he chose through which to make himself known (at least to me), although it was by no means certain that they were only symbols to him. When he spoke of foxes and horses it was with no shade of poetry or whimsey or condescension. His face became intense and I could easily imagine him in a kind of restricted paradise: just foxes, horses, himself, and a lot of Rousseau vegetation. Of all the animals, he said, only the horse lives in a state of uninterrupted insanity.

Renner took a large swallow from his glass and set it down with a noise. "For nineteen hundred years they've been doing that."

"Who? What?"

"Plato's learned men. Capitulating. I say nineteen hundred years, though it's longer, because Christ cut the ground from under them—the Scribes and Pharisees of old. He gave us a new law. Martyrdom, indecent as it sounds to our itching ears, is not supposed to be too much to suffer for it."

"Speak for yourself, Renner," I said.

"Aren't you a Christian?"

"Of course. But my idea of Christianity is the community fund, doing good, and brisk mottoes on the wall."

"Copulating with circumstance," Renner said.

I looked at the cardplayers and there they were, overwhelming aspects of human endeavor: the fat one and the Entrepreneur throwing themselves soulfully into their best cards, the table dumbly standing for it, the Irishman piled up warmly and lifelessly, except for his fingers flicking the cards and his eyes which blinked occasionally, keeping watch over the body. I caught Emil's eye, which he proceeded to twinkle at me, and he came over for our glasses. Renner kept his eyes down and so I was stuck with meeting Emil's smile. I could not bring myself to return it. I told him the beer was good, very—when he waited for more—*very* good beer. When he came from the bar with our glasses filled he explained in detail how the beer came to be so good and did his smile until I felt positively damp from it.

"A little tragedy took place in our department this afternoon," Renner said, after Emil had gone. "Victoria Marzak versus the super"—for whom Renner indicated the Entrepreneur; I was confused until I remembered their heads were alike. "It was three acts, beginning with Victoria giving the super hell because working conditions are so bad in the stock rooms (which they are). She delivered a nice little declaration of independence. I thought the day had finally arrived. The workers of the world were about to throw off their chains and forget their social security numbers. The super said nothing in this act.

"In the next, however, he went into action. He surpassed Victoria in both wrath and righteousness. His thesis, as much of it as I could understand, was that Victoria and the girls could not expect better conditions—for the duration. Victoria said it was the first she'd heard of our being a war plant. The super mentioned our ashtrays and picture frames, and said she ought to feel ashamed of herself, always complaining, when there were boys dying in foxholes—yes, boys who needed our products. Ashtrays in foxholes! I thought he was laying it on too thick at this point, even for him, and I did a foolish thing. We won't go into that now, as it might obscure the larger meaning of the tragedy.

"Act Three was classic, revealing the history of human progress, or the effects of original sin (reason darkened), depending on your taste in terminology. The super introduced Victoria to the supernatural element, which in our department goes by the name of Pressure From Above. He invoked Pressure as the first cause of all conditions, including working. In short, the less said about conditions, the better. Victoria wilted. But Pressure, besides being a just and jealous god, is merciful. The super forgave her trespasses, said he was working on a raise for her, and she went back to her job (under the same conditions), beating her sizable breast and crying *mea culpa* for having inveighed against them—conditions, that is—as things sacred to Pressure. Curtain."

Renner rubbed his eyes and gazed past me. Mr Ross had risen from the chicken livers and mushrooms. Emil stacked the dishes for removal.

"I want to pay you for everything," Mr Ross said, meaning, I presumed, the bread, butter, and beets. The cardplayers looked at each other wisely at this, as though the law had thus been fulfilled.

"In case you are wondering," Renner continued, "Victoria represents suffering humanity suffering as it was in the beginning, is now, and ever shall be, world without end."

"Amen," I said.

Renner's voice cracked and he began again. "How did the Austrian Socialists, the best organized working-class group in history and pacifists to boot, reconcile themselves to the war in 1914?"

"No doubt they organized committees," I said, "or took the ever-lovin' long view."

"Worse. Dressed in the Emperor's uniforms and crammed in boxcars ordinarily reserved for cattle, they rode off shouting—imagine—'Down with the Czar and Imperialism!'"

"A distinction to make a theologian blush," I said. "But tell me, what was this foolish thing you did in the second act?"

"I stood up to the super and told him a few things, mostly concerning the rights and dignity of man."

I considered the implications of this for a moment. "Then, as we say, you are no longer with the company?"

"Yes."

"You were fired?"

"Yes. Insubordination."

Emil was telling Mr Ross how much everything was. Mr Ross pulled out a couple of bills and pressed them blindly into Emil's hand.

"And the rest is for the house," Mr Ross said. The cardplayers sniffed at each other and shared their disgust. Emil thanked Mr Ross from the bottom of his heart, shook his hand, put it down, and took it up for a final shaking.

At the door Mr Ross turned smartly and waved a large farewell which seemed to include Renner and me and the poets playing pinochle. Then he vanished into the street.

"Good-bye, Mr Ross," Emil said plaintively, as if to his memory. Emil went to the card table, sat down, and fooled with his sleeves. The Entrepreneur, dealing, jerked his head at the door, snarled something in German, and went on dealing. The fat one nodded and belched lightly. The Irishman closed his eyes in a long blink. Emil grinned at his cards.

"That was Mr Ross," he said.

"So that was Mr Ross," the Entrepreneur said, attempting Yiddish dialect.

Abruptly Renner stood up, jolting our table sharply, his face all swollen and red, and started across the floor. Before I could get up and interfere, he came to a wavering halt. Looking at him were four surprised faces and there seemed to be nothing about them familiar or hateful to Renner. Evidently he was bewildered to find no super: he had seen his head a moment before. He gave me an ashamed look which was not without resentment. Then he walked back to our table, stuck his pipe, which was lying there, in his pocket, threw down some money, and went out the door.

THE VALIANT WOMAN

THEY HAD COME to the dessert in a dinner that was a shambles. "Well, John," Father Nulty said, turning away from Mrs Stoner and to Father Firman, long gone silent at his own table. "You've got the bishop coming for confirmations next week."

"Yes," Mrs Stoner cut in, "and for dinner. And if he don't eat anymore than he did last year—"

Father Firman, in a rare moment, faced it. "Mrs Stoner, the bishop is not well. You know that."

"And after I fixed that fine dinner and all." Mrs Stoner pouted in Father Nulty's direction.

"I wouldn't feel bad about it, Mrs Stoner," Father Nulty said. "He never eats much anywhere."

"It's funny. And that new Mrs Allers said he ate just fine when he was there," Mrs Stoner argued, and then spit out, "but she's a damned liar!"

Father Nulty, unsettled but trying not to show it, said, "Who's Mrs Allers?"

"She's at Holy Cross," Mrs Stoner said.

"She's the housekeeper," Father Firman added, thinking Mrs Stoner made it sound as though Mrs Allers were the pastor there.

"I swear I don't know what to do about the dinner this year," Mrs Stoner said.

Father Firman moaned. "Just do as you've always done, Mrs Stoner."

"Huh! And have it all to throw out! Is that any way to do?"

"Is there any dessert?" Father Firman asked coldly.

Mrs Stoner leaped up from the table and bolted into the kitchen, mumbling. She came back with a birthday cake. She plunged it in the center of the table. She found a big wooden match in her apron pocket and thrust it at Father Firman.

"I don't like this bishop," she said. "I never did. And the way he went and cut poor Ellen Kennedy out of Father Doolin's will!"

She went back into the kitchen.

"Didn't they talk a lot of filth about Doolin and the house-keeper?" Father Nulty asked.

"I should think they did," Father Firman said. "All because he took her to the movies on Sunday night. After he died and the bishop cut her out of the will, though I hear he gives her a pension privately, they talked about the bishop."

"I don't like this bishop at all," Mrs Stoner said, appearing with a cake knife. "Bishop Doran—there was the man!"

"We know," Father Firman said. "All man and all priest."

"He did know real estate," Father Nulty said.

Father Firman struck the match.

"Not on the chair!" Mrs Stoner cried, too late.

Father Firman set the candle burning—it was suspiciously large and yellow, like a blessed one, but he could not be sure. They watched the fluttering flame.

"I'm forgetting the lights!" Mrs Stoner said, and got up to turn them off. She went into the kitchen again.

The priests had a moment of silence in the candlelight.

"Happy birthday, John," Father Nulty said softly. "Is it fifty-nine you are?"

"As if you didn't know, Frank," Father Firman said, "and you the same but one."

Father Nulty smiled, the old gold of his incisors shining in the flickering light, his collar whiter in the dark, and raised his glass of water, which would have been wine or better in the by-gone days, and toasted Father Firman.

"Many of 'em, John."

"Blow it out," Mrs Stoner said, returning to the room. She waited by the light switch for Father Firman to blow out the candle.

Mrs Stoner, who ate no desserts, began to clear the dishes into the kitchen, and the priests, finishing their cake and coffee in a hurry, went to sit in the study.

Father Nulty offered a cigar.

"John?"

"My ulcers, Frank."

"Ah, well, you're better off." Father Nulty lit the cigar and crossed his long black legs. "Fish Frawley has got him a Filipino, John. Did you hear?"

Father Firman leaned forward, interested. "He got rid of the woman he had?"

"He did. It seems she snooped."

"Snooped, eh?"

"She did. And gossiped. Fish introduced two town boys to her, said, 'Would you think these boys were my nephews?' That's all, and the next week the paper had it that his two nephews were visiting him from Erie. After that, he let her believe he was going East to see his parents, though both are dead. The paper carried the story. Fish returned and made a sermon out of it. Then he got the Filipino."

Father Firman squirmed with pleasure in his chair. "That's

like Fish, Frank. He can do that." He stared at the tips of his fingers bleakly. "You could never get a Filipino to come to a place like this."

"Probably not," Father Nulty said. "Fish is pretty close to Minneapolis. Ah, say, do you remember the trick he played on us all in Marmion Hall?"

"That I'll not forget!" Father Firman's eyes remembered. "Getting up New Year's morning and finding the toilet seats all painted!"

"*Happy Circumcision!* Hah!" Father Nulty had a coughing fit.

When he had got himself together again, a mosquito came and sat on his wrist. He watched it a moment before bringing his heavy hand down. He raised his hand slowly, viewed the dead mosquito, and sent it spinning with a plunk of his middle finger.

"Only the female bites," he said.

"I didn't know that," Father Firman said.

"Ah, yes . . ."

Mrs Stoner entered the study and sat down with some sewing—Father Firman's black socks.

She smiled pleasantly at Father Nulty. "And what do you think of the atom bomb, Father?"

"Not much," Father Nulty said.

Mrs Stoner had stopped smiling. Father Firman yawned.

Mrs Stoner served up another: "Did you read about this communist convert, Father?"

"He's been in the Church before," Father Nulty said, "and so it's not a conversion, Mrs Stoner."

"No? Well, I already got him down on my list of Monsignor's converts."

"It's better than a conversion, Mrs Stoner, for there is more rejoicing in heaven over the return of . . . uh, he that was lost, Mrs Stoner, is found."

"And that congresswoman, Father?"

"Yes. A convert—she."

"And Henry Ford's grandson, Father. I got him down."

"Yes, to be sure."

Father Firman yawned, this time audibly, and held his jaw.

"But he's one only by marriage, Father," Mrs Stoner said. "I always say you got to watch those kind."

"Indeed you do, but a convert nonetheless, Mrs Stoner. Remember, Cardinal Newman himself was one."

Mrs Stoner was unimpressed. "I see where Henry Ford's making steering wheels out of soybeans, Father."

"I didn't see that."

"I read it in the *Reader's Digest* or some place."

"Yes, well . . ." Father Nulty rose and held his hand out to Father Firman. "John," he said. "It's been good."

"I heard Hirohito's next," Mrs Stoner said, returning to converts.

"Let's wait and see, Mrs Stoner," Father Nulty said.

The priests walked to the door.

"You know where I live, John."

"Yes. Come again, Frank. Good night."

Father Firman watched Father Nulty go down the walk to his car at the curb. He hooked the screen door and turned off the porch light. He hesitated at the foot of the stairs, suddenly moved to go to bed. But he went back into the study.

"Phew!" Mrs Stoner said. "I thought he'd never go. Here it is after eight o'clock."

Father Firman sat down in his rocking chair. "I don't see him often," he said.

"I give up!" Mrs Stoner exclaimed, flinging the holey socks upon the horsehair sofa. "I'd swear you had a nail in your shoe."

"I told you I looked."

"Well, you ought to look again. And cut your toenails, why don't you? Haven't I got enough to do?"

Father Firman scratched in his coat pocket for a pill, found
one, swallowed it. He let his head sink back against the chair
and closed his eyes. He could hear her moving about the room,
making the preparations; and how he knew them—the fumbling in the drawer for a pencil with a point, the rip of the page
from his daily calendar, and finally the leg of the card table
sliding up against his leg.

He opened his eyes. She yanked the floor lamp alongside
the table, setting the bead fringe tinkling on the shade, and
pulled up her chair on the other side. She sat down and smiled
at him for the first time that day. Now she was happy.

She swept up the cards and began to shuffle with the abandoned virtuosity of an old river-boat gambler, standing them
on end, fanning them out, whirling them through her fingers,
dancing them halfway up her arms, cracking the whip over
them. At last they lay before him tamed into a neat deck.

"Cut?"

"Go ahead," he said. She liked to go first.

She gave him her faint, avenging smile and drew a card, cast
it aside for another which he thought must be an ace from the
way she clutched it face down.

She was getting all the cards, as usual, and would have been
invincible if she had possessed his restraint and if her cunning
had been of a higher order. He knew a few things about leading
and lying back that she would never learn. Her strategy was
attack, forever attack, with one baffling departure: she might
sacrifice certain tricks as expendable if only she could have the
last ones, the heartbreaking ones, if she could slap them down
one after another, shatteringly.

She played for blood, no bones about it, but for her there
was no other way; it was her nature, as it was the lion's, and
for this reason he found her ferocity pardonable, more a defect
of the flesh, venial, while his own trouble was all in the will,
mortal. He did not sweat and pray over each card as she must,

but he did keep an eye out for reneging and demanded a cut now and then just to aggravate her, and he was always secretly hoping for aces.

With one card left in her hand, the telltale trick coming next, she delayed playing it, showing him first the smile, the preview of defeat. She laid it on the table—so! She held one more trump than he had reasoned possible. Had she palmed it from somewhere? No, she would not go that far; that would not be fair, was worse than reneging, which so easily and often happened accidentally, and she believed in being fair. Besides he had been watching her.

God smote the vines with hail, the sycamore trees with frost, and offered up the flocks to the lightning—but Mrs Stoner! What a cross Father Firman had from God in Mrs Stoner! There were other housekeepers as bad, no doubt, walking the rectories of the world, yes, but . . . yes. He could name one and maybe two priests who were worse off. One, maybe two. Cronin. His scraggly blonde of sixty—take her, with her everlasting banging on the grand piano, the gift of the pastor; her proud talk about the goiter operation at the Mayo Brothers', also a gift; her honking the parish Buick at passing strange priests because they were all in the game together. She was worse. She was something to keep the home fires burning. Yes sir. And Cronin said she was not a bad person really, but what was he? He was quite a freak himself.

For that matter, could anyone say that Mrs Stoner was a bad person? No. He could not say it himself, and he was no freak. She had her points, Mrs Stoner. She was clean. And though she cooked poorly, could not play the organ, would not take up the collection in an emergency, and went to card parties, and told all—even so, she was clean. She washed everything. Sometimes her underwear hung down beneath her dress like a paratrooper's pants, but it and everything she touched was clean. She washed constantly. She was clean.

She had her other points, to be sure—her faults, you might say. She snooped—no mistake about it—but it was not snooping for snooping's sake; she had a reason. She did other things, always with a reason. She overcharged on rosaries and prayer books, but that was for the sake of the poor. She censored the pamphlet rack, but that was to prevent scandal. She pried into the baptismal and matrimonial records, but there was no other way if Father was out, and in this way she had once uncovered a bastard and flushed him out of the rectory, but that was the perverted decency of the times. She held her nose over bad marriages in the presence of the victims, but that was her sorrow and came from having her husband buried in a mine. And he had caught her telling a bewildered young couple that there was only one good reason for their wanting to enter into a mixed marriage—the child had to have a name, and that—that was what?

She hid his books, kept him from smoking, picked his friends (usually the pastors of her colleagues), bawled out people for calling after dark, had no humor, except at cards, and then it was grim, very grim, and she sat hatchet-faced every morning at Mass. But she went to Mass, which was all that kept the church from being empty some mornings. She did annoying things all day long. She said annoying things into the night. She said she had given him the best years of her life. Had she? Perhaps—for the miner had her only a year. It was too bad, sinfully bad, when he thought of it like that. But all talk of best years and life was nonsense. He had to consider the heart of the matter, the essence. The essence was that housekeepers were hard to get, harder to get than ushers, than willing workers, than organists, than secretaries—yes, harder to get than assistants or vocations.

And she was a *saver*—saved money, saved electricity, saved string, bags, sugar, saved—him. That's what she did. That's what she said she did, and she was right, in a way. In a way, she was usually right. In fact, she was always right—in a way. And you could never get a Filipino to come way out here and live. Not a young one anyway, and he had never seen an old one. Not a Filipino. They liked to dress up and live.

Should he let it drop about Fish having one, just to throw a scare into her, let her know he was doing some thinking? No. It would be a perfect cue for the one about a man needing a woman to look after him. He was not up to that again, not tonight.

Now she was doing what she liked most of all. She was making a grand slam, playing it out card for card, though it was in the bag, prolonging what would have been cut short out of mercy in gentle company. Father Firman knew the agony of losing.

She slashed down the last card, a miserable deuce trump, and did in the hapless king of hearts he had been saving.

"Skunked you!"

She was awful in victory. Here was the bitter end of their long day together, the final murderous hour in which all they wanted to say—all he wouldn't and all she couldn't—came out in the cards. Whoever won at honeymoon won the day, slept on the other's scalp, and God alone had to help the loser.

"We've been at it long enough, Mrs Stoner," he said, seeing her assembling the cards for another round.

"Had enough, huh!"

Father Firman grumbled something.

"No?"

"Yes."

She pulled the table away and left it against the wall for the next time. She went out of the study carrying the socks, content and clucking. He closed his eyes after her and began to get under way in the rocking chair, the nightly trip to nowhere. He could hear her brewing a cup of tea in the kitchen and conversing with the cat. She made her way up the stairs, carrying the tea, followed by the cat, purring.

He waited, rocking out to sea, until she would be sure to be through in the bathroom. Then he got up and locked the front door (she looked after the back door) and loosened his collar going upstairs.

In the bathroom he mixed a glass of antiseptic, always afraid of pyorrhea, and gargled to ward off pharyngitis.

When he turned on the light in his room, the moths and beetles began to batter against the screens, the lighter insects humming . . .

Yes, and she had the guest room. How did she come to get that? Why wasn't she in the back room, in her proper place? He knew, if he cared to remember. The screen in the back room—it let in mosquitoes, and if it didn't do that she'd love to sleep back there, Father, looking out at the steeple and the blessed cross on top, Father, if it just weren't for the screen, Father. Very well, Mrs Stoner, I'll get it fixed or fix it myself. Oh, could you now, Father? I could, Mrs Stoner, and I will. In the meantime you take the guest room. Yes, Father, and thank you, Father, the house ringing with amenities then. Years ago, all that. She was a pie-faced girl then, not really a girl perhaps, but not too old to marry again. But she never had. In fact, he could not remember that she had even tried for a husband since coming to the rectory, but, of course, he could be wrong, not knowing how they went about it. God! God save us! Had she got her wires crossed and mistaken him all these years for *that*? *That!* Him! Suffering God! No. That was going too far. That was getting morbid. No. He must not think of that again, ever. No.

But just the same she had got the guest room and she had it yet. Well, did it matter? Nobody ever came to see him anymore, nobody to stay overnight anyway, nobody to stay very long . . . not anymore. He knew how they laughed at him. He had heard Frank humming all right—before he saw how serious and sad the situation was and took pity—humming, "Wedding Bells Are Breaking Up That Old Gang of Mine." But then they'd always laughed at him for something—for not being an athlete, for wearing glasses, for having kidney trouble . . . and mail coming addressed to Rev. and Mrs Stoner.

Removing his shirt, he bent over the table to read the volume left open from last night. He read, translating easily, "*Eisdem licet cum illis* . . . Clerics are allowed to reside only with women about whom there can be no suspicion, either because of a natural bond (as mother, sister, aunt) or of advanced age, combined in both cases with good repute."

Last night he had read it, and many nights before, each time as though this time to find what was missing, to find what obviously was not in the paragraph, his problem considered, a way out. She was not mother, not sister, not aunt, and *advanced age* was a relative term (why, she was younger than he was) and so, eureka, she did not meet the letter of the law— but, alas, how she fulfilled the spirit! And besides it would be a slimy way of handling it after all her years of service. He could not afford to pension her off, either.

He slammed the book shut. He slapped himself fiercely on the back, missing the wily mosquito, and whirled to find it. He took a magazine and folded it into a swatter. Then he saw it— oh, the preternatural cunning of it!—poised in the beard of St Joseph on the bookcase. He could not hit it there. He teased it away, wanting it to light on the wall, but it knew his thoughts and flew high away. He swung wildly, hoping to stun it, missed, swung back, catching St Joseph across the neck. The statue fell to the floor and broke.

Mrs Stoner was panting in the hall outside his door.

"What is it?"

"Mosquitoes!"

"What is it, Father? Are you hurt?"

"Mosquitoes—damn it! And only the female bites!"

Mrs Stoner, after a moment, said, "Shame on you, Father. She needs the blood for her eggs."

He dropped the magazine and lunged at the mosquito with his bare hand.

She went back to her room, saying, "Pshaw, I thought it was burglars murdering you in your bed."

He lunged again.

THE EYE

ALL THEM THAT dropped in at Bullen's last night was talking about the terrible accident that almost happened to Clara Beck—that's Clyde Bullen's best girl. I am in complete charge of the pool tables and cigar counter, including the punchboards, but I am not at my regular spot in front, on account of Clyde has got a hot game of rotation going at the new table, and I am the only one he will leave chalk his cue. While I am chalking it and collecting for games and racking the balls I am hearing from everybody how Clara got pulled out of the river by Sleep Bailey.

He is not one of the boys, Sleep, but just a nigger that's deef and lives over in jigtown somewhere and plays the piano for dances at the Louisiana Social Parlor. They say he can't hear nothing but music. Spends the day loafing and fishing. He's fishing—is the story—when he seed Clara in the river below the Ludlow road bridge, and he swum out and saved her. Had to knock her out to do it, she put up such a fight. Anyways he saved her from drownding. That was the story everybody was telling.

Clyde has got the idee of taking up a collection for Sleep, as it was a brave deed he done and he don't have nothing to his name but a tub of fishing worms. On the other hand, he don't need nothing, being a nigger, not needing nothing. But Clara is Clyde's girl and it is Clyde's idee and so it is going over pretty big as most of the boys is trying to stay in with Clyde and the rest is owing him money and can't help themselves. I chipped in two bits myself.

Clyde is just fixing to shoot when Skeeter Bird comes in and says, "Little cold for swimming, ain't it, Clyde?"

It upsets Clyde and he has to line up the thirteen ball again. I remember it is the thirteen 'cause they ain't nobody round here that's got the eye Clyde has got for them big balls and that thirteen is his special favor-ite, says it's lucky—it and the nine. I tell you this on account of Clyde misses his shot. Looked to me and anybody else that knowed Clyde's game that what Skeeter said upset his aim.

"What's eating you?" Clyde says to Skeeter, plenty riled. I can see he don't feel so bad about the thirteen getting away as he might of, as he has left it sewed up for Ace Haskins, that claims he once took a game from the great Ralph Greenleaf. "You got something to say?" Clyde says.

"No," Skeeter says, "only—"

"Only what?" Clyde wants to know.

"Only that Bailey nigger got hisself scratched up nice, Clyde."

"So I am taking up a little collection for him," Clyde says. "Pass the plate to Brother Bird, boys."

But Skeeter, he don't move a finger, just says, "Clara got banged up some, too, Clyde. Nigger must of socked her good."

None of us knowed what Skeeter was getting at, except maybe Clyde, that once took a course in mind reading, but we don't like it. And Clyde, I can tell, don't like it. The cue stick is shaking a little in his hand like he wants to use it on Skeeter and he don't shoot right away. He straightens up and says, "Well, he hadda keep her from strangling him while he was rescuing her, didn't he? It was for her own good."

"Yeah, guess so," Skeeter says. "But they both looked like they been in a mean scrap."

"That so?" Clyde says. "Was you there?"

"No, but I heard," Skeeter says.

"You heard," Clyde says. He gets ready to drop the fifteen.

"Yeah," Skeeter says. "You know, Clyde, that Bailey nigger is a funny nigger."

"How's that?" Clyde says, watching Skeeter close. "What's wrong with him?" Clyde holds up his shot and looks right at Skeeter. "Come on, out with it."

"Oh, I don't know as they's a lot wrong with him," Skeeter says. "I guess he's all right. Lazy damn nigger is all. Won't keep a job—just wants to play on the piano and fish."

"Never would of rescued Clara if he didn't," Clyde says. "And besides what kind of job you holding down?"

Now that gets Skeeter where it hurts on account of he don't work hisself, unless you call selling rubbers work or peddling art studies work. Yeah, that's what he calls them. Art studies. Shows a girl that ain't got no clothes on, except maybe her garters, and down below it says "Pensive" or "Evening in Paris." Skeeter sells them to artists, he says—he'll tell you that to your face—but he's always got a few left over for the boys at Bullen's.

Well, Skeeter goes on up front and starts in to study the slot machines. He don't never play them, just studies them. Somebody said he's writing a book about how to beat them, but I don't think he's got the mind for it, is my opinion.

Clyde is halfway into the next game when Skeeter comes back again. He has some of the boys with him now.

"All right, all right," Clyde says, stopping his game.

"You tell him, Skeeter," the boys says.

"Yeah, Skeeter, you tell me," Clyde says.

"Oh," Skeeter says, "it's just something some of them is saying, Clyde, is all."

"Who's saying?" Clyde says. "Who's saying what?"

"Some of them," Skeeter says, "over at the Arcade."

The Arcade, in case you don't know, is the other poolhall in town. Bullen's and the Arcade don't mix, and I guess Skeeter is about the only one that shows up regular in both places, on account of he's got customers in both places. I'd personally like to keep Skeeter out of Bullen's, but Clyde buys a lot of art studies off him and I can't say nothing.

After a spell of thinking Clyde says to Skeeter, "Spill it."

"May not be a word of truth to it, Clyde," Skeeter says. "You know how folks talk. And all I know is what I hear. Course I knowed a long time that Bailey nigger is a damn funny nigger. Nobody never did find out where he come from—St Louis, Chicago, New York, for all anybody knowed. And if he's stone deaf how can he hear to play the piano?"

"Damn the nigger," Clyde says. "What is they saying, them Arcade bastards!"

"Oh, not all of them is saying it, Clyde. Just some of them is saying it. Red Hynes, that tends bar at the El Paso, and them. Saying maybe the nigger didn't get them scratches on his face for nothing. Saying maybe he was trying something funny. That's a damn funny nigger, Clyde, I don't care what you say. And when you get right down to it, Clyde, kind of stuck up like. Anyways some of them at the Arcade is saying maybe the nigger throwed Clara in the river and then fished her out just to cover up. Niggers is awful good at covering up, Clyde."

Clyde don't say nothing to this, but I can tell he is thinking plenty and getting mad at what he's thinking—plenty. It's real quiet at Bullen's now.

"Maybe," Clyde says, "maybe they is saying what he was covering up from?"

"Yeah, Clyde," Skeeter says. "Matter of fact, they is. Yeah, some of them is saying maybe the nigger *raped* her!"

Bang! Clyde cracks the table with his cue stick. It takes a piece of pearl inlay right out of the apron board of the good, new table. Nobody says nothing. Clyde just stares at all the chalk dust he raised.

Then Skeeter says, "Raped her first, rescued her later, is what they is saying."

"What you going to do, Clyde?" Banjo Wheeler says.

"Clyde is thinking!" I say. "Leave him think!" But personally I never seed Clyde take that long just to think.

"Move," Clyde says.

The boys give Clyde plenty of room. He goes over to the rack and tips a little talcum in his hands. The boys is all watching him good. Then Clyde spits. I am right by the cuspidor and can see Clyde's spit floating on the water inside. Nobody says nothing. Clyde's spit is going around in the water and I am listening to hear what he is going to do. He takes the chalk out of my hand. He still don't say nothing. It is the first time he ever chalks his cue with me around to do it.

Then he says, "What kind of nigger is this Bailey nigger, Roy?"

Roy—that's me.

"Oh, just a no-good nigger, Clyde," I say. "Plays the piano at the Louisiana Social Parlor—*some* social parlor, Clyde—is about all I know, or anybody. Fishes quite a bit—just a lazy, funny, no-good nigger . . ."

"But he ain't no *bad* nigger, Roy?"

"Naw, he ain't *that*, Clyde," I say. "We ain't got none of them kind left in town."

"Well," Clyde says, "just so's he ain't no *bad* nigger."

Then, not saying no more, Clyde shoots and makes the ten ball in the side pocket. I don't have to tell you the boys is all pretty disappointed in Clyde. I have to admit I never knowed no other white man but Clyde to act like that. But maybe Clyde has his reasons, I say to myself, and wait.

Well, sir, that was right before the news come from the hospital. Ace is friendly with a nurse there is how we come to get it. He calls her on the phone to find out how Clara is. She is unconscious and ain't able to talk yet, but that ain't what makes all hell break loose at Bullen's. It's—un-mis-tak-able ev-i-dence of preg-nan-cy!

Get it? Means she was knocked up. Whoa! I don't have to tell you how that hits the boys at Bullen's. Some said they admired Clyde for not flying off the handle in the first place and some said they didn't, but all of them said they had let their good natures run away with their better judgments. They was right.

I goes to Ace, that's holding the kitty we took up for the nigger, and gets my quarter back. I have a little trouble at first as some of the boys has got there in front of me and collected more than they put in—or else Ace is holding out.

All this time Clyde is in the washroom. I try to hurry him up, but he don't hurry none. Soon as he unlocks the door and comes out we all give him the news.

I got to say this is the first time I ever seed Clyde act the way he do now. I hate to say it, but—I will. Clyde, he don't act much like a man. No, he don't, not a bit. He just reaches his cue down and hands it to me.

"Chalk it," he says. "Chalk it," is all he says. Damn if I don't almost hand it back to him.

I chalk his cue. But the boys, they can't stand no more.

Ace says he is going to call the hospital again.

"Damn it, Clyde," Banjo says. "We got to do something. Else they ain't going to be no white woman safe in the streets. What they going to think of you at the Arcade? I can hear Red Hynes and them laughing."

That is the way the boys is all feeling at Bullen's, and they say so. I am waiting with the rest for Clyde to hurry up and do something, or else explain hisself. But he just goes on, like nothing is the matter, and starts up a new game. It's awful quiet. Clyde gets the nine ball on the break. It hung on the lip of the pocket like it didn't want to, but it did.

"You sure like that old nine ball, Clyde," I say, trying to make Clyde feel easy and maybe come to his senses. I rack the nine for him. My hand is wet and hot and the yellow nine feels like butter to me.

"Must be the color of the nine is what he like," Banjo says.

Whew! I thought that would be all for Banjo, but no sir, Clyde goes right on with the game, like it's a compliment.

A couple of guys is whistling soft at what Banjo got away with. Me, I guess Clyde feels sorry for Banjo, on account of they is both fighters. Clyde was a contender for the state heavy title three years back, fighting under the name of Big Boy Bullen, weighing in at two thirty-three. Poor old Banjo is a broken-down carnival bum, and when he's drinking too heavy, like last night and every night, he forgets how old and beat up he is and don't know no better than to run against Clyde, that's a former contender and was rated in *Collyer's Eye*. Banjo never was no better than a welter when he was fighting and don't tip more than a hundred fifty-five right now. What with the drink and quail he don't amount to much no more.

And then Ace comes back from calling up the hospital and says, "No change; Clara's still unconscious."

"Combination," Clyde says. "Twelve ball in the corner pocket."

That's all Clyde has got to say. We all want to do something, but Banjo wants to do it the worst and he says, "No change, still unconscious. Knocked out and knocked up—by a nigger! Combination—twelve ball in the corner pocket!"

"Dummy up!" Clyde says. He slugs the table again and ruins a cube of chalk. He don't even look at Banjo or none of us. I take the whisk broom and brush the chalk away the best I could, without asking Clyde to move.

"Thanks," Clyde says, still not seeing nobody.

I feel kind of funny on account of Clyde never says thanks for nothing before. I wonder is it the old Clyde or is he feeling sick. Then, so help me, Clyde runs the table, thirteen balls. Ace don't even get a shot that game.

But, like you guessed, the boys won't hold still for it no more and is all waiting for Clyde to do something. And Clyde don't have to be no mind reader to know it. He gets a peculiar look in his eye that I seed once or twice before and goes over to Banjo— to—guess what?—to shake his hand. Yes sir, Clyde has got his hand out and is smiling—smiling at Banjo that said what he said.

Banjo just stands there with a dumb look on his face, not knowing what Clyde is all about, and they shake.

"So I'm yella, huh, Banjo?" That's what Clyde says to Banjo.

I don't know if Banjo means to do it, or can't help it, but he burps right in Clyde's face.

Boom! Clyde hits Banjo twice in the chin and mouth quick and drops him like a handkerchief. Banjo is all over the floor and his mouth is hanging open like a spring is busted and blood is leaking out the one side and he has got some bridge-work loose.

"Hand me the nine, Roy," Clyde says to me. I get the nine ball and give it to Clyde. He shoves it way into Banjo's mouth that is hanging open and bleeding good.

Then Clyde lets him have one more across the jaw and you can hear the nine ball rattle inside Banjo's mouth.

Clyde says, "Now some of you boys been itching for action all night. Well, I'm here to tell you I'm just the boy to hand it out. Tonight I just feel like stringing me up a black nigger by the light of the silvery moon! Let's get gaiting!"

Now that was the old Clyde for you. A couple of guys

reaches fast for cue sticks, but I am in charge of them and the tables, and I say, "Lay off them cue sticks! Get some two by fours outside!"

So we leaves old Banjo sucking on the nine ball and piles into all the cars we can get and heads down for the Louisiana Social Parlor. I am sitting next to Clyde in his car.

On the way Ace tells us when he called the hospital the second time he got connected with some doctor fella. Ace said this doctor was sore on account of Ace's girl, that's the nurse, give out information about Clara that she wasn't supposed to. But the doctor said as long as we all knowed so much about the case already he thought we ought to know it was of some months' standing, Clara's condition. Ace said he could tell from the way the doctor was saying it over and over that he was worried about what we was planning to do to the coon. Ace's girl must of copped out to him. But Ace said he thanked the doc kindly for his trouble and hung up and wouldn't give his right name when the doc wanted to know. We all knowed about the doctor all right—only one of them young intern fellas from Memphis or some place—and as for the some months' standing part we all knowed in our own minds what nigger bucks is like and him maybe burning with strong drink on top of it. Ace said he hoped the nurse wouldn't go and lose her job on account of the favor she done for us.

The only thing we seed when we gets to the Louisiana is one old coon by the name of Old Ivy. He is locking up. We asks him about Sleep Bailey, but Old Ivy is playing dumb and all he says is, "Suh? Suh?" like he don't know what we mean.

"Turn on them there lights," we says, "so's we can see."

Old Ivy turns them on.

"Where's the crowd," we says, "that's always around?"

"Done went," Old Ivy says.

"So they's done went," Skeeter says. "Well, if they's trying to steal that piano-playing nigger away they won't get very far."

"No, they won't get very far with that," Clyde says. "Hey, just seeing all them bottles is got me feeling kind of dry-like."

So we gets Old Ivy to put all the liquor on the bar and us boys refreshes ourselves. Skeeter tells Old Ivy to put some beer out for chasers.

Old Ivy says they is fresh out of cold beer.

"It don't have to be cold," Skeeter says. "We ain't proud."

Old Ivy drags all the bottled beer out on the bar with the other. Then he goes back into the kitchen behind the bar and we don't see him no more for a little.

"Hey, old nigger," Skeeter says. "Don't try and sneak out the back way."

"No, suh," Old Ivy says.

"Hey, Old Ivy," Clyde says. "You got something to eat back there?"

"Suh?" He just gives us that old *suh*. "Suh?"

"You heard him," Skeeter says.

"No, suh," Old Ivy says, and we seed him in the service window.

"Guess maybe he's deef," Skeeter says. "You old coon, I hope you ain't blind!" And Skeeter grabs a bottle of beer and lams it at Old Ivy's head. Old Ivy ducks and the big end of the bottle sticks in the wall and don't break. It is just beaverboard, the wall.

All us boys gets the same idee and we starts heaving the beer bottles through the window where Old Ivy was standing, but ain't no more.

"Hit the nigger baby!"

"Nigger in the fence!"

We keeps this up until we done run out of bottles, all except Skeeter that's been saving one. "Hey, wait," he says. "It's all right now, Grampaw. Come on, old boy, you can come out now."

But Old Ivy don't show hisself. I am wondering if he got hit on a rebound.

"Damn it, boy," Skeeter says. "Bring us some food. Or you want us to come back in there?"

"Suh?" It's that old *suh* again. "Yes, suh," Old Ivy says in the kitchen, but we don't see him.

Then we do. And Skeeter, he lets go the last bottle with all he's got. It hits Old Ivy right in the head. That was a mean thing Skeeter done, I think, but then I see it's only the cook's hat Old Ivy's got in his hand that got hit. He was holding it up like his head is inside, but it ain't.

The boys all laughs when they seed what Old Ivy done to fool Skeeter.

"Like in war when you fool the enemy," Clyde says.

"That's a smart nigger," I say.

"So that's a smart nigger, huh?" Skeeter says. "I'll take and show you what I do to smart niggers that gets smart with me!"

"Cut it out," Clyde says. "Leave him alone. He ain't hurting nothing. You just leave that old coon be." That is Clyde for you, always sticking up for somebody, even a nigger.

Clyde and me goes into the next room looking for a place to heave, as Clyde has got to. It is awful dark, but pretty soon our eyes gets used to it, and we can see some tables and chairs and a juke box and some beer signs on the walls. It must be where they do their dancing. I am just standing there ready to hold Clyde's head, as he is easing hisself, when I begins to hear a piano like a radio is on low. I can just barely pick it out, a couple a notes at a time, sad music, blues music, nigger music.

It ain't no radio. It is a piano on the other side of the room. I am ready to go and look into it when Clyde says, "It ain't nothing." Ain't nothing! Sometimes I can't understand Clyde for the life of me. But I already got my own idee about the piano.

About then Skeeter and Ace comes in the room yelling for Clyde in the dark, saying the boys out front is moving on to the next place. We hear a hell of a racket out by the bar, like they broke the mirror, and then it's pretty still and we know they is almost all left.

Skeeter gives us one more yell and Ace says, "Hey, Clyde, you fall in?" They is about to leave when Skeeter, I guess it is, hears the piano just like we been hearing it. All this time Clyde has got his hand over my mouth like he don't want me to say we is there.

Skeeter calls Old Ivy and says he should turn on the lights, and when Old Ivy starts that *suh* business again Skeeter lays one on him that I can hear in the dark.

So Old Ivy turns on the lights, a lot of creepy greens, reds, and blues. Then Clyde and me both seed what I already guessed—it's the Bailey nigger playing the piano—and Skeeter and Ace seed it is him and we all seed each other.

And right then, damn if the nigger don't start in to sing a song. Like he didn't know what was what! Like he didn't know what we come for! That's what I call a foxy nigger.

Skeeter yells at him to stop singing and to come away from the piano. He stops singing, but he don't move. So we all goes over to the piano.

"What's your name, nigger?" Skeeter says.

"Bailey," Sleep says, reading Skeeter's lips.

Old Ivy comes over and he is saying a lot of stuff like, "That boy's just a borned fool. Just seem like he got to put his foot in it some kind of way."

Sleep hits a couple a notes light on the piano that sounds nice and pretty.

"You know what we come for?" Skeeter says.

Sleep hits them same two notes again, nice and pretty, and shakes his head.

"Sure you don't know, boy?" Clyde says.

Sleep is just about to play them notes again when Skeeter hits him across the paws with a fungo bat. Then Sleep says, "I spect you after me on account of that Miss Beck I fish out of the river."

"That's right," Skeeter says. "You spect right."

"You know what they is saying uptown, Sleep?" I say.

"I heard," Sleep says.

"They is saying," I say, "you raped Clara and throwed her in the river to cover up."

"That's just a lie," Sleep says.

"Who says it's a lie?" Clyde says.

"That's just a white-folks lie," Sleep says. "It's God's truth."

"How you going to prove it?" Clyde says.

"Yeah," I say. "How you going to prove it?"

"How you going to prove it to them, son?" Old Ivy says.

"Here, ain't I?" Sleep says.

"Yeah, you's here all right, nigger," Skeeter says, "but don't you wish you wasn't!"

"If I'm here I guess I got no call to be scared," Sleep says. "Don't it prove nothing if I'm here, if I didn't run away? Don't that prove nothing?"

"Naw," Skeeter says. "It don't prove nothing. It's just a smart nigger trick."

"Wait till Miss Beck come to and talk," Sleep says. "I ain't scared."

"No," Old Ivy says, "you ain't scared. He sure ain't scared a bit, is he, Mr Bullen? That's a good sign he ain't done nothing bad, ain't it, Mr Bullen?"

"Well," Clyde says. "I don't know about that . . ."

Skeeter says, "You sure you feel all right, Clyde?"

"What you mean you don't know, Clyde?" Ace says. "Clara is knocked up and this is the bastard done it!"

"Who the hell else, Clyde?" I say. I wonder is Clyde dreaming or what.

"He ain't a bad boy like that, Mr Bullen," Old Ivy says, working on Clyde.

"I tell you what," Clyde says.

"Aw, stop it, Clyde," Skeeter and Ace both says. "We got enough!"

"Shut up!" Clyde says and he says it like he mean it.

"Listen to what Mr Bullen got to say," Old Ivy says.

"This is the way I seed it," Clyde says. "This ain't no open-and-shut case of rape—leastways not yet it ain't. Now the law—"

Skeeter cuts in and says, "Well, Clyde, I'll see you the first of the week." He acts like he is going to leave.

"Come back here," Clyde says. "You ain't going to tell no mob nothing till I got this Bailey boy locked up safe in the county jail waiting judgment."

"O.K., Clyde," Skeeter says. "That's different. I thought you was going to let him get away."

"Hell, no!" Clyde says. "We got to see justice did, ain't we?"

"Sure do, Clyde," Skeeter says.

Ace says, "He'll be nice and safe in jail in case we got to take up anything with him."

I knowed what they mean and so do Old Ivy. He says, "Better let him go right now, Mr Bullen. Let him run for it. This other way they just going to bust in the jailhouse and take him out and hang him to a tree."

"The way I seed it," Clyde says, "this case has got to be handled according to the law. I don't want this boy's blood on my hands. If he ain't to blame, I mean."

"That's just what he ain't, Mr Bullen," Old Ivy says. "But it ain't going to do no good to put him in that old jailhouse."

"We'll see about that," Clyde says.

"Oh, sure. Hell, yes!" Skeeter says. "We don't want to go and take the law in our own hands. That ain't our way, huh, Ace?"

"Cut it out," Clyde says.

"Maybe Miss Beck feel all right in the morning, son, and it going to be all right for you," Old Ivy says to Sleep. The old coon is crying.

So we takes Sleep in Clyde's car to the county jail. We makes him get down on the floor so's we can put our feet on him and guard him better. He starts to act up once on the way, but Skeeter persuades him with the fungo bat in the right place, *conk*, and he is pretty quiet then.

Right after we get him behind bars it happens.

Like I say, Clyde is acting mighty peculiar all night, but now he blows his top for real. That's what he does all right—plumb blows it. It is all over in a second. He swings three times—one, two, three—and Skeeter and Ace is out cold as Christmas, and I am holding this fat eye. Beats me! And I don't mind telling you I laid down quick with Skeeter and Ace, like I was out, till Clyde went away. Now you figure it out.

But I ain't preferring no charges on Clyde. Not me, that's his best friend, even if he did give me this eye, and Skeeter ain't, that needs Bullen's for his business, or Ace.

What happens to who? To the jig that said he pulled Clara out of the river?

You know that big old slippery elm by the Crossing? That's the one. But that ain't how I got the eye.

THE OLD BIRD, A LOVE STORY

UNEMPLOYED AND ELDERLY Mr Newman sensed there were others, some of them, just as anxious as he was to be put on. But he was the oldest person in the room. He approached the information girl, and for all his show of business, almost brusqueness, he radiated timidity. The man in front of him asked the girl a question, which was also Mr Newman's.

"Are they doing any hiring today?"

The girl gave the man an application, a dead smile, and told him to take a seat after he had filled the application out.

An answer, in any event, ready on her lips, she regarded Mr Newman. Mr Newman thought of reaching for an application and saying, "Yes, I'll take a seat," making a kind of joke out of the coincidence—the fellow before him looking for a job, too—only he could see from the others who had already taken seats it was no coincidence. They all had that superior look of people out of work.

"Got an application there for a retired millionaire?" Mr Newman said, attempting jauntiness. That way it would be easier for her to refuse him. Perhaps it was part of her job to weed out applicants clearly too old to be of any use to the company. Mr Newman had a real horror of butting in where he wasn't wanted.

The girl laughed, making Mr Newman feel like a regular devil, and handed him an application. The smile she gave him was alive and it hinted that things were already on a personal basis between him and her and the company.

"You'll find a pen at the desk," she said.

Mr Newman's bony old hand clawed at his coat pocket and unsnapped a large ancient fountain pen. "I carry my own! See?" In shy triumph he held up the fountain pen, which was orange. He unscrewed it, put it together, and fingered it as though he were actually writing.

But the girl was doing her dead smile at the next one.

Mr Newman went over to the desk. The application questioned him: Single? Married? Children of your own? Parents living? Living with parents? Salary (expect)? Salary (would take)? Mr Newman made ready with his fountain pen and in the ensuing minutes he did not lie about his age, his abilities, or past earnings. The salary he expected was modest. He was especially careful about making blots with his pen, which sometimes flowed too freely. He had noted before he started that the application was one of those which calls for the information to be printed. This he had done. Under "DO NOT WRITE BELOW THIS LINE" he had not written.

Mr Newman read the application over and rose to take it to the information girl. She pointed to a bench. Hesitating for a moment, Mr Newman seemed bent on giving it to her. He sat down. He got up. His face distraught, he walked unsteadily over to the girl.

Before she could possibly hear him, he started to stammer, "I wonder ... maybe it will make a difference," his voice both appealing for her mercy and saying it was out of the question—

indeed he did not desire it—that she should take a personal interest in him. Then he got control, except for his eyes, which, without really knowing it, were searching the girl's face for the live smile, like the first time.

"I used green ink," he said limply.

"Let's see." The girl took the application, gave both sides a darting scrutiny, looking for mistakes.

"Will it make any difference? If it does and I could have another application, I could—" Mr Newman had his orange fountain pen out again, as though to match the green on its tip with the ink on the application and thus fully account for what had come about.

"Oh no, I think that'll be all right," the girl said, finally getting the idea. "We're not that fussy." Mr Newman, however, still appeared worried. "No, that's fine—and neat, too," the girl said. "Mr *Newman*." She had spoken his name and there was her live smile. Mr Newman blushed, then smiled a little himself. With perspiring fingers he put the fountain pen together and snapped it in his pocket.

The girl returned the application. Mr Newman, lingering on, longed to confide in her, to tell her something of himself— why, for instance, he always used green ink; how famous and familiar a few years ago the initials "C. N." in green had been at the old place. Like his friend Jack P. Ferguson (died a few years back, it was in the papers) and the telegram. "Telegram" Ferguson, he was called, because he was always too busy to write. Green ink and telegrams, the heraldry of business. He wanted to tell her of the old days—the time he met Elbert Hubbard and Charley Schwab at a banquet.

Then on this side of the old days he saw a busy girl, busy being busy, who could never understand.

"I thank you," he said, going quickly back to his place on the bench to wait. He sat there rereading his application. Under "DO NOT WRITE BELOW THIS LINE" were some curious symbols. He guessed at their significance: CLN (Clean?); DSPN (Disposition?); PRSNLTY (Personality, no doubt about that one); PSE (Poise?); FCW (?); LYL (Loyal?); PSBLE LDR (Possible Leader); NTC (?). His fingers were damp with perspiration, and for fear he would present an untidy application, he laid it on his lap and held his hands open at his sides, letting them get cool and dry in case he had to shake hands with the interviewer.

When they were ready to see him, Mr Newman hustled into a small glass office and stood before a young man. A sign with wooden letters indicated that he was Mr Shanahan. Mr Shanahan was reading a letter. Mr Newman did not look directly at Mr Shanahan: it was none of Mr Newman's business —Mr Shanahan's letter—and he did not want to seem curious or expectant of immediate attention. This was their busy season.

Mr Shanahan, still reading the letter, had noiselessly extended a hand toward Mr Newman. A moment later, only then, Mr Newman saw the hand. Caught napping! A bad beginning! He hastened to shake the hand, recoiled in time. Mr Shanahan had only been reaching out for the application. Mr Newman gave it to Mr Shanahan and said, "Thank you," for some reason.

"Ah, yes. Have a seat." Mr Shanahan rattled the application in one hand. "What kind of work did you want to do?" Evidently he expected no answer, for he went on to say, "I don't have to tell you, Mr Newman, there's a labor shortage, especially in non-defense industries. That, and that alone, accounts for the few jobs we have to offer. We're an old-line house."

"Yes," Mr Newman said.

"And there aren't any office jobs," Mr Shanahan continued. "That's the kind of work you've always done?"

"Yes, it is," Mr Newman said. Mr Shanahan sucked a tooth sadly.

Mr Newman was ready now for the part about the company letting him know later.

"How'd you like a temporary job in our shipping room?" Mr Shanahan said, his eyes suddenly watchful.

For an instant Mr Newman succeeded in making it plain that he, like any man of his business experience, was meant for better things. A moment later, in an interesting ceremony which took place in his heart, Mr Newman surrendered his well-loved white collar. He knew that Mr Shanahan, with that dark vision peculiar to personnel men, had witnessed the whole thing.

"Well . . ." he said.

Mr Shanahan, the game bagged and bumping from his belt, got cordial now. "How are you, pretty handy with rope?"

He said it in such a flattering way that Mr Newman trembled under the desire to be worthy. "Yes, I am," he said.

"But can you begin right away?" It was the final test.

"Yes, I can!" Mr Newman said, echoing some of Mr Shanahan's spirit. "You bet I can!"

"Well then, follow me!"

Mr Shanahan guided Mr Newman through a maze of departments. On an elevator, going down, he revealed what the job paid to start. Mr Newman nodded vigorously that one could not expect too much to start. Mr Shanahan told him that he didn't have to tell him that they were a firm known far and wide for fair dealing and that if (for any reason) Mr Newman ever left them, it should be easy to get another position, and . . . Out of the elevator and in the lower depths, Mr Shanahan said he would like to make sure Mr Newman understood the job was only temporary. After the Christmas holidays things were pretty slow in their line. Otherwise, they would be glad to avail themselves of his services the year round. However, the experience Mr Newman would get here might very well prove invaluable to him in later life. Mr Newman nodded less vigorously now.

They came to a long table, flat against a wall, extending around a rafterish room fitted out for packing: tough twine and hairy manila rope on giant spools, brown paper on rollers, sticking tape bearing the company's name, crest, and slogan: "A modern house over 100 years *young.*"

Several men were packing things. Mr Shanahan introduced Mr Newman to one of them.

"This is your boss, Mr Hurley. This is Mr Newman. Mr Newman's pretty handy with rope. Ought to make an A-1 packer."

"Well . . ." Mr Newman said, embarrassed before the regular packers.

He shook Mr Hurley's hard hand.

"I sure hope so," Mr Hurley said grimly. "This is our busy season."

When Mr Shanahan had gone Mr Hurley showed Mr Newman where he could hang his coat. He told him what he would have to do and what he would be held responsible for. He cited the sad case of the shipment sent out last week to Fargo, North Dakota. The company had lost exactly double the amount of the whole sale, to say nothing of good will. Why? Faulty packing! He urged Mr Newman to figure it out for himself. He told Mr Newman that haste made waste, but that they were expected to get incoming orders out of the house on the same day. Not tomorrow. Not the next day. The same day. Finally Mr Hurley again brought up the case of the shipment sent to Fargo, and seemed pleased with the reaction it got. For Mr Newman frowned his forehead all out of shape and rolled his head back and forth like a sad old bell, as if to say, "Can such things be?"

"All right, Newman, let's see what you can do!" Mr Hurley slapped him on the shoulder like a football coach sending in a substitute. Mr Newman, gritting his false teeth, tackled his first assignment for the company: a half-dozen sets of poker chips, a box of rag dolls, 5,000 small American flags, and a boy's sled going to Waupaca, Wisconsin.

Mr Newman perspired . . . lost his breath, caught it, tried to break a piece of twine with his bare hands, failed, cut his nose on a piece of wrapping paper, bled, barked his shin on an ice skate, tripped, said a few cuss words to himself . . . perspired.

"We go to lunch at twelve in this section," Mr Hurley told him in a whisper a few minutes before that time. "If you want to wash up, go ahead now."

But Mr Newman waited until the whistle blew before he knocked off. He had a shipment he wanted to get off. It was ten after twelve when he punched out.

There was no crowd at the time clock and he had a chance to look the thing over. He tried to summon up a little interest, but all he felt with any intensity was the lone fact that he'd never had to punch a clock before. It had always been enough before that he live by one.

On his lunch hour he did not know where to go. The company had a place where you could eat your lunch, but Mr Newman had neglected to bring one. Quite reasonably he had not anticipated getting a job and starting on it the same day. After the usual morning of looking around, he had expected to go home and eat a bite with Mrs Newman.

He walked past a lunch stand twice before he could make certain, without actually staring in the window at the menu painted on the wall, that hamburgers were ten cents and coffee five. He entered the place, then, and ordered with assurance that he would not be letting himself in for more than he could afford. He did not have any money to spare. Would it be better, he wondered, to have payday come soon and get paid for a few days' work, or could he hold out for a week or so and really have something when he did get paid? Leaving the lunch stand, he walked in the direction of the company, but roundabout so he would not get back too soon. Say about fifteen minutes to one. That would give him time to go to the washroom.

"Where did you eat your lunch?" Mr Hurley asked him the first thing. "I didn't see you in the lunchroom."

"Oh, I ate out," Mr Newman said, gratified that he'd been missed until he saw that he had offended Mr Hurley by eating out. "I didn't bring my lunch today," he explained. "Didn't think I'd be working so soon."

"Oh." But Mr Hurley was still hurt.

"I heard they let you eat your lunch in the building," Mr Newman said, giving Mr Hurley his chance.

Mr Hurley broke down and told Mr Newman precisely where the employees' lunchroom was, where it wasn't, how to get there from the shipping room, how not to. There were two ways to get there, he said, and he guessed, as for him, he never went the same way twice in a row.

"You know how it is," Mr Hurley said, with a laugh, tying it in with life.

"Well, I guess so," Mr Newman said, with a laugh. Talking with Mr Hurley gave Mr Newman a good feeling. It was man-to-man or nothing with Hurley. Mr Newman, however, went back to work at four minutes to one.

During the afternoon Mr Newman developed a dislike for the fat fellow next to him, but when they teamed up on a big shipment of toys the fat fellow made some cynical remarks about the company and Mr Newman relaxed, thinking that his kind were harmless as rivals, that the company would be better off with employees like himself. And then was ashamed of himself, for he admired the fat fellow for his independence. Mr Newman regretted that he was too old for independence.

Toward the end of the day he was coming from getting a drink of water when he overheard Mr Hurley talking with Mr Shanahan.

"Yeah," Mr Hurley said, "when you said the old bird was handy with rope I thought, boy, he's old enough to think about using some on himself. My God, Shanahan, if this keeps up we'll have to draft them from the old people's home."

Mr Newman went for another drink of water. When he

returned to the shipping room they were all working and Mr Shanahan was not there.

Just before quitting time, Mr Hurley came over and congratulated Mr Newman on his first day's work. He said he thought Mr Newman would make out all right, and showed him an easier way to cut string. When he suggested that Mr Newman wash up before the whistle blew, Mr Newman did not have the faith to refuse. He could not look Mr Hurley in the eye now and say something about wanting to finish up a shipment. Any extraordinary industry on his part, he knew now, was useless. He was too old. That was all they could see when they looked at him. That was the only fact about him. He was an old bird.

"All right, Charley, see you in the morning," Mr Hurley said.

Mr Newman slowly brought himself to realize he was "Charley" to Mr Hurley. He had never before been "Charley" to anyone on such short acquaintance. Probably he would be "Old Charley" before long, which reminded him that Christmas was coming. There was no meaning beyond Christmas in all this sweat and humiliation, but that was enough. He would stick it out.

Mr Newman was impressed again with the vaultlike solemnity of the washroom. The strange dignity of the toilet booths, the resounding marble chips in the floor, the same as statehouses, the plenitude of paper, the rude music of water coursing, the fat washbowls, all resplendent and perfect of their kind, and towels, white as winding sheets, circulating without end . . .

Mr Newman, young here, luxuriated. Still he was sensible about it. The company was a big company and could no doubt stand a lot of wasting of towels and toilet paper, but Mr Newman, wanting to be fair, took only what he needed of everything. He would not knowingly abuse a privilege. He read a notice concerning a hospitalization service the company offered the employees. The sensibleness of such a plan appealed strongly to Mr Newman. He thought he would have to look into that, completely forgetting that he was only on temporary.

At the sound of the five-o'clock whistle Mr Newman hurried out and took his place in the line of employees at the time clock. When his turn came to punch out, clutching his time card, he was shaking all over. The clock would jam, or stamp the time in the wrong place, or at the last moment, losing confidence in the way he was holding the card, after all his planning, he would somehow stick it in the wrong way. Then there would be shouts from the end of the line, and everybody would know it was all on account of an old bird trying to punch out.

Mr Newman's heart stopped beating, his body followed a preconceived plan from memory in the lapse, and then his heart started up again. Mr Newman, a new friend to the machine, had punched out smoothly. One of the mass of company employees heading for home, Mr Newman, his old body at once tired and tingling, walked so briskly he passed any number of younger people in the corridors. His mood was unfamiliar to him, one of achievement and crazy gaiety. He recognized the information girl ahead of him, passed her, and said over his shoulder:

"Well, good night!"

She smiled in immediate reflex, but it was sobering to Mr Newman, though she did say good night, that she did not seem to remember him very well, for it had not been the live smile.

At the outside door it was snowing. Mr Newman bought a newspaper and let the man keep the two cents change. He meant to revive an old tradition with him by reading the paper on the streetcar. There was enough snow on the sidewalk to ease his swollen feet.

It was too crowded on the streetcar to open his paper and he had to stand all the way. His eyes on a placard, he considered the case of a man from Minneapolis who had got welcome relief. Hanging there on a strap, rocking with the elemental heave of the streetcar, he felt utterly weary, a gray old thing. What mattered above all else, though—getting a job—he had accomplished. This he told himself over and over until it became as real as his fatigue and mingled itself with the tortured noise of the streetcar.

His wife met him at the door. One glimpse of his face, he thought, was all she needed and she would know how to treat him tonight. Already she knew something was up and had seen the scratch on his nose. She only said:

"You stayed downtown all day, Charley."

"Yes, I did," he said.

She went to hang up his coat, hat, and scarf. He stepped across the familiar rug to the radiator. He stood there warming his hands and listening to her moving things in the kitchen. He could not bring himself to go there, as he did on any other night before supper, to talk of nothing important or particular, to let the water run till it got cold, to fill their glasses. He had too much to tell her tonight. He had forgotten to remove his rubbers.

"Come on now, Charley."

He took a few steps, hesitated a second, and went straight into the kitchen. He was immediately, as he knew he would be, uneasy. He could think of nothing insignificant to say. His eyes were not meeting hers. The glasses were filled with water. Suddenly he had to look at her. She smiled. It was hard to bear. He *did* have news. But now, he felt, she expected too much.

He bit his lips in irritation and snapped, "Why didn't you let me get the water?" That was beside the point, of course, but it gave him leeway to sit down at the table. He made a project of it. Trying to extend the note of normalcy, he passed things to her. He involved her subtly in passing them back. He wanted her to know there was a time and place for everything and now it was for passing. He invented an unprecedented interest in their silverware. His knife, fork, and spoon absorbed him.

"Where did we get this spoon?" he asked crossly.

It was all wasted. She had revamped her strategy. She appeared amused, and there was about her a determination deeper than his to wait forever. Her being so amused was what struck him as insupportable. He had a dismaying conviction that this was the truest condition of their married life. It ran, more or less, but always present, right through everything they did. She was the audience—that was something like it—and he was always on stage, the actor who was never taken quite seriously by his audience, no matter how heroic the role. The bad actor and his faithful but not foolish audience. Always! As now! It was not a hopeless situation, but only because she loved him.

She *did* love him. Overcome by the idea, he abandoned his silence. He heard himself telling her everything. Not exactly as it was, naturally, but still everything. Not at first about his being handy with rope, nothing about being "Charley" and an old bird, but quite frankly that he was working in the shipping room instead of the office. About Mr Shanahan, the interviewer—how nice he was, in a way. About the information girl who seemed to take quite an interest in him and who, to his surprise, had said good night to him. Mr Hurley, his department head, and how to get to the employees' lunchroom. The washroom, plenty of soap and towels, a clean place—clean as her kitchen; she should see it. Where he had lunch, not much of a place. The fat fellow next to him at the table, not exactly loyal to the company, but a very likable chap . . . and here—he dug into his shirt pocket—was a piece of their sticking tape, as she could see, with their name and trademark.

" 'A modern house,' " she read, " 'over 100 years young'— *young*—well, that's pretty clever."

"Oh, they're an old-line firm," Mr Newman said.

"I'll have to pack you a lunch then, Charley," she said. She had finally got into the adventure with him.

"I bought a paper tonight," he said. "It's in the other room."

With a little excited movement she parted the organdie curtains at the window. "My, Charley, just look at that!" Snowflakes tumbled in feathery confusion past the yellow light burning in the court, wonderfully white against the night, smothering the whole dirty, roaring, guilty city in innocence and silence and beauty.

Mr Newman squirmed warm inside the thought of everything he could think of—the snow falling, the glow in the kitchen, landing the job, Christmas coming, her . . .

Their supper got cold.

She let the curtains fall together, breathing, "My!"

Reluctantly Mr Newman assumed the duty he had as husband and only provider—not to be swept away by dreams and snowflakes. He said with the stern wisdom of his generation:

"Keeps up much longer it'll tie up transportation."

"But do you like that kind of work, Charley?"

He assured her most earnestly that he did, knowing she knew he'd do anything to get into an office again. He caught himself on the verge of telling her that working in the shipping room was just the way the company, since it was so old and reliable, groomed its new employees for service in the office. But that sounded too steep and ultimately disastrous. He had to confess it was only temporary work. This pained her, he could see, and he tried to get her mind on something else.

"I'll bet you had no idea your husband was so handy with rope."

He told her how it came on big spools, like telegraph wire. But she did not think this important.

"The people," he said, "the ones I've met at least—well, they all seem very nice."

"Then maybe they'll keep you after Christmas, Charley!"

He looked sharply at her and could tell she was sorry she'd said that. She understood what must follow. He opened his mouth to speak, said nothing, and then, closing his eyes to the truth, he said:

"Yes. You know, I think they will. I'm *sure* of it."

He coughed. That was not the way it was at all. It had happened again. He was the bad actor again. His only audience smiled and loved him.

PRINCE OF DARKNESS

I. MORNING

"I SHOULD'VE KNOWN you'd be eating breakfast, Father. But I was at your Mass and I said to myself that must be Father Burner. Then I stayed a few minutes after Mass to make my thanksgiving."

"Fine," Father Burner said. "Breakfast?"

"Had it, Father, thanking you all the same. It's the regret of my life that I can't be a daily communicant. Doctor forbids it. 'Fast every day and see how long you last,' he tells me. But I do make it to Mass."

"Fine. You say you live in Father Desmond's parish?"

"Yes, Father. And sometimes I think Father Desmond does too much. All the societies to look after. Plus the Scouts and the Legion. Of course Father Kells being so elderly and all . . ."

"We're all busy these days."

"It's the poor parish priest's day that's never done, I always say, Father, not meaning to slight the ladies, God love 'em."

Father Burner's sausage fingers, spelling his impatience over and over, worked up sweat in the folds of the napkin which he kept in view to provoke an early departure. "About this matter you say Father Desmond thought I might be interested in—"

"The Plan, Father." Mr Tracy lifted his seersucker trousers by the creases, crossed his shining two-tone shoes, and rolled warmly forward. "Father . . ."

Father Burner met his look briefly. He was wary of the fatherers. A backslider he could handle, it was the old story, but a red-hot believer, especially a talkative one, could be a devilish nuisance. This kind might be driven away only by prayer and fasting, and he was not adept at either.

"I guess security's one thing we're all after."

Father Burner grunted. Mr Tracy was too familiar to suit him. He liked his parishioners to be retiring, dumb, or frightened. There were too many references made to the priest's hard lot. Not so many poor souls as all that passed away in the wee hours, nor was there so much bad weather to brave. Mr Tracy's heart bled for priests. That in itself was a suspicious thing in a layman. It all led up to the Plan.

"Here's the Plan, Father . . ." Father Burner watched his eye peel down to naked intimacy. Then, half listening, he gazed about the room. He hated it, too. A fabulous brown rummage of encyclopedias, world globes, maps, photographs, holy pictures, mirrors, crucifixes, tropical fish, and too much furniture. The room reproduced the world, all wonders and horrors, less land than water. From the faded precipices of the walls photographs viewed each other for the most part genially across time. Three popes, successively thinner, raised hands to bless their departed painters. The world globes simpered in the shadows, heavy-headed idiot boys, listening. A bird in a blacked-out cage scratched among its offal. An anomalous buddha peeked beyond his dusty umbilicus at the trampled figures in the rug. The fish swam on, the mirrors and encyclopedias turned in upon themselves, the earless boys heard everything and understood nothing. Father Burner put his big black shoe on a moth and sent dust flecks crowding up a shaft of sunlight to the distant ceiling.

"Say you pay in $22.67 every month, can be paid semi-annually or as you please, policy matures in twenty years and pays you $35.50 a month for twenty years or as long as you live. That's the deal for you, Father. It beats the deal Father Desmond's got, although he's got a darned good one, and I hope he keeps it up. But we've gone ahead in the last few years, Father. Utilities are sounder, bonds are more secure, and this new legislation protects you one hundred per cent."

"You say Ed—Father Desmond—has the Plan?"

"Oh, indeed, Father." Mr Tracy had to laugh. "I hope you don't think I'm trying to high-pressure you, Father. It's not just a piece of business with me, the Plan."

"No?"

"No. You see, it's more or less a pet project of mine. Hardly make a cent on it. Looking out after the fathers, you might say, so they'll maybe look out after me—spiritually. I call it heavenly life insurance."

Slightly repelled, Father Burner nodded.

"Not a few priests that I've sold the Plan to remember me at the altar daily. I guess prayer's one thing we can all use. Anyway, it's why I take a hand in putting boys through seminary."

With that Mr Tracy shed his shabby anonymity for Father Burner, and grew executive markings. He became the one and only Thomas Nash Tracy—T. N. T. It was impossible to read the papers and not know a few things about T. N. T. He was in small loans and insurance. His company's advertising smothered the town and country; everybody knew the slogan "T. N. T. Spells Security." He figured in any financial drive undertaken by the diocese, was caught by photographers in orphanages, and sat at the heavy end of the table at communion breakfasts. Hundreds of nuns, thanks to his thoughtfulness, ate capon on Christmas Day, and a few priests of the right sort received baskets of scotch. He was a B. C. L., a Big Catholic Layman, and now Father Burner could see why. Father Burner's countenance softened at this intelligence, and T. N. T. proceeded with more assurance.

"And don't call it charity, Father. Insurance, as I said, is a better name for it. I have a little money, Father, which makes it possible." He tuned his voice down to a whisper. "You might say I'm moderately wealthy." He looked sharply at Father Burner, not sure of his man. "But I'm told there isn't any crime in that."

"I believe you need not fear for your soul on that account."

"Glad to hear it from you, a priest, Father. Ofttimes it's thrown up to me." He came to terms with reality, smiling. "I wasn't always so well off myself, so I can understand the temptation to knock the other fellow."

"Fine."

"But that's still not to say that water's not wet or that names don't hurt sometimes, whatever the bard said to the contrary."

"What bard?"

" 'Sticks and stones—' "

"Oh."

"If this were a matter of faith and morals, Father, I'd be the one to sit back and let you do the talking. But it's a case of common sense, Father, and I think I can safely say, if you listen to me you'll not lose by it in the long run."

"It could be."

"May I ask you a personal question, Father?"

Father Burner searched T. N. T.'s face. "Go ahead, Mr Tracy."

"Do you bank, Father?"

"*Bank?* Oh, bank—no. Why?"

"Let's admit it, Father," T. N. T. coaxed, frankly amused. "Priests as a class are an improvident lot—our records show it

—and you're no exception. But that, I think, explains the glory of the Church down through the ages."

"The Church is divine," Father Burner corrected. "And the concept of poverty isn't exactly foreign to Christianity or even to the priesthood."

"Exactly," T. N. T. agreed, pinked. "But think of the future, Father."

Nowadays when Father Burner thought of the future it required a firm act of imagination. As a seminarian twenty years ago, it had all been plain: ordination, roughly ten years as a curate somewhere (he was not the kind to be sent to Rome for further study), a church of his own to follow, the fruitful years, then retirement, pastor emeritus, with assistants doing the spade work, leaving the fine touches to him, still a hearty old man very much alive. It was not an uncommon hope and, in fact, all around him it had materialized for his friends. But for him it was only a bad memory growing worse. He was the desperate assistant now, the angry functionary aging in the outer office. One day he would wake and find himself old, as the morning finds itself covered with snow. The future had assumed the forgotten character of a dream, so that he could not be sure that he had ever truly had one.

T. N. T. talked on and Father Burner felt a mist generating on his forehead. He tore his damp hands apart and put the napkin aside. Yes, yes, it was true a priest received miserably little, but then that was the whole idea. He did not comment, dreading T. N. T.'s foaming compassion, to be spat upon with charity. Yes, as a matter of fact, it would be easier to face old age with something more to draw upon than what the ecclesiastical authorities deemed sufficient and would provide. Also, as T. N. T. pointed out, one never knew when he might come down with an expensive illness. T. N. T., despite himself, had something...The Plan, in itself, was not bad. He must not reject the olive branch because it came by buzzard.

But still Father Burner was a little bothered by the idea of a priest feathering his nest. Why? In other problems he was never the one to take the ascetic interpretation.

"You must be between thirty-five and forty, Father."

"I'll never see forty again."

"I'd never believe it from anyone else. You sure don't look it, Father."

"Maybe not. But I feel it."

"Worries, Father. And one big one is the future, Father. You'll get to be fifty, sixty, seventy—and what have you got?—not a penny saved. You look around and say to yourself—where did it go?"

T. N. T. had the trained voice of the good and faithful servant, supple from many such dealings. And still from time to time a faint draught of contempt seemed to pass through it which had something to do with his eyes. Here, Father Burner thought, was the latest thing in simony, unnecessary, inspired from without, participated in spiritlessly by the priest who must yet suffer the brunt of the blame and ultimately do the penance. Father Burner felt mysteriously purchasable. He was involved in an exchange of confidences which impoverished him mortally. In T. N. T. he sensed free will in its senility or the infinite capacity for equating evil with good—or with nothing—the same thing, only easier. Here was one more word in the history of the worm's progress, another wave on the dry flood that kept rising, the constant aggrandizement of decay. In the end it must touch the world and everything at the heart. Father Burner felt weak from a nameless loss.

"I think I can do us both a service, Father."

"I don't say you can't." Father Burner rose quickly. "I'll have to think about it, Mr Tracy."

"To be sure, Father." He produced a glossy circular. "Just let me leave this literature with you."

Father Burner, leading him to the door, prevented further

talk by reading the circular. It was printed in a churchy type, all purple and gold, a dummy leaf from a medieval hymnal, and entitled, "A Silver Lining in the Sky." It was evidently meant for clergymen only, though not necessarily priests, as Father Burner could instantly see from its general tone.

"Very interesting," he said.

"My business phone is right on the back, Father. But if you'd rather call me at my home some night—"

"No thanks, Mr Tracy."

"Allow me to repeat, Father, this isn't just business with me."

"I understand." He opened the door too soon for T. N. T. "Glad to have met you."

"Glad to have met you, Father."

Father Burner went back to the table. The coffee needed warming up and the butter had vanished into the toast. "Mary," he called. Then he heard them come gabbing into the rectory, Quinlan and his friend Keefe, also newly ordained.

They were hardly inside the dining room before he was explaining how he came to be eating breakfast so late—so late, see?—not *still*.

"You protest too much, Father," Quinlan said. "The Angelic Doctor himself weighed three hundred pounds, and I'll wager he didn't get it all from prayer and fasting."

"A pituitary condition," Keefe interjected, faltering. "Don't you think?"

"Yah, yah, Father, you'll wager"—Father Burner, eyes malignant, leaned on his knife, the blade bowing out bright and buttery beneath his fist—"and I'll wager you'll be the first saint to reach heaven with a flannel mouth!" Rising from the table, he shook Keefe's hand, which was damp from his pocket, and experienced a surge of strength, the fat man's contempt and envy for the thin man. He thought he might break Keefe's hand off at the wrist without drawing a drop of blood.

Quinlan stood aside, six inches or more below them, gazing up, as at two impossibly heroic figures in a hotel mural. Reading the caption under them, he mused, "Father Burner meets Father Keefe."

"I've heard about you, Father," Keefe said, plying him with a warmth beyond his means.

"Bound to be the case in a diocese as overstocked with magpies as this one." Father Burner threw a fresh napkin at a plate. "But be seated, Father Keefe." Keefe, yes, he had seen him before, a nobody in a crowd, some affair . . . the K. C. barbecue, the Youth Center? No, probably not, not Keefe, who was obviously not the type, too crabbed and introversive for Catholic Action. "I suppose," he said, "you've heard the latest definition of Catholic Action—the interference of the laity with the inactivity of the hierarchy."

"Very good," Keefe said uneasily.

Quinlan yanked off his collar and churned his neck up and down to get circulation. "Dean in the house? No? Good." He pitched the collar at one of the candles on the buffet for a ringer. "That turkey we met coming out the front door—think I've seen his face somewhere."

"Thomas Nash Tracy," Keefe said. "I thought you knew."

"The prominent lay priest and usurer?"

Keefe coughed. "They say he's done a lot of good."

Quinlan spoke to Father Burner: "Did you take out a policy, Father?"

"One of the sixth-graders threw a rock through his windshield," Father Burner said. "He was very nice about it."

"Muldoon or Ciesniewski?"

"A new kid. Public school transfer." Father Burner patted the napkin to his chin. "Not that I see anything wrong with insurance."

Quinlan laughed. "Let Walter tell you what happened to him a few days ago. Go ahead, Walter," he said to Keefe.

"Oh, that." Keefe fidgeted and, seemingly against his better judgment, began. "I had a little accident—was it Wednesday it rained so? I had the misfortune to skid into a fellow parked on Fairmount. Dented his fender." Keefe stopped and then, as though impelled by the memory of it, went on. "The fellow came raging out of his car at me. I thought there'd be serious trouble. Then he must have seen I was a priest, the way he calmed down, I mean. I had a funny feeling it wasn't because he was a Catholic or anything like that. As a matter of fact he wore a Masonic button." Keefe sighed. "I guess he saw I was a priest and ergo . . . knew I'd have insurance."

"Take nothing for your journey, neither staff, nor scrip," Quinlan said, "words taken from today's gospel."

Father Burner spoke in a level tone: "Not that I *still* see anything wrong with insurance. It's awfully easy," he continued, hating himself for talking drivel, "to make too much of little things." With Quinlan around he played the conservative; among the real right-handers he was the *enfant terrible*. He operated on the principle of discord at any cost. He did not know why. It was a habit. Perhaps it had something to do with being overweight.

Arranging the Dean's chair, which had arms, for himself, Quinlan sank into it, giving Keefe the Irish whisper. "Grace, Father."

Keefe addressed the usual words to God concerning the gifts they were about to receive. During the prayer Father Burner stopped chewing and did not reach for anything. He noted once more that Quinlan crossed himself sloppily enough to be a monsignor.

Keefe nervously cleared the entire length of his throat. "It's a beautiful church you have here at Saint Patrick's, Father." A lukewarm light appeared in his eyes, flickered, sputtered out, leaving them blank and blue. His endless fingers felt for his receding chin in the onslaught of silence.

"*I* have?" Father Burner turned his spoon abasingly to his bosom. "*Me!*" He jabbed at the grapefruit before him, his second, demolishing its perfect rose window. "I don't know why it is the Irish without exception are always laying personal claim to church property. The Dean is forever saying *my* church, *my* school, *my* furnace . . ."

"I'm sorry, Father," Keefe said, flushing. "And I'll confess I did think he virtually built Saint Patrick's."

"Out of the slime of the earth, I know. A common error." With sudden, unabated displeasure Father Burner recalled how the Dean, one of the last of the old brick and mortar pastors, had built the church, school, sisters' house, and rectory, and had named the whole thing through the lavish pretense of a popular contest. Opposed bitterly by Polish, German, and Italian minorities, he had effected a compromise between their bad taste (Saint Stanislaus, Saint Boniface, Saint Anthony) and his own better judgment in the choice of Saint Patrick's.

Quinlan, snorting, blurted, "Well, he did build it, didn't he?"

Father Burner smiled at them from the other world. "Only, if you please, in a manner of speaking."

"True," Keefe murmured humbly.

"Nuts," Quinlan said. "It's hard for me to see God in a few buildings paid for by the funds of the faithful and put up by a mick contractor. A burning bush, yes."

Father Burner, lips parched to speak an unsummonable cruelty, settled for a smoldering aside to the kitchen. "Mary, more eggs here."

A stuffed moose of a woman with a tabby-cat face charged in on swollen feet. She stood wavering in shoes sliced fiercely for corns. With the back of her hand she wiped some cream from the fuzz ringing her baby-pink mouth. Her hair poked through a broken net like stunted antlers. Father Burner pointed to the empty platter.

"Eggs," he said.

"Eggs!" she cried, tumbling her eyes like great blue dice among them. She seized up the platter and carried it whirling with grease into the kitchen.

Father Burner put aside the grapefruit. He smiled and spoke calmly. "I'll have to let the Dean know, Father, how much you like *his* plant."

"Do, Father. A beautiful church . . . 'a poem in stone'—was it Ruskin?"

"Ruskin? *Stones of Venice*," Father Burner grumbled. "*Sesame and Lilies*, I know . . . but I never cared for his *style*." He passed the knife lovingly over the pancakes on his plate and watched the butter bubble at the pores. "So much sweetness, so much light, I'm afraid, made Jack a dull boy."

Quinlan slapped all his pockets. "Pencil and paper, quick!"

"And yet . . ." Keefe cocked his long head, brow fretted, and complained to his upturned hands. "Don't understand how he stayed outside the Church." He glanced up hopefully. "I wonder if Chesterton gives us a clue."

Father Burner, deaf to such precious speculation, said, "In the nineteenth century Francis Thompson was the only limey worth his salt. It's true." He quartered the pancakes. "Of course, Newman."

"Hopkins has some good things."

"Good—yes, if you like jabberwocky and jebbies! I don't care for either." He dispatched a look of indictment at Quinlan.

"What a pity," Quinlan murmured, "Oliver Wendell couldn't be at table this morning."

"No, Father, you can have your Hopkins, you and Father Quinlan here. Include me out, as Sam Goldwyn says. Poetry—I'll take my poetry the way I take my liquor, neat."

Mary brought in the platter oozing with bacon and eggs.

"Good for you, Mary," Quinlan said. "I'll pray for you."

"Thank you, Father," Mary said.

Quinlan dipped the platter with a trace of obeisance to Father Burner.

"No thanks."

Quinlan scooped up the coffeepot in a fearsome rush and held it high at Father Burner, his arm so atremble the lid rattled dangerously. "Sure and will you be about having a sup of coffee now, Father?"

"Not now. And do you mind not playing the wild Irish wit so early in the day, Father?"

"That I don't. *But a relentless fate pursuing good Father Quinlan, he was thrown in among hardened clerics where but for the grace of God that saintly priest, so little understood, so much maligned . . .*" Quinlan poured two cups and passed one to Keefe. "For yourself, Father."

Father Burner nudged the toast to Keefe. "Father Quinlan, that saintly priest, models his life after the Rover Boys, particularly Sam, the fun-loving one."

Quinlan dealt himself a mighty *mea culpa*.

Father Burner grimaced, the flesh rising in sweet, concentric tiers around his mouth, and said in a tone both entrusting and ennobling Keefe with his confidence, "The syrup, if you please, Father." Keefe passed the silver pitcher which was running at the mouth. Father Burner reimmersed the doughy remains on his plate until the butter began to float around the edges as in a moat. He felt them both watching the butter. Regretting that he had not foreseen this attraction, he cast about in his mind for something to divert them and found the morning sun coming in too strongly. He got up and pulled down the shade. He returned to his place and settled himself in such a way that a new chapter was indicated. "Don't believe I know where you're located, Father."

"Saint Jerome's," Keefe said. "Monsignor Fiedler's."

"One of those P. N. places, eh? Is the boss sorry he ever started it? I know some of them are."

Keefe's lips popped apart. "I don't quite understand."

Quinlan prompted: "P. N.—Perpetual Novena."

"Oh, I never heard him say."

"You wouldn't, of course. But I know a lot of them that are." Father Burner stuck a morsel on his fork and swirled it against the tide of syrup. "It's a real problem all right. I was all out for a P. N. here during the depression. Thought it might help. The Dean was against it."

"I can tell you this," Keefe said. "Attendance was down from what it used to be until the casualties began to come in. Now it's going up."

"I was just going to say the war ought to take the place of the depression." Father Burner fell silent. "Terrible thing, war. Hard to know what to do about it. I tried to sell the Dean the idea of a victory altar. You've seen them. Vigil lights—"

"At a dollar a throw," Quinlan said.

"Vigil lights in the form of a V, names of the men in the service and all that. But even that, I guess— Well, like I said, I tried . . ."

"Yes, it is hard," Keefe said.

"God, the Home, and the Flag," Quinlan said. "The poets don't make the wars."

Father Burner ignored that. "Lately, though, I can't say how I feel about P. N.'s. Admit I'm not so strong for them as I was once. Ought to be some way of terminating them, you know, but then they wouldn't be perpetual, would they?"

"No, they wouldn't," Keefe said.

"Not *so* perpetual," Quinlan said.

"Of course," Father Burner continued, "the term itself, perpetual novena, is preposterous, a solecism. Possibly dispensation lies in that direction. I'm not theologian enough to say. Fortunately it's not a problem we have to decide." He laid his knife and fork across the plate. "Many are the consolations of the lowly curate. No decisions, no money worries."

"We still have to count the sugar," Quinlan said. "And put up the card tables."

"Reminds me," Father Burner said earnestly. "Father Desmond at Assumption was telling me they've got a new machine does all that."

"Puts up card tables?" Quinlan inquired.

"Counts the collection, wraps the silver," Father Burner explained, "so it's all ready for the bank. Mean to mention it to the Dean, if I can catch him right."

"I'm afraid, Father, he knows about it already."

Father Burner regarded Quinlan skeptically. "Does? I suppose he's against it."

"I heard him tell the salesman that's what he had his assistants for."

"Assistant, Father, not assistants. You count the collection, not me. I was only thinking of you."

"I was only quoting him, Father. *Sic*. Sorry."

"Not at all. I haven't forgotten the days I had to do it. It's a job has to be done and nothing to be ashamed of. Wouldn't you say, Father Keefe?"

"I dare say that's true."

Quinlan, with Father Burner still molesting him with his eyes, poured out a glass of water and drank it all. "I still think we could do with a lot less calculating. I notice the only time we get rid of the parish paper is when the new lists are published—the official standings. Of course it's a lousy sheet anyway."

Father Burner, as editor of the paper, replied: "Yes, yes, Father. We all know how easy it is to be wrathful or fastidious about these things—or whatever the hell it is you are. And we all know there *are* abuses. But contributing to the support of the Church is still one of her commandments."

"Peace, Père," Quinlan said.

"Figures don't lie."

"Somebody was telling me just last night that figures do lie. He looked a lot like you."

Father Burner found his cigarettes and shuffled a couple half out of the pack. He eyed Quinlan and the cigarettes as though it were as simple to discipline the one as to smoke the others. "For some reason, Father, you're damned fond of those particular figures."

Keefe stirred. "Which particular figures, Fathers?"

"It's the figures put out by the Cardinal of Toledo on how many made their Easter duty last year." Father Burner offered Keefe a cigarette. "I discussed the whole thing with Father Quinlan last night. It's his latest thesis. Have a cigarette?"

"No, thanks," Keefe said.

"So you don't smoke?" Father Burner looked from Keefe to Quinlan, blacklisting them together. He held the cigarette hesitantly at his lips. "It's all right, isn't it?" He laughed and touched off the match with his thumbnail.

"His Eminence," Quinlan said, "reports only fifteen percent of the women and five percent of the men made their Easter duty last year."

"So that's only three times as many women as men," Father Burner said with buried gaiety. "Certainly to be expected in any Latin country."

"But fifteen percent, Father! And five percent! Just think of it!" Keefe glanced up at the ceiling and at the souvenir plates on the molding, as though to see inscribed along with scenes from the Columbian Exposition the day and hour the end of the world would begin. He finally stared deep into the goldfish tank in the window.

Father Burner plowed up the silence, talking with a mouthful of smoke. "All right, all right, I'll say what I said in the first place. There's something wrong with the figures. A country as overwhelmingly Catholic as Spain!" He sniffed, pursed his lips, and said, "Pooh!"

"Yes," Keefe said, still balking. "But it *is* disturbing, Father Burner."

"Sure it's disturbing, Father Keefe. *Lots* of things *are*."

A big, faded goldfish paused to stare through the glass at them and then with a single lob of its tail slipped into a dark green corner.

Quinlan said, "Father Burner belongs to the school that's always seeing a great renascence of faith in the offing. The hour before dawn and all that. Tell it to Rotary on Tuesday, Father."

Father Burner countered with a frosty pink smile. "What would I ever do without you, Father? If you're trying to say I'm a dreadful optimist, you're right and I don't mind at all. I am—and proud of it!"

Ascending to his feet, he went to the right side of the buffet, took down the card index to parishioners, and returned with it to his place. He pushed his dishes aside and began to sort out the deadheads to be called on personally by him or Quinlan. The Dean, like all pastors, he reflected, left the dirty work to the assistants. "Why doesn't he pull them," he snapped, tearing up a card, "when they kick off! Can't very well forward them to the next world. Say, how many Gradys live at 909 South Vine? Here's Anna, Catherine, Clement, Gerald, Harvey, James A., James F.—which James is the one they call 'Bum'?"

"James F.," Quinlan said. "Can't you tell from the take? The other James works."

"John, Margaret, Matthew—that's ten, no eleven. Here's Dennis out of place. Patrick, Rita, and William—fourteen of them, no birth control there, and they all give. Except Bum. Nice account otherwise. Can't we find Bum a job? What's it with him, drink?"

Now he came to Maple Street. These cards were the remains of little Father Vicci's work among the magdalens. Ann Mason, Estelle Rogers, May Miller, Billie Starr. The names had the generic ring. Great givers when they gave—Christmas, $25; Easter, $20; Propagation of the Faith, $10; Catholic University, $10—but not much since Father Vicci was exiled to the sticks. He put Maple Street aside for a thorough sifting.

The doorbell rang. Father Burner leaned around in his chair. "Mary." The doorbell rang again. Father Burner bellowed. "Mary!"

Quinlan pushed his chair away from the table. "I'll get it."

Father Burner blocked him. "Oh, I'll get it! Hell of a bell! Why does he have a bell like that!" Father Burner opened the door to a middle-aged woman whose name he had forgotten or never known. "Good morning," he said. "Will you step in?"

She stayed where she was and said, "Father, it's about the servicemen's flag in church. My son Stanley—you know him—"

Father Burner, who did not know him, half nodded. "Yes, how is Stanley?" He gazed over her shoulder at the lawn, at the dandelions turning into poppies before his eyes.

"You know he was drafted last October, Father, and I been watching that flag you got in church ever since, and it's still the same, five hundred thirty-six stars. I thought you said you put a star up for all them that's gone in the service, Father."

Now the poppies were dandelions again. He could afford to be firm with her. "We can't spend all our time putting up stars. Sometimes we fall behind. Besides, a lot of the boys are being discharged."

"You mean there's just as many going in as coming out, so you don't have to change the flag?"

"Something like that."

"I see." He was sorry for her. They had run out of stars. He had tried to get the Dean to order some more, had even offered . . . and the Dean had said they could use up the gold ones first. When Father Burner had objected, telling him what it would mean, he had suggested that Father Burner apply for the curatorship of the armory.

"The pastor will be glad to explain how it works the next time you see him."

"Well, Father, if that's the way it is ..." She was fading down the steps. "I just thought I'd ask."

"That's right. There's no harm in asking. How's Stanley?"

"Fine, and thank you, Father, for your trouble."

"No trouble."

When he came back to the table they were talking about the junior clergyman's examinations which they would take for the first time next week. Father Burner interrupted, "The Dean conducts the history end of it, you know."

"I say!" Keefe said. "Any idea what we can expect?"

"You have nothing to fear. Nothing."

"Really?"

"Really. Last year, I remember, there were five questions and the last four depended on the first. So it was really only one question—if you knew it. I imagine you would've." He paused, making Keefe ask for it.

"Perhaps you can recall the question, Father?"

"Perfectly, Father. 'What event in the American history of the Church took place in 1541?'" Father Burner, slumping in his chair, smirked at Keefe pondering for likely martyrs and church legislation. He imagined him skipping among the tomes and statuary of his mind, winnowing dates and little known facts like mad, only at last to emerge dusty and downcast. Father Burner sat up with a jerk and assaulted the table with the flat of his hand. "Time's up. Answer: 'De Soto sailed up the Mississippi.'"

Quinlan snorted. Keefe sat very still, incredulous, silent, utterly unable to digest the answer, finally croaking, "How odd." Father Burner saw in him the boy whose marks in school had always been a consolation to his parents.

"So you don't have to worry, Father. No sense in preparing for it. Take in a couple of movies instead. And cheer up! The

Dean's been examining the junior clergy for twenty-five years and nobody ever passed history yet. You wouldn't want to be the first one."

Father Burner said grace and made the sign of the cross with slow distinction. "And, Father," he said, standing, extending his hand to Keefe, who also rose, "I'm glad to have met you." He withdrew his hand before Keefe was through with it and stood against the table knocking toast crumbs onto his plate. "Ever play any golf? No? Well, come and see us for conversation then. You don't have anything against talking, do you?"

"Well, of course, Father, I . . ."

Father Burner gave Keefe's arm a rousing clutch. "Do that!"

"I will, Father. It's been a pleasure."

"Speaking of pleasure," Father Burner said, tossing Quinlan a stack of cards, "I've picked out a few lost sheep for you to see on Maple Street, Father."

II. NOON

He hung his best black trousers on a hanger in the closet and took down another pair, also black. He tossed them out behind him and they fell patched at the cuffs and baggy across his unmade bed. His old suede jacket, following, slid dumpily to the floor. He stood gaping in his clerical vest and undershorts, knees knocking and pimply, thinking . . . what else? His aviator's helmet. He felt all the hooks blindly in the darkness. It was not there. "Oh, hell!" he groaned, sinking to his knees. He pawed among the old shoes and boxes and wrapping paper and string that he was always going to need. Under his golf bag he found it. So Mary had cleaned yesterday.

There was also a golf ball unknown to him, a Royal Bomber, with one small hickey in it. Father Desmond, he remembered, had received a box of Royal Bombers from a thoughtful parishioner. He stuck the helmet on his balding head to get it out of the way and took the putter from the bag. He dropped the ball at the door of the closet. Taking his own eccentric stance—a perversion of what the pro recommended and a dozen books on the subject—he putted the ball across the room at a dirty collar lying against the bookcase. A thready place in the carpet caused the ball to jump the collar and to loose a pamphlet from the top of the bookcase. He restored the pamphlet—Pius XI on "Atheistic Communism"—and poked the ball back to the door of the closet. Then, allowing for the carpet, he drove the ball straight, *click*, through the collar, *clop*. Still had his old putting eye. And his irons had always been steady if not exactly crashing. It was his woods, the tee shots, that ruined his game. He'd give a lot to be able to hit his woods properly, not to dub his drives, if only on the first tee—where there was always a crowd (mixed).

At one time or another he had played every hole at the country club in par or less. Put all those pars and birdies together, adding in the only two eagles he'd ever had, and you had the winning round in the state open, write-ups and action shots in the papers—photo shows Rev. Ernest "Boomer" Burner, par-shattering padre, blasting out of a trap. He needed only practice perhaps and at his earliest opportunity he would entice some of the eighth-grade boys over into the park to shag balls. He sank one more for good measure, winning a buck from Ed Desmond who would have bet against it, and put the club away.

Crossing the room for his trousers he noticed himself in the mirror with the helmet on and got a mild surprise. He scratched a little hair down from underneath the helmet to off-set the egg effect. He searched his eyes in the mirror for a sign of ill health. He walked away from the mirror, as though done with it, only to wheel sharply so as to see himself as others saw him, front and profile, not wanting to catch his eye, just to see himself . . .

Out of the top drawer of the dresser he drew a clean white silk handkerchief and wiped the shine from his nose. He chased his eyes over into the corner of the mirror and saw nothing. Then, succumbing to his original intention, he knotted the handkerchief at the crown of the helmet and completed the transformation of time and place and person by humming, vibrato, "Jeannine, I dream in lilac time," remembering the old movie. He saw himself over his shoulder in the mirror, a sad war ace. It reminded him that his name was not Burner, but Boerner, an impediment removed at the outset of the first world war by his father. In a way he resented the old man for it. They had laughed at the seminary; the war, except as theory, hardly entered there. In perverse homage to the old Boerner, to which he now affixed a proud "von," he dropped the fair-minded American look he had and faced the mirror sneering, scar-cheeked, and black of heart, the flying Junker who might have been. "*Himmelkreuzdonnerwetter!* When you hear the word 'culture,' " he snarled, hearing it come back to him in German, "reach for your revolver!"

Reluctantly he pulled on his black trousers, falling across the bed to do so, as though felled, legs heaving up like howitzers.

He lay still for a moment, panting, and then let the inner-spring mattress bounce him to his feet, a fighter coming off the ropes. He stood looking out the window, buckling his belt, and then down at the buckle, chins kneading softly with the effort, and was pleased to see that he was holding his own on the belt, still a good half inch away from last winter's high-water mark.

At the sound of high heels approaching on the front walk below, he turned firmly away from the window and considered for the first time since he posted it on the wall the prayer for priests sent him by a candle concern. "Remember, O most compassionate God, that they are but weak and frail human beings. Stir up in them the grace of their vocation which is in them by the imposition of the Bishops' hands. Keep them close to Thee, lest the enemy prevail against them, so that they may never do anything in the slightest degree unworthy of their sublime . . ." His eyes raced through the prayer and out the window . . .

He was suddenly inspired to write another letter to the Archbishop. He sat down at his desk, slipped a piece of paper into his portable, dated it with the saint's day it was, and wrote, "Your Excellency: Thinking my letter of some months ago may have gone amiss, or perhaps due to the press of busi-ness—" He ripped the paper from the portable and typed the same thing on a fresh sheet until he came to "business," using instead "affairs of the Church." He went on to signify—it was considered all right to "signify," but to re-signify?—that he was still of the humble opinion that he needed a change of lo-cation and had decided, since he believed himself ready for a parish of his own, a rural one might be best, all things consid-ered (by which he meant easier to get). He, unlike some priests of urban upbringing and experience, would have no objection to the country. He begged to be graced with an early reply. That line, for all its seeming docility, was full of dynamite and ought to break the episcopal silence into which the first letter had dissolved. This was a much stronger job. He thought it better for two reasons: the Archbishop was supposed to like outspoken people, or, that being only more propaganda talked up by the sycophants, then it ought to bring a reply which would reveal once and for all his prospects. Long overdue for the routine promotion, he had a just cause. He addressed the letter and placed it in his coat. He went to the bathroom. When he came back he put on the coat, picked up the suede jacket and helmet, looked around for something he might have forgot, a book of chances, a box of Sunday envelopes to be de-livered, some copy for the printer, but there was nothing. He lit a cigarette at the door and not caring to throw the match on the floor or look for the ashtray, which was out of sight again, he dropped it in the empty holy-water font.

Downstairs he paused at the telephone in the hall, scribbled "Airport" on the message pad, thought of crossing it out or tearing off the page, but since it was dated he let it stand and added "Visiting the sick," signing his initials, *E. B.*

He went through the wicker basket for mail. A card from the Book-of-the-Month Club. So it was going to be another war book selection this month. Well, they knew what they could do with it. He wished the Club would wake up and select some dandies, as they had in the past. He thought of *Studs Lonigan* —there was a book, the best thing since the Bible.

An oblique curve in the road: perfect, wheels parallel with the center line. So many drivers took a curve like that way over on the other fellow's side. Father Burner touched the lighter on the dashboard to his cigarette and plunged his hams deeper into the cushions. A cloud of smoke whirled about the little Saint Christopher garroted from the ceiling. Father Burner tugged viciously at both knees, loosening the binding black cloth, easing the seat. Now that he was in open country he wanted to enjoy the scenery—God's majesty. How about a sermon that would liken the things in the landscape to the people in a church? All different, all the same, the handiwork of God. Moral: it is right and meet for rocks to be rocks, trees to be trees, pigs to be pigs, but—and here the small gesture that says so much—what did that mean that men, created in the image and likeness of God, should be? And what—He thrust the sermon out of mind, tired of it. He relaxed, as before an open fireplace, the weight of dogma off his shoulders. Then he grabbed at his knees again, cursing. Did the tailor skimp on the cloth because of the ecclesiastical discount?

A billboard inquired: "Pimples?" Yes, he had a few, but he blamed them on the climate, the humidity. Awfully hard for a

priest to transfer out of a diocese. He remembered the plan he
had never gone through with. Would it work after all? Would
another doctor recommend a change? Why? He would only
want to know why, like the last bastard. Just a slight case of
obesity, Reverend. Knew he was a non-Catholic when he said
Reverend. Couldn't trust a Catholic one. Some of them were
thicker than thieves with the clergy. Wouldn't want to be
known as a malingerer, along with everything else.

Another billboard: "Need Cash? See T. N. T."

Rain. He knew it. No flying for him today. One more day
between him and a pilot's license. Thirteen hours yet and it
might have been twelve. Raining so, and with no flying, the
world seemed to him . . . a valley of tears. He would drive on
past the airport for a hamburger. If he had known, he would
have brought along one of the eighth-grade boys. They were always bragging among themselves about how many he had
bought them, keeping score. One of them, the Cannon kid, had
got too serious from the hamburgers. When he said he was
"contemplating the priesthood" Father Burner, wanting to
spare him the terrible thing a false vocation could be, had told
him to take up aviation instead. He could not forget the boy's
reply: *But couldn't I be a priest like you, Father?*

On the other hand, he was glad to be out driving alone.
Never had got the bang out of playing with the kids a priest
in this country was supposed to. The failure of the Tom Playfair tradition. He hated most sports. Ed Desmond was a sight
at a ball game. Running up and down the base lines, giving the
umpires hell, busting all the buttons off his cassock. Assumption rectory smelled like a locker room from all the equipment. Poor Ed.

The rain drummed on the engine hood. The windshield
wiper sliced back and forth, reminding him a little of a guillo-
tine. Yes, if he had to, he would die for the Faith.

From here to the hamburger place it was asphalt and slicker

than concrete. Careful. Slick. Asphalt. Remembered . . . Quinlan coming into his room one afternoon last winter when it was snowing—the idiot—prating:

> Here were decent godless people:
> Their only monument the asphalt road
> And a thousand lost golf balls . . .

That was Quinlan for you, always spouting against the status quo without having anything better to offer. Told him that. Told him golfers, funny as it might seem to some people, have souls and who's to save them? John Bosco worked wonders in taverns, which was not to say Father Burner thought he was a saint, but rather only that he was not too proud to meet souls halfway wherever it might be, in the confessional or on the fairways. Saint Ernest Burner, Help of Golfers, Pray for Us! (Quinlan's comeback.) Quinlan gave him a pain. Keefe, now that he knew what he was like, ditto. Non-smokers. Jansenists. First fervor is false fervor. They would cool. He would not judge them, however.

He slowed down and executed a sweeping turn into the parking lot reserved for patrons of the hamburger. He honked his horn his way, three shorts and a long—victory. She would see his car or know his honk and bring out two hamburgers, medium well, onions, pickle, relish, tomato, catsup—his way.

She came out now, carrying an umbrella, holding it ostensibly more over the hamburgers than herself. He took the tray from her. She waited dumbly, her eyes at a level with his collar.

"What's to drink?"

"We got pop, milk, coffee . . ." Here she faltered, as he knew she would, washing her hands of what recurrent revelation, rather than experience, told her was to follow.

"A nice cold bottle of beer." Delivered of the fatal words, Father Burner bit into the smoking hamburger. The woman turned sorrowfully away. He put her down again for native Protestant stock.

When she returned, sheltering the bottle under the umbrella, Father Burner had to smile at her not letting pious scruples interfere with business, another fruit of the so-called Reformation. Watch that smile, he warned himself, or she'll take it for carnal. He received the bottle from her hands. For all his familiarity with the type, he was uneasy. Her lowered eyes informed him of his guilt.

Was he immoderate? Who on earth could say? *In dubiis libertas*, not? He recalled his first church supper at Saint Patrick's, a mother bringing her child to the Dean's table. She's going to be confirmed next month, Monsignor. Indeed? Then tell me, young lady, what are the seven capital sins? Pride, Covetousness . . . Lust, Anger. Uh. The child's mother, one of those tough Irish females built like a robin, worried to death, lips silently forming the other sins for her daughter. Go ahead, dear. Envy. Proceed, child. Yes, Monsignor. Uh . . . Sloth. To be sure. That's six. One more. And . . . uh. Fear of the Lord, perhaps? Meekness? Hey, Monsignor, ain't them the Divine Counsels! The Dean, smiling, looking at Father Burner's plate, covered with chicken bones, at his stomach, fighting the vest, and for a second into the child's eyes, slipping her the seventh sin. *Gluttony*, Monsignor! The Dean gave her a coin for her trouble and she stood awkwardly in front of Father Burner, lingering, twisting her gaze from his plate to his stomach, to his eyes, finally quacking, Oh Fawther!

Now he began to brood upon his failure as a priest. There was no sense in applying the consolations of an anchorite to himself. He wanted to know one thing: when would he get a parish? When would he make the great metamorphosis from assistant to pastor, from mouse to rat, as the saying went? He was forty-three, four times transferred, seventeen years an ordained priest, a curate yet and only. He was the only one of his class still without a parish. The only one . . . and in his pocket, three days unopened, was another letter from his mother, kept waiting all these years, who was to have been his housekeeper. He could not bear to warm up her expectations again.

Be a chaplain? That would take him away from it all and there was the possibility of meeting a remote and glorious death carrying the Holy Eucharist to a dying soldier. It would take something like that to make him come out even, but then that, too, he knew in a corner of his heart, would be only exterior justification for him, a last bid for public approbation, a shortcut to nothing. And the chaplain's job, it was whispered, could be an ordeal both ignominious and tragic. It would be just his luck to draw an assignment in a rehabilitation center, racking pool balls and repairing ping-pong bats for the boys— the apostolic game-room attendant and toastmaster. Sure, Sarge, I'll lay you even money the Sox make it three straight in Philly and spot you a run a game to boot. You win, I lose a carton of Chesters—I win, you go to Mass every day for a week! Hard-headed holiness . . .

There was the painful matter of the appointment to Saint Patrick's. The Dean, an irremovable pastor, and the Archbishop had argued over funds and the cemetery association. And the Archbishop, losing though he won, took his revenge, it was rumored, by appointing Father Burner as the Dean's assistant. It was their second encounter. In the first days of his succession, the Archbishop heard that the Dean always said a green Mass on Saint Patrick's Day, thus setting the rubrics at nought. Furious, he summoned the Dean into his presence, but stymied by the total strangeness of him and his great age, he had talked of something else. The Dean took a different view of his narrow escape, which is what the chancery office gossips called it, and now every year, on repeating the error, he would say to the uneasy nuns, "Sure and nobody ever crashed the gates of hell for the wearing of the green." (Otherwise it was not often he did something to delight the hearts of the professional Irish.)

In the Dean's presence Father Burner often had the sensation of confusion, a feeling that someone besides them stood listening in the room. To free himself he would say things he neither meant nor believed. The Dean would take the other side and then . . . there they were again. The Dean's position in these bouts was roughly that of the old saints famous for their faculty of smelling sins and Father Burner played the role of the one smelled. It was no contest. If the Archbishop could find no words for the Dean there was nothing he might do. He might continue to peck away at a few stray foibles behind the Dean's back. He might point out how familiar the Dean was with the Protestant clergy about town. He did. It suited his occasional orthodoxy (reserved mostly to confound his critics and others much worse, like Quinlan, whom he suspected of having him under observation for humorous purposes) to disapprove of all such questionable ties, as though the Dean were entertaining heresy, or at least felt kindly toward this new "interfaith" nonsense so dear to the reformed Jews and freshwater sects. It was very small game, however. And the merest brush with the Dean might bring any one of a hundred embarrassing occasions back to life, and it was easy for him to burn all over again.

When he got his darkroom rigged up in the rectory the Dean had come snooping around and inquired without staying for an answer if the making of tintypes demanded that a man shun the light to the extent Father Burner appeared to. Now and again, hearkening back to this episode, the Dean referred to him as the Prince of Darkness. It did not end there. The title caught on all over the diocese. It was not the only one he had.

In reviewing a new historical work for a national Catholic magazine, he had attempted to get back at two Jesuits he knew in town, calling attention to certain tendencies—he meant nothing so gross as "order pride"—which, if not necessarily characteristic of any religious congregation within the Church, were still too often to be seen in any long view of history (which the book at hand did not pretend to take), and whereas the secular clergy, *per se*, had much to answer for, was it not true, though certainly not through any superior virtue, nor even as a consequence of their secularity—indeed, he would be a fool to dream that such orders as those founded, for instance, by Saint Benedict, Saint Francis, and Saint Dominic (Saint Ignatius was not instanced) were without their places in the heart of the Church, even today, when perhaps . . .

Anyway "secular" turned up once as "circular" in the review. The local Jesuits, writing in to the magazine as a group of innocent bystanders, made many subtle plays upon the unfortunate "circular" and its possible application to the person of the reviewer (their absolute unfamiliarity with the reviewer, they explained, enabled them to indulge in such conceivably dangerous whimsey). But the direction of his utterances, they thought, seemed clear, and they regretted more than they could say that the editors of an otherwise distinguished journal had found space for them, especially in wartime, or perhaps they did not rightly comprehend the course—was it something new?—set upon by the editors and if so . . .

So Father Burner was also known as "the circular priest" and he had not reviewed anything since for that magazine.

The mark of the true priest was heavy on the Dean. The mark was on Quinlan; it was on Keefe. It was on every priest he could think of, including a few on the bum, and his good friend and bad companion, Father Desmond. But it was not on him, not properly. They, the others, were stained with it beyond all disguise or disfigurement—indelibly, as indeed Holy Orders by its sacramental nature must stain, for keeps in this world and the one to come. "Thou art a priest forever." With him, however, it was something else and less, a mask or badge which he could and did remove at will, a temporal part to be played, almost only a doctor's or lawyer's. They, the others, would be lost in any persecution. The mark would doom them. But he, if that *dies irae* ever came—and it was every plump seminarian's apple-cheeked dream—could pass as the most harmless and useful of humans, a mailman, a bus rider, a husband. But would he? No. They would see. I, he would say, appearing unsought before the judging rabble, am a priest, of the order of Melchizedech. Take me. I am ready. *Deo gratias.*

Father Burner got out the money to pay and honked his horn. The woman, coming for the bottle and tray, took his money without acknowledging the tip. She stood aside, the bottle held gingerly between offended fingers, final illustration of her lambishness, and watched him drive away. Father Burner, applying a cloven foot to the pedal, gave it the gas. He sensed the woman hoping in her simple heart to see him wreck the car and meet instant death in an unpostponed act of God.

Under the steadying influence of his stomach thrust against the wheel, the car proceeded while he searched himself for a cigarette. He passed a hitchhiker, saw him fade out of view in the mirror overhead, gesticulate wetly in the distance. Was the son of a gun thumbing his nose? Anticlericalism. But pray that your flight be not in the winter . . . No, wrong text: he would not run away.

The road skirted a tourist village. He wondered who stayed in those places and seemed to remember a story in one of the religious scandal sheets . . . ILLICIT LOVE in steaming red type.

A billboard cried out, "Get in the scrap and—get in the scrap!" Some of this advertising, he thought, was pretty slick. Put out probably by big New York and Chicago agencies with crack men on their staffs, fellows who had studied at *Time.* How would it be to write advertising? He knew a few things about layout and type faces from editing the parish paper. He had read somewhere about the best men of our time being in advertising, the air corps of business. There was room for better taste in the Catholic magazines, for someone with a name in the secular field to step in and drive out the money-changers with their trusses, corn cures, non-tangle rosary beads, and crosses that glow in the dark. It was a thought.

Coming into the city limits, he glanced at his watch, but neglected to notice the time. The new gold strap got his eye. The watch itself, a priceless pyx, held the hour (time is money) sacred, like a host. He had chosen it for an ordination gift rather than the usual chalice. It took the kind of courage he had to go against the grain there.

"I'm a dirty stinker!" Father Desmond flung his arms out hard against the mattress. His fists opened on the sheet, hungry for the spikes, meek and ready. "I'm a dirty stinker, Ernest!"

Father Burner, seated deep in a red leather chair at the sick man's bedside, crossed his legs forcefully. "Now don't take on so, Father."

"Don't call me 'Father'!" Father Desmond's eyes fluttered open momentarily, but closed again on the reality of it all. "I don't deserve it. I'm a disgrace to the priesthood! I am not worthy! Lord, Lord, I am not worthy!"

A nurse entered and stuck a thermometer in Father Desmond's mouth.

Father Burner smiled at the nurse. He lit a cigarette and wondered if she understood. The chart probably bore the diagnosis "pneumonia," but if she had been a nurse very long she would know all about that. She released Father Desmond's wrist and recorded his pulse on her pad. She took the thermometer and left the room.

Father Desmond surged up in bed and flopped, turning with a wrench of the covers, on his stomach. He lay gasping like a fish out of water. Father Burner could smell it on his breath yet.

"Do you want to go to confession?"

"No! I'm not ready for it. I want to remember this time!"

"Oh, all right." It was funny, if a little tiresome, the way the Irish could exaggerate a situation. They all had access to the same two or three emotions. They all played the same battered barrel organ handed down through generations. Dying, fighting, talking, drinking, praying . . . wakes, wars, politics, pubs, church. The fates were decimated and hamstrung among them. They loved monotony.

Father Desmond, doing the poor soul uttering his last words in italics, said: "We make too good a thing out of confession, Ernest! Ever think of that, Ernest?" He wagged a nicotined finger. Some of his self-contempt seemed to overshoot its mark and include Father Burner.

Father Burner honked his lips—*plutt!* "Hire a hall, Ed."

Father Desmond clawed a rosary out from under his pillow.

Father Burner left.

He put the car in the garage. On the way to his room he passed voices in the Dean's office.

"Father Burner!" the Dean called through the door.

Father Burner stayed in the hallway, only peeping in, indicating numerous commitments elsewhere. Quinlan and Keefe were with the Dean.

"Apparently, Father, you failed to kill yourself." Then, for Keefe, the Dean said, "Father Burner fulfills the dream of the American hierarchy and the principle of historical localization. He's been up in his flying machine all morning."

"I didn't go up." Sullenness came and went in his voice. "It rained." He shuffled one foot, about to leave, when the Dean's left eyebrow wriggled up, warning, holding him.

"I don't believe you've had the pleasure." The Dean gave Keefe to Father Burner. "Father Keefe, sir, went through school with Father Quinlan—from the grades through the priesthood." The Dean described an arc with his breviary, dripping with ribbons, to show the passing years. Father Burner nodded.

"Well?" The Dean frowned at Father Burner. "Has the cat got your tongue, sir? Why don't you be about greeting Father O'Keefe—or Keefe, is it?"

"Keefe," Keefe said.

Father Burner, caught in the old amber of his inadequacy, stepped over and shook Keefe's hand once.

Quinlan stood by and let the drama play itself out.

Keefe, smiling a curious mixture more anxiety than amusement, said, "It's a pleasure, Father."

"Same here," Father Burner said.

"Well, good day, sirs!" The Dean cracked open his breviary and began to read, lips twitching.

Father Burner waited for them in the hall. Before he could explain that he thought too much of the Dean not to humor him and that besides the old fool was out of his head, the Dean proclaimed after them, "The Chancery phoned, Father Burner. You will hear confessions there tonight. I suppose one of those Cathedral jokers lost his faculties."

Yes, Father Burner knew, it was common procedure all right for the Archbishop to confer promotions by private interview, but every time a priest got called to the Cathedral it did not mean simply that. Many received sermons and it was most likely now someone was needed to hear confessions. And still Father Burner, feeling his pocket, was glad he had not remembered to mail the letter. He would not bother to speak to Quinlan and Keefe now.

III. NIGHT

"And for your penance say five Our Fathers and five Hail Marys and pray for my intention. And now make a good act of contrition. *Misereatur tui omnipotens Deus dimissis peccatis tuis . . ."* Father Burner swept out into the current of the prayer, stroking strongly in Latin, while the penitent, a miserable boy coming into puberty, paddled as fast as he could along the shore in English.

Finishing first, Father Burner waited for the boy to conclude. When, breathless, he did, Father Burner anointed the air and shot a whisper, "God bless you," kicking the window shut with the heel of his hand, ejecting the boy, an ear of corn shucked clean, into the world again. There was nobody on the other side of the confessional, so Father Burner turned on the signal light. A big spider drowsy in his web, drugged with heat and sins, he sat waiting for the next one to be hurled into his presence by guilt ruddy ripe, as with the boy, or, as with the old ladies who come early and try to stay late, by the spiritual famine of their lives or simply the desire to tell secrets in the dark.

He held his wrist in such a way as to see the sweat gleaming in the hairs. He looked at his watch. He had been at it since seven and now it was after nine. If there were no more kneeling in his section of the Cathedral at 9:30 he could close up and have a cigarette. He was too weary to read his office, though he had the Little Hours, Vespers, and Compline still to go. It was the last minutes in the confessional that got him— the insensible end of the excursion that begins with so many sinewy sensations and good intentions to look sharp at the landscape. In the last minutes how many priests, would-be surgeons of the soul, ended as blacksmiths, hammering out absolution anyway?

A few of the Cathedral familiars still drifted around the floor. They were day and night in the shadows praying. Meeting one of them, Father Burner always wanted to get away. They were collectors of priests' blessings in a day when most priests felt ashamed to raise their hands to God outside the ceremonies. Their respect for a priest was fanatic, that of the unworldly, the martyrs, for an emissary of heaven. They were so desperately disposed to death that the manner of dying was their greatest concern. But Father Burner had an idea there were more dull pretenders than saints among them. They inspired no unearthly feelings in him, as true sanctity was supposed to, and he felt it was all right not to like them. They spoke of God, the Blessed Virgin, of miracles, cures, and visitations, as of people and items in the news, which was annoying. The Cathedral, because of its location, described by brokers as exclusive, was not so much frequented by these wretches as it would have been if more convenient to the slums. But nevertheless a few came there, like the diarrheic pigeons, also a scandal to the neighborhood, and would not go away. Father Burner, from his glancing contact with them, had concluded that body odor is the real odor of sanctity.

Through the grating now Father Burner saw the young Vicar General stop a little distance up the aisle and speak to a couple of people who were possible prospects for Father Burner. "Anyone desiring to go to confession should do so at once. In a few minutes the priests will be gone from the confessionals." He crossed to the other side of the Cathedral.

Father Burner did not like to compare his career with the Vicar General's. The Archbishop had taken the Vicar General, a younger man than Father Burner by at least fifteen years, direct from the seminary. After a period of trial as Chancellor, he was raised to his present eminence—for reasons much pondered by the clergy and more difficult to discern than those obviously accounted for by intelligence, appearance, and, post factum, the loyalty consequent upon his selection over many older and possibly abler men. It was a medieval act of preference, a slap in the face to the monsignori, a rebuke to the principle of advancement by years applied elsewhere. The Vicar General had the quality of inscrutability in an ideal measure.

He did not seem at all given to gossip or conspiracy or even to that owlish secrecy peculiar to secretaries and so exasperating to others. He had possibly no enemies and certainly no intimates. In time he would be a bishop unless, as was breathed wherever the Cloth gathered over food and drink, he really was "troubled with sanctity," which might lead to anything else, the cloister or insanity.

The Vicar General appeared at the door of Father Burner's compartment. "The Archbishop will see you, Father, before you leave tonight." He went up the aisle, genuflected before the main altar, opened as a gate one of the host of brass angels surrounding the sanctuary, and entered the sacristies.

Before he would let hope have its way with him, Father Burner sought to recast the expression on the Vicar General's face. He could recall nothing significant. Very probably there had been nothing to see. Then, with a rush, he permitted himself to think this was his lucky day. Already he was formulating the way he would let the news out, providing he decided not to keep it a secret for a time. He might do that. It would be delicious to go about his business until the very last minute, to savor the old aggravations and feel none of the sting, to receive the old quips and smiles with good grace and know them to be toothless. The news, once out, would fly through the diocese. Hear about Burner at Saint Pat's, Tom? Finally landed himself a parish. Yeah, I just had it from McKenna. So I guess the A. B. wasn't so sore at the Round One after all. Well, he's just ornery enough to make a go of it.

Father Burner, earlier in the evening, had smoked a cigarette with one of the young priests attached to the Cathedral (a classmate of Quinlan's but not half the prig), stalling, hoping someone would come and say the Archbishop wanted to see him. When nothing happened except the usual small talk and introductions to a couple of missionaries stopping over, he had given up hope easily. He had seen the basis for his expectations as folly once more. It did not bother him after the fact was certain. He was amenable to any kind of finality. He had a light heart for a Ger—an American of German descent. And his hopes rose higher each time and with less cause. He was a ball that bounced up only. He had kept faith. And now—his just reward.

A little surprised he had not thought of her first, he admitted his mother into the new order of things. He wanted to open the letter from her, still in his coat, and late as it was send her a wire, which would do her more good than a night's sleep. He thought of himself back in her kitchen, home from the sem for the holidays, a bruiser in a tight black suit, his feet heavy on the oven door. She was fussing at the stove and he was promising her a porcelain one as big as a house after he got his parish. But he let her know, kidding on the square, that he would be running things at the rectory. It would not be the old story of the priest taking orders from his housekeeper, even if she was his mother (seminarians, from winter evenings of shooting the bull, knew only too well the pitfalls of parish life), or as with Ed Desmond a few years ago when his father was still living with him, the old man losing his marbles one by one, butting in when people came for advice and instructions, finally coming to believe he was the one to say Mass in his son's absence —no need to get a strange priest in—and sneaking into the box to hear confessions the day before they took him away.

He would be gentle with his mother, however, even if she talked too much, as he recalled she did the last time he saw her. She was well-preserved and strong for her age and ought to be able to keep the house up. Once involved in the social life of the parish she could be a valuable agent in coping with any lay opposition, which was too often the case when a new priest took over.

He resolved to show no nervousness before the Archbishop. A trifle surprised, yes—the Archbishop must have his due—but not overly affected by good fortune. If questioned, he would display a lot of easy confidence not unaccompanied by a touch of humility, a phrase or two like "God willing" or "with the help of Almighty God and your prayers, Your Excellency." He would also not forget to look the part—reliable, casual, cool, an iceberg, only the tip of his true worth showing.

At precisely 9:30 Father Burner picked up his breviary and backed out of the stall. But then there was the scuff of a foot and the tap of one of the confessional doors closing and then, to tell him the last penitent was a woman, the scent of apple blossoms. He turned off the light, saying "Damn!" to himself, and sat down again inside. He threw back the partition and led off, "Yes?" He placed his hand alongside his head and listened, looking down into the deeper darkness of his cassock sleeve.

"I . . ."

"Yes?" At the heart of the apple blossoms another scent bloomed: gin and vermouth.

"Bless me, Father, I . . . have sinned."

Father Burner knew this kind. They would always wait until the last moment. How they managed to get themselves into church at all, and then into the confessional, was a mystery. Sometimes liquor thawed them out. This one was evidently young, nubile. He had a feeling it was going to be adultery. He guessed it was up to him to get her under way.

"How long since your last confession?"

"I don't know . . ."

"Have you been away from the Church?"

"Yes."

"Are you married?"

"Yes."

"To a Catholic?"

"No."

"Protestant?"

"No."

"Jew?"

"No."

"Atheist?"

"No—nothing."

"Were you married by a priest?"

"Yes."

"How long ago was that?"

"Four years."

"Any children?"

"No."

"Practice birth control?"

"Yes, sometimes."

"Don't you know it's a crime against nature and the Church forbids it?"

"Yes."

"Don't you know that France fell because of birth control?"

"No."

"Well, it did. Was it your husband's fault?"

"You mean—the birth control?"

"Yes."

"Not wholly."

"And you've been away from the Church ever since your marriage?"

"Yes."

"Now you see why the Church is against mixed marriages. All right, go on. What else?"

"I don't know..."

"Is that what you came to confess?"

"No. Yes. I'm sorry, I'm afraid that's all."

"Do you have a problem?"

"I think that's all, Father."

"Remember, it is your obligation, and not mine, to examine your conscience. The task of instructing persons with regard to these delicate matters—I refer to the connubial relationship—

is not an easy one. Nevertheless, since there is a grave obligation imposed by God, it cannot be shirked. If you have a problem—"

"I don't have a *problem*."

"Remember, God never commands what is impossible and so if you make use of the sacraments regularly you have every reason to be confident that you will be able to overcome this evil successfully, with His help. I hope this is all clear to you."

"All clear."

"Then if you are heartily sorry for your sins for your penance say the rosary daily for one week and remember it is the law of the Church that you attend Mass on Sundays and holy days and receive the sacraments at least once a year. It's better to receive them often. Ask your pastor about birth control if it's still not clear to you. Or read a Catholic book on the subject. And now make a good act of contrition . . ."

Father Burner climbed the three flights of narrow stairs. He waited a moment in silence, catching his breath. He knocked on the door and was suddenly afraid its density prevented him from being heard and that he might be found standing there like a fool or a spy. But to knock again, if heard the first time, would seem importunate.

"Come in, Father."

At the other end of the long study the Archbishop sat behind an ebony desk. Father Burner waited before him as though expecting not to be asked to sit down. The only light in the room, a lamp on the desk, was so set that it kept the Archbishop's face in the dark, fell with a gentle sparkle upon his pectoral cross, and was absorbed all around by the fabric of the piped cloth he wore. Father Burner's eyes came to rest upon the Archbishop's freckled hand—ringed, square, and healthy.

"Be seated, Father."

"Thank you, Your Excellency."

"Oh, sit in this chair, Father." There were two chairs.

Father Burner changed to the soft one. He had a suspicion that in choosing the other one he had fallen into a silly trap, that it was a game the Archbishop played with his visitors: the innocent ones, seeing no issue, would take the soft chair, because handier; the guilty would go a step out of their way to take the hard one. "I called Saint Patrick's this morning, Father, but you were . . . out."

"I was visiting Father Desmond, Your Excellency."

"Father Desmond . . ."

"He's in the hospital."

"I know. Friend of his, are you, Father?"

"No, Your Excellency. Well"—Father Burner waited for the cock to crow the third time—"yes, I *know* the man." At once he regretted the scriptural complexion of the words and wondered if it were possible for the Archbishop not to be thinking of the earlier betrayal.

"It was good of you to visit Father Desmond, especially since you are not close to him. I hope he is better, Father."

"He is, Your Excellency."

The Archbishop got up and went across the room to a cabinet. "Will you have a little glass of wine, Father?"

"No. No, thanks, Your Excellency." Immediately he realized it could be another trap and, if so, he was caught again.

"Then I'll have a drop . . . *solus*." The Archbishop poured a glass and brought it back to the desk. "A little wine for the stomach's sake, Father."

Father Burner, not sure what he was expected to say to that, nodded gravely and said, "Yes, Your Excellency." He had seen that the Archbishop wore carpet slippers and that they had holes in both toes.

"But perhaps you've read Saint Bernard, Father, and recall where he says we priests remember well enough the apostolic counsel to use wine, but overlook the adjective 'little.' "

"I must confess I haven't read Saint Bernard lately, Your

Excellency." Father Burner believed this was somehow in his favor. "Since seminary, in fact."

"Not all priests, Father, have need of him. A hard saint . . . for hardened sinners. What is your estimate of Saint Paul?"

Father Burner felt familiar ground under his feet at last. There were the Pauline and Petrine factions—a futile business, he thought—but he knew where the Archbishop stood and exclaimed, "One of the greatest—"

"Really! So many young men today consider him . . . a bore. It's always the deep-breathing ones, I notice. They say he cuts it too fine."

"I've never thought so, Your Excellency."

"Indeed? Well, it's a question I like to ask my priests. Perhaps you knew that."

"No, I didn't, Your Excellency."

"So much the better then . . . but I see you appraising the melodeon, Father. Are you musical?"

"Not at all, Your Excellency. Violin lessons as a child." Father Burner laughed quickly, as though it were nothing.

"But you didn't go on with them?"

"No, Your Excellency." He did not mean it to sound as sad as it came out.

"What a pity."

"No great loss, Your Excellency."

"You are too . . . modest, Father. But perhaps the violin was not your instrument."

"I guess it wasn't, Your Excellency." Father Burner laughed out too loud.

"And you have the choir at Saint Patrick's, Father?"

"Not this year, Your Excellency. Father Quinlan has it."

"Now I recall . . ."

"Yes." So far as he was concerned—and there were plenty of others who thought so, too—Quinlan had played hell with the choir, canning all the women, some of them members for fifteen and twenty years, a couple even longer and practically living for it, and none of them as bad as Quinlan said. The liturgical stuff that Quinlan tried to pull off was all right in monasteries, where they had the time to train for it, but in a parish it sounded stodgy to ears used to the radio and split up the activity along sexual lines, which was really old hat in the modern world. The Dean liked it though. He called it "honest" and eulogized the men from the pulpit—not a sign that he heard how they brayed and whinnied and just gave out or failed to start—and each time it happened ladies in the congregation were sick and upset for days afterward, for he inevitably ended by attacking women, pants, cocktails, communism, cigarettes, and running around half naked. The women looked at the men in the choir, all pretty in surplices, and said to themselves they knew plenty about some of them and what they had done to some women.

"He's tried a little Gregorian, hasn't he—Father Quinlan?"

"Yes, Your Excellency," Father Burner said. "He has."

"Would you say it's been a success—or perhaps I should ask you first if you care for Gregorian, Father."

"Oh, yes, Your Excellency. Very much."

"Many, I know, don't . . . I've been told our chant sounds like a wild bull in a red barn or consumptives coughing into a bottle, but I will have it in the Cathedral, Father. Other places, I am aware, have done well with . . . light opera."

Father Burner frowned.

"We are told the people prefer and understand it. But at the risk of seeming reactionary, a fate my office prevents me from escaping in any event, I say we spend more time listening to the voice of the people than is good for either it or us. We have been too generous with our ears, Father. We have handed over our tongues also. When they are restored to us I wonder if we shall not find our ears more itching than before and our tongues more tied than ever."

Father Burner nodded in the affirmative.

"We are now entering the whale's tail, Father. We must go back the way we came in." The Archbishop lifted the lid of the humidor on the desk. "Will you smoke, Father?"

"No, thanks, Your Excellency."

The Archbishop let the lid drop. "Today there are few saints, fewer sinners, and everybody is already saved. We are all heroes in search of an underdog. As for villains, the classic kind with no illusions about themselves, they are . . . extinct. The very devil, for instance—where the devil is the devil today, Father?"

Father Burner, as the Archbishop continued to look at him, bit his lips for the answer, secretly injured that he should be expected to know, bewildered even as the children he toyed with in catechism.

The Archbishop smiled, but Father Burner was not sure at what—whether at him or what had been said. "Did you see, Father, where our brother Bishop Buckles said Hitler remains the one power on earth against the Church?"

Yes, Father Burner remembered seeing it in the paper; it was the sort of thing that kept Quinlan talking for days. "I did, Your Excellency."

"Alas, poor Buckles! He's a better croquet player than that." The Archbishop's hands unclasped suddenly and fell upon his memo pad. He tore off about a week and seemed to feel better for it. His hands, with no hint of violence about them now, came together again. "We look hard to the right and left, Father. It is rather to the center, I think, we should look—to ourselves, the devil in us."

Father Burner knew the cue for humility when he heard it. "Yes, Your Excellency."

With his chubby fingers the Archbishop made a steeple that was more like a dome. His eyes were reading the memo. "For instance, Father, I sometimes appear at banquets—when they can't line up a good foreign correspondent—banquets at which the poor are never present and at which I am unfailingly confronted by someone exceedingly well off who is moved to inform me that 'religion' is a great consolation to him. Opium, rather, I always think, perhaps wrongfully and borrowing a word from one of our late competitors, which is most imprudent of me, a bishop."

The Archbishop opened a drawer and drew out a sheet of paper and an envelope. "Yes, the rich have souls," he said softly, answering an imaginary objection which happened to be Father Burner's. "But if Christ were really with them they would not be themselves—that is to say, rich."

"Very true, Your Excellency," Father Burner said.

The Archbishop faced sideways to use an old typewriter. "And likewise, lest we forget, we would not be ourselves, that is to say—what? For we square the circle beautifully in almost every country on earth. We bring neither peace nor a sword. The rich give us money. We give them consolation and make of the eye of the needle a gate. Together we try to reduce the Church, the Bride of Christ, to a streetwalker." The Archbishop rattled the paper, Father Burner's future, into place and rolled it crookedly into the typewriter. "Unfortunately for us, it doesn't end there. The penance will not be shared so equitably. Your Christian name, Father, is—?"

"Ernest, Your Excellency."

The Archbishop typed several words and stopped, looking over at Father Burner. "I can't call to mind a single Saint Ernest, Father. Can you help me?"

"There were two, I believe, Your Excellency, but Butler leaves them out of his *Lives*."

"They would be German saints, Father?"

"Yes, Your Excellency. There was one an abbot and the other an archbishop."

"If Butler had been Irish, as the name has come to indicate,

I'd say that's an Irishman for you, Father. He does not forget to include a power of Irish saints." The Archbishop was Irish himself. Father Burner begged to differ with him, believing here was a wrong deliberately set up for him to right. "I am not Irish myself, Your Excellency, but some of my best friends are."

"Tut, tut, Father. Such tolerance will be the death of you." The Archbishop, typing a few words, removed the paper, signed it and placed it in the envelope. He got up and took down a book from the shelves. He flipped it open, glanced through several pages and returned it to its place. "No Ernests in Baring-Gould either. Well, Father, it looks as if you have a clear field."

The Archbishop came from behind the desk and Father Burner, knowing the interview was over, rose. The Archbishop handed him the envelope. Father Burner stuffed it hastily in his pocket and knelt, the really important thing, to kiss the Archbishop's ring and receive his blessing. They walked together toward the door.

"Do you care for pictures, Father?"

"Oh, yes, Your Excellency."

The Archbishop, touching him lightly on the arm, stopped before a reproduction of Raphael's Sistine Madonna. "There is a good peasant woman, Father, and a nice fat baby." Father Burner nodded his appreciation. "She could be Our Blessed Mother, Father, though I doubt it. There is no question about the baby. He is not Christ." The Archbishop moved to another picture. "Rembrandt had the right idea, Father. See the gentleman pushing Christ up on the cross? That is Rembrandt, a self-portrait." Father Burner thought of some of the stories about the Archbishop, that he slept on a cot, stood in line with the people sometimes to go to confession, that he fasted on alternate days the year round. Father Burner was thankful for such men as the Archbishop. "But here is Christ, Father." This time it was a glassy-eyed Christ whose head lay against the rough wood of the cross he was carrying. "That is Christ, Father. The Greek painted Our Saviour."

The Archbishop opened the door for Father Burner, saying, "And, Father, you will please not open the envelope until after your Mass tomorrow."

Father Burner went swiftly down the stairs. Before he got into his car he looked up at the Cathedral. He could scarcely see the cross glowing on the dome. It seemed as far away as the stars. The cross needed a brighter light or the dome ought to be painted gold and lit up like the state capitol, so people would see it. He drove a couple of blocks down the street, pulled up to the curb, opened the envelope, which had not been sealed, and read: "You will report on August 8 to the Reverend Michael Furlong, to begin your duties on that day as his assistant. I trust that in your new appointment you will find not peace but a sword."

DAWN

FATHER UDOVIC PLACED the envelope before the Bishop and stepped back. He gave the Bishop more than enough time to read what was written on the envelope, time to digest *The Pope* and, down in the corner, the *Personal*, and then he stepped forward. "It was in the collection yesterday," he said. "At Cathedral."

"Peter's Pence, Father?"

Father Udovic nodded. He'd checked that. It had been in with the special Peter's Pence envelopes, and not with the regular Sunday ones.

"Well, then..." The Bishop's right hand opened over the envelope, then stopped, and came to roost again, uneasily, on the edge of the desk.

Father Udovic shifted a foot, popped a knuckle in his big toe. The envelope was a bad thing all right. They'd never received anything like it. The Bishop was doing what Father Udovic had done when confronted by the envelope, thinking twice, which was what Monsignor Renton at Cathedral had done, and his curates before him, and his housekeeper who counted the collection. In the end, each had seen the envelope as a hot potato and passed it on. But the Bishop couldn't do that. He didn't know *what* might be inside. Even Father Udovic, who had held it up to a strong light, didn't know. That was the hell of it.

The Bishop continued to stare at the envelope. He still hadn't touched it.

"It beats me," said Father Udovic, moving backwards. He sank down on the leather sofa.

"Was there something else, Father?"

Father Udovic got up quickly and went out of the office—wondering how the Bishop would handle the problem, disappointed that he evidently meant to handle it by himself. In a way, Father Udovic felt responsible. It had been his idea to popularize the age-old collection—"to personalize Peter's Pence"—by moving the day for it ahead a month so that the Bishop, who was going to Rome, would be able to present the proceeds to the Holy Father personally. There had been opposition from the very first. Monsignor Renton, the rector at Cathedral, and one of those at table when Father Udovic proposed his plan, was ill-disposed to it (as he was to Father Udovic himself) and had almost killed it with his comment, "Smart promotion, Bruno." (Monsignor Renton's superior attitude was understandable. He'd had Father Udovic's job, that of chancellor of the diocese, years ago, under an earlier bishop.) But Father Udovic had won out. The Bishop had written a letter incorporating Father Udovic's idea. The plan had been poorly received in some rectories, which was to be expected since it disturbed the routine schedule of special collections. Father Udovic, however, had been confident that the people, properly appealed to, could do better than in the past with Peter's Pence. And the first returns, which had reached him that afternoon, were reassuring—whatever the envelope might be.

It was still on the Bishop's desk the next day, off to one side, and it was there on the day after. On the following day, Thursday, it was in the "In" section of his file basket. On Friday it was still there, buried. Obviously the Bishop was stumped.

On Saturday morning, however, it was back on the desk. Father Udovic, called in for consultation, had a feeling, a really satisfying feeling, that the Bishop might have need of him. If so, he would be ready. He had a plan. He sat down on the sofa.

"It's about this," the Bishop said, glancing down at the envelope before him. "I wonder if you can locate the sender."

"I'll do my best," said Father Udovic. He paused to consider whether it would be better just to go and do his best, or to present his plan of operation to the Bishop for approval. But the Bishop, not turning to him at all, was outlining what he wanted done. And it was Father Udovic's own plan! The Cathedral priests at their Sunday Masses should request the sender of the envelope to report to the sacristy afterwards. The sender should be assured that the contents would be turned over to the Holy Father, if possible.

"Providing, of course," said Father Udovic, standing and trying to get into the act, "it's not something . . ."

"Providing it's possible to do so."

Father Udovic tried not to look sad. The Bishop might express himself better, but he was saying nothing that hadn't occurred to Father Udovic first, days before. It was pretty discouraging.

He retreated to the outer office and went to work on a memo of their conversation. Drafting letters and announcements was the hardest part of his job for him. He tended to go astray without a memo, to take up with the tempting clichés that came to him in the act of composition and sometimes perverted the Bishop's true meaning. Later that morning he called Monsignor Renton and read him the product of many revisions, the two sentences.

"Okay," said Monsignor Renton. "I'll stick it in the bulletin. Thanks a lot."

As soon as Father Udovic hung up, he doubted that that was what the Bishop wished. He consulted the memo. The Bishop was very anxious that "not too much be made of this matter." Naturally, Monsignor Renton wanted the item for his parish bulletin. He was hard up. At one time he had produced the best bulletin in the diocese, but now he was written out, quoting more and more from the magazines and even from the papal encyclicals. Father Udovic called Monsignor Renton back and asked that the announcement be kept out of print. It would be enough to read it once over lightly from the pulpit, using Father Udovic's version because it said enough without saying too much and was, he implied, authorized by the Bishop. Whoever the announcement concerned would comprehend it. If published, the announcement would be subject to study and private interpretation. "Announcements from the pulpit are soon forgotten," Father Udovic said. "I mean—by the people they don't concern."

"You were right the first time, Bruno," said Monsignor Renton. He sounded sore.

The next day—Sunday—Father Udovic stayed home, expecting a call from Monsignor Renton, or possibly even a visit. There was nothing. That evening he called the Cathedral rectory and got one of the curates. Monsignor Renton wasn't expected in until very late. The curate had made the announcement at his two Masses, but no one had come to him about it. "Yes, Father, as you say, it's quite possible someone came to Monsignor about it. Probably he didn't consider it important enough to call you about."

"*Not important!*"

"Not important enough to call *you* about, Father. On *Sunday*."

"I see," said Father Udovic mildly. It was good to know that the curate, after almost a year of listening to Monsignor Renton, was still respectful. Some of the men out in parishes said Father Udovic's job was a snap and maintained that he'd landed it only because he employed the touch system of typing. Before hanging up, Father Udovic stressed the importance of resolving the question of the envelope, but somehow (words played tricks on him) he sounded as though he were accusing the curate of indifference. What a change! The curate didn't take criticism very well, as became all too clear from his sullen silence, and he wasn't very loyal. When Father Udovic suggested that Monsignor Renton might have neglected to make the announcement at his Masses, the curate readily agreed. "Could've slipped his mind all right. I guess you know what that's like."

Early the next morning Father Udovic was in touch with Monsignor Renton, beginning significantly with a glowing report on the Peter's Pence collection, but the conversation languished, and finally he had to ask about the announcement.

"Nobody showed," Monsignor Renton said in an annoyed voice. "What d'ya want to do about it?"

"Nothing right now," said Father Udovic, and hung up. If there had been a failure in the line of communication, he thought he knew where it was.

The envelope had reposed on the Bishop's desk over the weekend and through most of Monday. But that afternoon Father Udovic, on one of his appearances in the Bishop's office, noticed that it was gone. As soon as the Bishop left for the day, Father Udovic rushed in, looking first in the wastebasket, then among the sealed outgoing letters, for a moment actually expecting to see a fat one addressed in the Bishop's hand to the Apostolic Delegate. When he uncovered the envelope in the "Out" section of the file basket, he wondered at himself for looking in the other places first. The envelope had to be filed somewhere—a separate folder would be best—but Father Udovic didn't file it. He carried it to his desk. There, sitting down to it in the gloom of the outer office, weighing, feeling, smelling the envelope, he succumbed entirely to his first fears. He remembered the parable of the cockle. "An enemy hath done this." An enemy was plotting to disturb the peace of the diocese, to employ the Bishop as an agent against himself, or against some other innocent person, some unsuspecting priest or nun—yes, against Father Udovic. Why him? Why not? Only a diseased mind would contemplate such a scheme, Father Udovic thought, but that didn't make it less likely. And the sender, whoever he was, doubtless anonymous and judging others by himself, would assume that the envelope had already been opened and that the announcement was calculated to catch him. Such a person would never come forward.

Father Udovic's fingers tightened on the envelope. He could rip it open, but he wouldn't. That evening, enjoying instant coffee in his room, he could steam it open. But he wouldn't. In the beginning, the envelope might have been opened. It would have been so easy, pardonable then. Monsignor Renton's housekeeper might have done it. With the Bishop honoring the name on the envelope and the intentions of whoever wrote it, up to a point anyway, there was now a principle operating that just couldn't be bucked. Monsignor Renton could have it his way.

That evening Father Udovic called him and asked that the announcement appear in the bulletin.

"Okay. I'll stick it in. It wouldn't surprise me if we got some action now."

"I hope so," said Father Udovic, utterly convinced that Monsignor Renton had failed him before. "Do you mind taking it down verbatim this time?"

"Not at all."

In the next bulletin, an advance copy of which came to Father Udovic through the courtesy of Monsignor Renton, the announcement appeared in an expanded, unauthorized version.

The result on Sunday was no different.

During the following week, Father Udovic considered the possibility that the sender was a floater and thought of having the announcement broadcast from every pulpit in the diocese. He would need the Bishop's permission for that, though, and he didn't dare to ask for something he probably wouldn't get. The Bishop had instructed him not to make too much of the matter. The sender would have to be found at Cathedral, or not at all. If not at all, Father Udovic, having done his best, would understand that he wasn't supposed to know anymore about the envelope than he did. He would file it away, and some other chancellor, some other bishop, perhaps, would inherit it. The envelope was most likely harmless anyway, but Father Udovic wasn't so much relieved as bored by the probability that some poor soul was trusting the Bishop to put the envelope into the hands of the Holy Father, hoping for rosary beads blessed by him, or for his autographed picture, and enclosing a small offering, perhaps a spiritual bouquet. Toward the end of the week, Father Udovic told the Bishop that he liked to think that the envelope contained a spiritual bouquet from a little child, and that its contents had already been delivered, so to speak, its prayers and communions already credited to the Holy Father's account in heaven.

"I must say I hadn't thought of that," said the Bishop.

Unfortunately for his peace of mind Father Udovic wasn't always able to believe that the sender was a little child.

The most persistent of those coming to him in reverie was a middle-aged woman saying she hadn't received a special Peter's Pence envelope, had been out of town a few weeks, and so hadn't heard or read the announcement. When Father Udovic tried her on the meaning of the *Personal* on the envelope, however, the woman just went away, and so did all the other suspects under questioning—except one. This was a rich old man suffering from scrupulosity. He wanted his alms to be in secret, as it said in Scripture, lest he be deprived of his eternal reward, but not *entirely* in secret. That was as far as Father Udovic could figure the old man. Who was he? An audacious old Protestant who hated communism, or could some future Knight of St Gregory be taking his first awkward step? The old man was pretty hard to believe in, and the handwriting on the envelope sometimes struck Father Udovic as that of a woman. This wasn't necessarily bad. Women controlled the nation's wealth. He'd seen the figures on it. The explanation was simple: widows. Perhaps they hadn't taken the right tone in the announcement. Father Udovic's version had been safe and cold, Monsignor Renton's like a summons. It might have been emphasized that the Bishop, under certain circumstances, would *gladly* undertake to deliver the envelope. That might have made a difference. The sender would not only have to appreciate the difficulty of the Bishop's position, but abandon his own. That wouldn't be easy for the sort of person Father Udovic had in mind. He had a feeling that it wasn't going to happen. The Bishop would leave for Rome on the following Tuesday. So time was running out. The envelope could contain a check—quite the cruelest thought—on which payment would be stopped after a limited time by the donor, whom Father Udovic persistently saw as an old person not to be dictated to, or it could be nullified even sooner by untimely death. God, what a shame! In Rome, where the needs of the world, temporal as well as spiritual, were so well known, the Bishop would've been welcome as the flowers in May.

And then, having come full circle, Father Udovic would be hard on himself for dreaming and see the envelope as a whited sepulcher concealing all manner of filth, spelled out in letters snipped from newsprint and calculated to shake Rome's faith in him. It was then that he particularly liked to think of the sender as a little child. But soon the middle-aged woman would be back, and all the others, among whom the hottest suspect was a feeble-minded nun—devils all to pester him, and the last was always worse than the first. For he always ended up with the old man—and what if there was such an old man?

On Saturday, Father Udovic called Monsignor Renton and asked him to run the announcement again. It was all they could do, he said, and admitted that he had little hope of success.

"Don't let it throw you, Bruno. It's always darkest before dawn."

Father Udovic said he no longer cared. He said he liked to think that the envelope contained a spiritual bouquet from a little child, that its contents had already been delivered, its prayers and communions already...

"You should've been a nun, Bruno."

"Not sure I know what you mean," Father Udovic said, and hung up. He wished it were in his power to do something about Monsignor Renton. Some of the old ones got funny when they stayed too long in one place.

On Sunday, after the eight o'clock Mass, Father Udovic received a call from Monsignor Renton. "I told 'em if somebody didn't own up to the envelope, we'd open it. I guess I got carried away." But it had worked. Monsignor Renton had just talked with the party responsible for the envelope—a Mrs Anton—and she was on the way over to see Father Udovic.

"A woman, huh?"

"A widow. That's about all I know about her."

"A widow, huh? Did she say what was in it?"

"I'm afraid it's not what you thought, Bruno. It's money."

Father Udovic returned to the front parlor, where he had left Mrs Anton. "The Bishop'll see you," he said, and sat down. She wasn't making a good impression on him. She could've used a shave. When she'd asked for the Bishop, Father Udovic had replied instinctively, "He's busy," but it hadn't convinced her. She had appeared quite capable of walking out on him. He invoked the Bishop's name again. "Now one of the things the Bishop'll want to know is why you didn't show up before this."

Mrs Anton gazed at him, then past him, as she had when he'd tried to question her. He saw her starting to get up, and thought he was about to lose her. He hadn't heard the Bishop enter the room.

The Bishop waved Mrs Anton down, seated himself near the doorway at some distance from them, and motioned to Father Udovic to continue.

To the Bishop it might sound like browbeating, but Father Udovic meant to go on being firm with Mrs Anton. He hadn't forgotten that she'd responded to Monsignor Renton's threats. "Why'd you wait so long? You listen to the Sunday announcements, don't you?" If she persisted in ignoring him, she could make him look bad, of course, but he didn't look for her to do that, with the Bishop present.

Calmly Mrs Anton spoke, but not to Father Udovic. "Call off your trip?"

The Bishop shook his head.

In Father Udovic's opinion, it was one of his functions to protect the Bishop from directness of that sort. "How do we know what's in here?" he demanded. Here, unfortunately, he reached up the wrong sleeve of his cassock for the envelope. Then he had it. "What's in here? Money?" He knew from Monsignor Renton that the envelope contained money, but he hadn't told the Bishop, and so it probably sounded rash to him. Father Udovic could feel the Bishop disapproving of him, and Mrs Anton still hadn't answered the question.

"Maybe you should return the envelope to Mrs Anton, Father," said the Bishop.

That did it for Mrs Anton. "It's got a dollar in it," she said.

Father Udovic glanced at the Bishop. The Bishop was adjusting his cuffs. This was something he did at funerals and public gatherings. It meant that things had gone on too long. Father Udovic's fingers were sticking to the envelope. He still couldn't believe it. "Feels like there's more than that," he said.

"I wrapped it up good in paper."

"You didn't write a letter or anything?"

"Was I supposed to?"

Father Udovic came down on her. "You were supposed to do what everybody else did. You were supposed to use the envelopes we had printed up for the purpose." He went back a few steps in his mind. "You told Monsignor Renton what was in the envelope?"

"Yes."

"Did you tell him how much?"

"No."

"Why not?"

"*He* didn't ask me."

And *he* didn't have to, thought Father Udovic. One look at Mrs Anton and Monsignor Renton would know. Parish priests got to know such things. They were like weight-guessers, for whom it was only a question of ounces. Monsignor Renton shouldn't have passed Mrs Anton on. He had opposed the plan to personalize Peter's Pence, but who would have thought he'd go to such lengths to get even with Father Udovic? It was sabotage. Father Udovic held out the envelope and pointed to the *Personal* on it. "What do you mean by that?" Here was where the creatures of his dreams had always gone away. He leaned forward for the answer.

Mrs Anton leaned forward to give it. "I mean I don't want somebody else takin' all the credit with the Holy Father!"

Father Udovic sank back. It had been bad before, when she'd ignored him, but now it was worse. She was attacking the Bishop. If there were only a way to *prove* she was out of her

mind, if only she'd say something that would make all her remarks acceptable in retrospect . . . "How's the Holy Father gonna
know who this dollar came from if you didn't write anything?"

"I wrote my name and address on it. In ink."

"All right, Father," said the Bishop. He stood up and almost
went out of the room before he stopped and looked back at Mrs
Anton. "Why don't you send it by regular mail?"

"He'd never see it! That's why! Some flunky'd get hold of
it! Same as here! Oh, don't I know!"

The Bishop walked out, leaving them together—with the
envelope.

In the next few moments, although Father Udovic knew
he had an obligation to instruct Mrs Anton, and had the text
for it—"When thou dost an alms-deed, sound not a trumpet
before thee"—he despaired. He realized that they had needed
each other to arrive at their sorry state. It seemed to him, sitting there saying nothing, that they saw each other as two people who'd sinned together on earth might see each other in
hell, unchastened even then, only blaming each other for what
had happened.

DEATH OF A FAVORITE

I HAD SPENT most of the afternoon mousing—a matter of sport with me and certainly not of diet—in the sunburnt fields that begin at our back door and continue hundreds of miles into the Dakotas. I gradually gave up the idea of hunting, the grasshoppers convincing me that there was no percentage in stealth. Even to doze was difficult, under such conditions, but I must have managed it. At least I was late coming to dinner, and so my introduction to the two missionaries took place at table. They were surprised, as most visitors are, to see me take the chair at Father Malt's right.

Father Malt, breaking off the conversation (if it could be called that), was his usual dear old self. "Fathers," he said, "meet Fritz."

I gave the newcomers the first good look that invariably tells me whether or not a person cares for cats. The mean old buck in charge of the team did not like me, I could see, and would bear watching. The other one obviously did like me, but he did not appear to be long enough from the seminary to matter. I felt that I had broken something less than even here.

"My assistant," said Father Malt, meaning me, and thus unconsciously dealing out our fat friend at the other end of the table. Poor Burner! There was a time when, thinking of him, as I did now, as the enemy, I could have convinced myself I meant something else. But he *is* the enemy, and I was right from the beginning, when it could only have been instinct that told me how much he hated me even while trying (in his fashion!) to be friendly. (I believe his prejudice to be acquired rather than congenital, and very likely, at this stage, confined to me, not to cats as a class—there *is* that in his favor. I intend to be fair about this if it kills me.)

My observations of humanity incline me to believe that one of us—Burner or I—must ultimately prevail over the other. For myself, I should not fear if this were a battle to be won on the solid ground of Father Malt's affections. But the old man grows older, the grave beckons to him ahead, and with Burner pushing him from behind, how long can he last? Which is to say: How long can *I* last? Unfortunately, it is naked power that counts most in any rectory, and as things stand now, I am safe only so long as Father Malt retains it here. Could I—this impossible thought is often with me now—could I effect a reconciliation and alliance with Father Burner? Impossible! Yes, doubtless. But the question better asked is: *How* impossible? (Lord knows I would not inflict this line of reasoning upon myself if I did not hold with the rumors that Father Burner will be the one to succeed to the pastorate.) For I do like it here. It is not at all in my nature to forgive and forget, certainly not as regards Father Burner, but it is in my nature to come to terms (much as nations do) when necessary, and in this solution there need not be a drop of good will. No dog can make that statement, or take the consequences, which I understand are most serious, in the world to come. Shifts and ententes.

There is something fatal about the vocation of favorite, but it is the only one that suits me, and, all things considered—to dig I am not able, to beg I am ashamed—the rewards are adequate.

"We go through Chicago all the time," said the boss missionary, who seemed to be returning to a point he had reached when I entered. I knew Father Malt would be off that evening for a convention in Chicago. The missionaries, who would fill in for him and conduct forty hours' devotion on the side, belonged to an order just getting started in the diocese and were anxious to make a good impression. For the present, at least, as a kind of special introductory offer, they could be had dirt-cheap. Thanks to them, pastors who'd never been able to get away had got a taste of Florida last winter.

"Sometimes we stay over in Chicago," bubbled the young missionary. He was like a rookie ballplayer who hadn't made many road trips.

"We've got a house there," said the first, whose name in religion, as they say, was—so help me—Philbert. Later, Father Burner would get around it by calling him by his surname. Father Malt was the sort who wouldn't see anything funny about "Philbert," but it would be too much to expect him to remember such a name.

"What kind of a house?" asked Father Malt. He held up his hearing aid and waited for clarification.

Father Philbert replied in a shout, "The Order owns *a house* there!"

Father Malt fingered his hearing aid.

Father Burner sought to interpret for Father Philbert. "I think, Father, he wants to know what it's made out of."

"Red brick—it's red brick," bellowed Father Philbert.

"*My* house is red brick," said Father Malt.

"I *noticed* that," said Father Philbert.

Father Malt shoved the hearing aid at him.

"I know it," said Father Philbert, shouting again.

Father Malt nodded and fed me a morsel of fish. Even for a Friday, it wasn't much of a meal. I would not have been sorry to see this housekeeper go.

"All right, all right," said Father Burner to the figure lurking behind the door and waiting for him, always the last one, to finish. "She stands and looks in at you through the crack," he beefed. "Makes you feel like a condemned man." The housekeeper came into the room, and he addressed the young missionary (Burner was a great one for questioning the young): "Ever read any books by this fella Koestler, Father?"

"The Jesuit?" the young one asked.

"Hell, no, he's some kind of a writer. I know the man you mean, though. Spells his name different. Wrote a book—apologetics."

"That's the one. Very—"

"Dull."

"Well . . ."

"This other fella's not bad. He's a writer who's ahead of his time—about fifteen minutes. Good on jails and concentration camps. You'd think he was born in one if you ever read his books." Father Burner regarded the young missionary with absolute indifference. "But you didn't."

"No. Is he a Catholic?" inquired the young one.

"He's an Austrian or something."

"Oh."

The housekeeper removed the plates and passed the dessert around. When she came to Father Burner, he asked her privately, "What is it?"

"Pudding," she said, not whispering, as he would have liked.

"*Bread* pudding?" Now he was threatening her.

"Yes, Father."

Father Burner shuddered and announced to everybody, "No dessert for me." When the housekeeper had retired into the kitchen, he said, "Sometimes I think he got her from a hospital and sometimes, Father, I think she came from one of *your* fine institutions"—this to the young missionary.

Father Philbert, however, was the one to see the joke, and he laughed.

"My God," said Father Burner, growing bolder, "I'll never forget the time I stayed at your house in Louisville. If I hadn't been there for just a day—for the Derby, in fact—I'd have gone to Rome about it. I think I've had better meals here."

At the other end of the table, Father Malt, who could not have heard a word, suddenly blinked and smiled; the missionaries looked at him for some comment, in vain.

"He doesn't hear me," said Father Burner. "Besides, I think he's listening to the news."

"I didn't realize it was a radio too," said the young missionary.

"Oh, hell, yes."

"I think he's pulling your leg," said Father Philbert.

"Well, I thought so," said the young missionary ruefully.

"It's an idea," said Father Burner. Then in earnest to Father Philbert, whom he'd really been working around to all the time—the young one was decidedly not his type—"You the one drivin' that new Olds, Father?"

"It's not mine, Father," said Father Philbert with a meekness that would have been hard to take if he'd meant it. Father Burner understood him perfectly, however, and I thought they were two persons who would get to know each other a lot better.

"Nice job. They say it compares with the Cad in power. What do you call that color—oxford or clerical gray?"

"I really couldn't say, Father. It's my brother's. He's a layman in Minneapolis—St Stephen's parish. He loaned it to me for this little trip."

Father Burner grinned. He could have been thinking, as I was, that Father Philbert protested too much. "Thought I saw you go by earlier," he said. "What's the matter—didn't you want to come in when you saw the place?"

Father Philbert, who was learning to ignore Father Malt, laughed discreetly. "Couldn't be sure this was it. That house on the *other* side of the church, now—"

Father Burner nodded. "Like that, huh? Belongs to a Mason."

Father Philbert sighed and said, "It would."

"Not at all," said Father Burner. "I like 'em better than K. C.'s." If he could get the audience for it, Father Burner enjoyed being broad-minded. Gazing off in the direction of the Mason's big house, he said, "I've played golf with him."

The young missionary looked at Father Burner in horror. Father Philbert merely smiled. Father Burner, toying with a large crumb, propelled it in my direction.

"Did a bell ring?" asked Father Malt.

"His P. A. system," Father Burner explained. "Better tell him," he said to the young missionary. "You're closer. He can't bring me in on those batteries he uses."

"No bell," said the young missionary, lapsing into basic English and gestures.

Father Malt nodded, as though he hadn't really thought so.

"How do you like it?" said Father Burner.

Father Philbert hesitated, and then he said, "Here, you mean?"

"I wouldn't ask you that," said Father Burner, laughing. "Talkin' about that Olds. Like it? Like the Hydramatic?"

"No kiddin', Father. It's not mine," Father Philbert protested.

"All right, all right," said Father Burner, who obviously did not believe him. "Just so you don't bring up your vow of poverty." He looked at Father Philbert's uneaten bread pudding—"Had enough?"—and rose from the table, blessing himself. The other two followed when Father Malt, who was feeding me cheese, waved them away. Father Burner came around to us, bumping my chair—intentionally, I know. He stood behind Father Malt and yelled into his ear, "Any calls for me this aft?" He'd been out somewhere, as usual. I often thought he expected too much to happen in his absence.

"There was something..." said Father Malt, straining his memory, which was poor.

"*Yes?*"

"Now I remember—they had the wrong number."

Father Burner, looking annoyed and downhearted, left the room.

"They said they'd call back," said Father Malt, sensing Father Burner's disappointment.

I left Father Malt at the table reading his Office under the orange light of the chandelier. I went to the living room, to my spot in the window from which I could observe Father Burner and the missionaries on the front porch, the young one in the swing with his breviary—the mosquitoes, I judged, were about to join him—and the other two just smoking and standing around, like pool players waiting for a table. I heard Father Philbert say, "Like to take a look at it, Father?"

"Say, that's an idea," said Father Burner.

I saw them go down the front walk to the gray Olds parked at the curb. With Father Burner at the wheel they drove away. In a minute they were back, the car moving uncertainly—this I noted with considerable pleasure until I realized that Father Burner was simply testing the brakes. Then they were gone, and after a bit, when they did not return, I supposed they were out killing poultry on the open road.

That evening, when the ushers dropped in at the rectory, there was not the same air about them as when they came for pinochle. Without fanfare, Mr Bauman, their leader, who had never worked any but the center aisle, presented Father Malt with a traveling bag. It was nice of him, I thought, when he said, "It's from all of us," for it could not have come from all equally. Mr Bauman, in hardware, and Mr Keller, the druggist, were the only ones well off, and must have forked out plenty for such a fine piece of luggage, even after the discount.

Father Malt thanked all six ushers with little nods in which there was no hint of favoritism. "Ha," he kept saying. "You shouldn'a done it."

The ushers bobbed and ducked, dodging his flattery, and kept up a mumble to the effect that Father Malt deserved everything they'd ever done for him and more. Mr Keller came forward to instruct Father Malt in the use of the various clasps and zippers. Inside the bag was another gift, a set of military brushes, which I could see they were afraid he would not discover for himself. But he unsnapped a brush, and, like the veteran crowd-pleaser he was, swiped once or twice at his head with it after spitting into the bristles. The ushers all laughed.

"Pretty snazzy," said the newest usher—the only young blood among them. Mr Keller had made him a clerk at the store, had pushed through his appointment as alternate usher in the church, and was gradually weaning him away from his motor-cycle. With Mr Keller, the lad formed a block to Mr Bauman's power, but he was perhaps worse than no ally at all. Most of the older men, though they pretended a willingness to help him meet the problems of an usher, were secretly pleased when he bungled at collection time and skipped a row or overlapped one.

Mr Keller produced a box of ten-cent cigars, which, as a *personal* gift from him, came as a bitter surprise to the others. He was not big enough, either, to attribute it to them too. He had anticipated their resentment, however, and now produced a bottle of milk of magnesia. No one could deny the comic effect, for Father Malt had been known to recommend the blue bottle from the confessional.

"Ha!" said Father Malt, and everybody laughed.

"In case you get upset on the trip," said the druggist.

"You know it's the best thing," said Father Malt in all seriousness, and then even he remembered he'd said it too often before. He passed the cigars. The box went from hand to hand, but, except for the druggist's clerk, nobody would have one.

Father Malt, seeing this, wisely renewed his thanks for the bag, insisting upon his indebtedness until it was actually in keeping with the idea the ushers had of their own generosity. Certainly none of them had ever owned a bag like that. Father Malt went to the housekeeper with it and asked her to transfer his clothes from the old bag, already packed, to the new one. When he returned, the ushers were still standing around feeling good about the bag and not so good about the cigars. They'd discuss that later. Father Malt urged them to sit down. He seemed to want them near him as long as possible. They *were* his friends, but I could not blame Father Burner for avoiding them. He was absent now, as he usually managed to be when the ushers called. If he ever succeeded Father Malt, who let them have the run of the place, they would be the first to suffer—after me! As Father Malt was the heart, they were the substance of a parish that remained rural while becoming increasingly suburban. They dressed up occasionally and dropped into St Paul and Minneapolis, "the Cities," as visiting firemen into hell, though it would be difficult to imagine any other place as graceless and far-gone as our own hard little highway town—called Sherwood but about as sylvan as a tennis court.

They were regular fellows—not so priestly as their urban colleagues—loud, heavy of foot, wearers of long underwear in wintertime and iron-gray business suits the year round. Their idea of a good time (pilsener beer, cheap cigars smoked with the bands left on, and pinochle) coincided nicely with their understanding of "doing good" (a percentage of every pot went to the parish building fund). Their wives, also active, played cards in the church basement and sold vanilla extract and chances—

mostly to each other, it appeared—with all the revenue over cost going to what was known as "the missions." This evening I could be grateful that time was not going to permit the usual pinochle game. (In the midst of all their pounding—almost as hard on me as it was on the dining-room table—I often felt they should have played on a meat block.)

The ushers, settling down all over the living room, started to talk about Father Malt's trip to Chicago. The housekeeper brought in a round of beer.

"How long you be gone, Father—three days?" one of them asked.

Father Malt said that he'd be gone about three days.

"Three days! This is Friday. Tomorrow's Saturday. Sunday. Monday." Everything stopped while the youngest usher counted on his fingers. "Back on Tuesday?"

Father Malt nodded.

"Who's takin' over on Sunday?"

Mr Keller answered for Father Malt. "He's got some missionary fathers in."

"Missionaries!"

The youngest usher then began to repeat himself on one of his two or three topics. "Hey, Father, don't forget to drop in the U. S. O. if it's still there. I was in Chi during the war," he said, but nobody would listen to him.

Mr Bauman had cornered Father Malt and was trying to tell him where that place was—that place where he'd eaten his meals during the World's Fair; one of the waitresses was from Minnesota. I'd had enough of this—the next thing would be a diagram on the back of an envelope—and I'd heard Father Burner come in earlier. I went upstairs to check on him. For a minute or two I stood outside his room listening. He had Father Philbert with him, and, just as I'd expected, he was talking against Father Malt, leading up to the famous question with which Father Malt, years ago, had received the Sherwood appointment from the Archbishop: "Have dey got dere a goot meat shop?"

Father Philbert laughed, and I could hear him sip from his glass and place it on the floor beside his chair. I entered the room, staying close to the baseboard, in the shadows, curious to know what they were drinking. I maneuvered myself into position to sniff Father Philbert's glass. To my surprise, scotch. Here was proof that Father Burner considered Father Philbert a friend. At that moment I could not think what it was he expected to get out of a lowly missionary. My mistake, not realizing then how correct and prophetic I'd been earlier in thinking of them as two of a kind. It seldom happened that Father Burner got out the real scotch for company, or for himself *in* company. For most guests he had nothing—a safe policy, since a surprising number of temperance cranks passed through the rectory—and for unwelcome guests who would like a drink he kept a bottle of "scotch-type" whiskey, which was a smooth, smoky blend of furniture polish that came in a fancy bottle, was offensive even when watered, and cheap, though rather hard to get since the end of the war. He had a charming way of plucking the rare bottle from a bureau drawer, as if this were indeed an occasion for him; even so, he would not touch the stuff, presenting himself as a chap of simple tastes, of no taste at all for the things of this world, who would prefer, if anything, the rude wine made from our own grapes—if we'd had any grapes. Quite an act, and one he thoroughly enjoyed, holding his glass of pure water and asking, "How's your drink, Father? Strong enough?"

The housekeeper, appearing at the door, said there'd been a change of plans and some of the ushers were driving Father Malt to the train.

"Has he gone yet?" asked Father Burner.

"Not yet, Father."

"Well, tell him good-bye for me."

"Yes, Father."

When she had gone, he said, "I'd tell him myself, but I don't want to run into that bunch."

Father Philbert smiled. "What's he up to in Chicago?"

"They've got one of those pastors' and builders' conventions going on at the Stevens Hotel."

"Is he building?"

"No, but he's a pastor and he'll get a lot of free samples. He won't buy anything."

"Not much has been done around here, huh?" said Father Philbert.

He had fed Father Burner the question he wanted. "He built that fish pond in the back yard—for his minnows. That's the extent of the building program in his time. Of course he's only been here a while."

"How long?"

"Fourteen years," said Father Burner. *He* would be the greatest builder of them all—if he ever got the chance. He lit a cigarette and smiled. "What he's really going to Chicago for is to see a couple of ball games."

Father Philbert did not smile. "Who's playing there now?" he said.

A little irritated at this interest, Father Burner said, "I believe it's the Red Sox—or is it the Reds? Hell, how do I know?"

"Couldn't be the Reds," said Father Philbert. "The boy and I were in Cincinnati last week and it was the start of a long home stand for them."

"Very likely," said Father Burner.

While the missionary, a Cardinal fan, analyzed the pennant race in the National League, Father Burner sulked. "What's the best train out of Chicago for Washington?" he suddenly inquired.

Father Philbert told him what he could, but admitted that his information dated from some years back. "We don't make the run to Washington anymore."

"That's right," said Father Burner. "Washington's in the American League."

Father Philbert laughed, turning aside the point that he traveled with the Cardinals. "I thought you didn't know about these things," he said.

"About these things it's impossible to stay ignorant," said Father Burner. "Here, and the last place, and the place before that, and in the seminary—a ball, a bat, and God. I'll be damned, Father, if I'll do as the Romans do."

"What price glory?" inquired Father Philbert, as if he smelt heresy.

"I know," said Father Burner. "And it'll probably cost me the red hat." A brave comment, perhaps, from a man not yet a country pastor, and it showed me where his thoughts were again. He did not disguise his humble ambition by speaking lightly of an impossible one. "Scratch a prelate and you'll find a second baseman," he fumed.

Father Philbert tried to change the subject. "Somebody told me Father Malt's the exorcist for the diocese."

"Used to be." Father Burner's eyes flickered balefully.

"Overdid it, huh?" asked Father Philbert—as if he hadn't heard!

"Some." I expected Father Burner to say more. He could have told some pretty wild stories, the gist of them all that Father Malt, as an exorcist, was perhaps a little quick on the trigger. He had stuck pretty much to livestock, however, which was to his credit in the human view.

"Much scandal?"

"Some."

"Nothing serious, though?"

"No."

"Suppose it depends on what you call serious."

Father Burner did not reply. He had become oddly morose. Perhaps he felt that he was being catered to out of pity, or that

Father Philbert, in giving him so many opportunities to talk against Father Malt, was tempting him.

"Who plays the accordion?" inquired Father Philbert, hearing it downstairs.

"He does."

"Go on!"

"Sure."

"How can he hear what he's playing?"

"What's the difference—if he plays an accordion?"

Father Philbert laughed. He removed the cellophane from a cigar, and then he saw me. And at that moment I made no attempt to hide. "There's that damn cat."

"His assistant!" said Father Burner with surprising bitterness. "Coadjutor with right of succession."

Father Philbert balled up the cellophane and tossed it at the wastebasket, missing.

"Get it," he said to me fatuously.

I ignored him, walking slowly toward the door.

Father Burner made a quick movement with his feet, which were something to behold, but I knew he wouldn't get up, and took my sweet time.

Father Philbert inquired, "Will she catch mice?"

She! Since coming to live at the rectory, I've been celibate, it's true, but I daresay I'm as manly as the next one. And Father Burner, who might have done me the favor of putting him straight, said nothing.

"She looks pretty fat to be much of a mouser."

I just stared at the poor man then, as much as to say that I'd think one so interested in catching mice would have heard of a little thing called the mousetrap. After one last dirty look, I left them to themselves—to punish each other with their company.

I strolled down the hall, trying to remember when I'd last had a mouse. Going past the room occupied by the young missionary, I smiled upon his door, which was shut, confident that he was inside hard at his prayers.

The next morning, shortly after breakfast, which I took, as usual, in the kitchen, I headed for the cool orchard, to which I often repaired on just such a day as this one promised to be. I had no appetite for the sparrows hopping from tree to tree above me, but there seemed no way to convince them of that. Each one, so great is his vanity, thinks himself eminently edible. Peace, peace, they cry, and there is no peace. Finally, tired of their noise, I got up from the matted grass and left, leveling my ears and flailing my tail, in a fake dudgeon that inspired the males to feats of stunt flying and terrorized the young females most delightfully.

I went then to another favorite spot of mine, that bosky strip of green between the church and the brick sidewalk. Here, however, the horseflies found me, and as if that were not enough, visions of stray dogs and children came between me and the kind of sleep I badly needed after an uncommonly restless night.

When afternoon came, I remembered that it was Saturday, and that I could have the rectory to myself. Father Burner and the missionaries would be busy with confessions. By this time the temperature had reached its peak, and though I felt sorry for the young missionary, I must admit the thought of the other two sweltering in the confessionals refreshed me. The rest of the afternoon I must have slept something approaching the sleep of the just.

I suppose it was the sound of dishes that roused me. I rushed into the dining room, not bothering to wash up, and took my customary place at the table. Only then did I consider the empty chair next to me—the utter void. This, I thought, is a foreshadowing of what I must someday face—this, and Father Burner munching away at the other end of the table. And there was the immediate problem: no one to serve me. The young missionary smiled at me, but how can you eat a smile? The other two, looking rather wilted—to their hot boxes I wished them swift return—talked in expiring tones of reserved sins and did not appear to notice me. Our first meal together without Father Malt did not pass without incident, however. It all came about when the young missionary extended a thin sliver of meat to me.

"Hey, don't do that!" said Father Philbert. "You'll never make a mouser out of her that way."

Father Burner, too, regarded the young missionary with disapproval.

"Just this one piece," said the young missionary. The meat was already in my mouth.

"Well, watch it in the future," said Father Philbert. It was the word "future" that worried me. Did it mean that he had arranged to cut off my sustenance in the kitchen too? Did it mean that until Father Malt returned I had to choose between mousing and fasting?

I continued to think along these melancholy lines until the repast, which had never begun for me, ended for them. Then I whisked into the kitchen, where I received the usual bowl of milk. But whether the housekeeper, accustomed as she was to having me eat my main course at table, assumed there had been no change in my life, or was now acting under instructions from these villains, I don't know. I was too sickened by their meanness to have any appetite. When the pastor's away, the curates will play, I thought. On the whole I was feeling pretty glum.

It was our custom to have the main meal at noon on Sundays. I arrived early, before the others, hungrier than I'd been for as long as I could remember, and still I had little or no expectation of food at this table. I was there for one purpose—

to assert myself—and possibly, where the young missionary was concerned, to incite sympathy for myself and contempt for my persecutors. By this time I knew that to be the name for them.

They entered the dining room, just the two of them.

"Where's the kid?" asked Father Burner.

"He's not feeling well," said Father Philbert.

I was not surprised. They'd arranged between the two of them to have him say the six and eleven o'clock Masses, which meant, of course, that he'd fasted in the interval. I had not thought of him as the hardy type, either.

"I'll have the housekeeper take him some beef broth," said Father Burner. Damned white of you, I was thinking, when he suddenly whirled and swept me off my chair. Then he picked it up and placed it against the wall. Then he went to the lower end of the table, removed his plate and silverware, and brought them to Father Malt's place. Talking and fuming to himself, he sat down in Father Malt's chair. I did not appear very brave, I fear, cowering under mine.

Father Philbert, who had been watching with interest, now greeted the new order with a cheer. "Attaboy, Ernest!"

Father Burner began to justify himself. "More light here," he said, and added, "Cats kill birds," and for some reason he was puffing.

"If they'd just kill mice," said Father Philbert, "they wouldn't be so bad." He had a one-track mind if I ever saw one.

"Wonder how many that black devil's caught in his time?" said Father Burner, airing a common prejudice against cats of my shade (though I do have a white collar). He looked over at me. "Ssssss," he said. But I held my ground.

"I'll take a dog any day," said the platitudinous Father Philbert.

"Me, too."

After a bit, during which time they played hard with the

roast, Father Philbert said, "How about taking her for a ride in the country?"

"Hell," said Father Burner, "he'd just come back."

"Not if we did it right, she wouldn't."

"Look," said Father Burner. "Some friends of mine dropped a cat off the high bridge in St Paul. They saw him go under in mid-channel. I'm talking about the Mississippi, understand. Thought they'd never lay eyes on that animal again. That's what they thought. He was back at the house before they were." Father Burner paused—he could see that he was not convincing Father Philbert—and then he tried again. "That's a fact, Father. They might've played a quick round of golf before they got back. Cat didn't even look damp, they said. He's still there. Case a lot like this. Except now they're afraid of *him*."

To Father Burner's displeasure, Father Philbert refused to be awed or even puzzled. He simply inquired, "But did they use a bag? Weights?"

"Millstones," snapped Father Burner. "Don't quibble."

Then they fell to discussing the burial customs of gangsters —poured concrete and the rest—and became so engrossed in the matter that they forgot all about me.

Over against the wall, I was quietly working up the courage to act against them. When I felt sufficiently lionhearted, I leaped up and occupied my chair. Expecting blows and vilification, I encountered only indifference. I saw then how far I'd come down in their estimation. Already the remembrance of things past—the disease of noble politicals in exile—was too strong in me, the hope of restoration unwarrantably faint.

At the end of the meal, returning to me, Father Philbert remarked, "I think I know a better way." Rising, he snatched the crucifix off the wall, passed it to a bewildered Father Burner, and, saying "Nice Kitty," grabbed me behind the ears. "Hold it up to her," said Father Philbert. Father Burner held the crucifix up to me. "See that?" said Father Philbert to my face. I miaowed. "Take that!" said Father Philbert, cuffing me. He pushed my face into the crucifix again. "See that?" he said again, but I knew what to expect next, and when he cuffed me, I went for his hand with my mouth, pinking him nicely on the wrist. Evidently Father Burner had begun to understand and appreciate the proceedings. Although I was in a good position to observe everything, I could not say as much for myself. "Association," said Father Burner with mysterious satisfaction, almost with zest. He poked the crucifix at me. "If he's just smart enough to react properly," he said. "Oh, she's plenty smart," said Father Philbert, sucking his wrist and giving himself, I hoped, hydrophobia. He scuffed off one of his sandals for a paddle. Father Burner, fingering the crucifix nervously, inquired, "Sure it's all right to go on with this thing?" "It's the intention that counts in these things," said Father Philbert. "Our motive is clear enough." And they went at me again.

After that first taste of the sandal in the dining room, I foolishly believed I would be safe as long as I stayed away from the table; there was something about my presence there, I thought, that brought out the beast in them—which is to say very nearly all that was in them. But they caught me in the upstairs hall the same evening, one brute thundering down upon me, the other sealing off my only avenue of escape. And this beating was worse than the first—preceded as it was by a short delay that I mistook for a reprieve until Father Burner, who had gone downstairs muttering something about "leaving no margin for error," returned with the crucifix from the dining room, although we had them hanging all over the house. The young missionary, coming upon them while they were at me, turned away. "I wash my hands of it," he said. I thought he might have done more.

Out of mind, bruised of body, sick at heart, for two days and nights I held on, I know not how or why—unless I lived in hope of vengeance. I wanted simple justice, a large order in it-self, but I would never have settled for that alone. I wanted nothing less than my revenge.

I kept to the neighborhood, but avoided the rectory. I believed, of course, that their only strategy was to drive me away. I derived some little satisfaction from making my-self scarce, for it was thus I deceived them into thinking their plan to banish me successful. But this was my single comfort during this hard time, and it was as nothing against their crimes.

I spent the nights in the open fields. I reeled, dizzy with hunger, until I bagged an aged field mouse. It tasted bitter to me, this stale provender, and seemed, as I swallowed it, an ironic concession to the enemy. I vowed I'd starve before I ate another mouse. By way of retribution to myself, I stalked spar-rows in the orchard—hating myself for it but persisting all the more when I thought of those bird-lovers, my persecutors, before whom I could stand and say in self-redemption, "You made me what I am now. You thrust the killer's part upon me." Fortunately, I did not flush a single sparrow. Since *my* motive was clear enough, however, I'd had the pleasure of sin-ning against them and their ideals, the pleasure without the feathers and mess.

On Tuesday, the third day, all caution, I took up my post in the lilac bush beside the garage. Not until Father Malt re-turned, I knew, would I be safe in daylight. He arrived along about dinnertime, and I must say the very sight of him aroused a sentiment in me akin to human affection. The youngest usher, who must have had the afternoon off to meet him at the station in St Paul, carried the new bag before him into the rec-tory. It was for me an act symbolic of the counterrevolution to come. I did not rush out from my hiding place, however. I had suffered too much to play the fool now. Instead I slipped into the kitchen by way of the flap in the screen door, which they had not thought to barricade. I waited under the stove for my moment, like an actor in the wings.

Presently I heard them tramping into the dining room and seating themselves, and Father Malt's voice saying, "I had a long talk with the Archbishop." (I could almost hear Father Burner praying, Did he say anything about *me*?) And then, "Where's Fritz?"

"He hasn't been around lately," said Father Burner cunningly. He would not tell the truth and he would not tell a lie.

"You know, there's something mighty funny about that cat," said Father Philbert. "We think she's possessed."

I was astonished, and would have liked a moment to think it over, but by now I was already entering the room.

"*Possessed!*" said Father Malt. "Aw, no!"

"Ah, yes," said Father Burner, going for the meat right away. "And good riddance."

And then I miaowed and they saw me.

"Quick!" said Father Philbert, who made a nice recovery after involuntarily reaching for me and his sandal at the same time. Father Burner ran to the wall for the crucifix, which had been, until now, a mysterious and possibly blasphemous feature of my beatings—the crucifix held up to me by the one not scourging at the moment, as if it were the will behind my punishment. They had schooled me well, for even now, at the sight of the crucifix, an undeniable fear was rising in me. Father Burner handed it to Father Malt.

"Now you'll see," said Father Philbert.

"We'll leave it up to you," said Father Burner.

I found now that I could not help myself. What followed was hidden from them—from human eyes. I gave myself over entirely to the fear they'd beaten into me, and in a moment, according to their plan, I was fleeing the crucifix as one truly possessed, out of the dining room and into the kitchen, and from there, blindly, along the house and through the shrubbery, ending in the street, where a powerful gray car ran over me—and where I gave up the old ghost for a new one.

Simultaneously, reborn, redeemed from my previous fear, identical with my former self, so far as they could see, and still in their midst, I padded up to Father Malt—he still sat gripping the crucifix—and jumped into his lap. I heard the young missionary arriving from an errand in Father Philbert's *brother's* car, late for dinner he thought, but just in time to see the stricken look I saw coming into the eyes of my persecutors. This look alone made up for everything I'd suffered at their hands. Purring now, I was rubbing up against the crucifix, myself effecting my utter revenge.

"What have we done?" cried Father Philbert. He was basically an emotional dolt and would have voted then for my canonization.

"I ran over a cat!" said the young missionary excitedly. "I'd swear it was this one. When I looked, there was nothing there!"

"Better go upstairs and rest," growled Father Burner. He sat down—it was good to see him in his proper spot at the low end of the table—as if to wait a long time, or so it seemed to me. I found myself wondering if I could possibly bring about his transfer to another parish—one where they had a devil for a pastor and several assistants, where he would be able to start at the bottom again.

But first things first, I always say, and all in good season, for now Father Malt himself was drawing my chair up to the table, restoring me to my rightful place.

THE POOR THING

HER PENSION FROM the store wasn't enough. She tried to conceal this from Mrs Shepherd, saying she *preferred* to be doing something, but knew she sounded like a person in need of a job, and she had, after all, come to an employment agency. Mrs Shepherd, however, found a word for it. "Oh, you mean you want to *supplement* your income." And to that Teresa could agree.

The next day Mrs Shepherd called. She was in a spot, she said, or she wouldn't ask Teresa to consider what she had to offer. It wasn't the kind of position Teresa was down for, but perhaps she'd accept it on a temporary basis.

"You know, Mrs Shepherd, I don't *have* to work."

"My dear, I know you don't. You just want to supplement your income."

"Yes, and I like to be doing something."

"My dear, I know how you feel."

"And I'm down for light sewing."

"Of course you are. I don't know what ever made me think

of you for this—except they want a nice refined person that's a Catholic."

Teresa, dreaming over the compliment, heard Mrs Shepherd say, "This party isn't offering enough. In fact, I hate to tell you what it is. Say, I wonder if you'd just let me call them back and maybe I can get you more money. If I can't, I don't want you to even consider it. How's that?"

"Well, all right," Teresa said, "but I don't have to work."

When Mrs Shepherd called again, Teresa said it wasn't very much money and not in her line at all and would not be persuaded—until Mrs Shepherd said something indirectly about their friendship.

The next morning Teresa got on the streetcar and rode out into the suburbs. Mrs Shepherd had referred to Teresa's charge-to-be as a semi-invalid. The poor thing who met Teresa at the door in a wheelchair wore an artificial flower in her artificial hair, but had the face of a child, small, sweet, gay. Her name was Dorothy. She had always been Dolly to everybody, however, and it did seem to fit her.

Teresa could truthfully say to Mrs Shepherd, who called up that evening to ask how things were going, that the poor dear was no trouble at all, neat as a pin, nice as you please, and that they were already calling each other by their first names. Mrs Shepherd was glad to hear it, she said, but she hadn't forgotten that Teresa was down for light sewing. Teresa only had to say the word if she wanted to make a change.

Teresa's duties were those of a companion. She went home at night, and had Saturdays and Sundays off. Dolly's sister, a teacher, got breakfast in the morning and was home in time to prepare dinner. For lunch, Teresa served green tea, cinnamon toast, and a leafy vegetable. Over Dolly's protests, she did some housecleaning. At first Dolly tried to help. Then she tried to get Teresa to give it up and listen to the radio.

That was how Dolly spent the day, dialing from memory,

charting her course at fifteen-minute intervals, from Fred Waring in the morning to Morton Downey at night. In between came the dramatic programs that Teresa, as a working person, had scarcely known about. Dolly was a great one for writing in to the stations. She'd been in correspondence with CBS all during all the criminal trials of Lord Henry Brinthrop (of Black Swan Hall) in "Our Gal Sunday." She was one of those faithful listeners who plead with the networks to bring back deceased characters, but it wasn't the lovable ones who concerned her. She said some of the bad ones got off too easily, "just dying." One afternoon she chanced to dial to "Make Believe Ballroom," a program of popular recordings, and got the idea that it should include *some* sacred music. (After a week of constant listening, they heard the announcer read Dolly's letter and ask listeners for their views. Dolly, expecting trouble, wrote another letter, but that was the last they heard of her suggestion.)

They were getting to know each other. Dolly, who had always been an invalid, said she'd hoped in the past that something might be done for her. Now, however, she was resigned to God's will (she had visited St Anne de Beaupré in Canada, where it had not been God's will to cure her, and Lourdes was too far and expensive), but, really, she wasn't to be pitied, she said, when you considered the poor souls in the "leopard colonies." The sufferings of the "leopards" were much with Dolly, and she sent them a dollar a month, wishing it might be more. They often discussed the leopards—too often to suit Teresa. Dolly had read a great deal about them and knew of the most frightful cases, which she told about, she said, to excite sympathy in herself and others. Teresa said she was having nightmares from hearing about the cases (in fact she wasn't). "Which one? Which one?" Dolly wanted to know, but Teresa wouldn't lie anymore to her. Dolly said she was sorry. She didn't stop her awful stories, however.

Mrs Shepherd called again. "Still getting along famously?"

Teresa, a little disturbed to hear Mrs Shepherd speak of her as a party she'd "placed," which sounded so permanent, said that she had no complaints.

One rainy afternoon when it was so dark they should have had a light, and with the radio off on account of lightning, Dolly said, "Teresa, I consider you my best friend." For some reason Teresa was moved to say that she might have married. The first time she had been too young, or so she had been told, and the second time, also the last time, she had been living with some people who hadn't wanted her to leave them. They hadn't been relatives or close friends, or even friends until she moved in, just people with whom she'd roomed, that was all. Dolly seemed to understand. Teresa could not say that she did, now, but was grateful to Dolly for not scolding or ridiculing her—others had.

Dolly said, "If you'd got married, Teresa, just think—maybe you wouldn't be here today. Now tell me how you got your first raise at the store."

Dolly, for someone who liked to talk, was a good listener, though she occasionally missed the point, or discovered one that Teresa could never find. "You want to hear that again? I declare, Dolly, you're a funny one."

So Teresa told her again how she'd seen this notice in the paper that the store had declared a dividend and how she'd worried all night over what she knew she must do in the morning. The first thing, then, after hanging up her coat and hat, she went to the supervisor of the sewing room. The supervisor sat on an elevated chair, a kind of throne in that mean setting, and stared down on the girls below.

"How'd she look, Teresa?"

Teresa made the face she'd made the first time, now an indispensable feature of the story.

"What'd you do then, Teresa?"

"I said, 'If you please, Miss Merck, I see by the paper the store declared a dividend.' "

Dolly clapped her hands. "How'd she look then?"

"My lands, do I have to go through it all again?"

"Please."

Teresa made the face again.

"Then what?"

"I said, 'If the store can declare a dividend they ought to be able to pay me more than five dollars a week. It's not very much to live on.' "

Dolly crushed her hands to her face. "Oh, Teresa, you shouldn't have said it!"

"Of course," Teresa said, "that was years ago. They have to pay good now."

"Go on, Teresa."

Now Miss Merck was getting down from her throne and directing Teresa to follow her into the cloakroom.

"Oh, oh," Dolly said. "Now you're gonna catch it."

"I thought she was going to show me the door."

"Show me how she walked, Teresa."

Teresa stood up and did a slow goose step across the room.

"Oh, Lord, Teresa! Don't I pity you!"

Teresa growled a little, which was not in the original Miss Merck, or even in the part as she'd previously played it for Dolly, and it was a great success. Dolly swooned, her head toppling back on her pillow, her eyes closed against the reality of Miss Merck, but still peeking. When she had recovered, Teresa continued—as Miss Merck herself:

"Girl, you're a poor hand with a needle!"

"Oh, you were not!" cried Dolly.

"Of course I wasn't," said Teresa, "but that was part of her game."

"No!"

"Oh, yes."

"Go on."

"Girl, how can you expect to be kept on at the present wage, let alone get a raise?"

"Oh, Teresa, you're gonna lose your job!"

"I'll admit I was going for my hat and coat," said Teresa, pausing to remember.

"Is that all?"

"You know it isn't."

"All right, Teresa."

"But"—and to Miss Merck's voice something nastier had been added—"sewing isn't everything. Do *I* sew, girl?"

"What'd she mean? What'd she mean?"

"You know what she meant. She came right out with it then. She wanted me to be her assistant, at seven dollars a week. And she said not to tell the other girls about the dividend."

"That's not all, Teresa. You're not telling it all."

"That's how I got my raise. That's what you asked to hear."

"Please, Teresa."

"All right—and when she died I got her job."

"*Died!*"

"Yes."

"You got her job when she died—?"

"Of cancer."

"*Cancer!*"

And now it was just as though they were back on the leopards, with Dolly telling how, one by one, their members fell off. For Teresa the story ended in the raise and promotion, not in her succession to the throne on Miss Merck's death or the cause of it.

"I'm glad I'm not a cancer person," Dolly would say when they were looking up birthdays in the almanac. Dolly was fascinated by the Crab in the zodiac, and by Leo, her sign, which reminded her of the early Christian martyrs. "I wouldn't be afraid to die that way, would you, Teresa?"

"I certainly would."

"So would *I!*"

Teresa made a mistake when she mentioned her brother and his family and the good time she'd had with them one summer, long ago, at a lake cottage. (She remembered telling her little niece and nephew that she'd like to be one of the cows they saw standing in a flooded meadow, and they'd thought she really meant it. They'd told strangers, in an eating place where they'd stopped, that their aunt wanted to be a cow. "Oh, no, Teresa," cried Dolly, going deeper into the matter. "And have some rough farmer . . .") The trouble was that Dolly was forever asking if the little drowning victims she read about weren't just the age of Teresa's little nephew or niece, and wasn't it a wonder they hadn't all drowned in Wisconsin? Teresa would snap, "They're grown-up now," or, "They don't go there anymore."

Dolly gave Teresa a package for her niece and nephew one day, saying it was hard to find something that boys and girls both liked. She wouldn't tell Teresa what was in the package— it was a secret. "Hold it to your ear. Just tell them that. Say it a hundred times to yourself, Teresa, so you won't forget." When Teresa got home, she looked inside the package, and a good thing she had. All done up in tissue paper was an old sea shell, with a little card, "Your unknown friend, Dolly S." When Dolly asked how they'd liked the gift, Teresa said she hadn't given it to them yet. Finally, one day, tired of being asked about it, she said, "They liked it fine. They use it all the time."

Dolly was tight. She took the longest time rooting in her purse for the three cents she owed Teresa for a stamp. (She wanted Teresa to buy stamps one at a time, as if expecting the market to break, but Teresa secretly bought a supply and retailed them to Dolly as needed.) And one week Teresa paid the paper boy and never did get it back. Dolly hated the time when she must send her dollar to the leopards. "Well," she'd say, as if she were a woman in her first pregnancy, "it won't be long now." When the day arrived, sweat broke out all over the poor thing. "Oh, come on, cheer up," Teresa said about the third time this happened, and tossed a dollar into her lap.

Dolly would not take it, she said, taking it. She tried to swear Teresa to a like amount regularly, saying they could rotate the months, which came too often for one. "Pledge yourself, Teresa."

"I won't do it, not for you or anybody. And besides I may not be here."

"Oh, Teresa, don't say that!"

Then Dolly tried to convert Teresa to her special devotions. But Teresa was wary of coming under Dolly's spiritual guidance, embarrassed too at the thought of praying with anyone unless in church. When Dolly persisted, rattling off the indulgences to be gained here and there (she kept books and knew exactly how many days she had coming), Teresa said it was her privilege to worship as she pleased.

One Monday morning, when Dolly met Teresa at the front door, she held some little wads of paper in her outstretched hand.

"What's all this?"

"Go ahead and draw one, Teresa. See what you have to practice this week." Teresa drew one. Dolly, after shaking the wads like dice, opened her hand and selected one.

"What's yours, Teresa?"

" 'Kindness to others.' I can't read the rest."

"Is it 'Alms for the leopards'?"

"I guess it is. What's yours?"

Dolly sighed, " 'More prayers for the poor souls in purgatory.' "

In the ensuing weeks, Dolly's assignments all had to do with prayer, for a variety of beneficiaries, and Teresa was stuck with "kindness to others" and "alms." Dolly kept the extra wads on her person, and so Teresa had no opportunity to investigate the possibility of fraud. Dolly went on as though she had much the worst of it, and to hear her tell it, she didn't have a free minute from her prayers.

When Teresa gave a short answer, Dolly would remind her that she was supposed to be practicing kindness that week. Sometimes Dolly would ask the silliest questions.

"Do you smoke, Teresa?"

"Once in a while is all."

"Teresa! I know you don't. You don't look it."

"Then why'd you ask?"

"I don't call that kindness to others, Teresa."

Teresa, for her part, did not blame the priest for not coming every week to hear Dolly's confession, a principal complaint with her. Once, when he was there, Teresa had heard Dolly confess, "I missed my morning prayers two times, Father."

"Is that all?"

"Is that all!"

The next time Dolly complained about the priest's not coming often enough, Teresa said, "If you told him half the things you do, you wouldn't want him to come so often. You never think to tell him all those mean things you say about the woman across the way. Don't forget Our Lord was a Jew."

"Teresa! Our Lord was a Galilean. And remember what you're practicing this week."

When Dolly pouted, and she might if the programs were good enough to hold her, Teresa was glad for the rest. Too soon, she knew, Dolly would roll into the next room and start up some fool thing.

"Teresa, have your brother come out sometime and see where you work."

"Huh! I don't have to work. Why would he want to come 'way out here? He's got a nice place of his own."

"Hasn't he got a car, Teresa?"

"He doesn't need a car."

"How old do you think I am, Teresa?"

"How do I know how old you are?"

"Oh, go ahead, guess."

"Why should I guess how old you are?"

"Oh, go ahead, Teresa."

"Eighty."

"Teresa!"

With that little baby face she had, though, she really looked younger than she was (younger than Teresa, in fact), and she knew it. But then she never did a lick of work in her life—but how could she, the poor thing!

Dolly had one very bad habit. They might be talking about the leopards when, suddenly, sitting perfectly still in her wheelchair, she'd catch Teresa's eye. Then, giggling slightly, she would push up her wig, inch by inch, showing more and more scalp. When this started now, Teresa looked the other way and left the room. The first time it happened, however, she'd seen all of Dolly's bone-white head. Teresa didn't know what this meant —Dolly didn't call it anything and Teresa wouldn't ask—but it certainly wasn't very nice. She thought of reporting it to Dolly's sister, but did not, each time hoping it wouldn't happen again.

But finally she did call Mrs Shepherd and say she didn't know how much longer she could stay on the job. She really felt sorry for the poor thing, but she had to think of herself too. Mrs Shepherd asked Teresa to give it another chance—at least until something turned up in her line, which might be any day now—and Teresa said, "Well, all right . . ."

For a week they were engaged in preparations for the priest, who had finally accepted Dolly's invitation to dinner—for Saturday, however—and Teresa knew he intended to eat and run, pleading confessions to be heard, and she certainly didn't blame

him. She had been asked to work Saturday and to stay overnight because, as Dolly put it, "it might be late before it's all
over." She planned to serve ginger ale later on, after she read
her poems to him. (Dolly gave Teresa a copy of every one she
wrote, and on some days she wrote many. Teresa kept only
one, because it was a little like *Trees*.

> A sight more lovely and sweet
> Nowhere on earth have I seen
> Than the little bundles of meat
> In mothers' arms I mean.)

Teresa cleaned the whole house, and Dolly got out the sick-
call kit and checked over the candles, crucifix, and cotton.
Teresa asked what she was doing—getting ready to be sick
while she had the priest in the house to pray over her? Dolly
said she knew what she was doing. She said the priest might
want to inspect the kit.

"Teresa, what dress are you going to wear tomorrow night?"

"I don't know."

"Teresa, why don't you wear your nice blue one with the
white collar and cuffs?"

"You can't fool me, Dolly. I know you. You want me to look
like the maid."

Dolly smiled and said, "Well?"

More than just put out, really hurt, Teresa retired to the
other side of the house, taking the vacuum cleaner with her.
Dolly was afraid of the vacuum cleaner, and the rest of the
morning Teresa kept it going strong. Often, if she craved a little peace and quiet, she would switch it on in another room
and just let it run while she read a magazine. And sometimes
when Dolly came snooping, Teresa got up and started after her
with the vacuum cleaner, sending her wheeling and squealing
back to her radio.

That day, while Dolly was in the bathtub, Teresa phoned Mrs Shepherd. She'd had enough, she said, and was quitting at the end of the day. It was Friday, and Dolly's sister would be home over Saturday and Sunday, and maybe by Monday they'd have somebody else. Anyway, she was through. No, she wasn't mad. She was just through. She couldn't be mad at the poor thing, though that one could be very mean. Mrs Shepherd, who must have sensed it was no use, said she understood, said she was grateful to Teresa, and would just have to buckle down and find somebody else. She thought something in light sewing would turn up very soon. In fact, she had a lead.

Teresa returned to Dolly thinking—and what if they can't find anybody to look after the poor thing?—and feeling sorry for her, until she said, "Next fall, Teresa, with winter coming on and everything, people will be looking for work. You're lucky to be here, Teresa."

"Huh! I don't have to work. I own property in Florida." Teresa's property, which she'd never seen, had cost fourteen hundred dollars in 1928, and she'd always told Dolly what they'd told her, that it would be worth a lot more someday. Recently it had been appraised at "Twenty-five dollars or maybe fifty."

When Dolly's sister came home, Teresa gave her the bad news. She was sorry, she said, going at once for her coat and things. Maybe they'd be able to get somebody by Monday. Dolly cried. Dolly's sister, paying up only when Teresa had her coat on, offered her an extra dollar as a bonus, but Teresa said, "No, thanks," and hoped they understood. A dollar!

That evening Teresa celebrated by eating in a new cafeteria, and after dinner she saw a double feature. The next day, Saturday, she slept late. Toward sundown she thought of Dolly: now she's dusting the furniture from her wheel chair, now she's got the wig in her hands, tying the flower into it, now she's waiting by the door for the priest to come, now they're sitting down to it, now they're eating the cake Teresa had baked, and now, much too soon for the poor thing, before she could read her poems, the priest had gone, and the unopened bottle of ginger ale chilled on in the refrigerator.

By Sunday afternoon Teresa was getting tired of her little apartment and beginning to consider a quick visit to her relatives downstate. But that evening Mrs Shepherd called.

"Teresa?"

"Yes."

"Remember that lead I spoke to you about?"

"Yes."

"I'm afraid it fell through."

"Oh." Teresa was afraid of what was coming.

"Teresa, will you help me out—try it just one more week, maybe just a day or two, just until I get someone?"

"Oh, no . . ."

"You won't reconsider?"

"Oh, no . . ."

"Teresa, I already told them you'd come tomorrow. I mean I was sure you'd help me out of this spot. I mean I just knew you'd do it for me."

"But, Mrs Shepherd . . ."

"As a friend, Teresa?"

Teresa was holding her breath for fear she'd weaken.

"Good night, Teresa, and thanks anyway."

A few minutes later Mrs Shepherd called again.

"I told them you weren't coming, Teresa," said Mrs Shepherd as though she expected to be thanked for it. "Teresa, that Dolly—did you ever notice anything about her?"

"What about her? She's been an invalid all her life."

"I mean—did she seem all right—otherwise?"

"Well, I wouldn't say she's crazy—if that's what you mean."

"Then I don't understand it. She said you stole some money

from her and that's why you quit. She says that's why you won't come back . . ."

Teresa lay awake until shortly before the alarm went off in the morning. At the usual time, she got on the streetcar and rode out into the suburbs. Coming up the walk, she saw Dolly's face at the level of the window sill, waiting. As always, the door chain, protection against burglars and rapists, was on, but after a moment, Dolly admitted her. "You poor thing!" Dolly cried.

Before Teresa could say a word, Dolly put the blame on herself. Having the priest over, she said, had upset her so. The money had not been stolen. She had just forgotten all about paying out for the bottle of ginger ale. "And it's still there, Teresa, untouched. Oh, let's have a glass! Let's do! In honor of your coming back!" Dolly twirled herself down the hall, calling back, "You'll have to get it down, Teresa. After all, you're the one put it 'way up there by the ice cubes." Then in a gay reproving voice, "Teresa, this wouldn't have happened if you hadn't done *that*!"

THE DEVIL WAS THE JOKER

MR McMASTER, a hernia case convalescing in one of the four-bed wards, was fat and fifty or so, with a candy-pink face, sparse orange hair, and popeyes. ("Eyes don't permit me to read much," he had told Myles Flynn, the night orderly, more than once.) On his last evening in the hospital, as he lay in his bed smoking, his hands clasped over a box of Havanas that rested on the soft dais of his stomach, he called Myles to his bedside. He wanted to thank him, he said, and, incidentally, he had no use for "that other son of a bitch"—meaning the other orderly, an engineering student, who had prepped him for surgery. "A hell of a fine engineer he'll make. You, though, you're different—more like a doctor than an orderly—and I was surprised to hear from one of the Sisters today that you're not going into the medical field." Mr McMaster said he supposed there must be other reasons for working in a hospital, but he didn't sound as though he knew any.

Myles said he'd been four years in a seminary, studying for the priesthood—until "something happened." There he stopped.

Mr McMaster grinned. "To make a long story short," he said.

Myles shook his head. He'd told Mr McMaster all there was for him to tell—all he knew. He'd simply been asked to leave, he said, and since that day, three months before, he'd just been trying to make himself useful to society, here in the hospital. Mr McMaster suddenly got serious. He wondered, in a whisper, whether Myles was "a cradle Catholic," as if that had something to do with his expulsion, and Myles said, "Yes. Almost have to be with a name like mine." "Not a-tall," said Mr McMaster. "That's the hell of it. The other day I met a Jew by the name of Buckingham. Some Buckingham!"

Scenting liquor on the patient's breath, Myles supposed that Mr McMaster, like so many salesmen or executives on their last evening, wanted to get a good night's rest, to be ready for the morrow, when he would ride away in a taxicab to the daily battle of Chicago.

Again Mr McMaster asked if Myles was a cradle Catholic, and when Myles again told him he was, Mr McMaster said, "Call me Mac," and had Myles move the screen over to his bed. When they were hidden from the others in the ward, Mac whispered, "We don't know who they may be, whatever they say." Then he asked Myles if he'd ever heard of the Clementine Fathers. Myles had. "I'm with them," Mac said. "In a goodwill capacity." He described the nature of his work, which was meeting the public, lay and clerical (the emphasis was on the latter), and "building good will" for the Clementine order and finding more readers for the *Clementine*, the family-type magazine published by the Fathers.

Myles listened patiently because he considered it part of his job to do so, but the most he could say for the magazine was that it was probably good—of its kind. Yes, he'd heard the Fathers' radio program. The program, "Father Clem Answers Your Question," was aimed at non-Catholics but it had many faithful listeners among the nuns at the hospital. And the pamphlets put out by the Fathers, many of them written by Father Clem—Myles knew them well. In the hospital waiting rooms, they were read, wrung, and gnawed upon by their captive audience. "Is Father Clem a real person?" Myles asked. "Yes, and no," Mac said, which struck Myles as descriptive of the characters created by Father Clem, an author who tackled life's problems through numberless Joans, Jeans, Bobs, and Bills, clear-thinking college kids who, coached from the wings by jolly nuns and priests, invariably got the best of the arguments they had with the poor devils they were always meeting—atheists, euthanasianists, and the like. "Drive a car?" Mac asked. Myles said yes.

Mac then said he wanted it understood he wasn't making Myles any promises, but he thought there might be a job opening up with the Fathers soon, a job such as his own. "Think it over," Mac said, and Myles did—needing only a moment. He thought of his correspondence with the hierarchy, of the nice replies, all offering him nothing. For his purposes, the job with the Fathers, unsuited as he was to it, could be ideal. Traveling around from diocese to diocese, meeting pastors and even bishops face to face in the regular course of the work, he might make the vital connection that would lead him, somehow, to the priesthood. Without a bishop he'd never get into another seminary—a bishop was more necessary than a vocation—but Myles had more than meeting the right bishop to worry about. He had lost his clerical status, and was now 1-A in the draft. The call-up might come any day.

Working with Mac would be action of a positive sort, better than continuing his fruitless correspondence, better than following such advice as he'd had from acquaintances—or even from the confessional, where, too hopefully, he'd taken his problems. There he had been told to go into business or science and get ahead, or into government and make a success of *that*, after which, presumably, he could come—tottering—before the bishops of the land as a man of proved ability and, what was more important, a man of stability. When the wise old confessor realized, however, that Myles not only had been cast aside by the Church but was likely to be wanted soon by the State, there had been no problem at all. His counsel had flowed swift and sure: "Enlist! Don't wait to be drafted!"

"Don't think of it as just a job," Mac said now. "Try to think of it as the Fathers do, and as I hope I do. Think of it as the Work."

Myles, thinking of it as a stepping-stone to ordination, said he'd like to be considered for the job.

Mac said that of course the Fathers would have the last say, but his word would carry some weight with them, since Myles, if accepted, would be working under him—at first, anyway. He then asked Myles to bring a glass of ice water, and easy on the water. Myles, returning with a glass of ice, noted a bottle in bed with Mac, tucked under the sheet at his side like a nursing infant. He left them together, behind the screen.

Two days later Myles was summoned by telegram to an address in the Loop. He found the place, all right—an old building with grillwork elevators affording passengers a view of the cables. Mac was waiting for Myles at the cigar stand downstairs. As they rode up to the Fathers' floor, he advised Myles to forget all about his past as a seminarian, reasoning that if this was mentioned to the Fathers, it might make a bad impression. Myles had to agree with that, if reluctantly.

At the fifth floor, which the Fathers shared with a number of tailors, publishers, and distributors of barbers' supplies, Mac hustled Myles into the washroom. Myles' black overcoat, suit, and tie were all wrong, Mac said. He told Myles to take off his coat and then he suggested that they switch ties. This they did, morosely. Mac's suit, a double-breasted Glen plaid with a precipitous drape and trousers that billowed about his disproportionately thin legs, would "just carry" the black tie, he said, and presumably his tie, with its spheres, coils, and triangles suggesting the spirit of Science and Industry, would carry Myles' black suit. "Don't want 'em to think they're hiring a creep," Mac said.

There was no trouble at all with the Fathers. Mac evidently stood high with them. He told them that Myles had gone to the University of Illinois for a time, which was news to Myles. He let it pass, though, because he remembered a conversation at the hospital during which, assuming Illinois to be Mac's old school, he had said that he'd once attended a football game at Illinois—or almost had. He had been dragooned into joining the Boy Scouts, Myles had explained, and had marched with his troop to the stadium for the season opener, admission free to Scouts, but on reaching the gates, he had remained outside, in a delayed protest against the Scouts and all their pomps. He had spent the afternoon walking under the campus elms. "Then you were there," Mac had said, which Myles had taken to mean that Mac felt as he did about those beautiful old trees.

Mac delivered a little pep talk, chiefly for the benefit of the three Fathers in the office, Myles suspected, although the words were spoken to him. He could think of nothing to say. He was more impressed by the charitable than the catechetical aspects of the Fathers' work. And yet, little as he might value their radio program, their pamphlets, their dim magazine, it would be work with which he could associate himself with some enthusiasm. It would suit his purposes far better than going into business or staying on at the hospital.

"The Work is one hundred percent apostolic," said one of the Fathers.

Myles remembered that the Fathers ran several institutions for juvenile delinquents. "I know something of your trade schools," he said quickly.

"Would that we had more of them," said the Father sitting behind the desk. He had bloodied his face and neck in shaving. "You have to move with the times." He seemed to be the boss. On the wall behind him hung a metal crucifix, which could have come off a coffin, and a broken airplane propeller, which must have dated from the First World War. "How do you stand in the draft?" he asked Myles.

"All clear," said Mac, answering for him. Myles let that pass, too. He could tell Mac the facts later.

When Myles heard what the salary would be, he was glad he had other reasons for taking the job. The money would be the least important part of it, Mac put in, and Myles could see what he meant. But Myles didn't care about the money; he'd live on bread and water—and pamphlets. The salary made him feel better about not telling Mac and the Fathers that he intended to use his new position, if he could, to meet a bishop. The expense allowance, too, impressed him as decidedly pre-war. Mac, however, seemed to be hinting not at its meanness but at Myles' possible profligacy when, in front of two more Fathers, who had come in to meet Myles, he said, "You'll have to watch your expenses, Flynn. Can't have you asking for reimbursements, you understand." As Myles was leaving, one of the new arrivals whispered to him, "I was on the road myself for a bit and I'd dearly love to go out again. Mr McMaster, he's a grand companion. You'll make a great team."

Three days later the team was heading north in Mac's car, a lightweight black Cadillac, a '41—a good year for a Cadillac, Mac said, and the right car for the job: impressive but not showy, and old enough not to antagonize people.

Myles was not sorry to be leaving Chicago. The nuns and nurses at the hospital had been happy to see him go—happy, they said, that he'd found a better job. This showed Myles how little they had ever understood him and his reasons for being at the hospital; he'd known all along that they had very little sense of vocation.

Speaking of the nurses, Myles told Mac that the corporal works of mercy had lost all meaning in the modern world, to which Mac replied that he wouldn't touch nursing with a ten-foot pole. Nursing might be a fine career for a girl, he allowed, and added, "A lot of 'em marry above themselves—marry money."

They were like two men in a mine, working at different levels, in different veins, and lost to each other. Mac, who apparently still thought of Myles as a doctor, wanted to know how much the interns and nurses knocked down and what their private lives were like—said he'd heard a few stories. When Myles professed ignorance, Mac seemed to think he was being secretive, as if the question went against the Hippocratic oath. He tried to discuss medicine, with special reference to his diet, but failed to interest Myles. He asked what the hospital did with the stiffs, and received no pertinent information, because the question happened to remind Myles of the medieval burial confraternities and he sailed into a long discussion of their blessed work, advocating its revival in the modern world.

"All free, huh?" Mac commented. "The undertakers would love that!"

Myles strove in vain for understanding, always against the wind. Mac had got the idea that Myles, in praising the burial fraternities, was advocating a form of socialized medicine, and he held on to it. "Use logic," he said. "What's right for the undertakers is right for the doctors."

They rode in silence for a while. Then Mac said, "What you say about the nurses may be true, but you gotta remember they don't have it easy." He knew how Myles felt about hospital work, he said, but instead of letting it prey on his mind, Myles should think of other things—of the better days ahead.

J. F. POWERS

Mac implied that Myles' talk about the corporal works was just a cover-up for his failure to get into anything better.

Myles restated his position. Mac, with noticeable patience, said that Myles was too hard on people—too critical of the modern world. "Give it time," he said. When Myles persisted, Mac said, "Let's give it a rest, huh? You wanna take it awhile?" He stopped the car and turned the wheel over to Myles. After watching him pass a Greyhound bus, he appeared to be satisfied that the car was in good hands, and went to sleep.

The first night on the road they stopped in a small town, at the only hotel, which had no bar, and Mac suggested that they go out for a drink. In a tavern, the bartender, when he found out they were from Chicago, showed them his collection of matchbooks with nudes on the cover.

"I have a friend that'll get you all that you want," Mac said to him. "You better avert your eyes, son," he said to Myles. "This is some of that modern world you don't like. He doesn't like our modern world," Mac said to the bartender.

"Maybe he don't know what he's missing."

The bartender seemed anxious to make a deal until Mac asked him to put down a little deposit "as evidence of good faith."

"Do I have to?"

"To me it's immaterial," Mac said. "But I notice it sometimes speeds delivery."

"I can wait."

"All right, if you're sure you can. You write your name and address on a slip of paper and how many you want." While the bartender was doing this, Mac called over to him, "Don't forget your zone number."

"We don't have 'em in this town."

"Oh," Mac said. He gave Myles a look, the wise, doped look of a camel.

The bartender brought the slip of paper over to Mac.

"They gotta be as good as them I got—or better," he said, and walked away.

Mac, watching him, matched him word for step: "When-you-gonna-get-those-corners-sawed-off-your-head?"

Leaving the tavern with Mac, Myles saw the wind take the slip of paper up the street.

"My friend can do without that kind of business," Mac said.

Mac began operations on a freezing cold day in central Wisconsin, and right away Myles was denied his first opportunity. While Mac went into a chancery office to negotiate with the bishop, who would (or would not) grant permission to canvass the diocese, Myles had to wait outside in the car, with the engine running; Mac said he was worried about the battery. This bishop was one with whom Myles had already corresponded unsuccessfully, but that was small consolation to him, in view of his plan to plead his case before as many bishops as possible, without reference to past failures. How he'd manage it with Mac in attendance, he didn't know. Perhaps he could use the initial interview for analysis only and, attempting to see the bishop as an opponent in a game, try to uncover his weakness, and then call back alone later and play upon it. Myles disapproved of cunning, and rather doubted whether he could carry out such a scheme. But he also recalled that puzzling but practical advice, "Be ye therefore wise as serpents and simple as doves," the first part of which the bishops themselves, he believed, were at such pains to follow in their dealings with him.

The next day Mac invited Myles to accompany him indoors when he paid his calls upon the pastors. The day was no warmer but Mac said nothing about the battery. He said, "You've got a lot to learn, son," and proceeded to give Myles some pointers. In some dioceses, according to Mac, the bishop's permission was all you needed; get that, and the pastors—always excepting a few incorrigibles—would drop like ripe fruit. Unfortunately, in such dioceses the bishop's permission wasn't always easy to obtain. Of course you got in to see bishops personally (this in reply to a question from Myles), but most of the time you were working with pastors. There were two kinds of pastors, Mac said—those who honestly believed they knew everything and those who didn't. With the first, it was best to appear helpless (as, in fact, you were) and try to get them interested in doing your job for you. With the other kind, you had to appear confident, promise them the moon—something they were always looking for anyway—tell them a change might come over their people if they were exposed to the pamphlets and the *Clementine*. Of course, no pastor had a right to expect such a miracle, but many did expect it even so, if the pamphlets and the *Clementine* hadn't been tried in the parish before. You'd meet some, though, Mac said, who would be cold, even opposed, to the Work, and offensive to you, and with them you took a beating—but cheerfully, hoping for a change of heart later. More than one of that kind had come around in the end, he said, and one of them had even written a glowing letter to the Fathers, complimenting them on the high type of layman they had working for them, and had placed an order for a rack of pamphlets on condition that Mac received credit for it. Then there were the others—those who would do everything they could to help you, wanted to feed you and put you up overnight, but they, for some reason, were found more often in the country, or in poor city parishes, where little could be accomplished and where you seldom went.

On the third day out, they came across one of the incorrigibles. He greeted them with a snarl. "You guys're a breed apart," he said. Myles was offended, but Mac, undaunted, went into his routine for cracking hard nuts. "Don't know much about this job, I'm ashamed to say," he said, "but it's sure a lot of fun learning." The pastor, instead of going out of his way to help a cheerful soul like Mac (and a nervous one like Myles), ordered them out of the rectory, produced a golf club when they didn't go and, when they did, stood at the front window, behind a lace curtain, until they drove off.

Before the end of the first week, Myles discovered that Mac wasn't really interested in getting permission to canvass a parish house-to-house. He said he just didn't care that much about people. What he liked was cooperation; he liked to have a pastor in the pulpit doing the donkey work and the ushers in the aisles dispensing pencil stubs and subscription blanks, with him just sitting at a card table in the vestibule after Mass, smiling at the new subscribers as they passed out, making change, and croaking, "God love you." That was what Mac called "a production." He operated on a sliding scale—a slippery one, Myles thought. In a big, well-to-do parish, where the take would be high, Mac cut prices. He was also prepared to make an offering toward the upkeep of the church, or to the pastor's favorite charity (the latter was often the former), and to signify his intention beforehand. He had to hustle, he said, in order to meet the stiff competition of the missionaries; a layman, even if he represented a recognized religious order, was always at a disadvantage. Fortunately, he said, there were quite a few secular pastors who, though they didn't care for the orders, didn't consider the struggling Clementines a menace. But there weren't many pastors with flourishing parishes who would cooperate with Mac or with anybody. They were sitting pretty, Mac said, and they knew it. If he now and then succeeded with one of them, it was only because he was liked personally—or, as it seemed to Myles, because of what Mac called "the package deal." The package deal didn't actually involve the Work, Mac was careful to explain, but it sometimes helped it. And, Myles felt, compromised it.

The package deal always began with Mac's opening his bag of tricks. It was a Gladstone bag, which he had got from a retired cookie salesman. When open, it looked like a little stadium, and where the cookies had once been on display, in their individual plastic sections, ranged in tiers, there were now rosaries, medals, scapulars—religious goods of the usual quality, which didn't catch the eye in many rectories. But there were also playing cards with saints as face cards—in one deck the Devil was the joker—and these were new to some priests, as they were to Myles, and had strong educational appeal. Children could familiarize themselves with the lives of the saints from them, and there were other decks, which taught Christian doctrine. Mac had a new kind of rosary, too. It was made of plastic, to fit the hand, and in function and appearance it was similar to an umpire's ball-and-strike indicator. Each time a little key was punched, the single dial, which showed the Mysteries—Sorrowful, Joyful, and Glorious—revolved a notch, and for the Ave Marias there was a modest tick, for the Pater Nosters an authoritative click. Mac had difficulty explaining the new rosary's purpose to some priests—*not* to replace the old model, the traditional beads on a string, but to facilitate prayer while driving, for the new rosary was easily attached to the steering wheel. "Of course, you still have to say the prayers," Mac would say.

Mac gave freely from his bag. Other things, however, he sold —just as an accommodation, he said, to priests, whose work naturally left them little time for shopping. He seemed to have a friend in every business that a parish priest might have to deal with. Myles saw him take large orders for automatic bingo cards (with built-in simulated corn counters), and the trunk of the car was full of catalogues and of refills for the grab bag. "There's one for you, Father," he'd say, presenting a pastor with one of the new rosaries. Later, speaking earnestly of power lawn mowers, of which he happened to have a prospectus showing pictures and prices, he'd say, "That's practically cost minus, Father. He"—referring to a friend—"can't do better than that, I know."

One day, when they were driving along, Myles, at the wheel, asked about Mac's friends.

"Friends? Who said I had any?" Mac snapped.

"I keep hearing you talking about your friends."

"Is that *so*?" Some miles later, after complete silence, Mac said, "I'm a man of many friends—and I don't make a dime on any of 'em." Still later, "The Fathers know all about it."

This Myles doubted. The Fathers were forbidden to engage in business for profit, he knew, and he believed that Mac, as their representative, was probably subject to the same prohibition. It was a question, though, whether Mac was primarily the Fathers' representative or his friends' or his own. It was hard to believe that *everyone* was only breaking even. And Myles felt sure that if the Fathers knew about the package deal, they'd think they had to act. But a replacement for Mac would be hard to find. The *Clementine*, as Myles was discovering, was not an easy magazine to sell. The pamphlets weren't moving well, either.

Without knowing it at the time, Myles saw a variation of the package deal worked on a pastor who met them in his front yard, baying, "I know all about you! Go!" Myles was more than ready to go, but Mac said, "You know, Monsignor, I believe you do know about me." "Don't call me Monsignor!" "My mistake, Father." Mac's voice was as oil being poured out. "Father, something you said just now makes me want to say something to you, only it's not anything I care to say in front of others." "Whatever you have to say can be said now," the pastor mumbled. "Believe me, Father, I can't say it—not in front of this boy," Mac said, nodding at Myles. Then, in a stage whisper to Myles, "You better go, son." Myles hesitated, expecting to hear the pastor overrule Mac, but nothing of the sort happened, and Myles went out and sat in the car. Mac and the pastor, a fierce-looking, beak-nosed Irish type, began to walk slowly around the yard, and presently disappeared behind the rectory. Then, after a bit, there was Mac, coming out the front door and calling to Myles from the porch, "Come on in!" Myles went in and shook hands with the pastor, actually a gentle silver-haired man. He asked them to stay for lunch, but Mac graciously refused, insisting it would be too much trouble for the housekeeper. On the following Sunday morning, this same pastor, a marvelous speaker, preached in behalf of the Work, calling the *Clementine* "that dandy little magazine" at all five Masses. Myles attended them all, while Mac hobnobbed with the ushers in the vestibule. Between Masses, the two of them, sitting at the card table, worked like bookmakers between races. Afterward, when they were driving away, Mac announced that the team had had its most successful day. That evening, in a new town, relaxing in the cocktail lounge of their hotel, Mac gave up his secret. He said he had diagnosed the pastor perfectly and had taken the pledge from him—that was all. Seeing that Myles disapproved, he said, "It so happened I needed it." Myles, who was getting to know Mac, couldn't quarrel with that.

Mac and Myles moved constantly from town to town and diocese to diocese, and almost every night Myles had the problem of locating suitable accommodations. He soon saw that he would not be able to afford the hotels and meals to which Mac was accustomed, and finally he complained. Mac looked hurt. He said, "We don't do the Work for profit, you know." He only got by himself, he said, by attributing part of his living expenses to the car. He wasn't misusing the swindle sheet, though; he was adapting it to circumstances beyond his control. There really *were* expenses. "I don't have to tell you that," he said. "The Fathers, God love 'em, just don't understand how prices have gone up." Myles' predecessor, a fellow named Jack, had put up in "the more reasonable hotels and rooming houses," and Mac suggested that Myles do the same, for a while. "Later, when you're doing better, you could stay in regular hotels."

"Is that what Jack did—later?" Myles asked.

"No. Jack seemed to like the kind of places he stayed in." Jack, in fact, had quit the Work in order to stay on in one of them, and was now engaged to the landlady. "In some ways, Jack wasn't meant for the Work," Mac added. "But we had some fine times together and I hated to see him go. He was a damn fine driver. Not that that's everything."

It had become an important part of Myles' job to do all the driving and put the car away at night and bring it around to the hotel in the morning for Mac and his luggage. More and more, Mac rode in the back seat. (He said he preferred the ashtray there.) But there was no glass between the front and back seats, and the arrangement did not interfere with conversation or alter Mac's friendliness. Occasionally, they'd arrive in a town late at night—too late for Myles to look for one of the more reasonable places—and Mac would say, mercifully, "Come on. Stay with me." And on those nights Mac would pick up the tab. This could also happen even when they arrived in plenty of time for Myles to look around, provided the drive had been a long one and Myles had played the good listener.

The association between the two was generally close, and becoming closer. Mac talked frankly about his ex-friends, of whom there were many—mostly former associates or rivals in the general-merchandise field, double-crossers to a man. The first few times this happened, Myles controlled his desire to tell Mac that by damning others, as he did, he damned the whole human race—damned himself, in fact. One day, after Mac had finished with his old friends and with his wife (who was no good), and was beginning to go to work on the Jews (who also had given him nothing but trouble), Myles did tell him. He presented an idea he held to be even greater than the idea of brotherhood. It was the doctrine of the Mystical Body of

Christ. Humanity was one great body, Myles explained, all united with Christ, the Saviour. Mac acted as though the doctrine were a new one on him. "One great body, huh? Sounds like the Mystical Knights of the Sea," he said, and talked for a while of Amos and Andy and of the old days when they'd been Sam and Henry. That was the afternoon that Mac got onto the subject of his dream.

Mac's dream—as he spoke, the snow was going from gray to ghostly blue and the lights were coming on in the houses along the way—was to own a turkey ranch and a church-goods store. What he really wanted was the ranch, he said, but he supposed he'd have to play it safe and have the store, too. Turkeys could be risky. With the general revival of interest in religion, however, a well-run church-goods store would be sure to succeed. He'd sell by mail, retail and wholesale, and there'd be discounts for everybody—not just for the clergy, though, of course, he'd have to give them the usual break. The store would be a regular clearinghouse: everything from holy cards to statues—products of all the leading manufacturers.

"Sort of a supermarket?" Myles asked, thinking of chalices and turkeys roosting all in a row.

"That's the idea."

"It'd be nice if there were one place in this country where you could get an honest piece of ecclesiastical art," Myles said.

"I'd have that, too, later," Mac said. "A custom department."

They were getting along very well, different as they were. Mac *was* a good traveling companion, ready wherever they went with a little quick information about the towns ("Good for business," "All Swedes," "Wide open"), the small change of real knowledge.

One day, when they were passing through Superior, Wisconsin, Mac said that originally the iron-ore interests had planned to develop the town. Property values had been jacked up, however, by operators too smart for their own good, and everything had gone to Duluth, with its relatively inferior harbor. That was how Superior, favored by nature, had become what it was, a small town with the layout of a metropolis.

"It's easier to move mountains than greedy hearts," Myles commented.

"I wouldn't know," Mac said.

Myles found the story of Superior instructive—positively Biblical, he said. Another case of man's greed. The country thereabouts also proved interesting to Myles, but difficult for Mac when Myles began to expound on the fished-out lakes (man's greed), the cut-over timberland (man's greed), the poor Indians (the *white* man's greed). The high-grade ore pits, Mac foolishly told him, were almost exhausted.

"Exhausted for what?" Myles asked.

"Steel," said Mac, who didn't realize the question had been rhetorical.

"This car!" said Myles, with great contempt. "War!" Looking into the rearview mirror, he saw Mac indulging in what was becoming a habit with him—pulling on his ear lobes.

"What *are* you?" Mac finally demanded. "Some kind of a new damn fool?"

But Myles never gave up on him. He went right on making his points, laying the ground for an awakening; it might never come to Mac, but Myles carried on as if it might at any moment. Mac, allied with the modern world for better or worse, defended the indefensible and fought back. And when logic failed him, he spluttered, "You talk like you got holes in your head," or, "Quit moanin'!" or, "Who you think you are, buster—the Pope?"

"This is when you're *really* hard to take!" Mac said one day, when the news from Korea was bad and Myles was most telling. Myles continued obliviously, perceiving moral links between Hiroshima and Korea and worse things to come, and predicting universal retribution, weeping, and gnashing of teeth. "And why?" he said. "Greed!"

"Greed! Greed! Is that all you can think about? No wonder they had to get rid of you!"

A few miles of silence followed, and then a few well-chosen words from Mac, who had most certainly been thinking, which was just what Myles was always trying to get him to do. "Are you sure the place you escaped from was a seminary?" he asked.

But Myles let him see he could take even this, turning the other cheek so gracefully that Mac could never know his words were touching a sore spot.

Later that day, in the middle of a sermon from Myles, they passed a paddy wagon and Mac said, "They're looking for you." Ever after, if Myles discoursed too long or too well on the state of the modern world, there came a tired but amiable croaking from the back seat, "They're looking for you."

At night, however, after the bars closed, it was *Mac* who was looking for Myles. If they were staying at the same hotel, he'd knock at Myles' door and say, "Care to come over to the room for a drink?" At first, Myles, seeing no way out of it, would go along, though not for a drink. He drank beer when he drank, or wine, and there was never any of either in Mac's room. It was no fun spending the last hour of the day with Mac. He had a lot of stories, but Myles often missed the point of them, and he knew none himself—none that Mac would appreciate, anyway. What Cardinal Merry del Val had said to Cardinal Somebody Else—the usual seminary stuff. But Mac found a subject to interest *him*. He began denying that Myles was a cradle Catholic. Myles, who had never seen in this accident of birth the personal achievement that Mac seemed to see, would counter, "All right. What if I weren't one?"

"You see? You see?" Mac would say, looking very wise and drunk. Then, as if craving and expecting a confession, he'd say, "You can tell *me*."

Myles had nothing to tell, and Mac would start over again,

on another tack. Developing his thought about what he called Myles' "ideas," he would arrive at the only possible conclusion: Myles wasn't a Catholic at all. He was probably only a smart-aleck convert who had come into the Church when the coming was good, and only *thought* he was in.

"Do you deny the possibility of conversion?" Myles would ask, though there was small pleasure in theologizing with someone like Mac.

Mac never answered the question. He'd just keep saying, "You call yourself a *Catholic*—a *cradle* Catholic?"

The first time Myles said no to Mac's invitation to come over and have one, it worked. The next time, Mac went back to his room only to return with his bottle, saying, "Thought you might like to have one in your pajamas." That was the night Myles told Mac, hopefully, that whiskey was a Protestant invention; in Ireland, for example, it had been used, more effectively than the penal laws, to enslave the faithful. "Who're you kiddin'!" Mac wailed.

Mere admonishment failed with Mac. One day, as they were driving through primitive country, Myles delivered a regular sermon on the subject of drink. He said a man possessed by drink was a man possessed by the Devil. He said that Mac, at night, was very like a devil, going about hotel corridors "as a roaring lion goeth about seeking whom he may devour." This must have hit Mac pretty hard, for he said nothing in his own defense; in fact, he took it very well, gazing out at the pine trees, which Myles, in the course of his sermon, had asked him to consider in all their natural beauty. That afternoon, they met another hard nut—and Mac took the pledge again, which closed the deal for a production on the following Sunday, and also, he seemed to think, put him into Myles' good graces. "I wish I could find one that could give it to me and make it stick," he said.

"Don't come to me when I'm a priest," said Myles, who had still to see his first bishop.

That night Mac and the bottle were at the door again. Myles, in bed, did not respond. This was a mistake. Mac phoned the office and had them bring up a key and open Myles' door, all because he thought Myles might be sick. "I love that boy!" he proclaimed, on his way back to his room at last. Later that night Myles heard him in the corridor, at a little distance, with another drunk. Mac was roaring, "I'm seein' who I may devour!"

More and more, Myles and Mac were staying together in the same hotels, and Myles, though saving money by this arrangement (money, however, that he never saw), wondered if he wasn't paying too much for economy. He felt slightly kept. Mac only wanted him handy late at night, it seemed, so as to have someone with whom to take his pleasure, which was haranguing. Myles now understood better why Jack had liked the places he stayed in. Or was this thing that Mac was doing to him nightly something new for Mac? Something that Myles had brought upon himself? He was someone whom people looking for trouble always seemed to find. It had happened to him in the hospital, in the seminary, in the Boy Scouts. If a million people met in one place, and he was there, he was certain that the worst of them would rise as a man and make for him.

But Mac wasn't always looking for trouble. One afternoon, for no reason at all, he bought Myles a Hawaiian sports shirt. "For next summer," Mac said, as if they would always be together. The shirt was a terrible thing to look at—soiled merchandise picked up at a sale—but it might mean something. Was it possible that Mac, in his fashion, liked him?

"A fellow like you might handle that end of it," Mac said one day in the car. He had been talking about the store part of his dream and how he would put out a big catalogue in which it would be wise for manufacturers—and maybe religious orders, too—to buy advertising if they expected to do business with him. "Interested?" he asked.

Myles was definitely not interested, but he was touched by the offer, since it showed that Mac trusted him. It was time to put matters straight between them. Myles spoke then of *his* dream—of the great desire he had to become a priest. Not a punch-drunk seminary professor or a fat cat in a million-dollar parish, he said, but a simple shepherd ministering gently to the poorest of God's poor. He wouldn't mind being a priest-worker, like those already functioning so successfully in France, according to reports reaching him. "That can't happen here," Mac said. Myles, however, saw difficult times ahead for the nation— Here Mac started to open his mouth but grabbed instead for his ears. Myles felt pretty sure that there would soon be priest-workers slaving away in fields and factories by day and tending to the spiritual needs of their poor fellow-workers by night.

"Poor?" Mac asked. "What about the unions? When I think what those boys take home!"

Myles then explored the more immediate problem of finding a bishop to sponsor him.

Mac said he knew several quite well and he might speak to them.

"I wish you would," Myles said. "The two I've seen looked impossible." Then, having said that much—too much—he confessed to Mac his real reason for taking the job: the urgency of his position with regard to Selective Service.

Immediately, Mac, who had not been paying much attention, released an ear for listening. He appeared ill-disposed toward Myles' reluctance to serve in the armed forces, or, possibly, toward such frankness.

"I can't serve two masters," Myles said. Mac was silent; he'd gone absolutely dead. "Are you a veteran?" Myles asked.

"Since you ask," Mac said, "I'll tell you. I served and was wounded—honorably—in both World Wars. If there's another one, I hope to do my part. Does that answer your question?" Myles said that it did, and he could think of nothing to say just then that wouldn't hurt Mac's feelings.

That night, Mac, in his cups, surpassed himself. He got through with the usual accusations early and began threatening Myles with "exposure." "Dodgin' the draft!" Mac howled. "I oughta turn you in."

Myles said he hadn't broken the law *yet*.

"But you *intend* to," Mac said. "I oughta turn you in."

"I'll turn myself in when the time comes," Myles said.

"Like hell you will. You'll go along until they catch up with you. Then they'll clap you in jail—where you belong."

"Maybe you're right," Myles said, thinking of St Paul and other convicts.

"Then you'll wish you were in the Army—where you belong. I'm not sure it's not my duty to report you. Let's see your draft card."

Myles let him see it.

" 'Flynn, Myles'—that you? How do I know you're not somebody else by the same name?"

Myles made no reply. Had prohibition been so wrong, he wondered.

"Don't wanna incriminate yourself, huh? Hey, you're 1-A! Didja see that?"

Myles explained, as he had before, that he was awaiting his induction notice.

"Bet you are! Bet you can hardly wait! I'd better hold onto this." Mac slipped Myles' draft card into his pocket.

In the morning, Myles got the card back. Mac, sober, returned it, saying he'd found it in his room, where Myles (who had not been there) must have dropped it. "Better hold on to that," Mac said.

The next night Myles managed to stay in a rooming house, out of reach, but the following night they were together again, and Mac asked to see Myles' draft card again. Myles wouldn't give it up. "I deny your authority," he said, himself emboldened by drink—two beers.

"Here's my authority!" Mac cried. He loosened his trousers and pulled up his shirt in front, exposing a stomach remarkably round, smooth, veined, and, in places, blue, like a world globe. There was a scar on it. "How d'ya think I got that?"

"Appendicitis," Myles said.

There was no doubt of it. The scar testified to Mac's fraudulence as nothing else had, and for once Mac seemed to know it. He'd strayed into a field in which he believed Myles to be supreme. Putting his stomach away, he managed a tone in which there was misgiving, outrage, and sarcasm. "That's right. That's right. You know everything. You were a bedpan jockey. I forgot about that."

Myles watched him, amused. Mac might have saved himself by telling the truth or by quickly laughing it off, but he lied on. "Shrapnel—some still inside," he said. He coughed and felt his stomach, as if his lungs were there, but he didn't get it out again. "Not asking *you* to believe it," he said. "Won't show *you* my other wound."

"Please don't," said Myles. He retired that night feeling that he had the upper hand.

One week later, leaving a town in Minnesota where they had encountered a difficult bishop, Mac ordered Myles to stop at a large, gabled rectory of forbidding aspect. As it turned out, however, they enjoyed a good dinner there, and afterward the pastor summoned three of his colleagues for a little game of blackjack—in Mac's honor, Myles heard him say as the players trooped upstairs.

Myles spent the evening downstairs with the curate. While they were eating some fudge the curate had made that afternoon, they discovered that they had many of the same enthusiasms and prejudices. The curate wanted Myles to understand that the church was not his idea, loaded up, as it was, with junk. He was working on the pastor to throw out most of the statues and all the vigil lights. It was a free-talking, free-swinging session, the best evening for Myles since leaving the seminary. In a nice but rather futile tribute to Myles, the curate said that if the two of them were pastors, they might, perhaps, transform the whole diocese. He in no way indicated that he thought there was anything wrong with Myles because he had been asked to leave the seminary. He believed, as Myles did, that there was no *good* reason for the dismissal. He said he'd had trouble getting through himself and he thought that the seminary, as an institution, was probably responsible for the way Stalin, another aspirant to the priesthood, had turned out. The curate also strongly disapproved of Mac, and of Myles' reasons for continuing in the Work. He said the Clementines were a corny outfit, and no bishop in his right mind, seeing Myles with Mac, would ever take a chance on him. The curate thought that Myles might be playing it too cautious. He'd do better, perhaps, just to go around the country, hitchhiking from see to see, washing dishes if he had to, but calling on bishops personally—as many as he could in the time that remained before he got his induction notice.

"How many bishops have you actually seen?" the curate asked.

"Three. But I couldn't say anything with Mac right there. I would've gone back later, though, if there'd been a chance at all with those I saw."

The curate sniffed. "How could you tell?" he asked. "I thought you were desperate. You just *can't* be guided entirely by private revelation. You have a higher injunction: 'Seek, and you shall find.' Perhaps you still haven't thought this thing *through*. I wonder. Perhaps you don't pray enough?"

Myles, noticing in the curate a tendency to lecture and feeling that he'd suffered one "perhaps" too many, defended himself, saying, "The man we met today wouldn't let us set foot on church property in his diocese. What can you do with a bishop like that?"

"The very one you should have persevered with! Moses, you may remember, had to do more than look at the rock. He had to strike it."

"Twice, unfortunately," murmured Myles, not liking the analogy. Moses, wavering in his faith, had struck twice and had not reached the Promised Land; he had only seen it in the distance, and died.

"It may not be too late," the curate said. "I'd try that one again if I were you."

Myles laughed. "*That* one was your own bishop," he said.

"The bishop said that?" The curate showed some alarm and seemed suddenly a lot less friendly. "Is that why you're here, then—why Mac's here, I mean?"

"I couldn't tell you why I'm here," Myles said. In Mac's defense, he said, "I don't think he's mentioned the Work here." It was true. Mac and the pastor had hit it off right away, talking of other things.

"I heard him trying to sell the pastor a new roof—a copper one. Also an oil burner. Does he deal in *those* things?" the curate asked.

"He has friends who do." Myles smiled. He wanted to say more on this subject to amuse the curate, if that was still possible; he wanted to confide in him again; he wanted to say whatever would be necessary to save the evening. But the shadow of the bishop had fallen upon them. There were only crumbs on the fudge plate; the evening had ended. It was bedtime, the curate said. He offered Myles a Coke, which Myles refused, then showed him to a couch in the parlor, gave him a blanket, and went off to bed.

Some time later—it was still night—Mac woke Myles and they left the rectory. Mac was sore; he said he'd lost a bundle. He climbed into the back seat and wrapped himself in the car rug. "A den of thieves. I'm pretty sure I was taken. Turn on the heater." And then he slept while Myles drove away toward the dawn.

The next day, as they were having dinner in another diocese, another town, another hotel—Mac looked fresh; he'd slept all day—Myles told him that he was quitting.

"Soon?" said Mac.

"Right away."

"Give me a little time to think about it."

After dinner, Mac drew one of his good cigars out of its aluminum scabbard. "What is it? Money? Because if it is—" Mac said, puffing on the cigar, and then, looking at the cigar and not at Myles, he outlined his plans. He'd try to get more money for Myles from the Fathers, more take-home dough and more for expenses. He'd sensed that Myles had been unhappy in some of those flea bags; Myles might have noticed that they'd been staying together oftener. Ultimately, if the two of them were still together and everything went right, there might be a junior partnership for Myles in the store. "No," Mac said, looking at Myles. "I can see that's not what you want." He turned to the cigar again and asked, "Well, why not?" He invited Myles up to his room, where, he said, he might have something to say that would be of interest to him.

Upstairs, after making himself a drink, Mac said that he just might be able to help Myles in the only way he wanted to be helped. He was on fairly good terms with a number of bishops, as Myles might have gathered, but an even better bet would be the Clementines. Myles could join the order as a lay brother—*anybody* could do that—swiftly win the confidence of his superiors, then switch to the seminary, and thus complete his studies for the priesthood. "I might be able to give you such a strong recommendation that you could go straight into the seminary," Mac said. "It would mean losing you, of course. Don't like that part. Or *would* it? What's to stop us from going on together, like now, after you get your degree?"

"After *ordination*?" Myles asked.

"There you are!" Mac exclaimed. "Just shows it's a natural —us working as a team. What I don't know, you do."

While Mac strengthened his drink just a little—he was cutting down—Myles thanked him for what he'd done to date and also for what he was prepared to do. He said that he doubted, however, that he was meant for the Clementines or for the community life, and even if he were, there would still be the problem of finding a bishop to sponsor him. "Oh, *they'd* do all that," Mac said. Myles shook his head. He was quitting. He had to intensify his efforts. He wasn't getting to see many bishops, was he? Time was of the essence. He had a few ideas he wanted to pursue on his own (meaning he had one—to have another crack at the curate's bishop). The induction notice, his real worry, might come any day.

"How d'ya know you're all right physically?" Mac asked him. "You don't look very strong to me. I took you for a born 4-F. For all you know, you might be turned down and out lookin' for a job. In the circumstances, I couldn't promise to hold this one open forever."

With the usual apprehension, Myles watched Mac pour another drink. Could Mac want so badly for an underpaid chauffeur, he wondered. Myles' driving was his only asset. As a representative of the Fathers, he was a flop, and he knew it, and so did Mac. Mac, in his own words, was the baby that delivered the goods. But no layman could be as influential as Mac claimed to be with the Fathers, hard up though they were for men and money. Mac wouldn't be able to help with any bishop in his right mind. But Mac did want him around, and Myles, who could think of no one else who did, was almost tempted to stay as long as he could. Maybe he *was* 4-F.

Later that evening Mac, still drinking, put it another way, or possibly said what he'd meant to say earlier. "Hell, you'll never pass the mental test. Never let a character like you in the Army." The Fathers, though, would be glad to have Myles, if Mac said the word.

Myles thanked him again. Mac wanted him to drive the car, to do the Work, but what he wanted still more, it was becoming clear, was to have a boon companion, and Myles knew he just couldn't stand to be it.

"You're not my type," Mac said. "You haven't got it—the velocity, I mean—but maybe that's why I like you."

Myles was alone again with his thoughts, walking the plank of his gloom.

"Don't worry," Mac said. "I'll always have a spot in my heart for you. A place in my business."

"In the supermarket?"

Mac frowned. Drinking, after a point, made him appear a little cross-eyed. "I wish you wouldn't use that word," he said distinctly. "If y'wanna know, your trouble's words. Make y'self harda take. Don't *have* to be jerk. Looka you. Young. Looka me. Dead. Not even Catholic. Bloody Orangeman. 'S truth."

Myles couldn't believe it. And then he could, almost. He'd never seen Mac at Mass on Sundays, either coming or going, except when they were working, and then Mac kept to the vestibule. The bunk that Mac had talked about Myles' being a cradle Catholic began to make sense.

"Now you're leaving the Work, I tell you," Mac was saying "Makes no difference now." They were in Minnesota, staying in a hotel done in the once popular Moorish style, and the ceiling light and the shades of the bed lamps, and consequently the walls and Myles' face, were dead orange and Mac's face was bloody orange.

Myles got up to leave.

"Don't go," Mac said. He emptied the bottle.

But Myles went, saying it was bedtime. He realized as he said it that he sounded like the curate the night before.

Ten minutes later Mac was knocking at Myles' door. He was in his stocking feet, but looked better, like a drunk getting a hold on himself.

"Something to read," he said. "Don't feel like sleeping."

Myles had some books in his suitcase, but he left them there. "I didn't get a paper," he said.

"Don't want that," Mac said. He saw the Gideon Bible on the night stand and went over to it. "Mind if I swipe this?"

"There's probably one in your room."

Mac didn't seem to hear. He picked up the Gideon. "The Good Book," he said.

"I've got a little Catholic Bible," Myles said. The words came out of themselves—the words of a diehard proselytizer.

"Have you? Yeah, that's the one I want."

"I can't recommend it," Myles said, on second thought. "You better take the other one, for reading. It's the King James."

"Hell with that!" Mac said. He put the King James from him.

Myles went to the suitcase and got out his portable Bible. He stood with it at the door, making Mac come for it, and then, still withholding it, led him outside into the corridor, where he finally handed it over.

"How you feel now, about that other?" Mac asked.

For a moment, Myles thought he was being asked about his induction, which Mac ordinarily referred to as "that other," and not about Mac's dark secret. When he got Mac's meaning, he said, "Don't worry about me. I won't turn you in."

In the light of his activities, Mac's not being a Catholic was in his favor, from Myles' point of view; as an honest faker Mac was more acceptable, though many would not see it that way. There was something else, though, in Mac's favor—something unique; he was somebody who liked Myles just for himself. He had been betrayed by affection—and by the bottle, of course.

Myles watched Mac going down the corridor in his stocking feet toward his room, holding the Bible and swaying just a little, as if he were walking on calm water. He wasn't so drunk.

The next morning Mac returned the Bible to Myles in his room and said, "I don't know if you realize it or not, but I'm sorry about last night. I guess I said a lot of things I shouldn't have. I won't stand in your way any longer." He reached into his pocket and took out his roll. "You'll need some of this," he said.

"No, thanks," Myles said.

"You sure?"

Myles was sure.

"Forget anything I might have said." Mac eased over to the window and looked out upon the main street. "I don't know what, but I might have said something." He came back to Myles. He was fingering his roll, holding it in both hands, a fat red squirrel with a nut. "You sure now?"

Myles said yes, he was sure, and Mac reluctantly left him.

Myles was wondering if that had been their good-bye when, a few minutes later, Mac came in again. His manner was different. "I'll put it to you like this," he said. "You don't say anything about me and I won't say anything about you. Maybe we both got trouble. You know what I'm talking about?"

Myles said that he thought he knew and that Mac needn't worry.

"They may never catch you," Mac said, and went away again. Myles wondered if *that* had been their good-bye.

Presently Mac came in again. "I don't remember if I told you this last night or not. I know I was going to, but what with one thing and another last night, and getting all hung up—"

"Well?"

"Kid"—it was the first time Mac had called him that—"I'm not a Catholic."

Myles nodded.

"Then I did say something about it?"

Myles nodded again. He didn't know what Mac was trying now, only that he was trying something.

"I don't know what I am," Mac said. "My folks weren't much good. I lost 'em when I was quite young. And you know about my wife." Myles knew about her. "No damn good."

Myles listened and nodded while all those who had ever failed Mac came in for slaughter. Mac ordinarily did this dirty work in the car, and it had always seemed to Myles that they threw out the offending bodies, one by one, making room for the fresh ones. It was getting close in the room. Mac stood upright amid a wreckage of carcasses—with Myles.

"You're the only one I can turn to," he said. "I'd be afraid to admit to anyone else what I've just admitted to you—I mean to a priest. As you know, I'm pretty high up in the Work, respected, well thought of, and all that, and you can imagine what your average priest is going to think if *I* come to him—to be baptized!"

The scene rather appealed to Myles, but he looked grave.

"I know what you're thinking," Mac said. "Don't think I don't know the awful risk I'm taking now, with my immortal soul and all. Gives me a chill to think of it. But I still can't bring myself to do the right thing. Not if it means going to a priest. Sure to be embarrassing questions. The Fathers could easily get wind of it back in Chicago."

Myles was beginning to see what Mac had in mind.

"As I understand it, you don't have to be a priest to baptize people," Mac continued. "*Anybody* can do it in an emergency. You know that, of course."

Myles, just a step ahead of him, was thinking of the pastors who'd been deceived into giving Mac the pledge. It looked a lot like the old package deal.

"We could go over there," Mac said, glancing at the washbowl in the corner. "Or there's my room, if it'd be more appropriate." He had a bathroom.

Myles hardened. "If you're asking *me* to do it," he said, "the answer's no." Myles was now sure that Mac had been baptized before—perhaps many times, whenever he had need of it. "I couldn't give you a proper certificate anyway," Myles added. "You'd want that."

"You mean if I wanted to go on with it and come into the Catholic Church? All the way in? Is that what you mean?"

Myles didn't mean that at all, but he said, "I suppose so."

"Then you do get me?" Mac demanded.

Myles stiffened, knowing that he was in grave danger of being in on Mac's conversion, and feeling, a moment later, that this—this conversion—like the pledge and baptism, must have happened before. He hastened to say, "No. I don't get you and I don't *want* to."

Mac stood before him, silent, with bowed head, the beaten man, the man who'd asked for bread and received a stone, who'd asked for a fish and got a serpent.

But no, Mac wasn't that at all, Myles saw. He was the serpent, the nice old serpent with Glen-plaid markings, who wasn't *very* poisonous. He'd been expecting tenderness, but he had caught the forked stick just behind the head. The serpent was quiet. Was he dead? "I give you my word that I'll never tell anybody what you've told me," Myles said. "So far as I'm concerned, you're a Catholic—a cradle Catholic if you like. I hold no grudge against you for anything you've said, drunk or sober. I hope you'll do the same for me."

"I will that," Mac said, and began to speak of their "relationship," of the inspiration Myles had been to him from the very first. There was only one person responsible for the change in his outlook, he said, and it might interest Myles to know that *he* was that person.

Myles saw that he'd let up on the stick too soon. The serpent still had plenty left. Myles pressed down on him. "I want out, Mac," he said. "I'm not a priest yet. I don't *have* to listen to this. If you want me to spill the beans to the Fathers, just keep it up."

The serpent was very quiet now. Dead?

"You do see what I mean?" Myles said.

"Yeah, now I see," Mac said. He was looking only a little hurt; the flesh above his snow-white collar was changing pinks, but he was looking much better, seemingly convinced that Myles, with an excuse to harm him, and with the power to do so, would not. Mac was having his remarkable experience after all—almost a conversion. "Had you wrong," he confessed. "Thought sure you'd squeal. Thought sure you'd be the type that would. Hope you don't mind me saying that. Because you got my respect now."

Myles could see, however, that Mac liked him less for having it. But he had Mac's respect, and it was rare, and it made the day rare.

"Until I met you, why— Well, *you* know." Mac stopped short.

Myles, with just a look, had let him feel the stick.

"We'll leave it at that," Mac said.

"If you will, I will," said Myles. He crossed the room to the washbowl, where he began to collect his razor, his toothbrush, and the shaving lotion that Mac had given him. When he turned around with these things in his hands, he saw that Mac had gone. He'd left a small deposit of gray ash on the rug near the spot where he'd coiled and uncoiled.

Later that morning Myles, as a last service and proof of good will, went to the garage and brought Mac's car around to the hotel door, and waited there with it until Mac, smoking his second cigar of the day, appeared. Myles helped him stow his luggage and refused his offer to drive him to the railroad station, if that was where Myles wanted to go. Myles had not told Mac that he intended to hitchhike back to the last town, to confront the difficult bishop and strike the rock a second time. After shaking hands, Mac began, "If I hear of anything—" but Myles silenced him with a look, and then and there the team split up.

Mac got into the Cadillac and drove off. Watching, Myles saw the car, half a block away, bite at the curb and stop. And he saw why. Mac, getting on with the Work, was offering a lift to two men all in black, who, to judge by their actions, didn't really want one. In the end, though, the black car consumed them, and slithered out of view.

A LOSING GAME

FATHER FABRE, COMING from the bathroom, stopped and knocked at the pastor's door—something about the door had said, Why not? No sound came from the room, but the pastor had a ghostly step and there he was, opening the door an inch, giving his new curate a glimpse of the green eyeshade he wore and of the chaos in which he dwelt. Father Fabre saw the radio in the unmade bed, the correspondence, pamphlets, the folding money, and all the rest of it—what the bishop, on an official visitation, barging into the room and then hurriedly backing out, had passed off to the attending clergy as "a little unfinished business."

"Yes? Yes?"

"How about that table you promised me?"

The pastor just looked at him.

"The one for my room, remember? Something to put my typewriter on."

"See what I can do."

The pastor had said that before. Father Fabre said, "I'm using the radiator now."

The pastor nodded, apparently granting him permission to continue using it.

Father Fabre put down the old inclination to give up. "I thought you said you'd fix me up, Father."

"See what I can do, Father."

"Now?"

"Busy now."

The pastor started to close the door, which was according to the rules of their little game, but Father Fabre didn't budge, which was not according to the rules.

"Tell you what I'll do, Father," he said. "I'll just look around in the basement and you won't have to bother. I know how busy you are." Father Fabre had a strange feeling that he was getting somewhere with the pastor. Everything he'd said so far had been right, but he had to keep it up. "Of course I'll need to know the combination." He saw the pastor buck and shudder at the idea of telling anyone the combination of the lock that preserved his treasures.

"Better go with you," the pastor said, feeling his throat.

Father Fabre nodded. This was what he'd had in mind all the time. While the pastor was inside his room looking for his collar (always a chance of meeting a parishioner on the stairs), Father Fabre relaxed and fell to congratulating himself. He had been tough and it had worked. The other thing had proved a waste of time.

After a bit, though, Father Fabre took another view of the situation, knowing as he did so that it was the right one, that the door hadn't just happened to shut after the pastor, that the man wasn't coming out. Oh, that was it. The pastor had won again. He was safe in his room again, secure in the knowledge that his curate wouldn't knock and start up the whole business again, not for a while anyway.

Father Fabre went away. Going downstairs, he told himself that though he had lost, he had extended the pastor as never before, and would get the best of him yet.

Father Fabre sensed John, the janitor, before he saw him sitting in the dark under the staircase, at one of his stations. He might be found in this rather episcopal chair, which was also a hall-tree, or on a box in the furnace room, or in the choir loft behind the organ, or in the visiting priest's confessional. There were probably other places which Father Fabre didn't know about. John moved around a lot, foxlike, killing time.

Father Fabre switched on the light. John pulled himself together and managed a smile, his glasses as always frosted over with dust so that he seemed to be watching you through basement windows.

"John, you know that lock on the door to the church basement?"

John nodded.

"It's not much of a lock. Think we can open it?"

John frowned.

"A tap on the side?"

John shook his head.

"No?"

"Sorry, Father."

"So." Father Fabre turned away.

"Will you need a hammer, Father?"

"Don't think I'll need one. Sure you won't come along?"

"Awful busy, Father." But John found time to get up and accompany Father Fabre to the iron staircase that led to the church basement. There they parted. Father Fabre snapped the light switch on the wall. He wasn't surprised when nothing happened. He left the door open for light. A half flight down, pausing, he hearkened to John's distant footsteps, rapidly climbing, and then he went winding down into the gloom. At the bottom he seated himself on a step and waited.

Soon he heard a slight noise above. Rounding the last turn, descending into view, was the pastor. "Oh, there you are," said Father Fabre, rising.

The pastor voiced no complaint—and why should he? He'd lost a trick, but Father Fabre had taken it honorably, according to the rules, in a manner worthy of the pastor himself.

Father Fabre was up on his toes, straining to see.

The pastor was fooling with something inside the fuse box on the wall, standing up to it, his back almost a shield against Father Fabre's eyes. Overhead a bulb lit up. So that was it, thought Father Fabre, coming down to earth—and to think that he'd always blamed the wiring for the way some of the lights didn't work around the church and rectory, recommending a general checkup, prophesying death by conflagration to the pastor. Father Fabre, rising again, saw the pastor screw in another fuse where none had been before. That would be the one controlling the basement lights.

The pastor dealt next with the door, dropping into a crouch to dial the lock.

Father Fabre leaned forward like an umpire for the pitch, but saw at once that it would be impossible to lift the combination. He scraped his foot in disgust, grinding a bit of fallen plaster. The pastor's fingers tumbled together. He seemed to be listening. After a moment, he began to dial again, apparently having to start all over.

"There," he said finally. He removed the lock, threw open the door, but before he went in, he stepped over to the fuse box. The overhead light went out. Father Fabre entered the basement, where he had been only once before, and not very far inside then. The pastor secured the door behind them. From a convenient clothes tree he removed a black cap and put it on—protection against the dust? Father Fabre hadn't realized that the pastor, who now looked like a burglar in an insurance ad, cared. The pastor glanced at him. Quickly Father Fabre looked away. He gazed around him in silence.

It was impossible to decide what it all meant. In the clothes tree alone, Father Fabre noted a cartridge belt, a canteen stenciled with the letters U.S., a pair of snowshoes, an old bicycle tire of wrinkled red rubber, a beekeeper's veil. One of Father Fabre's first services to the pastor had been to help John carry two workbenches into the basement. At that time he had thought the pastor must have plans for a school in which manual training would be taught. Now he felt that the pastor had no plans at all for any of the furniture and junk. A few of the unemployed statues when seen at a distance, those with their arms extended, appeared to be trying to get the place straightened up, carrying things, but on closer examination they, too, proved to be preoccupied with a higher kind of order, and carrying crosiers.

The pastor came away from a rack containing billiard cues, ski poles, and guns.

"Here," he said, handing an air rifle to Father Fabre.

Father Fabre accepted the gun, tipped it, listening to the BB shot bowling up and down inside. "What's this for?"

"Rats."

"Couldn't kill a rat with this, could I?"

"Could."

But Father Fabre noticed that the pastor was arming himself with a .22 rifle. "What's that?" he asked covetously.

"This gun's not accurate," said the pastor. "From a shooting gallery."

"What's wrong with trapping 'em?"

"Too smart."

"How about poison?"

"Die in the walls."

The pastor moved off, bearing his gun in the way that was supposed to assure safety.

Father Fabre held his gun the same way and followed the pastor. He could feel the debris closing in, growing up behind him. The path ahead appeared clear only when he looked to either side. He trailed a finger in the dust on a table top, revealing the grain. He stopped. The wood was maple, he thought, maple oiled and aged to the color of saddle leather. There were little niches designed to hold glasses. The table was round, a whist table, it might be, and apparently sound. Here was a noble piece of furniture that would do wonders for his room. It could be used for his purposes, and more. That might be the trouble with it. The pastor was strong for temperance. It might not be enough for Father Fabre to deplore the little niches.

"Oh, Father."

The pastor retraced his steps.

"This might do," Father Fabre said grudgingly, careful not to betray a real desire. There was an awful glazed green urn thing in the middle of the table which Father Fabre feared would leave scratches or a ring. A thing like that, which might have spent its best days in a hotel, by the elevators, belonged on the floor. Father Fabre wanted to remove it from the table, but he controlled himself.

"Don't move," said the pastor. "Spider."

Father Fabre held still while the pastor brushed it off his back. "Thanks." Father Fabre relaxed and gazed upon the table again. He had to have it. He would have it.

But the pastor was moving on.

Father Fabre followed in his steps, having decided to say nothing just then, needing more time to think. The important thing was not to seem eager. "It isn't always what we want that's best for us," the pastor had said more than once. He loved to speak of Phil Mooney—a classmate of Father Fabre's —who had been offered a year of free study at a major secular university, but who had been refused permission by the bishop. Young Mooney, as the pastor said, had taken it so well ... "This—how about this?" said Father Fabre. He had stopped before a nightstand, a little tall for typing. "I could saw the legs off some."

The pastor, who had paused, now went ahead again, faster.

Father Fabre lifted his gun and followed again, wondering if he'd abused the man's sensibilities, some article of the accumulator's creed. He saw a piano stool well suited to his strategy. This he could give up with good grace. "Now here's something," he said. "I wouldn't mind having this." He sounded as though he thought he could get it too.

The pastor glanced back and shook his head. "Belongs upstairs."

"Oh, I see," said Father Fabre submissively. There was no piano in the rectory, unless that, too, was in the pastor's room.

The pastor, obviously pleased with his curate's different tone, stopped to explain. "A lot of this will go upstairs when we're through remodeling."

Father Fabre forgot himself. "*Remodeling!*" he said, and tried to get the pastor to look him in the eye.

The pastor turned away.

Father Fabre, who was suddenly seeing his error, began to reflect upon it. There was no material evidence of remodeling, it was true, but he had impugned the pastor's good intentions. Was there a pastor worth his salt who didn't have improvements in mind, contractors and costs on the brain?

They moved deeper into the interior. Above them the jungle joined itself in places now. Father Fabre passed under the full length of a ski without taking notice of it until confronted by its triangular head, arching down at him. He shied away. Suddenly the pastor stopped. Father Fabre pulled up short, cradling his gun, which he'd been using as a cane. Something coiled on the trail?

"How's this?" said the pastor. He was trying the drawers of a pitiful old sideboard affair with its mirrors out and handles

maimed, a poor, blind thing. "Like this?" he said. He seemed
to have no idea what they were searching for.

"I need something to type on," Father Fabre said bluntly.

The pastor hit the trail again, somehow leaving the impression that Father Fabre was the one who was being difficult.

They continued to the uttermost end of the basement. Here
they were confronted by a small mountain of pamphlets. In the
bowels of the mountain something moved.

The pastor's hands shifted on his gun. "They're in there,"
he whispered, and drew back a pace. He waved Father Fabre to
one side, raised the gun, and pumped lead into the pamphlets.
Sput-flub. Sput-flub. Sput-spong-spit.

Father Fabre reached for his left leg, dropped to his knees,
his gun clattering down under him. He grabbed up his trouser
leg and saw the little hole bleeding in his calf. It hurt, but not
as much as he would've thought.

The pastor came over to examine the leg. He bent down.
"Just a flesh wound," he said, straightening up. "You're lucky."

"*Lucky!*"

"Tire there at the bottom of the pile. Absorbed most of the
fire power. Bullet went through and ricocheted. You're lucky.
Here." The pastor was holding out his hand.

"Oh, no," said Father Fabre, and lowered his trouser leg
over the wound.

The pastor seemed to be surprised that Father Fabre
wouldn't permit him to pinch the bullet out with his dirty
fingers.

Father Fabre stood up. The leg held him, but his walking
would be affected. He thought he could feel some blood in
his sock. "Afraid I'll have to leave you," he said. He glanced
at the pastor, still seeking sympathy. And there it was, at
last, showing in the pastor's face, some sympathy, and words
were on the way—no, caught again in the log jam of the man's
mind and needing a shove if they were to find their way down

to the mouth, and so Father Fabre kept on looking at the pastor, shoving ...

"Sorry it had to happen," muttered the pastor. Apparently that was going to be all. He was picking up Father Fabre's gun.

Painfully, Father Fabre began to walk. Sorry! That it *had* to happen! Anyone else, having fired the shot, would've been only too glad to assume the blame. What kind of man was this? This was a man of very few words, as everyone knew, and he had said he was sorry. How sorry then? Sorry enough?

Father Fabre stopped. "How about this?" he said, sounding as if he hadn't asked about the maple table before. It was a daring maneuver, but he was giving the pastor a chance to reverse himself without losing face, to redeem himself ...

The pastor was shaking his head.

Father Fabre lost patience. He'd let the old burglar shoot him down and this was what he got for it. "Why not?" he demanded.

The pastor was looking down, not meeting Father Fabre's eye. "You don't have a good easy chair, do you?"

Father Fabre, half turning, saw what the pastor had in mind. There just weren't any words for the chair. Father Fabre regarded it stoically—the dust lying fallow in the little mohair furrows, the ruptured bottom—and didn't know what to say. It would be impossible to convey his true feelings to the pastor. The pastor really did think that this was a good easy chair. There was no way to get at the facts with him. But the proper study of curates is pastors. "It's *too* good," Father Fabre said, making the most of his opportunity. "If I ever sat down in a chair like that I might never get up again. No, it's not for me."

Oh, the pastor was pleased—the man was literally smiling. Of a self-denying nature himself, famous for it in the diocese, he saw the temptation that such a chair would be to his curate.

"No?" he said, and appeared, besides pleased, relieved.

"No, thanks," said Father Fabre briskly, and moved on. It

might be interesting to see how far he could go with the man—but some other time. His leg seemed to be stiffening.

When they arrived back at the door, the pastor, in a manner that struck Father Fabre as too leisurely under the circumstances, racked the guns, hung up his cap, boxed the dust out of his knees and elbows, all the time gazing back where they'd been—not, Father Fabre thought, with the idea of returning to the rats as soon as he decently could, but with the eyes of a game conservationist looking to the future.

"I was thinking I'd better go to the hospital with this," said Father Fabre. He felt he ought to tell the pastor that he didn't intend to let the bullet remain in his leg.

He left the pastor to lock up, and limped out.

"Better take the car," the pastor called after him.

Father Fabre pulled up short. "*Thanks*," he said, and began to climb the stairs. The hospital was only a few blocks away, but it hadn't occurred to him that he might have walked there. He was losing every trick. Earlier he had imagined the pastor driving him to the hospital, and the scene there when they arrived—how it would be when the pastor's indifference to his curate's leg became apparent to the doctors and nurses, causing their hearts to harden against him. But all this the pastor had doubtless foreseen, and that was why he wasn't going along. The man was afraid of public opinion.

At the hospital, however, they only laughed when Father Fabre told them what had happened to him, and when, after they had taken the bullet out, he asked if they had to report the matter to the police. Just laughed at him. Only a flesh wound, they said. They didn't even want him to keep off the leg. It had been a mistake for him to ask. Laughed. Told him just to change his sock. But he arranged for the pastor to get the bill. And, on leaving, although he knew nothing would come of it, he said, "I thought you were required by law to report *all* gunshot cases."

When he returned to the rectory, the pastor and John were talking softly in the upstairs hall. They said nothing to him, which he thought strange, and so he said nothing to them. He was lucky, he guessed, that they hadn't laughed. He limped into his room, doubting whether John had even been told, and closed the door with a little bang. He turned and stood still. Then, after a few moments in which he realized why the pastor and John were in the hall, he limped over to the window—to the old mohair chair.

Ruefully, he recalled his false praise of the chair. How it had cost him! For the pastor had taken him at his word. After the shooting accident, the pastor must have been in no mood to give Father Fabre a table in which he seemed only half interested. Nothing would do then but that the wounded curate be compensated with the object of his only enthusiasm in the basement. No one knew better than the pastor where soft living could land a young priest, and yet there it was—luxury itself, procured by the pastor and dragged upstairs by his agent and now awaiting his curate's pleasure. And to think it might have been the maple table!

They clearly hadn't done a thing to the chair. The dust was all there, every grain intact. They were waiting for him, the pastor and John, waiting to see him sitting in it. He thought of disappointing them, of holing up as the pastor had earlier. But he just couldn't contend with the man anymore that day. He didn't know how he'd ever be able to thank them, John for carrying it up from the basement, the pastor for the thing itself, but he limped over to the door to let them in. Oh, it was a losing game.

DEFECTION OF A FAVORITE

I WAS WAITING in the lobby, sitting in a fairly clean overshoe, out of the draft and near a radiator, dozing, when the monthly meeting of the ushers ended and the men began to drift up from the church basement. Once a meeting got under way, the majority of the ushers, as well as Father Malt, their old pastor, liked to wind it up and break for the rectory, for pinochle and beer. Father Malt, seeing me, called "Fritz!" and I came, crossing in front of Mr Cormack, the new man, who muttered "Bad luck!" and blessed himself. I hadn't thought much about him before, but this little action suggested to me that his eyes were failing or that he was paranoidal, for, though a black cat, I have a redeeming band of white at my throat.

While I waited for the ushers to put their hats and coats on, I thought I saw their souls reflected in their mufflers, in those warm, unauthentic plaids and soiled white rayons and nylons, a few with fringe work, some worn as chokers in the nifty, or *haute*-California, manner, and some tucked in between coat and vest in a way that may be native to our part of Minnesota.

Father Malt and I went out the door together. Going bare-footed, as nature intended, I was warned of the old ice beneath the new-fallen snow. Father Malt, however, in shoes and over-shoes, walked blindly, and slipped and fell.

When several ushers took hold of Father Malt, Mr Keller, the head usher, a druggist and a friend of physicians, spoke with authority. "Don't move him! That's the worst thing you can do! Call an ambulance!"

Three ushers thought to cover Father Malt with their over-coats (three others, too late with theirs, held them in their hands), and everyone just stood and stared, as I did, at the old priest, my friend and protector, lying under the mound of over-coats, with the indifferent snow settling down as upon a new grave. I began to feel the cold in my bones and to think that I should certainly perish if I were locked out on such a night. I heard Mr Keller ordering Mr Cormack to the rectory to phone for an ambulance. Reluctantly—not through any deficiency in my sorrow—I left the scene of the accident, crossed the snowy lawn, and entered the rectory with Mr Cormack.

After Mr Cormack had summoned an ambulance, he called his old pastor, Father O'Hannon, of St Clara's, Minneapolis (of which Sherwood, our town, was gradually becoming a suburb), and asked him to be at the hospital, in case Father Malt should be in danger of death and in need of extreme unction. "The assistant here, Father Burner, isn't around. His car's gone from the garage, and there's no telling when that one'll be back," said Mr Cormack, sounding lonesome for his old parish. At St Clara's, he'd evidently been on more intimate terms with the priests. His last words to Father O'Hannon, "We could sure use someone like you out here," gave me the idea that he had gone fishing for Father Burner's favor but had caught one of the white whale's flukes. Now, like so many of us, he dreamed of getting even someday. I could only wish him luck as he left the rectory.

I watched at the window facing upon the tragedy, enduring

the cold draft there for Father Malt's sake, until the ambulance came. Then I retired to the parlor register and soon fell asleep —not without a prayer for Father Malt and many more for myself. With Father Burner running the rectory, it was going to be a hard, hard, and possibly fatal winter for me.

The ironic part was that Father Burner and I, bad as he was, had a lot in common. We disliked the same people (Mr Keller, for instance), we disliked the same dishes (those suited to Father Malt's dentures), but, alas, we also disliked each other. This fault originated in Father Burner's raw envy of me—which, however, I could understand. Father Malt didn't improve matters when he referred to me before visitors, in Father Burner's presence, as *the* assistant. I was realist enough not to hope for peace between us assistants as long as Father Malt lived. But it did seem a shame that there was no way of letting Father Burner know I was prepared—if and when his position improved —to be his friend and favorite, although not necessarily in that order. (For some reason, I seem to make a better favorite than friend.) As it was Father Burner's misfortune to remain a curate too long, it was mine to know that my life of privilege— my preferred place at table, for example—appeared to operate at the expense of his rights and might be the cause of my ultimate undoing. It was no good wishing, as I sometimes did, that Father Malt were younger—he was eighty-one—or that I were older, that we two could pass on together when the time came.

Along toward midnight, waking, I heard Father Burner's car pull into the driveway. A moment later the front porch cracked under his heavy step. He entered the rectory, galoshes and all, and, as was his custom, proceeded to foul his own nest wherever he went, upstairs and down. Finally, after looking, as he always did, for the telephone messages that seemingly never came, or, as he imagined, never got taken down, he went out on the front porch and brought in more snow and the evening paper. He sat reading in the parlor—it was then midnight—

still in his dripping galoshes, still in perfect ignorance of what had befallen Father Malt *and* me. Before he arrived, the telephone had been ringing at half-hour intervals—obviously the hospital, or one of the ushers, trying to reach him. The next time, I knew, it would toll for me.

Although I could see no way to avoid my fate, I did see the folly of waiting up for it. I left the parlor to Father Burner and went to the kitchen, where I guessed he would look last for me, if he knew anything of my habits, for I seldom entered there and never stayed long. Mrs Wynn, the housekeeper, loosely speaking, was no admirer of mine, nor I of her womanly disorder.

I concealed myself in a basket of clean, or at least freshly laundered, clothes, and presently, despite everything, I slept.

Early the following day, when Father Burner came downstairs, he had evidently heard the news, but he was late for his Mass, as usual, and had time for only one wild try at me with his foot. However, around noon, when he returned from the hospital, he paused only to phone the chancery to say that Father Malt had a fractured hip and was listed as "critical" and promptly chased me from the front of the house to the kitchen. He'd caught me in the act of exercising my claws on his new briefcase, which lay on the hall chair. The briefcase was a present to himself at Christmas—no one else thought quite so much of him—but he hadn't been able to find a real use for it and I think it piqued him to see that I had.

"I want that black devil kept out of my sight," he told Mrs Wynn, before whom he was careful to watch his language.

That afternoon I heard him telling Father Ed Desmond, his friend from Minneapolis, who'd dropped by, that he favored the wholesale excommunication of household pets from homes and particularly from rectories. He mentioned me in the same breath with certain parrots and hamsters he was familiar with. Although he was speaking on the subject of clutter, he said nothing about model railroads, Father Desmond's little vice, or about photography, his own. The term "household pet" struck me as a double-barreled euphemism, unpetted as I was and denied the freedom of the house.

And still, since I'd expected to be kicked out into the weather, and possibly not to get that far alive, I counted my deportation to the kitchen as a blessing—a temporary one, however. I had no reason to believe that Father Burner's feeling about me had changed. I looked for something new in persecutions. When nothing happened, I looked all the harder.

I spent my days in the kitchen with Mrs Wynn, sleeping when I could, just hanging around in her way when I couldn't. If I wearied of that, as I inevitably did, I descended into the cellar. The cellar smelled of things too various—laundry, coal, developing fluid, and mice—and the unseemly noise of the home-canned goods digesting on the shelves, which another might never notice, reached and offended my ears. After an hour down there, where the floor was cold to my feet, I was ready to return to the kitchen and Mrs Wynn.

Mrs Wynn had troubles of her own—her husband hit the jar —but they did nothing to Christianize her attitude toward me. She fed me scraps, and kicked me around, not hard but regularly, in the course of her work. I expected little from her, however. She was another in the long tradition of unjust stewards.

Father Burner's relatively civil conduct was harder to comprehend. One afternoon, rising from sleep and finding the kitchen door propped open, I forgot myself and strolled into the parlor, into his very presence. He was reading *Church Property Administration*, a magazine I hadn't seen in the house before. Having successfully got that far out of line—as far as the middle of the room—I decided to keep going. As if by chance, I came to my favorite register, where, after looking about to estimate the shortest distance between me and any suitable places of refuge in the room, I collapsed around the heat. There was still no intimation of treachery—only peace surpassing all understanding, only the rush of warmth from the register, the winds of winter outside, and the occasional click and whisper of a page turning in *Church Property Administration.*

Not caring to push my luck, wishing to come and doze another day, wanting merely to establish a precedent, I got up and strolled back into the kitchen—to think. I threw out the possibility that Father Burner had suffered a lapse of memory, had forgotten the restriction placed on my movements. I conceived the idea that he'd lost, or was losing, his mind, and then, grudgingly, I gave up the idea. He was not trying to ignore me. He was ignoring me without trying. I'd been doing the same thing to people for years, but I'd never dreamed that one of them would do it to me.

From that day on, I moved freely about the house, as I had in Father Malt's time, and Mrs Wynn, to add to the mystery, made no effort to keep me with her in the kitchen. I was thus in a position to observe other lapses or inconsistencies in Father Burner. Formerly, he'd liked to have lights burning all over the house. Now that he was paying the bill, the place was often shrouded in darkness. He threw out the tattered rugs at the front and back doors and bought rubber mats—at a saving, evidently, for although one mat bore the initial "B," the other had an "R," which stood for nobody but may have been the closest thing he could get to go with the "B." I noticed, too, that he took off his galoshes before entering the house, as though it were no longer just church property but home to him.

I noticed that he was going out less with his camera, and to the hospital more, not just to visit Father Malt, to whom he'd never had much to say, but to visit the sick in general.

In former times, he had been loath to go near the hospital during the day, and at night, before he'd leave his bed to make a sick call, there had had to be infallible proof that a patient was in danger of death. It had been something awful to hear him on the line with the hospital in the wee hours, haggling, asking if maybe they weren't a little free and easy with their designation "critical," as, indeed, I believe some of them liked to be. He'd tried to get them to change a patient's "critical" to "fair" (which meant he could forget about that one), and acted as though there were some therapeutic power about the word, if the hospital could just be persuaded to make use of it. Father Malt, with his hearing aid off, was virtually deaf, Mrs Wynn roomed down the street, and so I had been the one to suffer. "Oh, go on, go on," I'd wanted to say. "Go on over there, or don't go—but hang up! Some of us want to sleep!" There were nights when I'd hardly sleep a wink—unlike Father Burner, who, even if he *did* go to the hospital, would come bumbling back and drop off with his clothes on.

In general, I now found his attitude toward his duties altered, but not too much so, not extreme. If he'd had a night of sick calls, he'd try to make up for it with a nap before dinner. His trouble was still a pronounced unwillingness to take a total loss on sacrifice.

I found other evidence of the change he was undergoing—outlines of sermons in the wastebasket, for instance. In the past, he'd boasted that he thought of whatever he was going to say on Sunday in the time it took him to walk from the altar to the pulpit. He was not afraid to speak on the parishioners' duty to contribute generously to the support of the church, a subject neglected under Father Malt, who'd been satisfied with what the people wanted to give—very little. Father Burner tried to get them interested in the church. He said it was a matter of pride—pride in the good sense of the word. I felt he went too far, however, when, one Sunday, he told the congregation that it was their church *and* their rectory. There had always been too many converts hanging around the house for instruction, and now there were more of them than in Father Malt's day. The house just wasn't large enough for all of us.

Father Desmond, noting how little time Father Burner now had for himself (and for Father Desmond), suggested that the chancery be petitioned for help ("There's just too much work here for one man, Ernest"), but Father Burner said no, and so resisted what must have been the worst of all possible temptations to him, the assistant's sweet dream—to have an assistant. He said he'd go it alone. It almost seemed as if he were out to distinguish himself, not in the eyes of others—something he'd always worked at—but in his own eyes.

At any rate, he was beginning to act and talk like a real pastor. When Father Desmond came over or phoned, they talked of construction and repairs. Father Desmond, one of our most promising young pastors, was building a new school—with undue emphasis, it seemed to me, on the gymnasium. Father Burner, lacking authority to do more, made needed repairs. He had the rectory kitchen painted and purchased a Mixmaster for Mrs Wynn. He had the windows in the church basement calked and installed a small institutional kitchen there, thus showing all too clearly that he intended to go in for parish suppers, which he'd abominated in the past as the hardest part of the priesthood.

Father Desmond and Father Burner now spoke fluently a gibberish that only a building pastor could comprehend. They talked of organs, bells, and bulletin boards, coin counters, confessional chairs and hearing devices, flooring, kneeler pads, gym seats, radiation, filing systems, electric fans, mops, and brooms, and all by their difficult trade names—Wurlitzer, Carillonic, Confessionaire, Confession-Ease, Speed Sweep, the Klopp (coin counter); Vakumatic, Scrubber-Vac, Kardex, Mopmaster, and many more. And shrubbery and trees.

There was a great need for trees in Sherwood—a need that, I daresay, had never occurred to Father Malt, or, presumably, to many of the older inhabitants of the town. The new people, who lived in "ranch houses" and worked in Minneapolis, seemed to like trees, and so, in his new phase, did Father Burner.

"When spring comes," he said, in cold January, 'I'll plant some maples."

Father Desmond, who knew where Father Burner's thoughts were hiding, said, "Someday you'll build, too, Ernest."

After fourteen months in the hospital, Father Malt was moved to the sisters' infirmary in St Paul, where there were supposed to be other patients, including old priests, of similar tastes and outlook. In our busy rectory, the seasons had come and gone without pause, the seasons as we observed them—baseball, football, Christmas, basketball, and Lent again. There were further improvements, or at least changes. Father Burner got Mrs Wynn a white radio for her kitchen and thereby broke the tradition of silence we'd had under Father Malt, who hadn't even listened to Cedric Adams and the ten o'clock news.

I spent my mornings in the parlor and thus escaped the full effect of Mrs Wynn's programs, but in the parlor, or wherever I went in the house, I heard those same voices, always at the same hour, always repeating themselves, and for a while, at first, I took a certain interest in those miserable lives. Can a woman over thirty-five find love again? Should a girl, the ward of a man twenty years older, marry him? For these questions, as time went on, I could see there would be no answers.

In our rectory, another question was being asked, and for this question there had to be an answer. Father Burner was pastor of the church in all but name, and could hope, with good reason, that this, too, would be added unto him in time, if he worked and prayed hard enough. During the first weeks after the accident, Father Burner and Father Desmond had discussed the physical aspects of Father Malt's case—what kind of cast, the number and type of pins, and all the rest. Lately, however, they'd been taking another line, more to the point and touching upon Father Burner's chances.

The difficulty lay, of course, in Father Malt's refusal to give himself up to the life of an invalid. Nothing could be done about appointing his successor until he actually resigned or died. No one, of course, openly suggested that he do either. It was up to him to decide. Father Desmond believed that, sooner or later, the Archbishop would go to Father Malt and precipitate a solution of the problem. But even the Archbishop was powerless to force Father Malt to resign against his will. As long as Father Malt wished, as long as he lived, he would be pastor, and this was according to canon law. Father Malt was an "irremovable pastor," well liked by the people of the parish, a favorite at the chancery, where, however, it was known—according to Father Desmond—that Father Burner was doing a bang-up job.

Father Burner was the rare one who hadn't asked for help, who was going it alone, with just two monks, down from St John's, to assist him over weekends. He would go on retreat in June for five days (he wasn't much on card games, though), but he planned no regular vacation. He worked like a dog. He lost weight. He was tired. I was edified.

In May, I heard Father Desmond say, "Ernest, it's time to widen your circle of friends," and so Father Burner, rather unwillingly, tried to give a poker party at the rectory. Father Desmond, popular (as Father Burner wasn't) with the older men, a surprising number of whom claimed to have sold him on sobriety, invited several pastors and, significantly, no curates. But only two of those invited showed up—Father Kling and Father Moore. They belonged to the active set, a kind of Jockey Club for pastors, which maintained a floating poker game, a duck-blind, and a summer lodge. They gambled, hunted, and fished in common.

On the evening of the party, when they came into the dining room, where the cards and chips were laid out, I could see that Father Desmond had led them to believe that Father Burner, of all people, was playing host to an almost official session. Father Kling, a forceful man, glanced at Father Moore, a mild one, and remarked that he'd understood others were coming. With good grace, however, he and Father Moore sat down to play.

Father Desmond, who seemed to regard his function as essentially one of public relations, started right in to plump for Father Burner. "It's a shame somebody doesn't tell the old man to retire," he said, referring to Father Malt. "It's not fair to Ernest, here, and it's not fair to the parish. This place needs a young man, with young ideas." I, for one, wasn't surprised by the utter silence that followed these remarks. Father Kling and Father Moore, as even Father Desmond should've known, were not so young themselves, nor were they so hot on young ideas.

Father Burner wisely stayed out of it. Father Desmond continued along the same lines, however, until Father Kling commented dryly, "It's his hip, not his mind, that's gone wrong, isn't it?" and drained his highball.

"He's had quite a time of it, hasn't he?" said Father Moore gently. "Poor Dutch."

"How about poor Ernest?" asked Father Desmond.

"Uh, yes, of course," said Father Moore.

Father Desmond seemed to realize that he was doing no good and shut up. At least he might have waited, I thought, until they were feeling better. Father Kling had a little pile in front of him, and perhaps he'd remember where he got it. That was the only thing in Father Burner's favor when Mrs Wynn came into the dining room and announced the Archbishop and another priest.

I followed Father Burner out of the dining room, but stopped at the door to the parlor, into which Mrs Wynn had shown the guests. I preferred to enter unobserved.

When Father Burner attempted to kiss the episcopal ring, the Archbishop put his hand behind him. He reserved the ring-kissing business for ceremonial occasions, as everyone knew, but it was customary to make a try for it.

At Father Burner's invitation, the Archbishop and his companion, a young priest whose eyes looked as though he'd been driving all day, sat down, and at that juncture Father Desmond and the two other poker players came in to declare themselves. While they, too, tried to get at the Archbishop's ring, I slipped into the parlor unseen and then along the wall until I came to the library table. There, back out of view, at the intersection of the crossbars supporting the table, I took up my position.

The Archbishop said that they'd been passing the church, on their way back from a confirmation tour along the northern marches of the diocese, when he thought of dropping in on Father Burner.

"It's good to see you all together," he said, looking them over. He liked to have his priests associating with one another, I knew, and not seeking other company to excess—except, of course, when necessary at parish functions.

The Archbishop asked about Father Malt (I daresay His Excellency, of those present, had seen him last), and Father Burner and Father Desmond, replying, sounded a little too broken up to suit my taste, or to sound much like themselves.

When the conversation came around to Father Burner and the fine work he was doing, Father Desmond ran it into the ground. He fed the most leading questions to Father Burner, who expressed himself well, I thought, although referring too often to the Archbishop for a higher opinion on trivial matters. It galled me to see Father Desmond turning the occasion into a grease job all around. Father Burner, possibly recognizing this but not able to turn Father Desmond off, excused himself and went down the hallway to the kitchen.

Father Desmond, speaking in a near whisper, as if he were

telling a secret, said, "You know, Your Excellency, Father's taken some nice shots of the Cathedral at night. If you'd care to see them . . ."

"I believe I've seen them," said the Archbishop. He was looking over Father Desmond's shoulder, disapprovingly, at his own smiling picture on the wall—not one of Father Burner's shots, however.

"Yes," said Father Desmond. "But he doesn't have time for much anymore."

The Archbishop nodded, and got up from his chair. "Excuse me, Father," he said. He crossed the room to the bookcase.

Mrs Wynn entered the parlor with a tray of wineglasses, which she placed on the table.

Father Burner followed her with a bottle. I was happy to see that he'd had good luck with the cork. Later on, when the Archbishop had left, they'd switch back to bourbon (except Father Desmond, who was on 7UP). For some reason, sacramental wine, taken daily, spoiled them for other wines.

"This is hardly the time, but it may be the place to ask you," said Father Burner, handing the Archbishop his glass, "but with Father Malt off the scene, Your Excellency, I was wondering if I dare go ahead with a tuck-pointing job on the church. I've been considering it—only academically, that is, Your Excellency, because it'll run into quite a lot of money." The Archbishop was silent. Father Burner started up again, in a manner feeble for him. "In the pastor's temporary absence, the disposition of these matters . . ."

"Couldn't it wait a bit, Father?" asked the Archbishop. It was a tense moment, a difficult reply indeed, when one tried to analyze it, as I did. At its best, it could mean that Father Burner would soon be empowered to make decisions concerning the church; at its worst, it could mean that the Archbishop expected Father Malt to recover and take over again, or, what was most likely, that he was not considering the question at all, regarded it as out of order, ill-timed, and impertinent. I felt that the Archbishop understood the reason for it, however. Father Burner had been overwhelmed by the visit, and flattered that others, particularly Father Kling and Father Moore, should be present to witness it. Such a visit—not an official visitation—could be enough to make him. It had been a great night for Father Burner until he popped that question.

When, a few minutes later, the Archbishop got up to leave, I came out from under the library table, went over to Father Burner, and brushed up against his trouser leg, purring.

The Archbishop, hearing me, I think, before he saw me, gazed down and said, "Do you like animals, Father?"

"Yes, Your Excellency," said Father Burner, who was only a dog-lover at best, and where I was concerned, I know, his answer was a barefaced lie—until he made it. From that moment on—there was no doubt of it—he loved me.

"This one, I see, likes you," said the Archbishop, smiling. "Some believe it to be an infallible sign, the best of character references."

Father Burner blushed and said, "I wish I could believe in that sign, Your Excellency."

I trotted over to the Archbishop, selected his black trouser leg from all the others, and brushed against it, nicely purring. Everyone laughed.

"*Credo!*" cried Father Burner.

I was not surprised when, on the following morning, Father Burner invited me to join him at table for breakfast. I had wanted my elevation to my former place to happen of itself, to be a voluntary act on Father Burner's part, as mine had been on his account, and for that reason, and because I wanted Mrs Wynn to get a good eyeful, I'd remained in the kitchen, awaiting, as it were, my nomination. After offering Mass, Father Burner came and sought me.

"Where's Fritz?" he asked.

"Who?" said Mrs Wynn.

"Fritz," Father Burner said. "My cat."

"Oh, him," said Mrs Wynn, who, it occurred to me, represented the sort of person who could live in the thick of history and never know the difference.

I walked out from under the kitchen table. Father Burner knelt and lifted me into his arms. He carried me into the dining room and pulled my old chair away from the wall and up to the table. We both sat down—to what I hoped would be only the first of many pleasant meals together.

I ate my bacon right royally and ruminated on the events of the evening before. I could not honestly say that I'd planned the splendid thing I'd done. It had more or less happened—unless, of course, I was both kinder and wiser than I believed myself to be. I was eating high on the hog again, I had my rightful place back, my reward for patience, and I was only sorry that Father Burner still had to wait for his. His buds had been pinched off at the start, but his roots had grown strong and deep. If he managed to flower, he'd be the classic type of late-blooming pastor. Until then he had me at his side, to him everything I'd been to Father Malt—friend and favorite, and, more, the very symbol and prefigurement of power. I actually liked him, I discovered. I liked him for what I'd done for him. But why had I done it? I didn't really know why. I work at times in ways so inscrutable that even I cannot tell what good or evil I am up to.

Before we'd finished breakfast, Father Desmond phoned—to discuss the Archbishop's visit, I gathered, for Father Burner said, "I've decided not to talk anymore about it, Ed." I could almost hear Father Desmond squawking, "Whatta ya mean, Ernest?" "Maybe that's part of the trouble," Father Burner said. "We're talkin' it to death." Evidently Father Desmond took offense at that, for Father Burner spoke quickly, out of context.

"Why don't you come for dinner sometime, Ed? When? Well, come tomorrow. Come early. Good."

Father Burner hung up, bounced over to the table, chucked me fondly behind the ears, took a banana out of the fruit bowl, and went whistling off to his car—off to do the work of the parish, to return a defective length of hose, to visit the sick and pregnant, to drive to Minneapolis for more informal conferences with building experts, lay and clerical. He had several projects going ahead—academically, that is: the tuck pointing, a new decorating job inside the church, and outside, possibly, a floodlight on the dome, which I thought a paltry affair better left in the dark.

Before lunch that day, he returned with a half dozen mousetraps. He seemed to want me to follow him around the house, and therefore I attended him most faithfully, while he set the traps in what he regarded as likely places. I rather expected to be jollied about my indifference to mousing. There was none of that, however, and what might have been an embarrassing experience for me became instead an occasion of instruction. Using a pencil for a mouse, Father Burner showed me how the trap worked, which was quite unnecessary but a nice gesture, I thought.

That evening—with Father Burner still in the mood to exterminate—we appeared together for the first time in public, at the monthly meeting of the ushers. In the future, Father Burner announced, all notices of the sort now being posted on the bulletin board at the rear of the church would have to emanate from his office (which, strictly speaking, was his bedroom) and carry his signature. This was a cruel but unavoidable check to Mr Keller, who had become too prolific for his own good. He used the drugstore typewriter and special engraved cards bearing his name and title, and he took an authoritarian tone in matters of etiquette ("Keep your feet off the kneelers," "Don't stand in the back of the church," "Ask the usher to find you a seat—that's what he's there for," etc.), and in other matters (Lost and Found, old-clothes collections, ticket sales, and the like) he made it sound as though these were all services and causes thought up and sponsored by him personally. I felt that he was not far from posting bargains in real estate, another means of livelihood for him at the drugstore, when Father Burner stepped in. Mr Keller took it well—too well, I thought. He murmured a few meek words about trying to spare Father Burner the trouble, as he'd spared Father Malt the trouble. (He now visited Father Malt regularly at the infirmary.) Before we left, he asked Father Burner to lead the ushers in the usual prayer for Father Malt's swift recovery.

It was early afternoon the next day when Father Burner remembered the mousetraps. I accompanied him on his rounds, but there was nothing I liked about the business before us. First we went to the pantry and kitchen, where Mrs Wynn constantly dropped and mislaid quantities of food. Any mouse caught in a trap there, I thought, deserved to die for his gluttony. None had. In the cellar, however, Father Burner had snared two young ones, both from a large family whose members I saw from time to time. My record with them had been good, and they, in turn, had played fair with me and had committed no obvious depredations to make me look bad. When their loss was noted, the others, I feared, would blame me—not for the crime itself but for letting it happen within my precinct.

Father Burner removed the little bodies from the traps, and then, with the best of intentions and with a smile, which only made it worse, he did a terrible thing. He extended a hand to me, a hand curled in kindness, inviting me to banquet on the remains. I turned away in a swoon, physically sick and sick at heart. I made my way upstairs, wanting to be alone. I considered bitterly others I'd known and trusted in the past. Always, except with Father Malt, when I'd persuaded myself to take a

chance on one of them, there'd be something like this. I tried
to forget, or to sleep it off, which proved impossible. I knew
what I had to do before I could begin to forget, and so I did it. I
forgave Father Burner. It was another lesson in charity, one
that cost me more than my going to bat for him with the
Archbishop, but I'm afraid it was entirely lost on him.

Father Desmond came for dinner that afternoon at four, which
I thought rather early even for "early." When he arrived, I was
in the front hall having a go at the briefcase. He went right past
me. I could see that he had something on his mind.

"I just couldn't stay away," he said, taking a chair across
from Father Burner in the parlor. "I've got what I *think* is good
news, Ernest."

Father Burner glanced up from *Church Property Administration* and shook his head. "I don't want to hear it," he said,
"if it's about you-know-what."

"I'll just tell you what I *know* to be true," Father Desmond
said, "and let it go at that."

"Whatever it is, it can wait," said Father Burner. I could see,
however, that he'd listen if he was primed again.

Father Desmond bore down on him. "Sure, I know, you'll
get it in the mail—when you get it. That's what you figure. I
admire your restraint, Ernest, but let's not be superstitious
about it, either."

Father Burner, sprawling in his chair, rolled and unrolled
Church Property Administration. Then, making a tube of it,
he put it to his eye and peered through it, down his black leg, a
great distance, and appeared finally to sight the silver glow on
the toe of his big black shoe, which lay in the sunlight. "All
right, Ed," he said. "Let's have it."

"All right, then," said Father Desmond. "Here it is. I have it
on reliable authority—that is to say, my spies tell me—the
Archbishop visited the infirmary today." I interpreted "spies"

to mean some little nun or other on whom Father Desmond bestowed sample holy cards.

Father Burner, taking a long-suffering tone in which there was just a touch of panic, said, "Ed, you know he does that all the time. You'll have to do better than that."

Father Desmond tried to come up with more. "He had *words* with Dutch."

Father Burner flung himself out of his chair. He engaged in swordplay with the air, using *Church Property Adminis-tration*. "How do you mean 'he had words'? You don't mean to say they quarreled?"

Father Desmond could only reply, "I just mean they talked at *some* length."

Father Burner gave a great snort and threw *Church Property Administration* across the room. It clattered against the bookcase, a broken sword. He wheeled and walked the floor, demanding, "Then why'd you say they had words? Why make something out of nothing? Why not tell it straight, Ed? Just once, huh?" He was standing over Father Desmond.

"You're under a strain, Ernest," said Father Desmond, getting up from his chair. "Maybe I shouldn't have said anything about it at all."

Father Burner stared at him. "*Said?* Said *what?* That's just it, Ed—you haven't said anything." He took another walk around the room, saying the word "nothing" over and over to himself.

Father Desmond cut in, "All right, Ernest, I'm sorry," and sat down in his chair.

Then Father Burner, too, sat down, and both men were overcome by quiet and perhaps shame. Several minutes passed. I was sorry for Father Burner. He'd sacrificed his valuable silence to his curiosity and received nothing in return.

I addressed the briefcase, making my claws catch and pop in the soft, responsive leather. I wished that I were plucking instead at the top of Father Desmond's soft head.

Father Desmond glanced over at me and then at Father Burner.

"Why do you let him do that?" he asked.

"He likes to."

"Yeah?" said Father Desmond. "Does he ever bring you a mouse?"

With one paw poised, I listened for Father Burner's answer.

"You don't see any around, do you?" he said.

Well done, I thought, and renewed my attack on the briefcase. I had the feeling that Father Desmond still wanted to tell the world what he'd do to me if it were his briefcase, but, if so, he denied himself and got out a cigar.

"What'd you think of the plans for that rectory in South Dakota?" he asked.

"Not bad," said Father Burner, looking around for his *Church Property Administration*.

"There it is," said Father Desmond, as if it were always misplacing itself. He went over by the bookcase, picked up the magazine, and delivered it to Father Burner.

I curled up to nap. I could see that they were going to have one of their discussions.

When I heard the back door open, I supposed it was Mrs Wynn coming in to start dinner, but it was Mr Keller. I saw him advancing gravely up the hallway, toward me, carrying a traveling bag that I recognized as one the ushers had given Father Malt. Instantly I concluded that Father Malt had passed away in the night, that the nuns had failed to inform Father Burner, and had instead told Mr Keller, the faithful visitor, to whom they'd also entrusted the deceased's few belongings.

Mr Keller set down the bag and, without looking into the parlor, started back the way he'd come, toward the back door. Father Burner and Father Desmond, at the sight of the bag, seemed unable to rise from their chairs, powerless to speak.

After a moment, I saw Father Malt emerging from the

kitchen, on crutches, followed by Mr Keller. He worked his way up the hallway, talking to himself. "Somebody painted my kitchen," I heard him say.

I beheld him as one risen from the dead. He looked the same to me but different—an imperfect reproduction of himself as I recalled him, imperfect only because he appeared softer, whiter, and, of course, because of the crutches.

Not seeing me by the hatrack, he clumped into the parlor, nodded familiarly to Father Burner and Father Desmond, and said, again to himself, "Somebody changed my chairs around."

Father Desmond suddenly shot up from his chair, said, "I gotta go," and went. Mr Keller seemed inclined to stick around. Father Burner, standing, waited for Father Malt to come away from the library table, where he'd spotted some old copies of *Church Property Administration*.

Father Malt thrust his hand under the pile of magazines, weighed it, and slowly, with difficulty, turned on his crutches, to face Father Burner.

They stared at each other, Father Malt and Father Burner, like two popes themselves not sure which one was real.

I decided to act. I made my way to the center of the room and stood between them. I sensed them both looking at me, then *to* me—for a sign. Canon law itself was not more clear, more firm, than the one I lived by. I turned my back on Father Burner, went over to Father Malt, and favored him with a solemn purr and dubbed his trouser leg lightly with my tail, reversing the usual course of prerogative between lord and favorite, switching the current of power. With a purr, I'd restored Father Malt's old authority in the house. Of necessity—authority as well as truth being one and indivisible—I'd unmade Father Burner. I was sorry for him.

He turned and spoke harshly to Mr Keller. "Why don't you go see if you left the back door open?"

When Father Burner was sure that Mr Keller had gone, he

faced Father Malt. The irremovable pastor stood perspiring on his crutches. As long as he lived, he had to be pastor, I saw; his need was the greater. And Father Burner saw it, too. He went up to Father Malt, laid a strong, obedient hand on the old one that held tight to the right crutch, and was then the man he'd been becoming.

"Hello, boss," he said. "Glad you're back."

It was his finest hour. In the past, he had lacked the will to accept his setbacks with grace and had derived no merit from them. It was difficult to believe that he'd profited so much from my efforts in his behalf—my good company and constant example. I was happy for him.

ZEAL

SOUTH OF ST PAUL the conductor appeared at the head of the coach, held up his ticket punch, and clicked it.

The Bishop felt for his ticket. It was there.

"I know it's not a pass," said Father Early. He had been talking across the aisle to one of the pilgrims he was leading to Rome, but now he was back on the subject of the so-called clergy pass. "But it is a privilege."

The Bishop said nothing. He'd meant to imply by his silence before, when Father Early brought up the matter, that there was nothing wrong with an arrangement which permitted the clergy to travel in parlor cars at coach rates. The Bishop wished the arrangement were in effect in all parts of the country, and on all trains.

"But on a run like this, Bishop, with these fine coaches, I daresay there aren't many snobs who'll go to the trouble of filling out the form."

The Bishop looked away. Father Early had a nose like a parrot's and something on it like psoriasis that held the Bishop's attention—unfortunately, for Father Early seemed to think it was his talk. The Bishop had a priest or two in his diocese like Father Early.

"Oh, the railroads, I daresay, mean well."

"Yes," said the Bishop distantly. The voice at his right ear went on without him. He gazed out the window, up at the limestone scarred by its primeval intercourse with the Mississippi, now shrunk down into itself, and there he saw a cave, another cave, and another. Criminals had been discovered in them, he understood, and ammunition from the Civil War, and farther down the river, in the high bluffs, rattlesnakes were said to be numerous still.

"Bishop, I don't think I'm one to strain at a gnat." (The Bishop glanced at Father Early's nose with interest.) "But I must say I fear privilege more than persecution. Of course the one follows the other, as the night the day."

"Is it true, Father, that there are rattlesnakes along here?"

"Very likely," said Father Early, hardly bothering to look out the window. "Bishop, I was dining in New York, in a crowded place, observed by all and sundry, when the management tried to present me with a bottle of wine. Well!"

The Bishop, spying a whole row of caves, thought of the ancient Nile. Here, though, the country was too fresh and frigid. Here the desert fathers would've married early and gone fishing. The aborigines, by their fruits, pretty much proved that. He tried again to interrupt Father Early. "There must be a cave for you up there, somewhere, Father."

Father Early responded with a laugh that sounded exactly like ha-ha, no more or less. "I'll tell you a secret, Bishop. When I was in seminary, they called me Crazy Early. I understand they still do. Perhaps you knew."

"No," said the Bishop. Father Early flattered himself. The Bishop had never heard of him until that day.

"I thought perhaps Monsignor Reed had told you."

"I seldom see him." He saw Reed only by accident, at somebody's funeral or jubilee celebration or, it seemed, in railroad
stations, which had happened again in Minneapolis that morning. It was Reed who had introduced Father Early to him then.
Had Reed known what he was doing? It was six hours to Chicago, hours of this . . .

"I suppose you know Macaulay's *England*, Bishop."

"No." There was something to be gained by a frank admission of ignorance when it was assumed anyway.

"Read the section dealing with the status of the common
clergy in the eighteenth century. I'm talking about the Anglican clergy. Hardly the equal of servants, knaves, figures of
fun! The fault of the Reformation, you say? Yes, of course"—
the Bishop had in no way signified assent—"but I say it could
happen anywhere, everywhere, any time! Take what's going on
in parts of Europe today. When you consider the status of the
Church there in the past, and the overwhelmingly catholic
population even now. I wonder, though, if it doesn't take
something to bring us to our senses from time to time—*now*
what do you say, Bishop?"

If the conductor hadn't been upon them, the Bishop
would've said there was probably less danger of the clergy getting above themselves than there was of their being accepted
for less than they were; or at least for less than they were supposed to be; or was that what Father Early was saying?

The conductor took up their tickets, placed two receipts
overhead, one white and one blue. Before he moved on, he advised the Bishop to bring his receipt with him, the blue one,
when he moved into the parlor car.

The Bishop nodded serenely.

Beside him, Father Early was full of silence, and opening
his breviary.

The Bishop, who had expected to be told apologetically
that it was a matter of no importance if he'd used his clergy

pass, had an uncomfortable feeling that Father Early was praying for him.

At Winona, the train stopped for a minute. The Bishop from his window saw Father Early on the platform below talking to an elderly woman. In parting, they pecked at each other, and she handed him a box. Returning to his seat, he said he'd had a nice visit with his sister. He went to the head of the coach with the box, and came slowly back down the aisle, offering the contents to the pilgrims. "Divinity? Divinity?" The Bishop, when his turn came, took a piece, and consumed it. Then he felt committed to stay with Father Early until Chicago.

It was some time before Father Early returned to his seat —from making the acquaintance of Monsignor Reed's parishioners. "What we did was split the responsibility. Miss Culhane's in charge of Monsignor's people. Of course, the ultimate responsibility is mine." Peering up the aisle at two middle-aged women drawing water from the cooler, Father Early said, "The one coming this way now," and gazed out the window.

Miss Culhane, a paper cup in each hand, smiled at the Bishop. He smiled back.

When Miss Culhane had passed, Father Early said, "She's been abroad once, and that's more than most of 'em can say. She's a secretary in private life, and it's hard to find a man with much sense of detail. But I don't know . . . From what I've heard already I'd say the good people don't like the idea. I'm afraid they think she stands between them and me."

The other woman, also carrying paper cups, came down the aisle, and again Father Early gazed out the window. So did the Bishop. When the woman had gone by, Father Early commented dryly, "Her friend, whose name escapes me. Between the two of 'em, Bishop . . . Oh, it'll be better for all concerned when Monsignor joins us."

The Bishop knew nothing about this. Reed had told him nothing. "*Monsignor?*"

"Claims he's allergic to trains."

"*Reed?*"

Again Father Early treated the question as rhetorical. "His plane doesn't arrive until noon tomorrow. We sail at four. That doesn't give us much time in New York."

The Bishop was putting it all together. Evidently Reed was planning to have as much privacy as he could on the trip. Seeing his little flock running around loose in the station, though, he must have felt guilty—and then the Bishop had happened along. Would Reed do this to him? Reed had done this to him. Reed had once called the Bishop's diocese the next thing to a titular see.

"I'm sorry he isn't sailing with us," said Father Early.

"Isn't he?"

"He's got business of some kind—stained glass, I believe—that'll keep him in New York for a few days. He may have to go to Boston. So he's flying over. I wonder, Bishop, if he isn't allergic to boats too." Father Early smiled at the Bishop as one good sailor to another.

The Bishop wasn't able to smile back. He was thinking how much he preferred to travel alone. When he was being hustled into the coach by Reed and Father Early, he hadn't considered the embarrassment there might be in the end; together on the train to Chicago and again on the one to New York and then crossing on the same liner, apart, getting an occasional glimpse of each other across the barriers. The perfidious Reed had united them, knowing full well that the Bishop was traveling first class and that Father Early and the group were going tourist. The Bishop hoped there would be time for him to see Reed in New York. According to Father Early, though, Reed didn't want them to look for him until they saw him. The Bishop wouldn't.

Miss Culhane, in the aisle again, returned with more water. When she passed, the Bishop and Father Early were both looking out the window. "You can't blame 'em," Father Early said. "I wish he'd picked a man for the job. No, they want more than a man, Bishop. They want a priest."

"They've got you," said the Bishop. "And Monsignor will soon be with you."

"Not until we reach Rome."

"*No?*" The Bishop was rocked by this new evidence of Reed's ruthlessness. Father Early and the group were going to Ireland and England first, as the Bishop was, but they'd be spending more time in those countries, about two weeks.

"No," said Father Early. "He won't."

The Bishop got out his breviary. He feared that Father Early would not be easily discouraged. The Bishop, if he could be persuaded to join the group, would more than make up for the loss of Reed. To share the command with such a man as Father Early, however, would be impossible. It would be to serve under him—as Reed may have realized. The Bishop would have to watch out. It would be dangerous for him to offer Father Early plausible excuses, to point out, for instance, that they'd be isolated from each other once they sailed from New York. Such an excuse, regretfully tendered now, could easily commit him to service on this train, and on the next one, and in New York—and the Bishop wasn't at all sure that Father Early wouldn't find a way for him to be with the group aboard ship. The Bishop turned a page.

When Father Early rose and led the pilgrims in the recitation of the rosary, the Bishop put aside his breviary, took out his beads and prayed along with them. After that, Father Early directed the pilgrims in the singing of "Onward, Christian Soldiers"—which was *not* a Protestant hymn, not originally, he said. Monsignor Reed's parishioners didn't know the words, but Father Early got around that difficulty by having everyone sing the notes of the scale, the ladies *la*, the men *do*. The Bishop cursed his luck and wouldn't even pretend to sing. Father Early was in the aisle, beating time with his fist, exhorting some by name to contribute more to the din, clutching others (males) by the shoulders until they did. The Bishop grew afraid that even he might not be exempt, and again sought the protection of his breviary.

He had an early lunch. When he returned to his seat, it was just past noon, and Father Early was waiting in the aisle for him.

"How about a bite to eat, Bishop?"

"I've eaten, Father."

"You eat early, Bishop."

"I couldn't wait."

Father Early did his little ha-ha laugh. "By the way, Bishop, are you planning anything for the time we'll have in Chicago between trains?" Before the Bishop, who was weighing the significance of the question, could reply, Father Early told him that the group was planning a visit to the Art Institute. "The Art Treasures of Vienna are there now."

"I believe I've seen them, Father."

"In Vienna, Bishop?"

"Yes."

"Well, they should be well worth seeing again."

"Yes. But I don't think I'll be seeing them." Not expecting the perfect silence that followed—this from Father Early was more punishing than his talk—the Bishop added, "Not today." Then, after more of that silence, "I've nothing planned, Father." Quickly, not liking the sound of that, "I do have a few things I might do."

Father Early nodded curtly and went away.

The Bishop heard him inviting some of the group to have lunch with him.

During the rest of the afternoon, the indefatigable voice of Father Early came to the Bishop from all over the coach, but the man himself didn't return to his seat. And when the train pulled into the station, Father Early wasn't in the coach. The Bishop guessed he was with the conductor, to whom he had a lot to say, or with the other employees of the railroad, who never seem to be around at the end of a journey. Stepping out of the coach, the Bishop felt like a free man.

Miss Culhane, however, was waiting for him. She introduced him to an elderly couple, the Doyles, who were the only ones in the group not planning to visit the Art Institute. Father Early, she said, understood that the Bishop wasn't planning to do anything in Chicago and would be grateful if the Bishop would keep an eye on the Doyles there. They hadn't been there before.

The Bishop showed them Grant Park from a taxicab, and pointed out the Planetarium, the Aquarium, the Field Museum. "Thought it was the stockyards," Mr Doyle commented on Soldier Field, giving Mrs Doyle a laugh. "I'm afraid there isn't time to go there," the Bishop said. He was puzzled by the Doyles. They didn't seem to realize the sight-seeing was for them. He tried them on foot in department stores until he discovered from something Mrs Doyle said that they were bearing with him. Soon after that they were standing across the street from the Art Institute, with the Bishop asking if they didn't want to cross over and join the group inside. Mr Doyle said he didn't think they could make it over there alive—a reference to the heavy traffic, serious or not, the Bishop couldn't tell, but offered to take them across. The Doyles could not be tempted. So the three of them wandered around some more, the Doyles usually a step or two behind the Bishop. At last, in the lobby of the Congress Hotel, Mrs Doyle expressed a desire to sit down. And there they sat, three in a row, in silence, until it was time to take a cab to the station. On the way over, Mr Doyle, watching the meter, said, "These things could sure cost you."

In the station the Bishop gave the Doyles a gentle shove in the direction of the gate through which some members of the group were passing. A few minutes later, after a visit to the newsstand, he went through the gate unaccompanied. As soon as he entered his Pullman his ears informed him that he'd reckoned without Mr Hope, the travel agent in Minneapolis. Old pastors wise in the ways of the world and to the escapist urge to which so many of the men, sooner or later, succumbed, thinking it only a love of travel, approved of Mr Hope's system. If Mr Hope had a priest going somewhere, he tried to make it a pair; dealt two, he worked for three of a kind; and so on—and nuns, of course, were wild, their presence eminently sobering. All day the Bishop had thought the odds safely against their having accommodations in the same Pullman car, but he found himself next door to Father Early.

They had dinner together. In the Bishop's view, it was fortunate that the young couple seated across the table was resilient from drink. Father Early opened up on the subject of tipping.

"These men," he said, his glance taking in several waiters, and his mouth almost in the ear of the one who was serving them, a cross-looking colored man, "are in a wonderful position to assert their dignity as human beings—which dignity, being from God, may not be sold with impunity. And for a mere pittance at that! Or, what's worse, bought!"

The Bishop, laying down his soup spoon, sat gazing out the window, for which he was again grateful. It was getting dark. The world seen from a train always looked sadder then. Indiana. Ohio next, but he wouldn't see it. Pennsylvania, perhaps, in the early morning, if he didn't sleep well.

"I see what you mean," he heard the young woman saying, "but I just charge it up to expenses."

"Ah, ha," said Father Early. "Then you don't see what I mean."

"Oh, don't I? Well, it's not important. And *please*—don't explain."

The Bishop, coloring, heard nothing from Father Early and thanked God for that. They had been coming to this, or something like it, inevitably they had. And again the Bishop suffered the thought that the couple was associating him with Father Early.

When he had served dessert across the table, the waiter addressed himself to Father Early. "As far as I'm concerned, sir, you're right," he said, and moved off.

The young woman, watching the waiter go, said, "He can't do that to me."

Airily, Father Early was saying, "And this time tomorrow we'll be on our way to Europe."

The Bishop was afraid the conversation would lapse entirely —which might have been the best thing for it in the long run— but the young man was nodding.

"Will this be your first trip?" asked the young woman. She sounded as though she thought it would be.

"My fifth, God willing," Father Early said. "I don't mean that as a commentary on the boat we're taking. Only as a little reminder to myself that we're all of us hanging by a thread here, only a heart's beat from eternity. Which doesn't mean we shouldn't do our best while here. On the contrary. Some people think Catholics oppose progress here below. Look on your garbage can and what do you see? Galvanized. Galvan was a Catholic. Look on your light bulb. Watts. Watt was a Catholic. The Church never harmed Galileo."

Father Early, as if to see how he was doing, turned to the Bishop. The Bishop, however, was dining with his reflection in the window. He had displayed a spark of interest when Father Early began to talk of the trip, believing there was to be a change of subject matter, but Father Early had tricked him.

"And how long in Rome?" asked the young woman.

"Only two days. Some members of the group intend to stay longer, but they won't return with me. Two days doesn't seem long enough, does it? Well, I can't say that I care for Rome. I didn't feel at home there, or anywhere on the Continent. We'll have two good weeks in the British Isles."

"Some people don't travel to feel at home," said the young woman.

To this Father Early replied, "Ireland first and then England. It may interest you to know that about half of the people in the group are carrying the complete works of Shakespeare. I'm hoping the rest of the group will manage to secure copies of the plays and read them before we visit Stratford."

"It sounds like a large order," said the young woman.

"Paperback editions are to be had everywhere," Father Early said with enthusiasm. "By the way, what book would you want if you were shipwrecked on a desert island?"

Apparently the question had novelty for the young man. "That's a hard one," he said.

"Indeed it is. Chesterton, one of the great Catholic writers, said he'd like a manual of shipbuilding, but I don't consider that a serious answer to the question. I'll make it two books because, of course, you'd want the Bible. Some people think Catholics don't read the Bible. But who preserved Scripture in the Dark Ages? Holy monks. Now what do you say? No. Ladies first."

"I think I'd like that book on shipbuilding," said the young woman.

Father Early smiled. "And you, sir?"

"Shakespeare, I guess."

"I was hoping you'd say that."

Then the Bishop heard the young woman inquiring:

"Shakespeare wasn't a Catholic, was he?"

The Bishop reached for his glass of water, and saw Father Early observing a moment of down-staring silence. When he spoke his voice was deficient. "As a matter of fact, we don't know. Arguments both ways. But we just don't know. Perhaps it's better that way," he said, and that was all he said. At last he was eating his dinner.

When the young couple rose to leave, the Bishop, who had been waiting for this moment, turned in time to see the young man almost carry out Father Early's strict counsel against tipping. With one look, however, the young woman prevailed over him. The waiter came at once and removed the tip. With difficulty, the Bishop put down the urge to comment. He wanted to say that he believed people should do what they could do, little though it might be, and shouldn't be asked to attempt what was obviously beyond them. The young woman, who probably thought Father Early was just tight, was better off than the young man.

After the waiter came and went again, Father Early sat back and said, "I'm always being surprised by the capacity ordinary people have for sacrifice."

The Bishop swallowed what—again—would have been his comment. Evidently Father Early was forgetting about the young man.

"Thanks for looking after the Doyles. I would've asked you myself but I was in the baggage car. Someone wanted me to say hello to a dog that's going to South Bend. No trouble, were they? What'd you see?"

The Bishop couldn't bring himself to answer either question. "It's hard to know what other people want to do," he said. "They might've had a better guide."

"I can tell you they enjoyed your company, Bishop."

"Oh?" The Bishop, though touched, had a terrible vision of himself doing the capitals of the world with the Doyles.

Father Early handed the Bishop a cigar. "Joe Quirke keeps me well supplied with these," he said, nodding to a beefy middle-aged man two tables away who looked pleased at having caught Father Early's eye. "I believe you know him."

"I met him," the Bishop said, making a distinction. Mr Quirke had sat down next to him in the club car before dinner, taken up a magazine, put it down after a minute, and offered to buy the Bishop a drink. When the Bishop (who'd been about to order one) refused, Mr Quirke had apparently taken him for a teetotaler with a past. He said he'd had a little problem until Father Early got hold of him.

Father Early was discussing the youth eating with Mr Quirke. "Glenn's been in a little trouble at home—and at school. Three schools, I believe. Good family. I have his father's permission to leave him with the Christian Brothers in Ireland, if they'll have him."

When Glenn got up from the table, the Bishop decided he didn't like the look of him. Glenn was short-haired, long-legged, a Doberman pinscher of a boy. He loped out of the diner, followed by Mr Quirke.

Two problems, thought the Bishop, getting ready to happen —and doubtless there were more of them in the group. Miss Culhane, in her fashion, could make trouble.

"There's something I'd like to discuss with you, Bishop."

The Bishop stiffened. Now it was coming, he feared, the all-out attempt to recruit him.

Father Early was looking across the table, at the empty places there. "You realize they'd been drinking?"

The Bishop refused to comment. *Now what?*

"It wouldn't surprise me if they met on this train."

"Yes, well . . ."

"Bishop, in my opinion, the boy is or has been a practicing Catholic."

In the Bishop's opinion, it was none of Father Early's business. He knew what Father Early was getting at, and he didn't like it. Father Early was thinking of taking on more trouble.

"I believe the boy's in danger," Father Early said. "Real danger."

The Bishop opened his mouth to tell Father Early off, but not much came out. "I wouldn't call him a boy." The Bishop felt that Father Early had expected something of the sort from him, nothing, and no support. Father Early had definitely gone into one of his silences. The Bishop, fussing with his cuffs, suddenly reached, but Father Early beat him to the checks.

Father Early complimented the waiter on the service and food, rewarding him with golden words.

The Bishop was going to leave a tip, to be on the safe side, but apparently the waiter was as good as his word. They left the diner in the blaze of his hospitality.

The Bishop had expected to be asked where in New York he'd be saying Mass in the morning, but when they arrived at their doors, Father Early smiled and put out his hand. It certainly looked like good-bye.

They shook hands.

And then, suddenly, Father Early was on his knees, his head bowed and waiting for the Bishop's blessing.

His mind was full of the day and he was afraid he was in for one of those nights he'd had on trains before. He kept looking at his watch in the dark, listening for sounds of activity next door, and finally he admitted to himself that he was waiting for Father Early to come in. So he gave Father Early until midnight—and then he got dressed and went out to look for him.

Up ahead he saw Glenn step into the corridor from an end room and go around the corner. The Bishop prepared to say hello. But when he was about to pass, the atmosphere filled up with cigarette smoke. The Bishop hurried through it, unrecognized, he hoped, considering the lateness of the hour and the significance of another visit to the club car, as it might appear to Glenn, who could have observed him there earlier in the evening.

The club car was empty except for a man with a magazine in the middle of the car, the waiter serving him a drink, and the young man and Father Early at the tail end of the train, seated on a sofa facing upon the tracks. The Bishop advanced with difficulty to the rear. The train was traveling too fast.

Father Early glanced around. He moved over on the sofa to make room for the Bishop, and had the young man move. The Bishop sat down beside the young man, who was now in the middle.

"One I went to—we're talking about fairs, Bishop—had an educated donkey, as the fellow called it. This donkey could tell one color from another—knew them all by name. The fellow had these paddles, you've seen them, painted different colors. Red, green, blue, brown, black, orange, yellow, white—oh, all colors . . ."

The Bishop, from the tone of this, sensed that nothing had been resolved and that Father Early's objective was to keep the young man up all night with him. It was a siege.

"The fellow would say, 'Now, Trixie'—I remember the little donkey's name. You might've seen her at some time."

The young man shook his head.

" 'Now, Trixie,' the fellow would say, 'bring me the yellow paddle,' and that's what she'd do. She'd go to the rack, where all the paddles were hanging, pick out the yellow one, and carry it to the fellow. Did it with her teeth, of course. Then the fellow would say, 'Trixie, bring me the green paddle.' "

"And she brought the green one," said the young man patiently.

"That's right. The fellow would say, 'Now, Trixie, bring me the paddles that are the colors of the flag.' " Father Early addressed the Bishop: "Red, white, and blue."

"Yes," said the Bishop. What an intricate instrument for good a simple man could be! Perhaps Father Early was only a fool, a ward of heaven, not subject to the usual penalties for meddling. No, it was zeal, and people, however far gone, still expected it from a man of God. But, even so, Father Early ought to be more careful, humbler before the mystery of iniquity. And still . . .

"My, that was a nice little animal, that Trixie." Father Early paused, giving his attention to the signal lights blinking down the tracks, and continued. "Red, green, all colors. Most fairs have little to recommend them. Some fairs, however, are worthwhile." Father Early stood up. "I'll be right back," he said, and went to the lavatory.

The Bishop was about to say something—to keep the ball rolling—when the young man got up and left, without a word.

The Bishop sat where he was until he heard the lavatory door open and shut. Then he got up to meet Father Early. Father Early looked beyond the Bishop, toward the place where the young man had been, and then at the Bishop. He didn't appear to blame the Bishop at all. Nothing was said.

They walked in the direction from which Father Early had just come. The Bishop thought they were calling it a day, but Father Early was onto something else, trying the waiter on baseball.

"Good night, Father."

"Oh?" said Father Early, as if he'd expected the Bishop to stick around for it.

"Good night, Father." The Bishop had a feeling that baseball wouldn't last, that the sermon on tipping was due again.

"Good night, Bishop."

The Bishop moved off comically, as the train made up for lost time. Entering his Pullman car, he saw the young man, who must have been kept waiting, disappear into the room Glenn had come out of earlier.

The Bishop slept well that night, after all, but not before he thought of Father Early still out there, on his feet and trying, which was what counted in the sight of God, not success. *Thinkest thou that I cannot ask my Father, and he will give me presently more than twelve legions of angels?*

"Would you like me to run through these names with you, Bishop, or do you want to familiarize yourself with the people as we go along?"

"I'd prefer that, I think. And I wish you'd keep the list, Miss Culhane."

"I don't think Father Early would want you to be without it, Bishop."

"No? Very well, I'll keep it then."

BLUE ISLAND

ON THE DAY the Daviccis moved into their house, Ethel was visited by a Welcome Wagon hostess bearing small gifts from local merchants, but after that by nobody for three weeks, only Ralph's relatives and door-to-door salesmen. And then Mrs Hancock came smiling. They sat on the matching green chairs which glinted with threads of what appeared to be gold. In the picture window, the overstimulated plants grew wild in pots.

Mrs Hancock had guessed right about Ethel and Ralph, that they were newlyweds. "Am I right in thinking you're of Swedish descent, Mrs Davicky? You, I mean?"

Ethel smiled, as if taking a compliment, and said nothing.

"I only ask because so many people in the neighborhood are. I'm not, myself," said Mrs Hancock. She was unnaturally pink, with tinted blue hair. Her own sharp-looking teeth were transparent at the tips. "But you're so fair."

"My maiden name was Taylor," Ethel said. It was, and it wasn't—it was the name she'd got at the orphanage. Wanting a cigarette, she pushed the silver box on the coffee table toward Mrs Hancock.

Mrs Hancock used one of her purple claws to pry up the first cigarette from the top layer. "A good old American name like mine."

She was making too much of it, Ethel thought, and wondered about Mrs Hancock's maiden name.

"Is your husband in business, Mrs Davicky?"

"Yes, he is." Ethel put the lighter—a simple column of silver, the mate to the box—to Mrs Hancock's cigarette and then to her own.

"Not here in Blue Island?"

"No." From here on, it could be difficult. Ralph was afraid that people in the neighborhood would disapprove of his business. "In Minneapolis." The Mohawk Inn, where Ethel had worked as a waitress, was first-class—thick steaks, dark lights, an electric organ—but Ralph's other places, for which his brothers were listed as the owners, were cut-rate bars on or near Washington Avenue. "He's a distributor," Ethel said, heading her off. "Non-alcoholic beverages mostly." It was true. Ralph had taken over his family's wholesale wine business, never much in Minneapolis, and got it to pay by converting to soft drinks.

Mrs Hancock was noticing the two paintings which, because of their size and the lowness of the ceiling, hung two feet from the floor, but she didn't comment on them. "Lovely, lovely," she said, referring to the driftwood lamp in the picture window. A faraway noise came from her stomach. She raised her voice. "But you've been lonely, haven't you? I could see it when I came in. It's this neighborhood."

"It's very nice," said Ethel quickly. Maybe Mrs Hancock was at war with the neighbors, looking for an ally.

"I suppose you know Mrs Nilgren," said Mrs Hancock, nodding to the left.

"No, but I've seen her. Once she waved."

"She's nice. Tied down with children, though." Mrs Hancock nodded to the right. "How about old Mrs Mann?"

"I don't think anybody's there now."

"The Manns are away! California. So you don't know anybody yet?"

"No."

"I'm surprised you haven't met some of them at the Cashway."

"I never go there," Ethel said. "Ralph—that's my husband—he wants me to trade at the home-owned stores."

"Oh?" Mrs Hancock's stomach cut loose again. "I didn't know people still felt that way." Mrs Hancock looked down the street, in the direction of the little corner store. "Do they do much business?"

"No," said Ethel. The old couple who ran it were suspicious of her, she thought, for buying so much from them. The worst of it was that Ralph had told her to open a charge account, and she hadn't, and she never knew when he'd stop there and try to use it. There was a sign up in the store that said: In God We Trust—All Others Pay Cash.

"I'll bet that's it," Mrs Hancock was saying. "I'm afraid people are pretty clannish around here—and the Wagners have so many friends. They live one-two-three-five houses down." Mrs Hancock had been counting the houses across the street. "Mr Wagner's the manager of the Cashway."

Ethel was holding her breath.

"I'm afraid so," said Mrs Hancock.

Ethel sighed. It was Ralph's fault. She'd always wanted to trade at the Cashway.

Mrs Hancock threw back her head, inhaling, and her eyelids, like a doll's, came down. "I'm afraid it's your move, Mrs Davicky."

Ethel didn't feel that it was her move at all and must have shown it.

Mrs Hancock sounded impatient. "Invite 'em in. Have 'em in for a morning coffee."

"I couldn't do that," Ethel said. "I've never been to a coffee." She'd only read about coffees in the women's magazines to which Ralph had subscribed for her. "I wouldn't know what to do."

"Nothing to it. Rolls, coffee, and come as you are. Of course nobody really does, not really." Mrs Hancock's stomach began again. "Oh, shut up," she said to it. "I've just come from one too many." Mrs Hancock made a face, showing Ethel a brown mohair tongue. She laughed at Ethel. "Cheer up. It wasn't in this neighborhood."

Ethel felt better. "I'll certainly think about it," she said.

Mrs Hancock rose, smiling, and went over to the telephone. "You'll do it right now," she said, as though being an older woman entitled her to talk that way to Ethel. "They're probably dying to get inside this lovely house."

After a moment, Ethel, who was already on her feet, having thought that Mrs Hancock was leaving, went over and sat down to telephone. In the wall mirror she saw how she must appear to Mrs Hancock. When the doorbell had rung, she'd been in too much of a hurry to see who it was to do anything about her lips and hair. "Will they know who I am?"

"Of course." Mrs Hancock squatted on the white leather hassock with the phone book. "And you don't have to say I'm coming. Oh, I'll come. I'll be more than happy to. You don't need me, though. All you need is confidence."

And Mrs Hancock was right. Ethel called eight neighbors, and six could come on Wednesday morning, which Mrs Hancock had thought would be the best time for her. Two of the six even sounded anxious to meet Ethel, and, surprisingly, Mrs Wagner was one of these.

"You did it all yourself," said Mrs Hancock.

"With your help," said Ethel, feeling indebted to Mrs

Hancock, intimately so. It was as if they'd cleaned the house together.

They were saying good-bye on the front stoop when Ralph rolled into the driveway. Ordinarily at noon he parked just outside the garage, but that day he drove in—without acknowledging them in any way. "Mr Daveechee," Ethel commented. For Mrs Hancock, after listening to Ethel pronounce her name for all the neighbors, was still saying "Davicky."

Mrs Hancock stayed long enough to get the idea that Ralph wasn't going to show himself. She went down the front walk saying, " 'Bye now."

While Mrs Hancock was getting into her car, which seemed a little old for the neighborhood, Ralph came out of the garage.

Mrs Hancock waved and nodded—which, Ethel guessed, was for Ralph's benefit, the best Mrs Hancock could do to introduce herself at the distance. She drove off. Too late, Ralph's hand moved up to wave. He stared after Mrs Hancock's moving car with a look that just didn't belong to him, Ethel thought, a look that she hadn't seen on his face until they moved out to Blue Island.

During lunch, Ethel tried to reproduce her conversation with Mrs Hancock, but she couldn't tell Ralph enough. He wanted to know the neighbors' names, and she could recall the names of only three, Mrs Wagner, one of them, was very popular in the neighborhood, and her husband . . .

"You go to the Cashway then. Some of 'em sounded all right, huh?"

"Ralph, they all sounded all right, real friendly. The man next door sells insurance. Mr Nilgren."

Ethel remembered that one of the husbands was a lawyer and told Ralph that. He left the table. A few minutes later Ethel heard him driving away.

It had been a mistake to mention the lawyer to Ralph. It

had made him think of the shooting they'd had at the Bow Wow, one of the joints. There had been a mix-up, and Ralph's home address had appeared in the back pages of one of the papers when the shooting was no longer news. Ethel doubted that the neighbors had seen the little item. Ralph might be right about the lawyer, though, who would probably have to keep up with everything like that.

Ralph wouldn't have worried so much about such a little thing in the old days. He was different now. It was hard to get him to smile. Ethel could remember how he would damn the Swedes for slapping higher and higher taxes on liquor and tobacco, but now, when she pointed out a letter some joker had written to the paper suggesting a tax on coffee, or when she showed him the picture of the wife of the Minnesota senator— the fearless one—christening an ore boat with a bottle of milk, which certainly should've given Ralph a laugh, he was silent.

It just made Ethel sick to see him at the windows, watching Mr Nilgren, a sandy-haired, dim-looking man who wore plaid shirts and a red cap in the yard. Mr Nilgren would be raking out his hedge, or wiring up the skinny little trees, or washing his car if it was Sunday morning, and there Ralph would be, behind a drape. One warm day Ethel had seen Mr Nilgren in the yard with a golf club, and had said, "He should get some of those little balls that don't go anywhere." It had been painful to see Ralph then. She could almost *hear* him thinking. He would get some of those balls and give them to Mr Nilgren as a present. No, it would look funny if he did. Then he got that sick look that seemed to come from wanting to do a favor for someone who might not let him do it.

A couple of days later Ethel learned that Ralph had gone to an indoor driving range to take golf lessons. He came home happy, with a club he was supposed to swing in his spare time. He'd made a friend, too, another beginner. They were going to have the same schedule and be measured for clubs. During his second lesson, however, he quit. Ethel wasn't surprised, for Ralph, though strong, was awkward. She was better than he was with a hammer and nails, and he mutilated the heads of screws. When he went back the second time, it must have been too much for him, finding out he wasn't any better, after carrying the club around the house for three days. Ethel asked about the other beginner, and at first Ralph acted as though she'd made him up, and then he hotly rejected the word "friend," which she'd used. Finally he said, "If you ask me, that bastard's played before!"

That was just like him. At the coffee, Ethel planned to ask the women to come over soon with their husbands, but she was afraid some of the husbands wouldn't take to Ralph. Probably he could buy insurance from Mr Nilgren. He would want to do something for the ones who weren't selling anything, though—if there were any like that—and they might misunderstand Ralph. He was used to buying the drinks. He should relax and take the neighbors as they came. Or move.

She didn't know why they were there anyway. It was funny. After they were married, before they left on their honeymoon, Ralph had driven her out to Blue Island and walked her through the house. That was all there was to it. Sometimes she wondered if he'd won the house at cards. She didn't know why they were there when they could just as well be living at Minnetonka or White Bear, where they could keep a launch like the one they'd hired in Florida—and where the houses were far apart and neighbors wouldn't matter so much. What were they waiting for? Some of the things they owned, she knew, were for later. They didn't need sterling for eighteen in Blue Island. And the two big pictures were definitely for later.

She didn't know what Ralph liked about his picture, which was of an Indian who looked all in sitting on a horse that looked all in, but he had gone to the trouble of ordering it from a regular art store. Hers was more cheerful, the palace of the Doge of Venice, Italy. Ralph hadn't wanted her to have it at first. He was really down on anything foreign. (There were never any Italian dishes on the menu at the Mohawk.) But she believed he liked her for wanting that picture, for having a weakness for things Italian, for him—and even for his father and mother, whom he was always sorry to see and hadn't invited to the house. When they came anyway, with his brothers, their wives and children (and wine, which Ralph wouldn't touch), Ralph was in and out, upstairs and down, never long in the same room with them, never encouraging them to stay when they started to leave. They called him "Rock" or "Rocky," but Ralph didn't always answer to that. To one of the little boys who had followed him down into the basement, Ethel had heard him growl, "The name's Ralph" —that to a nine-year-old. His family must have noticed the change in Ralph, but they were wrong if they blamed her, just because she was a little young for him, a blonde, and not a Catholic—not that Ralph went to church. In fact, she thought Ralph would be better off with his family for his friends, instead of counting so much on the neighbors. She liked Ralph's family and enjoyed having them in the house.

And if Ralph's family hadn't come around, the neighbors might even think they weren't properly married, that they had a love nest going there. Ethel didn't blame the neighbors for being suspicious of her and Ralph. Mr Nilgren in his shirt and cap that did nothing for him, he belonged there, but not Ralph, so dark, with his dark blue suits, pearl-gray hats, white jacquard shirts—and with her, with her looks and platinum hair. She tried to dress down, to look like an older woman, when she went out. The biggest thing in their favor, but it wasn't noticeable yet, was the fact that she was pregnant.

Sometimes she thought Ralph must be worrying about the baby—as she was—about the kind of life a little kid would have in a neighborhood where his father and mother didn't know anybody. There were two preschool children at the Nilgrens'. Would they play with the Davicci kid? Ethel didn't ever want to see that sick look of Ralph's on a child of hers.

That afternoon two men in white overalls arrived from Minneapolis in a white truck and washed the windows inside and out, including the basement and garage. Ralph had sent them. Ethel sat in the dining room and polished silver to the music of *Carmen* on records. She played whole operas when Ralph wasn't home.

In bed that night Ralph made her run through the neighbors again. Seven for sure, counting Mrs Hancock. "Is that all?" Ethel said she was going to call the neighbor who hadn't been home. "When?" When she got the number from Mrs Hancock. "When's that?" When Mrs Hancock phoned, if she phoned . . . And that was where Ralph believed Ethel had really fallen down. She didn't have Mrs Hancock's number—or address— and there wasn't a Hancock listed for Blue Island in the phone book. "How about next door?" Mrs Nilgren was still coming. "The other side?" The Manns were still away, in California, and Ralph knew it. "They might come back. Ever think of that? You don't wanna leave them out." *Them*, he'd said, showing Ethel what was expected of her. He wanted those husbands. Ethel promised to watch for the return of the Manns. "They could come home in the night." Ethel reminded Ralph that a person in her condition needed a lot of sleep, and Ralph left her alone then.

Before Ralph was up the next morning, Ethel started to clean the house. Ralph was afraid the house cleaning wouldn't be done right (*he* spoke of her condition) and wanted to get another crew of professionals out from Minneapolis. Ethel said it wouldn't look good. She said the neighbors expected them to do their own house cleaning—*and window washing*. Ralph shut up.

When he came home for lunch, Ethel was able to say that Mrs Hancock had called and that the neighbor who hadn't been home could come to the coffee. Ethel had talked to her, and she had sounded very friendly. "That's three of 'em, huh?" Ethel was tired of that one, but told him they'd *all* sounded friendly to her. "Mrs Hancock okay?" Mrs Hancock was okay. More than happy to be coming. Ralph asked if Ethel had got Mrs Hancock's phone number and address. No. "Why not?" Mrs Hancock would be there in the morning. That was why— and Ralph should get a hold on himself.

In the afternoon, after he was gone, Ethel put on one of her new conservative dresses and took the bus to Minneapolis to buy some Swedish pastry. She wanted something better than she could buy in Blue Island. In the window of the store where they'd bought Ralph's Indian, there were some little miniatures, lovely New England snow scenes. She hesitated to go in when she saw the sissy clerk was on duty again. He had made Ralph sore, asking how he'd like to have the Indian framed in birch bark. The Mohawk was plastered with birch bark, and Ralph thought the sissy recognized him and was trying to be funny. "This is going into my home!" Ralph had said, and ordered the gold frame costing six times as much as the Indian. However, he'd taken the sissy's advice about having a light put on it. Ethel hesitated, but she went in. In his way, the sissy was very nice, and Ethel went home with five little Old English prints. When she'd asked about the pictures in the window, the New England ones, calling them "landscapes," he'd said "snowscapes" and looked disgusted, as if they weren't what she should want.

When she got home, she hung the prints over the sofa where there was a blank space, and they looked fine in their shiny black frames. She didn't say anything to Ralph, hoping he'd notice them, but he didn't until after supper. "Hey, what *is* this?" he said. He bounced off the sofa, confronting her.

"Ralph, they're cute!"

"Not in my home!"

"Ralph, they're humorous!" The clerk had called them that. Ralph called them drunks and whores. He had Ethel feeling ashamed of herself. It was hard to believe that she could have felt they were just fat and funny and just what their living room needed, as the clerk had said. Ralph took them down. "Man or woman sell 'em to you?" Ethel, seeing what he had in mind, knew she couldn't tell him where she'd got them. She lied. "I was in Dayton's . . ."

"A woman—all right, then *you* can take 'em back!"

She was scared. Something like that was enough to make Ralph regret *marrying* her—and to remind her again that she couldn't have made him. If there had been a showdown between them, he would've learned about her first pregnancy. It would've been easy for a lawyer to find out about that. She'd listened to an old doctor who'd told her to go ahead and have it, that she'd love her little baby, who hadn't lived, but there would be a record anyway. She wasn't sorry about going to a regular hospital to have it, though it made it harder for her now, having that record. She'd done what she could for the baby. She hated to think of the whole thing, but when she did, as she did that evening, she knew she'd done her best.

It might have been a bad evening for her, with Ralph brooding on her faults, if a boy hadn't come to the door selling chances on a raffle. Ralph bought all the boy had, over five dollars' worth, and asked where he lived in the neighborhood. "I live in Minneapolis."

"Huh? Whatcha doin' way out here then?" The boy said it was easier to sell chances out there. Ethel, who had been doing the dishes, returned to the sink before Ralph could see her. He went back to his *Reader's Digest*, and she slipped off to bed, early, hoping his mind would be occupied with the boy if she kept out of sight.

He came to bed after the ten o'clock news. "You awake?" Ethel, awake, but afraid he wanted to talk neighbors, moaned remotely. "If anybody comes to the door sellin' anything, make sure it's somebody local."

In the morning, Ralph checked over the silver and china laid out in the dining room and worried over the pastry. "Fresh?" Fresh! She'd put it in the deep freeze right away and it hadn't even thawed out yet. "Is that *all*?" That was all, and it was more than enough. She certainly didn't need a whole quart of whipping cream. "Want me to call up for something to go with this?" No. "Turkey or a ham? I maybe got time to go myself if I go right now." He carried on like that until ten o'clock, when she got rid of him, saying, "You wouldn't want to be the only man, Ralph."

Then she was on her own, wishing Mrs Hancock would come early and see her through the first minutes.

But Mrs Wagner was the first to arrive. After that, the neighbors seemed to ring the bell at regular intervals. Ethel met them at the door, hung their coats in the hall closet, returning each time to Mrs Wagner in the kitchen. They were all very nice, but Mrs Wagner was the nicest.

"Now let's just let everything be," she said after they'd arranged the food in the dining room. "Let's go in and meet your friends."

They found the neighbors standing before the two pictures. Ethel snapped on the spotlights. She heard little cries of pleasure all around.

"Heirlooms!"

"Is Mr Davitchy a collector?"

"Just likes good things, huh?"

"I just love this lamp."

"I just *stare* at it when I go by."

"So do I."

Ethel, looking at her driftwood lamp, her plants, and beyond, stood in a haze of pleasure. Earlier, when she was giving her attention to Mrs Nilgren (who was telling about the trouble "Carl" had with his trees), Ethel had seen Ralph's car cruise by, she thought, and now again, but this time there was no doubt of it. She recognized the rather old one parked in front as Mrs Hancock's, but where was Mrs Hancock?

"Hello, everybody!"

Mrs Hancock had let herself in, and was hanging up her coat.

Ethel disappeared into the kitchen. She carried the coffeepot, which had been on *low*, into the dining room, where they were supposed to come and help themselves. She stood by the pot, nervous, ready to pour, hoping that someone would look in and see that she was ready, but no one did.

She went to see what they were doing. They were still sitting down, listening to Mrs Hancock. She'd had trouble with her car. That was why she was late. She saw Ethel. "I can see you want to get started," she said, rising. "So do I."

Ethel returned to the dining room and stood by the coffeepot.

Mrs Hancock came first. "Starved," she said. She carried off her coffee, roll, and two of the little Swedish cookies, and Ethel heard her in the living room rallying the others.

They came then, quietly, and Ethel poured. When all had been served, she started another pot of coffee, and took her cup and a cookie—she wasn't hungry—into the living room.

Mrs Hancock, sitting on the hassock, had a bottle in her hand. On the rug around her were some brushes and one copper pan. "Ladies," she was saying, "now here's something new." Noticing Ethel, Mrs Hancock picked up the pan. "How'd you like to have this for your kitchen? Here."

Ethel crossed the room. She carried the pan back to where she'd been standing.

"This is no ordinary polish," continued Mrs Hancock, shaking the bottle vigorously. "This is what is known as liquefied ointment. It possesses rare medicinal properties. It renews wood. It gives you a base for polishing—something to shine that simply wasn't there before. There's nothing like it on the market—not in the polish field. It's a Shipshape product, and you all know what that means." Mrs Hancock opened the bottle and dabbed at the air. "Note the handy applicator." Snatching a cloth from her lap, she rubbed the leg of the coffee table—"remove all foreign matter first"—and dabbed at the leg with the applicator. "This does for wood what liniment does for horses. It relaxes the grain, injects new life, *soothes* the wood. Well, how do you like it?" she called over to Ethel.

Ethel glanced down at the pan, forgotten in her hand.

"Pass it around," said Mrs Hancock.

Ethel offered the pan to Mrs Nilgren, who was nearest.

"I've seen it, thanks."

Ethel moved to the next neighbor.

"I've seen it."

Ethel moved on. "Mrs Wagner, have you?"

"Many times"—with a smile.

Ethel looked back where she'd been standing before she started out with the pan—and went the other way, finally stepping into the hallway. There she saw a canvas duffel bag on the side of which was embossed a pennant flying the word SHIPSHAPE. And hearing Mrs Hancock—"And this is new, girls. Can you all see from where you're sitting?"—Ethel began to move again. She kept right on going.

Upstairs, in the bedroom, lying down, she noticed the pan in her hand. She shook it off. It hit the headboard of the bed, denting the traditional mahogany, and came to rest in the satin furrow between Ralph's pillow and hers. Oh, God! In a minute, she'd have to get up and go down to them and do *something*— but then she heard the coat hangers banging back empty in the

closet downstairs, and the front door opening and, finally, closing. There was a moment of perfect silence in the house before
her sudden sob, then another moment before she heard someone coming, climbing the carpeted stairs.

Ethel foolishly thought it would be Mrs Wagner, but of
course it was Mrs Hancock, after her pan.

She tiptoed into the room, adjusted the venetian blind, and
seated herself lightly on the edge of the bed. "Don't think I
don't know how you feel," she said. "Not that it shows yet. I
wasn't *sure*, dear." She looked into Ethel's eyes, frightening her.

As though only changing positions, Ethel moved the hand
that Mrs Hancock was after.

"My ointment would fix that, restore the surface," said Mrs
Hancock, her finger searching the little wound in the headboard. She began to explain, gently—like someone with a terrible temper warming up: "When we first started having these
little Shipshape parties, they didn't tell each other. They do
now, oh, yes, or they would if I'd let them. I'm on to them.
They're just in it for the mops now. You get one, you know, for
having the party in your home. It's collapsible, ideal for the
small home or travel. But the truth is you let me down! Why,
when you left the room the way you did, you didn't give them
any choice. Why, I don't think there's one of that crowd—with
the exception of May Wagner—that isn't using one of my free
mops! Why, they just walked out on me!"

Ethel, closing her eyes, saw Mrs Hancock alone, on the hassock, with her products all around her.

"It's a lot of pan for the money," Mrs Hancock was saying
now. She reached over Ethel's body for it. "You'll love your little pan," she said, fondling it.

Ethel's eyes were resisting Mrs Hancock, but her right hand
betrayed her.

"Here?" Mrs Hancock opened a drawer, took out a purse,
and handed it over, saying, "Only $12.95."

Ethel found a five and a ten.

"You *do* want the ointment, don't you? The pan and the large bottle come to a little more than this, but it's not enough to worry about."

Mrs Hancock got up, apparently to leave.

Ethel thought of something. "You do live in Blue Island, don't you?" Ralph would be sure to ask about that—if she had to tell him. And she would!

"Not anymore, thank God."

Ethel nodded. She wasn't surprised.

Mrs Hancock, at the door, peeked out—reminding Ethel of a bored visitor looking for a nurse who would tell her it was time to leave the patient. "You'll find your ointment and mop downstairs," she said. "I just know everything's going to be all right." Then she smiled and left.

When, toward noon, Ethel heard Ralph come into the driveway, she got out of bed, straightened the spread, and concealed the pan in the closet. She went to the window and gazed down upon the crown of his pearl-gray hat. He was carrying a big club of roses.

THE PRESENCE OF GRACE

O N A F I N E Sunday morning in June, Father Fabre opened the announcement book to familiarize himself with the names of the deceased in the parish for whom Masses would be offered in the coming week, and came upon a letter from the chancery office. The letter, dated December, dealt with the Legion of Decency pledge which should have been administered to the people at that time. Evidently Father Fabre was supposed to read it at the nine-thirty and eleven o'clock Masses that morning. He went to look for the pastor.

Father Fabre, ordained not quite a year, had his hands full at Trinity. It wasn't a well-run parish. The pastor was a hard man to interest in a problem. They saw each other at meals. Father Fabre had been inside the pastor's bedroom, the seat of all his inactivity, only once; Miss Burke, the housekeeper, never. The press of things was very great in the pastor's room, statues, candlesticks, cases of sacramental wine, bales of pious literature and outdated collection envelopes, two stray pews and a prie-dieu, the implements and furniture of his calling. There was a large table-model radio in his bed, and he obviously slept and made the bed around it. That was about it.

Father Fabre found the pastor in the dining room. "Little late for this, isn't it?" he said. He held out the letter which had wintered in the pastor's room.

"Don't watch me eat," said the pastor, a graying dormouse. He had had the six-thirty and eight o'clocks, and was breaking his fast—not very well, Father Fabre thought, still trying to see what was in the bowl. Shredded wheat *and* oatmeal? Something he'd made himself? Not necessarily. Miss Burke could make dishes like that.

The pastor shifted into a sidesaddle position, bending one of his narrow shoulders over the bowl, obstructing the curate's view.

Father Fabre considered the letter in his hand... *immoral motion pictures/demoralizing television/indecent plays/vulgar radio programs/pernicious books/vicious papers and periodicals/degrading dance halls/and unwholesome taverns* ... Was this the mind, the tongue of the Church? "Little late for this, isn't it?"

"No."

"I thought we were supposed to give it a long time ago." On the Sunday within the Octave of the Immaculate Conception, in fact. On that day, Trinity, pledgeless, had been unique among the churches of the diocese—so he'd bragged to friends, curates who were unhappy about the pledge, as he was, and he hadn't really blamed them for what they'd said out of envy, that it had been his duty to repair the omission at his Masses.

"Weren't we?"

"No."

"*No?*"

The dormouse shook his head a half inch. The spoon in his right hand was a precision instrument, scraping up the last of whatever had filled the bowl. Grain.

"I don't feel right about this," Father Fabre said, going away with the letter. He went to the sacristy to vest for the nine-thirty, talking to himself. It *was* a little late for the pledge. *No.* The Sunday within the Octave *had* been the day for it. *No.*

The white fiddleback chasuble he was putting on had been spoiled on Christmas. He'd been vesting, as now, when the pastor, writing out a Mass card for a parishioner, had flicked his pen at the floor to get the ink flowing. Father Fabre had called his attention to the ink spots on the chasuble. " 'S not ink," he'd said. Asked what it was, he'd said, " 'S not ink," and that was all he'd say. For a time, after that, Father Fabre wondered if the pastor's pen could contain some new kind of writing fluid—not ink—and thought perhaps the spots would disappear. The spots, the *'s not ink* spots, were still there. But a recent incident seemed to explain the pastor's odd denials. "Not a ball point, is it?" he'd said to Father Fabre, who was about to fill his fountain pen from the big bottle in the office. "*No*, Father," said Father Fabre, presenting his pen for inspection. "Takes ink," said the pastor. "*Yes*, Father." The pastor pointed to the big bottle from which Father Fabre customarily filled his pen, and said, "Why don't you try that?" "Say, that's an idea," said Father Fabre, going the pastor one better. "Better go and flush your pen with water first," said the pastor. And the funny part was that Father Fabre had gone and flushed his pen before filling it from the big bottle that time. "I think you'll like *that*," said the pastor. *That* was *Quink*. The dormouse had the casuist's gift, and more.

He escaped much of man's fate. Instead of arguing his way out of a jam, or confessing himself in error, the pastor simply denied everything. It was simple—as simple as when he, as priest, changed the bread and wine into the body and blood of Christ. But he had no power from his priesthood to deny the undeniable, for instance that he'd spoiled a good chasuble. When he said " 'S not ink," nothing was changed. He could really slow you up, though, if you were inclined to disagree with him and to be rational about it.

When the pastor entered the sacristy before the nine-thirty, Father Fabre was ready for him. "Father," he said, "I can't give this pledge in conscience—not as it's given in some parishes. I can't ask the people to rise as a body and raise their right hands, to repeat after me words which many of them either don't understand the full meaning of, or don't mean to abide by. I don't see anything *wrong* with giving it to those who mean to keep it." He'd wrangled against the pledge in the seminary. If it was "not an oath," as some maintained, wasn't it administered by a priest in church, and didn't it cheapen the clergy to participate in such a ceremony, and one which many merely paid lip service to? Didn't the chancery use the word "invite" and wasn't "demand" the word for the way the thing was rammed through in some parishes? Couldn't outsiders, with some justice, call the whole procedure totalitarian? What *did* Rome think of it? Wasn't it a concession to the rather *different* tone in America, a pacifier?

But the pastor had gone, saying, "Just so you give it."

Father Fabre got behind his servers and started them moving toward the altar. He saw the pastor in front of a battery of vigil lights, picking up the burned matches. Parishioners who had used them would be surprised to know that the pastor blew out all the lights after the last Mass. "Fire hazard," he'd said, caught in the act.

Before the eleven o'clock, after resting a few minutes between Masses in his room, he went to the bathroom and called down the laundry chute to Miss Burke in the kitchen. "Don't set a place for me. I'm invited out for dinner." He stood ready at the chute to cut her off but heard only a sigh and something about the pastor having said the same thing. He hadn't expected to get away with it so easily. They were having another critical period, and it was necessary, as before, to stand up to her. "I hope I let you know soon enough," he said. She should be happy, with them both gone. She wouldn't have to cook at all. And he was doing her the honor of pretending that she planned their meals ahead.

"Father!"

"Yes, Miss Burke."

"Is it Mrs Mathers' you're going to?"

He delayed his reply in the hope that she'd see the impertinence of the question, and when this should have been accomplished, he said, "I hope I let you know in time."

He heard the little door slam at the other end of the chute. Then, as always in time of stress, she was speaking intimately to friendly spirits who, of course, weren't there, and then wailing like the wind. "Sure she was puttin' it around she'd have him over! But we none of us"—by which Father Fabre assumed she meant the Altar and Rosary Society—"thought he'd go *there*! Oh, Lord!"

He'd lost the first fall to the pastor, but he'd thrown Miss Burke.

Going downstairs, he heard the coin machines start up in the pastor's room, the tambourines of the separator, the castanets of the counter. The pastor was getting an early start on the day's collections. He wore a green visor in his room and worked under fluorescent tubes. Sometimes he worked a night shift. It was like a war plant, his room, except that no help was wanted. The pastor lived to himself, in a half-light.

In the hallway downstairs, John, the janitor, sitting in the umbrella chair, was having coffee. The chair had a looking-glass back, and when John turned his head he appeared to have two faces.

"Thought you had the day off," said Father Fabre.

"Always plenty to do around here, Father."

"I suppose." They knew each other well enough now for

John not to get off that old one about wanting to spend the day with his family.

"She's really rarin' in there," John said. "I had to come out here." He glanced down at the floor, at the cup of muddy water cooling there, and then fearfully in the direction of the kitchen. This did not impress Father Fabre, however, who believed that the janitor and the housekeeper lived in peace. "Not her responsibility," John said.

Father Fabre, knowing he was being tempted, would not discuss the housekeeper with the janitor. Curates came and went, and even pastors, but the janitor, a subtle Slav, stayed on at Trinity.

"I told her it was none of her business."

"*What* isn't?"

"If you want to go there, that's your business," John said. "I had to come out here." John reached down for his cup, without looking, because his hand knew right where it was. "I don't blame you for being sore at her, Father." ("I'm not," Father Fabre murmured, but John, drinking, smiled into his cup.) "I told her it's your business what you do. 'He's old enough,' I said."

"What's she got against Mrs Mathers?" Father Fabre asked, wondering if Mrs Mathers was any match for the housekeeper. A natural leader vs. a mental case. It might be close if the Altar and Rosary Society took sides. But the chances were that Miss Burke would soon be fighting on another front. Impossible for her to wage as many wars as she declared.

"Hell, you know how these old maids are, Father," John was saying. "Just needs a man. *You* can understand that."

Father Fabre, calling it a draw with John, turned away and left.

The other guests at Mrs Mathers' didn't act like Catholics. Mr Pint, a small man in his sixties, was surprisingly unfriendly, and his daughter, though rather the opposite, went at Father

Fabre the wrong way. It might have been the absence of excess respect in her manner that he found unsettling. But Mrs Mathers, a large motherly but childless widow with puffy elbows, had baked a cake, and was easy to take.

They were all on the back porch of her second floor flat, watching Mr Pint make ice cream.

"Let me taste it, Dad," Velma said.

"I can't be standin' here all day with this cream gettin' soft on me," Mr Pint said.

Velma pouted. She had on a purple dress which reminded Father Fabre of the purple veils they'd had on the statues in church during Passiontide. Otherwise there was nothing lenten about Velma, he thought.

"If you taste it now," he said, "it'll just take that much longer to harden."

Mr Pint, who might have agreed with that, said nothing. He dropped a handful of rock salt into the freezer, a wood-and-iron affair that must have been as old as he was, and sank again to his knees. He resumed cranking.

Father Fabre smiled at Mrs Mathers. Parishioners expected a priest to be nice and jolly, and that was how he meant to be at Mrs Mathers'. With Mr Pint setting the tone, it might not be easy. Father Fabre hadn't expected to be the second most important person there. The cake, he believed, had not been baked for him.

"Your good suit," said Mrs Mathers. She snatched a *Better Homes and Gardens* from a pile of such magazines and slid it under Mr Pint's knees.

"Sir Walter Reilly," said Velma, looking at Father Fabre to see if he followed her.

He nodded, doubting her intelligence, wondering if she was bright enough to be a nurse. Mrs Mathers was a registered nurse.

"Aw, come on," Velma said. "Let me taste it, Dad."

Mr Pint churned up a chunk of ice and batted it down with the heel of his hand. "By Dad!" he breathed, a little god invoking himself.

Mrs Mathers wisely retired to the kitchen. Velma, after a moment, ingloriously followed.

Father Fabre gazed over the porch railing. With all the apartment buildings backed up together, it was like a crowded harbor, but with no sign of life—a port of plague. Miss Burke, he remembered, had warned him not to go. John, however, had said go. Mr Pint's shirt had broken out in patches of deeper blue, and his elastic suspenders, of soft canary hue, were stained a little. Pity moved Father Fabre to offer the helping hand, prudence stayed it, then pity rose again. "Let me take it awhile," he said quietly.

But Mr Pint, out to deny his size and years, needed no help, or lost in his exertions, had not heard.

Father Fabre went inside, where he found the women, by contrast, laughing and gay. Velma left off tossing the salad, and Mrs Mathers' stirring spoon hung expectantly in mid-air. "I'm afraid I wasn't much help out there," he said.

"That's just Dad's way," Mrs Mathers said. "Come in here a minute, Father, if you want to see something nice."

Mrs Mathers led him into a little room off the kitchen. She wanted him to see her new day bed. He felt the springs as she had and praised the bed in her terms. He meant it when he said he wished he had one, and sat down on it. Mrs Mathers left the room, and returned a moment later whispering that she believed in flushing the toilet before she made coffee. That was the quickest way to bring fresh water into the house. Father Fabre, rising from the day bed, regretted that he wouldn't be able to pass this household hint on to Miss Burke.

Then, leaving the room, they met Mr Pint, all salt and sweat, coming in from the back porch. He came among them as one from years at sea, scornful of soft living, suspicious of the womenfolk and young stay-at-home males.

The women followed Mr Pint, and Father Fabre followed the women, into the dining room.

"You're a sight," said Velma.

"Your good blue shirt," said Mrs Mathers. She went down the hall after Mr Pint.

"We're going to eat in a minute," Velma said to Father Fabre. "You want to wash or anything?"

"No, thanks," he said. "I never wash."

He had tried to be funny, but Velma seemed ready to believe him.

Mrs Mathers, looking upset, entered the dining room.

"Should I take off her plate?" Velma asked.

"Leave it on in case she does come," Mrs Mathers said.

"Father, you know Grace."

"No, I don't think so."

"Grace Halloran. She's in the Society."

"Of course." Of course he knew Grace, a maiden lady. He saw her almost daily, a shadow moving around the sanctuary, dusting the altar rail and filling vases with flowers—paid for by herself, the pastor said. Her brother was a big builder of highways. She wasn't the kind to use her means and position, however, to fraternize with the clergy. "Maybe she's just late," he said, rather hoping she wouldn't make it. The present company was difficult enough to assimilate.

Mr Pint appeared among them again, now wearing a white shirt. Had he brought an extra? Or had Mrs Mathers given him one which had belonged to her late husband? Father Fabre decided it would be unwise to ask.

They sat down to eat. It was like dining in a convent, with Velma in the role of the nun assigned to him, plying him with food. "Pickles?" He took one and passed the dish to Mr Pint.

"He can't eat 'em," Velma said.

"That's too bad," said Father Fabre.

Mrs Mathers, brooding, said, "I can't understand Grace, though heaven knows she can be difficult sometimes."

"If she'd only come," said Velma.

"Yes," said Father Fabre.

"Vel had to work last Sunday and didn't get a chance to meet her," said Mrs Mathers.

"That's too bad," said Father Fabre.

"Grace was my best friend," Mrs Mathers said. "In the Society, I mean."

Father Fabre frowned. *Was?*

"I was dying to meet her," said Velma, looking at Father Fabre.

"Very nice person," he said.

"I just can't understand it," declared Mrs Mathers, without conviction. Then: "It's no surprise to me! You soon find out who your friends are!"

Father Fabre applied his fingers to the fried chicken. "Well," he said, "she doesn't know what she's missing." Grace's plate, however, seemed to reject the statement. "Did she know I was coming?"

"Oh, indeed, she did, Father! That's what makes me so blamed mad!"

Velma went to answer the telephone. "Yoo-hoo! It's for you-hoo!" she called.

"She means you," Mrs Mathers said to Father Fabre, who wondered how she could have known.

He went to the bedroom, where Mrs Mathers, never knowing when she'd be called for special duty, had her telephone. When he said "Hello" there was a click and then nothing. "Funny," he said, returning to the table. "Nobody there."

"Vel," Mrs Mathers asked, "was *that* Grace?"

"She didn't say, Mildred. Wouldn't she say who she was if she was Grace?"

"It was Grace," said Mrs Mathers quietly. She looked unwell.

There was a rattle of silverware. "Eat your dinner, Mildred," said Mr Pint, and she did.

After dinner, they retired to the living room. Soon, with Mrs Mathers and Mr Pint yawning on the sofa, Velma said, "I met some Catholic priests that were married, once." She had taken the chair near Father Fabre's. They were using the same ash tray.

"Were they Greek or Russian?"

She seemed to think he was joking. "They were with their wives, two of them—I mean they were two couples—but they said the ones that weren't married could have dates with girls if they wanted to."

He nodded. "It's only been observed among us since the eleventh century—celibacy." Velma looked doubtful. "It may be overrated," he added, smiling.

"I never tried it," Velma said.

"Yes, well . . . in some parts of the world, even now, there are married Catholic priests."

"That's what these were," Velma said.

"Maybe they were *Old* Catholics," he said.

"No, they weren't, not at all."

He looked across the room at the couple on the sofa. Mr Pint appeared to be asleep, but Mrs Mathers was trying to fight it with a *Good Housekeeping*. "That's a sect," he said, getting back to Velma. "They go by that name. Old Catholics."

"I wouldn't say they were that," she said.

He was ready to drop it.

"I met them in Chicago," she said.

"I understand Old Catholics are strong there," he said. "Comparatively."

There was a lull during which Velma loaded her cigarette case and Father Fabre surveyed the room—the bookcase with no books in it, only plants and bric-a-brac, and the overstuffed furniture rising like bread beneath the slipcovers, which rivaled nature in the tropics for color and variety of growing things, and the upright piano with the mandolin and two photographs on top: one would be the late Mr Mathers and somewhere in the other, a group picture of graduating nurses, would be the girl he had married, now stout, being now what she had always been becoming. Mrs Mathers was openly napping now. The room was filled with breathing, hers and Mr Pint's in unison, and the sun fell upon them all and upon the trembling ferns.

"Mildred says you can't have dates."

Father Fabre looked Velma right in the eye. "That's right." He'd drifted long enough. He'd left the conversation up to her from the beginning, and where had it got him? "I take it you're not a Catholic."

"Oh, no," she said, "but I see all your movies."

"I beg your pardon."

"I liked *The Miracle of the Bells* the best. But they're all swell."

He felt himself drifting again.

"I enjoyed reading *The Cardinal*," she said.

So had he. He wondered if a start could be made there.

Mrs Mathers, whom he'd thought asleep, said, "Why don't you tell Father what you told me, Vel?"

"Mildred!" cried Velma.

Father Fabre blushed, thinking Velma must have remarked favorably on his appearance.

"About the church of your choice," said Mrs Mathers.

"Oh, that. I told Mildred *The Miracle of the Bells* made me want to be a Catholic."

Mr Pint came to and mumbled something.

Father Fabre decided to face up to him. "Do you like to go to the movies, Mr Pint?"

"No, sir." Mr Pint was not looking Father Fabre in the eye, but it was as though he didn't think it necessary—yet.

"Why, Dad," Mrs Mathers said, "you took me last Sunday night."

"Not to those kind, I didn't. Whyn't you let me finish? By Dad, I ain't so old I can't remember what I did a week back."

"Who said anybody was old?" Velma asked.

"Stop showin' off," Mr Pint said. "I heard who said it."

Mrs Mathers clucked sadly, too wise to defend herself.

Mr Pint blinked at her. "You made me go," he said.

Mrs Mathers saw her chance. "Ho, ho," she laughed. "I'd just like to see anybody *make* you do anything!"

"You can say that again! Tell him about your office, Dad," Velma said, but Mr Pint would not.

From the women, however, Father Fabre learned that Mr Pint had asked "them"—his employers, presumably—to build him an office of glass so that he could sit in it, out of the dirt and noise, and keep an eye on the men who worked under him.

"Why shouldn't they do it," said Mrs Mathers, "when he saves them all the money he does?"

Father Fabre, about to address Mr Pint directly, rephrased his question. "He has men under him? I mean—many?"

"Five," said Mrs Mathers. "Before he came, they had six. He gets more out of five men than they did out of six."

"Two he brought with him," Velma said. "They've been with Dad for years."

Father Fabre nodded. Mr Pint, with his entourage, was like a big-time football coach, but what was Mr Pint's work?

Velma, who had switched on the radio, cried, "Lee!"

Father Fabre watched the women closely. Evidently "Lee" was the announcer and not some entertainer to follow on the program. His sponsor, a used car dealer, whose name and address he gave, dispensed with commercial announcements on Sunday, he said, and presented music suited to the day. They

sat quietly listening to *How Are Things in Glocca Morra?*
Then to *The Rosary*, one of Mrs Mathers' favorite pieces, she
said. Then to *Cryin' in the Chapel*. Father Fabre wanted to
go home.

Lee came on again with the business about no commercials
and also threw in the correct time. (Mr Pint pulled out his
watch.) Lee warned motorists to be careful on the highways.

"Don't judge by this. You should hear him on weekdays,"
Velma said. "Does he ever kid the sponsors!"

"He's a good disc jockey or he wouldn't be on the air," Mrs
Mathers said tartly. "But he's no Arthur Godfrey." It sounded
to Father Fabre as though she'd been over this ground with
Velma before. "Do you ever get Arthur, Father?"

"Can't say that I do, Mrs Mathers."

"He might give you some ideas for your sermons."

"My radio isn't working."

"I'll take Lee," Velma said. She rose and went down the hall
to the bathroom.

Mrs Mathers whispered, "Father, did I tell you she wanted
to call in for them to play a song for you? *Our Lady of Fatima*
or something. She wanted it to come over the air while you
were here. A surprise."

"No," he said. "You didn't tell me about that."

"I told her not to do it. I said maybe you wouldn't want it."

"No, I wouldn't." He was grateful to Mrs Mathers.

Showing a little interest, Mr Pint inquired uneasily, "What
do you think of this disc jockey business?" He got up and turned
off the radio.

"I'm afraid I don't know much about it," Father Fabre
said, surprised to find himself engaged in conversation with
Mr Pint.

"Sounds kind of fishy to me," said Mr Pint, sitting down
again. He had opened up some, not much, but some. "You
know it's just playing phonograph records?"

"Yes," said Father Fabre, and then wondered if he'd said the right thing. Mr Pint might have wanted to tell him about it. Fearing a lull, he plunged. "Certainly was good ice cream."

"Glad you liked it."

After the long winter, gentle spring, the sap running... "That's a good idea of yours when you make ice cream—bringing an extra shirt, I mean."

There was a bad silence, the worst of the afternoon, crippling every tongue. Even Velma, back with them, was quiet. Mr Pint was positively stony. Finally, as if seeing no other way, Mrs Mathers explained:

"Mr Pint lives here, Father."

"He does?"

"Yes, Father."

"I guess I didn't know."

"I guess I didn't tell you."

"No reason why you should've," he said quickly. "You do have quite a bit of room here." He seemed to be perspiring. "Certainly do get the sun." He never would have thought it. Was there a chance that Mr Pint, who acted so strangely, was not her lover? He took a good look at Mr Pint. Was there a chance that he was? In either case, Mrs Mathers had planned well. Father Fabre, taking out his handkerchief, blew his nose politely and dabbed at his cold, damp neck. He was in very good health and perspired freely. The fat flowery arms of the overstuffed chair held him fast while the hidden mouth devoured him. The trembling ferns frankly desired him. He just never would have thought it.

"You should see my little room at the Y," Velma said. "So dark." She was looking at Father Fabre, but he could think of nothing to say.

Mrs Mathers sighed. "Vel, you *could* stay here, you know. She could, too." Mrs Mathers appealed to Father Fabre. "The day bed is always ready."

"Oh, well," said Velma.

"So I had this extra bedroom," Mrs Mathers said, as if coming to the end of a long explanation, "and I thought I might as well have the income from it—what's your opinion, Father?"

"Swell," he said. In the future he ought to listen to Miss Burke and stay away from John, with his rotten talk against her. A very sound person, Miss Burke, voices, visions, and all. He ought to develop a retiring nature, too, stick close to the pastor, maybe try to get a job in his war plant. "I hate to rush off," he said, rising.

"Don't tell me it's time for devotions," said Mrs Mathers.

They went down the street together. "You know, Father," said Mrs Mathers, "I almost asked them to come along with us."

"You did?" Mrs Mathers was hard to figure. He'd heard that hospital life made iconoclasts.

"What'd you think of Vel?"

"Who? Oh, fine." He didn't know what he thought of Vel. "What does she do?"

"She's with the telephone company, Father. She thinks she's in line for a supervisor's, but I don't know. The seniority system is the one big thing in her favor. Of course, it wouldn't come right away."

"I suppose not," Father Fabre said. "She seems quite young for that."

"Yes, and they're pretty careful about those jobs."

"What I understand." He was in line for a pastor's himself. They were pretty careful about those jobs too. "What does Mr Pint do?"

"Didn't I tell you?"

"No," he said bleakly.

Mr Pint was an engineer. "But he never touches a wrench. He's like an executive."

"Where?"

"At the hospital, Father."

"At City?"

"At Mercy, Father."

Oh, God, he thought, the nuns were going to be in on it too. They walked the next block in silence.

"Who plays the mandolin?" he asked.

"He does."

They walked another block in silence. "I don't want to get TV," she said plaintively. She brightened at the sight of a squirrel.

"Don't care for TV?"

"No, it's not that. I just don't know how long I'll keep my apartment."

Was Mrs Mathers saying that she'd get out of town, or only that she'd move to another parish? If so, she was a little late. By feasting at their board, he had blessed the union, if any, in the eyes of the parish. What a deal! It was too late for him to condemn the enamored couple, one of whom was out of his jurisdiction anyway (in parting, he had shaken Mr Pint's hand). It was a bad situation, bad in itself and bad because it involved him. Better, though, that they live in sin than marry in haste. That was something, however, that it would take theologians (contemplating the dangers of mixed marriage, the evil of divorce) to see. He knew what the parishioners would think of that.

And the pastor . . .

At the church, at the moment of parting, he said, "You're going to be early for devotions." That was all. To thank her, as he wanted to, for the good dinner would be, in a way, to thank her for compromising him with parish and pastor. It was quite enough that he say nothing to hurt her, and go.

"I've got some things to do around the side altars," Mrs Mathers said.

He nodded, backing away.

"You suppose Grace'll be inside?" she called after him, just as if all were now well between her and her best friend in the Society.

He had his back to her and kept going, plowed on, nodding though, vigorously nodding like one of the famous yes-horses of Odense. For a moment he entertained the idea that Mrs Mathers was a mental case, which would explain everything, but it wouldn't do. Mrs Mathers remained a mystery to him.

In the rectory, he started up the front stairs for his room. Then he went back down, led by sounds to the converts' parlor. There he found a congregation of middle-aged women dressed mostly in navy blues and blacks, unmistakably Altar and Rosary, almost a full consistory, and swarming.

"Could I be of any service to you ladies?"

The swarming let up. "Miss Burke said we should wait in here," someone said.

He hadn't seen who had spoken. "For me?" he said, looking them over. He saw Grace sorrowing in their midst.

"No, Father," said someone else, also hidden from him. "We're here to see the pastor."

"Oh," he said.

"*He* went out on a sick call," said someone else.

"Oh," he said, and escaped.

One minute later he was settling down in the garage, on the bottom rung of a folding ladder, the best seat he could find. He picked up a wrench, got grease on his fingers, and remembered that Mr Pint never touched a wrench. He wondered where he'd gone wrong, if there was anything he might have done, or might yet do. There was nothing. He attributed his trouble to his belief, probably mistaken, that the chancery had wanted a man at Trinity to compensate for the pastor. Father Fabre had tried to be that man, one who would be accessible to the people. The pastor strenuously avoided people. He was happy with the machines in his room, or on a picnic with himself, topped off perhaps with a visit to the zoo. The assistant was the one to see at Trinity. Naturally there were people who would try to capitalize on his inexperience. The pastor gave him a lot of rope. Some pastors wouldn't let their curates dine out with parishioners—with good reason, it appeared. The pastor was watchful, though, and would rein in the rope on the merest suspicion. Father Fabre was thinking of the young lady of charm and education who had come to him after Mass one Sunday with the idea of starting up a study club at Trinity. He'd told the pastor and the pastor had told him, "It's under study." You might think that would be the end of it. It had been, so far as the young lady was concerned, but that evening at table Father Fabre was asked by the dormouse if he knew about young ladies.

"Know about them?"

"Ummm." The dormouse was feasting on a soda cracker.

"No," said Father Fabre, very wise.

"Well, Father, I had them all in a sodality some years ago." (Ordinarily untalkative to the point of being occult, the pastor spoke now as a man compelled, and Father Fabre attended his every word. The seminary professors had harped on the wisdom of pastors, as against the all-consuming ignorance of curates.) It seemed that the pastor, being so busy, didn't notice how the young ladies showed up for induction during the few years of the sodality's existence at Trinity, but from the day he did, there had been no more of that. (*What?* Father Fabre wondered but did not interrupt.) The pastor was not narrow-minded, he said, and he granted that a young woman might wear a bit of paint on her wedding day. But when sodalists, dedicated to the Blessed Virgin, the Mother of God, Mary Immaculate, presented themselves at the communion rail in low-necked evening gowns, wearing lipstick, stuff in their eyes, and with their hair up in the permanent wave, why then, Gentlemen—the pastor used that word, causing Father Fabre to blink and then to realize he was hearing a speech the pastor must have given at a clergy conference—there was something wrong somewhere and that was why he had suppressed the sodality in his parish.

By God, thought Father Fabre, nodding vigorously, the pastor had a point! Here was something to remember if he ever got a church of his own.

It must have touched the pastor to see his point so well taken by his young curate, for he smiled. "You might say the scales dropped from my eyes," he said.

But by then Father Fabre, gazing at the cracker flak on the pastor's black bosom, had begun to wonder what all this had to do with a study club.

"A study club's just another name for a sodality," the pastor prompted. "See what I mean?"

Father Fabre did not, not unless the pastor meant that young ladies were apt to belong to either and that, therefore, his curate would do well to steer clear of both. Hear their sins, visit them in sickness and prison, give them the Sacrament. Beyond that, there wasn't much to be done for or about them. In time they would get old and useful. The pastor, for his part, had put them away in the cellar part of his mind to ripen like cheese. But the good ladies of the Altar and Rosary were something else again. Nuns could not have kept the church cleaner, and the good ladies, unlike nuns, didn't labor under the illusion that they were somehow priests, only different, and so weren't always trying to vault the communion rail to the altar.

"You want to be one of these 'youth priests,' Father?"

"I haven't thought much about it."

"Good."

But, as the pastor must have noticed, Father Fabre had wanted to get some "activities" going at Trinity, believing that his apostolate lay in the world, with the people, as the pastor's obviously didn't. Well, he had failed. But he wasn't sorry.

Wasn't there enough to do at Trinity, just doing the regular chores? For the poor, the sick and dying, yes, anything. But non-essentials he'd drop, including dining out with parishioners, and major decisions he'd cheerfully hand over to the pastor. (He still thought the man who rented owls to rid you of pigeons might have something, for that was nature's way, no cruel machines or powders. But he'd stop agitating for the owls, for that was another problem for the pastor, to solve or, probably, not to solve.) Of course the parish was indifferently run, but wasn't it a mistake to keep trying to take up *all* the slack? He'd had himself under observation, of late. It seemed to him his outlook was changing, not from a diminution of zeal, not from loss of vision, but from growing older and wiser. At least he hoped so. He was beginning to believe he wasn't the man to compensate for the pastor—not that he'd ask for a transfer. The bishop was a gentle administrator but always seemed to find a place in one of the salt mines for a young man seeking a change. Father Fabre's predecessor in the curate's job at Trinity had been antisocial, which some of the gadabout clergy said could be a grievous fault in a parish priest, but he hadn't asked for a change—it had come to him—and now he was back in the seminary, as a professor with little pocket money, it was true, but enjoying food and handball again. That afternoon, sitting in the garage, Father Fabre envied him.

The pastor handed a wicker basket to Father Fabre, and himself carried a thermos bottle. He showed no surprise at finding his curate waiting for him in the garage and asked no questions. Father Fabre, the moment he saw the basket and bottle, understood that the pastor was returning from a picnic, and that Miss Burke, telling the ladies he'd gone on a sick call, thought it part of her job to create a good impression whenever possible, part of being loyal, the prime requisite. Who but the pastor would have her for a housekeeper?

They walked to the back door at the pastor's pace.

"Some coffee in here for you," the pastor said, jiggling the thermos bottle.

"Thanks," said Father Fabre, but he'd not be having any of that.

"One of the bears died at Como," the pastor said. "One of the babies."

"That's too bad," said Father Fabre. He pushed in the door for the pastor, then stood aside. "Some women to see you in the converts' parlor," he said, as the pastor passed in front of him.

The pastor nodded. Women in the converts' parlor; he would see them.

"I don't know," Father Fabre said. "It may concern me— indirectly." Then, staring down at the kitchen linoleum, he began an account of his afternoon at Mrs Mathers'. At the worst part—his chagrin on learning of the setup there—the pastor interrupted. He filled an unwashed cup from the sink with the fluid from the thermos bottle, gave it to Father Fabre to drink, and watched to see that he did. Father Fabre drank Miss Burke's foul coffee to the dregs and chewed up a few grounds. When he started up his account again, the pastor interrupted.

"That's enough," he said.

Father Fabre, for a moment, thought he was in for it. But when he looked into the pastor's eyes, there was nothing in them for him to fear, nor was there fear, nor even fear of fear, bravado. The pastor's eyes were blue, blank and blue.

Father Fabre followed the pastor at a little distance, out of the kitchen, down the hallway. "Will you need me?" he said.

With an almost imperceptible shake of his head, the pastor walked into the converts' parlor, leaving the door ajar as always when dealing with women.

Father Fabre stayed to listen, out of sight of those inside. He soon realized that it had been a mistake to omit all mention of Velma in his account, as he had, thinking her presence at Mrs

Mathers' incidental, her youth likely to sidetrack the pastor, to arouse memories of so-called study clubs and suppressed sodalists. Why, if the pastor was to hear the details, didn't they tell him that Grace had been invited to dinner? Then there would have been five of them. The pastor was sure to get the wrong impression. To hear the ladies tell it, Mr Pint and Father Fabre were as bad as sailors on leave, kindred evil spirits double-dating a couple of dazzled working girls. The ladies weren't being fair to Father Fabre or, he felt, even to Mr Pint. He wondered at the pastor's silence. When all was said and done, there was little solidarity among priests—a nest of tables scratching each other.

In the next room, it was the old, old story, right from Scripture, the multitude crying, "Father, this woman was taken in adultery. The law commandeth us to stone such a one. What sayest thou?" The old story with the difference that the pastor had nothing to say. Why didn't he say, She that is without sin among you, let her first cast a stone at her! But there was one close by who could and would speak, who knew what it was to have the mob against him, and who was not afraid. With chapter and verse he'd atomize 'em. *This day thou shouldst be pastor.* Yes, it did look that way, but he'd wait a bit, to give the pastor a chance to redeem himself. He imagined how it would be if he hit them with that text. They, hearing him, would go out one by one, even the pastor, from that day forward his disciple. And he alone would remain, and the woman. And he, lifting up himself, would say, Woman, where are they that accused thee? Hath no one condemned thee? Who would say, No one, master. Neither will I condemn thee. Go, and sin no more.

"Think he can handle it?"

Whirling, Father Fabre beheld his tempter. "Be gone, John," he said, and watched the janitor slink away.

Father Fabre, after that, endeavored to think well of the pastor, to discover the meaning in his silence. Was this forbearance?

It seemed more like paralysis. The bomb was there to be used, but the pastor couldn't or wouldn't use it. He'd have to do something, though. The ladies, calmed at first by his silence, sounded restless. Soon they might regard his silence not as response to a grave problem but as refusal to hold council with them.

"We don't feel it's any of our business to know *what* you intend to do, Father, but we would like some assurance that something will be done. It that asking too much?"

The pastor said nothing.

"We thought you'd know what to do, Father," said another. "What would be best for all concerned, Father. Gosh, I don't know what to think!"

The pastor cleared his throat, touched, possibly, by the last speaker's humility, but he said nothing.

"I wonder if we've made ourselves clear," said the one who had spoken before the last one. She wasn't speaking to the pastor but to the multitude. "Maybe that's what comes from trying to describe everything in the best possible light." (Father Fabre remembered the raw deal they'd given him.) "Not *all* of us, I'm afraid, believe that man's there against Mildred's will."

" 'S not so."

Father Fabre gasped. Oh, no! Not that! But yes, the pastor had spoken.

"Father, do you mean to say we're lying?"

"*No.*"

Father Fabre shook his head. In all arguments with the pastor there was a place like the Sargasso Sea, and the ladies had reached it. It was authority that counted then, as Father Fabre knew, who had always lacked it. The ladies hadn't taken a vow of obedience, though, and they might not take " 'S not so" for an answer. They might very well go to the chancery. At the prospect of that, of the fine slandering he'd get there, and realizing only then that he and the pastor were in the same boat, Father Fabre began to consider the position as defined by

" 'S not so" and "No." The pastor was saying (a) that the situation, as reported by the ladies, was not so, and (b) that the ladies were not lying. He seemed to be contradicting himself, as was frequently the case in disputations with his curate. This was no intramural spat, however. The pastor would have to make sense for a change, to come out on top. *Could* the dormouse be right? And the ladies wrong in what they thought? What if what they thought was just not so? *Honi soit qui mal y pense!*

One said, "I just can't understand Mildred," but Father Fabre thought he could, now. At no time had Mrs Mathers sounded guilty, and that—her seeming innocence—was what had thrown everything out of kilter. When she said Mr Pint lived with her, when she said she was thinking of giving up her apartment, she had sounded not guilty but regretful, regretful and flustered, as though she knew that her friends and even her clergy were about to desert her. Mrs Mathers was a veteran nurse, the human body was her work bench, sex probably a matter of technical concern, as with elderly plumbers who distinguish between the male and female connections. It was quite possible that Mrs Mathers had thought nothing of letting a room to a member of the opposite sex. She could not have known that what was only an economy measure for her would appear to others as something very different—and so, in fact, it had become for her, in time. Mrs Mathers and Mr Pint were best described as victims of their love for each other. It was true love, of that Father Fabre was now certain. He had only to recollect it. If it were the other kind, Mrs Mathers never would have invited him over—and Grace—to meet Mr Pint. Mr Pint, non-Catholic and priest-shy, had never really believed that Mrs Mathers' friends would understand, and when Grace defaulted, he had become sullen, ready to take on anybody, even a priest, which showed the quality of his regard for Mrs Mathers, that he meant to marry her willy-nilly, in or out of the Church.

There must be no delay. All Mrs Mathers needed now, all she'd ever needed, was a little time—and help. If she could get Mr Pint to take instructions, they could have a church wedding. Velma, already Catholic in spirit, could be bridesmaid. That was it. The ladies had done their worst—Father Fabre's part in the affair was criminally exaggerated—but the pastor, the angelic dormouse, had not failed to sniff out the benign object of Mrs Mathers' grand plan. Or what would have been its object. The ladies could easily spoil everything.

One of the ladies got sarcastic. "Would it be too much to ask, then, just what you do mean?"

The pastor said nothing.

Then the one who earlier had succeeded in getting him to clear his throat said, "Father, it's not always easy for us to understand everything you say. Now, Father, I always get a lot out of your sermons—why, some I've heard on television aren't half as good—but I don't kid myself that I can understand *every* word you say. Still waters run deep, I guess, and I haven't got the education I should have. So, Father, would you please tell us what you mean, in words we can all understand?"

It would have surprised Father Fabre if, after all that, the pastor had said nothing.

" '*S not so*," he said.

Father Fabre had to leave then, for devotions.

In the sacristy, he slipped into his cassock, eased the zipper past the spot where it stuck, pawed the hangers for his surplice, found it on the floor. The altar boys had come, but he wasn't in the mood for them, for the deceptive small talk that he seemed to do so well, from ballplayers to St John Bosco in one leap, using the Socratic method to get them to do their own thinking and then breaking off the conversation when he'd brought out the best in them. It wasn't necessary with the two on hand—twins who were going to be priests anyway, according to them at the age of ten. They had fired the censer too soon, and it would be petering out after the rosary, when it would be needed for benediction. He stood at the door of the sacristy and gazed out into the almost empty church. It was the nice weather that kept people away from devotions, it was said, and it was the bad weather that kept them away in the wintertime. He saw Mrs Mathers kneeling alone in prayer. The pastor had done well for her, everything considered, but not well enough, Father Fabre feared. He feared a scandal. Great schisms from little squabbles grew . . .

And great affirmations! He'd expected the pastor to dismiss the ladies in time for devotions, but he hadn't expected them to come, not in such numbers, and he took it as a sign from heaven when they didn't kneel apart from Mrs Mathers, the woman taken in adultery, or thereabouts, a sign that the pastor had triumphed, as truth must always triumph over error, sooner or later, always: that was heaven's promise to pastors. Life was a dark business for everyone in it, but the way for pastors was ever lit by flares of special grace. Father Fabre, knowing full well that he, in spirit, had been no better than the ladies, thanked God for the little patience he'd had, and asked forgiveness for thinking ill of the pastor, for coveting his authority. He who would have been proud to hurl the ready answer at Mrs Mathers' persecutors, to stone them back, to lose the ninety-nine sheep and save not the one whose innocence he would have violated publicly then as he had in his heart, in his heart humbled himself with thoughts of his unworthiness, marveled at the great good lesson he'd learned that day from the pastor, that Solomon. But the pastor, he knew, was zealous in matters affecting the common weal, champion of decency in his demesne, and might have a word or two for his curate at table that evening, and for Mrs Mathers there would certainly be a just poke or two from the blunt sword of his mercy.

Father Fabre, trailing the boys out of the sacristy, gazed upon the peaceful flock, and then beyond, in a dim, dell-like recess of the nave used for baptism, he saw the shepherd carrying a stick and then he heard him opening a few windows.

LOOK HOW THE FISH LIVE

IT HAD BEEN a wonderful year in the yard, which was four city lots and full of trees, a small forest and game preserve in the old part of town. Until that day, there hadn't been a single casualty, none at least that he knew about, which was the same thing and sufficient where there was so much life coming and going: squirrels, both red and gray, robins, flickers, mourning doves, chipmunks, rabbits. These creatures, and more, lived in the yard, and most of these he'd worried about in the past. Some, of course, he'd been too late for, and perhaps that was best, being able to bury what would have been his responsibility.

Obviously the children had been doing all they could for some time, for when he happened on the scene the little bird was ensconced in grass twisted into a nesting ring, soggy bread and fresh water had been set before it—the water in a tiny pie tin right under its bill—and a birdhouse was only inches away, awaiting occupancy. Bird, food and drink, and house were all in a plastic dishpan.

"Dove, isn't it?" said his wife, who had hoped to keep him off such a case, he knew, and now was easing him into it.

"I don't know," he said, afraid that he did. It was a big little bird, several shades of gray, quills plainly visible because the feathers were only beginning. Its bill was black and seemed too long for it. "A flicker maybe," he said, but he didn't think so. No, it was a dove, because where were the bird's parents? Any bird but the dove would try to do something. Somewhere in the neighborhood this baby dove's mother was posing on a branch like peace itself, with no thought of anything in her head.

"God," he groaned.

"Where *are* the worms?" said his wife.

"We can't find any," said the oldest child.

"Here," he said, taking the shovel from her. He went and dug near some shrubbery with the shovel, which was probably meant for sand and gravel. With this shovel he had buried many little things in the past. The worms were deeper than he could go with such a shovel, or they were just nowhere. He pried up two flagstones. Only ants and one many-legged worm that he didn't care to touch.

He had found no worms, and when he came back to the bird, when he saw it, he was conscious of returning empty-handed. His wife was going into the house.

"That bird can't get into that house," he said. "It's for wrens."

"We know it," said the oldest child.

He realized then that he had pointed up an obvious difficulty that the two girls had decently refrained from mentioning in front of the bird and the two younger children, the boys. But he hadn't wanted them to *squeeze* the dove into the wrenhouse. "Well, you might as well leave it where it is. Keep the bird in the shade."

"That's what we're doing."

"We put him in the dishpan so we could move him around in the shade."

"Good. Does it eat or drink anything?"

"Of course."

He didn't like the sound of that. "Did you *see* it eat or drink anything?"

"No, she did."

"You saw it eat or drink?" he said to the younger girl.

"Drink."

"It didn't eat?"

"I didn't see him eat. He maybe did when we weren't watching."

"Did it drink like this?" He sipped the air and threw back his head, swallowing.

"More like this." The child threw back her head only about half as far as he had.

"Are you sure?"

"Of course."

He walked out into the yard to get away from them. He didn't know whether the bird had taken any water. All he knew was that one of the children had imitated a bird drinking—rather, had imitated him imitating a chicken. He didn't even know whether birds threw back their heads in drinking. Was the dove a bird that had to have its mother feed it? Probably so. And so probably, as he'd thought when he first saw the bird, there was no use. He was back again.

"How does it seem? Any different?"

"How do you mean?"

"Has it changed any since you found it?"

The little girls looked at each other. Then the younger one spoke: "He's not so afraid."

He was touched by this, in spite of himself. Now that they'd found the bird, she was saying, it would be all right. Was ever a bird in worse shape? With food it couldn't eat, water it probably hadn't drunk and wouldn't, and with a house it couldn't get into—and *them*! Now they punished him with their faith in themselves and the universe, and later, when these had failed and the bird began to sink, they would punish him some more, with their faith in him. He knew what was the best thing for the bird. When the children took their naps, then maybe he could do the job. He was not soft. He had flooded gophers out of their labyrinthine ways and beheaded them with the shovel; he had purged a generation of red squirrels from the walls and attic of the old house when he moved in, knowing it was them or him. But why did animals and birds do this to him? Why did children?

"Why'd you pick this bird up? Why didn't you leave it where it was? The mother might've found it then."

"She couldn't lift him, could she?"

"Of course not."

"Well, he can't fly."

"No, but if you'd left it where it fell, the mother might see it. The mother bird has to feed a baby like this." Why couldn't she lift it? Why couldn't the two parents get together and just put it back in the nest? Why, down through the ages, hadn't birds worked out something for such an emergency? As he understood it, they were descended from reptiles and had learned how to grow feathers and fly. The whale had gone to sea. But he didn't know whether he believed any of this. Here was a case that showed how incompetent nature really was. He was tired of such cases, of nature passing the buck to him. He hated to see spring and summer come to the yard, in a way. They meant death and mosquitoes to him.

It had been the worst year for mosquitoes that anyone could remember, and in Minnesota that was saying a lot. He had bought a spraying outfit, and DDT at $2.50 a quart, which, when you considered that there was no tax on it, made you think. A quart made two gallons, but he was surprised how quickly it went. The words on the bottle "Who enjoys your yard—you or the mosquitoes?" had stayed with him, however. He had engaged professionals, with a big machine mounted on a truck, to blow a gale of poison through the yard. (In other years, seeing such an operation in other yards, he had worried about the bees.) The squirrels and rabbits in residence had evacuated the trees and lily beds while he stood by, hoping that they and the birds understood it was an emergency measure. He believed, however, that the birds received too much credit for eating annoying insects. Wasps, he knew, consumed great numbers of mosquitoes—but what about *them*? The mosquito hawk, a large, harmless insect, was a great killer of mosquitoes, but was itself killed by birds—by martins. That was the balance of nature for you. Balance for whom? You had to take steps yourself—drastic steps. Too drastic?

"Now I want you to show me exactly where you found this bird."

The little girls looked at each other.

"Don't say anything. Just take me to the exact spot."

They walked across the yard as if they really knew where they were going, and he and the little boys followed. The girls appeared to agree on the spot, but he supposed the one was under the influence of the other. The older one put out a foot and said, "Here."

He hadn't realized they were being that exact. It was surprising how right they were. Fifty or sixty feet overhead, in a fork of a big white oak, he saw a nest, definitely a dove's nest, a jerry-built job if he ever saw one, the sky visible between the sticks, and something hanging down. He moved away and gazed up again. It was only a large dead leaf, not what he'd feared, not a baby bird hanging by its foot. He felt better about having had the yard sprayed. The machine on the truck was very powerful, powerful enough to bend back the bushes and small trees, but he doubted that it had blown the baby dove out of the nest. This was just an unusually bad nest and the bird had fallen out. Nature had simply failed again.

"The nest! I see it! See?"

"Yes." He walked away from them, toward the garage. He hadn't called the nest to their attention because restoring the bird was out of the question for him—it was a job for the fire department or for God, whose eye is on the sparrow—but that didn't mean that the children might not expect him to do it.

"Just keep the bird in the shade," he called from the garage. He drove down to the office, which he hadn't planned to visit that day, and spent a few hours of peace there.

And came home to another calamity. In the kitchen, the little girls were waiting for him. Something, they said, had jumped out of the lilies and pushed one of the young bunnies that hadn't been doing anything, just eating grass near the playhouse. A weasel, they thought. Their mother hadn't seen it happen, had only heard the bunny crying, and had gone up to bed. There was no use going to her. They were in possession of what information there was. He should ask them.

"Don't go out there!"

"Why not?"

"Mama says if the bunny has the rabies it might bite."

He stood still in thought. Most of his life had been spent in a more settled part of the country. There was a great deal he didn't know about wildlife, even about the red squirrel and the yellow-jacket wasp, with which he had dealt firsthand, and he knew it. He could be wrong. But there was something ridiculous about what they were suggesting. "Did you see whatever it was that pushed the rabbit?"

"Of course!" said the older girl. It was this that distinguished her from all others in the house.

"What did it look like?"

"It went so fast."

This was ground they'd covered before, but he persevered, hoping to flush the fact that would explain everything. "What color was it?"

"Kind of—like the rabbit. But it went so fast."

This, too, was as before. "Maybe it was the mama rabbit," he said, adding something new. The more he thought about it, the more he liked it. "Maybe she didn't want the young one to come out in the open—in the daytime, I mean. Maybe she was just teaching it a lesson." He didn't know whether rabbits did that, but he did know that this particular mother was intelligent. He had first noticed her young ones, just babies then, in a shallow hole alongside a tiny evergreen that he had put a wire fence around, and that he'd draped with Shoo—rope soaked with creosote, advertised as very effective against dogs, rabbits, and rodents of all kinds. And as for the punishment the young rabbit had taken from whatever it was, he had once seen a mother squirrel get tough with a little one that had strayed from the family tree.

"Would she hurt the young rabbit?" said the younger girl.

"She might. A little."

"This one was hurt a lot," said the eyewitness. She spoke with authority.

"Maybe it was a cat," he said, rallying. "You say it was about the same size."

The children didn't reply. It seemed to him that they did not trust him. His mama-rabbit theory was too good to be true. They believed in the weasel.

"A weasel would've killed it," he said.

"But if he saw *me*?"

"*Did* he see you?"

"Of course."

"Did you see *him*?"

"Of course!" cried the child, impatient with the question. She didn't appear to realize that she was cornered, that having seen the attacker she should be able to describe it. But she was under no obligation to be logical. He decided to wait a few years.

Out in the yard he scrutinized the ground around the play-house for blood and fur, and saw none. He stepped to the edge of the lilies. Each year the lilies were thicker and less fruitful of flowers, and a gardener would have thinned them out. A gardener, though, would have spoiled this yard—for the fairies who, the children told him, played there. He didn't enter the lilies because he didn't want to encounter what he might.

Passing through the kitchen, he noticed that the children were cutting up a catalogue, both pasting. Apparently the older one could no longer get the younger one to do all the scissor work. "How's the bird?"

"We don't know."

He stopped and got them in focus. "Why don't you know?"

"We haven't looked at it."

"Haven't looked at it! Why haven't you?"

"We've been doing this."

"This is why."

It was a mystery to him how, after crooning over the helpless creature, after entangling him in its fate, they could be this way. This was not the first time, either. "Well, get out there and look at it!"

On the way out to look at it himself, he met them coming back. "He's all right," the older one said grumpily.

"Looks the same, huh?" He didn't catch what they said in reply, which wasn't much anyway. He found the bird where he'd last seen it, beside the back porch. He had expected it to be dying by now. Its ribs showed clearly when it breathed, which was alarming, but he remembered that this had worried him when he first saw the bird. It did seem to be about the same.

He passed through the kitchen and, seeing the children all settled down again, he said, "Find a better place for it. It'll soon be in the sun."

A few moments later, he was intervening. They had the whole yard and yet they were arguing over two patches of shade, neither of which would be good for more than a few minutes. He carried the dishpan out into the yard, and was annoyed that they weren't following him, for he wanted them to see what he was doing and why. He put the dishpan down where the sun wouldn't appear again until morning. He picked it up again. He carried it across the yard to the foot of the white oak. On the ground, directly below the nest, there was and would be sun until evening, but near the trunk there would be shade until morning.

The bird was breathing heavily, as before, but it was in no distress—unless this was distress. He thought not. If the bird had a full coat of feathers, its breathing wouldn't be so noticeable.

He was pleasantly surprised to see a mature dove high above him. The dove wasn't near the nest, wasn't watching him— was just looking unconcerned in another part of the tree—but it was in the right tree. He tried to attract its attention, making what he considered a gentle bird noise. It flew away, greatly disappointing him.

He knelt and lifted the tin of water to the bird's mouth. This he did with no expectation that it would drink, but it did, it definitely did. The bird kept its bill in the water, waggling it once or twice, spilling some, and raised its head slightly—not as a chicken would. He tried a little bread, unsuccessfully. He tried the water again, and again the bird drank. The bread was refused again and also the water when it was offered the third time. This confirmed him in his belief that the bird had been drinking before. This also proved that the bird was able to make decisions. After two drinks, the bird had said, in effect, no more. It hadn't eaten for some time, but it was evidently still sound in mind and body. It might need only a mother's care to live.

He went into the house. In the next two hours, he came to the window frequently. For a while he tried to believe that there might be maternal action at the foot of the oak while he wasn't watching. He knew better, though. All he could believe was that the mother might be staying away because she regarded the dishpan as a trap—assuming, of course, that she had spotted the baby, and assuming also that she gave a damn, which he doubted.

Before dinner he went out and removed the birdhouse and then the bird from the dishpan, gently tipping it into the grass, not touching it. The nest the children had twined together slid with it, but the bird ended up more off than on the nest. There was plenty of good, growing grass under the dove, however. If, as the children claimed, the bird could move a little and if the mother did locate it, perhaps between them—he credited the baby with some intelligence—they might have enough sense to hide out in the lilies of the valley only a few feet away. There would be days ahead of feeding and growth before the little bird could fly, probably too many days to pass on the ground in the open. Once the mother assumed her responsibility, however, everything would become easier—that is, possible. *He* might even build a nest nearby. (One year there had been a dove's nest in a chokecherry tree, only ten feet off the ground.) Within a few yards of the oak there were aged lilac bushes, almost trees, which would be suitable for a nest. At present, though, with the mother delinquent, the situation was impossible.

He looked up into the trees for her, in vain, and then down at the orphan. It had moved. It had taken up its former position precisely in the center of the little raft of grass the children had made for it, and this was painful to see, this little display of order in a thing so small, so dumb, so sure.

It would not drink. He set the water closer, and the bread, just in case, and carried away the dishpan and the birdhouse. He saw the bowel movement in the bottom of the dishpan as a good omen, but was puzzled by the presence of a tiny dead bug of the beetle family. It could mean that the mother had been in attendance, or it could mean that the bug had simply dropped dead from the spraying, a late casualty.

After dinner, standing on the back porch, he heard a disturbance far out in the yard. Blue jays, and up to no good, he thought, and walked toward the noise. When he reached the farthest corner of the yard, the noise ceased, and began again. He looked into the trees across the alley. Then he saw two catbirds in the honeysuckle bushes only six feet away and realized that he had mistaken their rusty cries for those of blue jays at some distance. The catbirds hopped, scolding, from branch to branch. They moved to the next bush, but not because of him, he thought. It was then that he saw the cat in the lilies. He stamped his foot. The cat, a black-and-white one marked like a Holstein cow, plowed through the lilies and out into the alley where the going was good, and was gone. The catbirds followed, flying low, belling the cat with their cries. In the distance he heard blue jays, themselves marauders, join in, doing their bit to make the cat's position known. High overhead he saw two dopey doves doing absolutely nothing about the cat, heard their little dithering noise, and was disgusted with them. It's a wonder you're not extinct, he thought, gazing up at them. They chose that moment to show him the secret of their success.

He walked the far boundaries of the yard, stopping to gaze back at the old frame house, which was best seen at a distance. He had many pictures of it in his mind, for it changed with the seasons, gradually, and all during the day. The old house always looked good to him: in spring when the locust, plum, lilacs, honeysuckle, caragana, and mock orange bloomed around it; in summer, as it was now, almost buried in green; in autumn when the yard was rolling with nuts, crashing with leaves, and the mountain-ash berries turned red; and in winter when, under snow and icicles, with its tall mullioned windows sparkling, it reminded him of an old-fashioned Christmas card. For a hundred years it had been painted barn or Venetian red, with forest-green trim. In winter there were times when the old house, because of the light, seemed to be bleeding; the red then was profound and alive. Perhaps it knew something, after all, he thought. In January the yellow bulldozers would come for it and the trees. One of the old oaks, one that had appeared to be in excellent health, had recently thrown down half of itself in the night. "Herbal suicide," his wife had said.

Reaching the other far corner of the yard, he stood considering the thick black-walnut tree, which he had once, at about this time of year, thought of girdling with a tin shield to keep off the squirrels. But this would have taken a lot of tin, and equipment he didn't own to trim a neighboring maple and possibly an elm, and so he had decided to share the nuts with the squirrels. This year they could have them all. Few of the birds would be there when it happened, but the squirrels—there were at least a dozen in residence—were in for a terrible shock.

He moved toward the house, on the street side of the yard, on the lookout for beer cans and bottles that the college students from their parked cars tossed into the bushes. He knew, from several years of picking up after them, their favorite brand.

He came within twenty yards of the white oak, and stopped. He didn't want to venture too near in case the mother was engaged in feeding the baby, or was just about to make up her mind to do so. In order to see, however, he would have to be a little closer. He moved toward the white oak in an indirect line, and stopped again. The nest was empty. His first thought was that the bird, sensing the approach of darkness, had wisely retreated into the shelter of the lilies of the valley nearby, and then he remembered the recent disturbance on the other side of the yard. The cat had last been seen at what had appeared a safe distance then. He was looking now for feathers, blood, bones. But he saw no such signs of the bird. Again he considered the possibility that it was hiding in the lilies of the valley. When he recalled the bird sitting in the very center of the nest, it did not seem likely that it would leave, ever—unless persuaded by the mother to do so. But he had no faith in the mother, and instead of searching the lilies, he stood where he was and studied the ground around him in a widening circle. The cat could've carried it off, of course, or—again—the bird could be safe among the lilies.

He hurried to the fallen oak. Seeing the little bird at such a distance from the nest, and not seeing it as he'd expected he would, but entire, he had been deceived. The bird was not moving. It was on its back, not mangled but dead. He noted the slate-black feet. Its head was to one side on the grass. The one eye he could see was closed, and the blood all around it, enamel-bright, gave the impression, surprising to him, that it had poured out like paint. He wouldn't have thought such a little thing would even have blood.

He went for the shovel with which he'd turned up no worms for the bird earlier that day. He came back to the bird by a different route, having passed on the other side of a big tree, and saw the little ring of grass that had been the bird's nest. It now looked like a wreath to him.

He dug a grave within a few feet of the bird. The ground was mossy there. He simply lifted up a piece of it, tucked in the bird, and dropped the sod down like a cover. He pounded it once with the back side of the shovel, thinking the bird would rest easier there than in most ground.

When he looked up from his work, he saw that he had company: Mr and Mrs Hahn, neighbors. He told them what had happened, and could see that Mr Hahn considered him soft. He remembered that Mr Hahn, who had an interest such as newspapers seemed to think everybody ought to have in atomic explosions, didn't care to discuss the fallout.

The Hahns walked with him through the yard. They had heard there were no mosquitoes there now.

"Apparently it works," he said.

"The city should spray," said Mrs Hahn.

"At least the swamps," said Mr Hahn, who was more conservative.

He said nothing. They were perfectly familiar with his theory: that it was wet enough in the lily beds, in the weeds along the river, for mosquitoes to breed. When he argued that there just weren't enough swamps to breed that many mosquitoes, people smiled, and tried to refute his theory—confirmed it—by talking about how little water it took, a birdbath, a tin can somewhere. "In my opinion, they breed right here, in this yard and yours."

"Anyway, they're not here now," said Mrs Hahn.

He received this not as a compliment but as a polite denial of his theory. They were passing under the mulberry tree. In the bloody atmosphere prevailing in his mind that evening, he naturally thought of the purple grackle that had hung itself from a high branch with a string in the previous summer. "I'm sick of it all."

"Sick of *what*?" said Mrs Hahn.

The Hahns regarded him as a head case, he knew, and probably wouldn't be surprised if he said that he was sick of them. He had stopped trying to adjust his few convictions and prejudices to company. He just let them fly. Life was too short. "Insects, birds, and animals of all kinds," he said. "Nature."

Mr Hahn smiled. "There'd be too many of those doves if things like that didn't happen."

"I suppose."

Mr Hahn said: "Look how the fish live."

He looked at the man with interest. This was the most remarkable thing Mr Hahn had ever said in his presence. But, of course, Mr Hahn didn't appreciate the implications. Mr Hahn didn't see himself in the picture at all.

"That includes children," he said, pursuing his original line. It was the children who were responsible for bringing the failures of nature to his attention.

Mrs Hahn, who seemed to feel she was on familiar ground, gaily laughed. "Everybody who has them complains about them."

"*And* women," he added. He had almost left women out, and they belonged in. They were responsible for the children and the success of *Queen for a Day*.

"And men," he added when he caught Mr Hahn smiling at the mention of women. Men were at the bottom of it all.

"That doesn't leave much, does it?" said Mr Hahn.

"No." Who *was* left? God. It wasn't surprising, for all problems were at bottom theological. He'd like to put a few questions to God. God, though, knowing his thoughts, knew his questions, and the world was already in possession of all the answers that would be forthcoming from God. Compassion for the Holy Family fleeing from Herod was laudable and meritorious, but it was wasted on soulless rabbits fleeing from soulless weasels. Nevertheless it was there just the same, or something very like it. As he'd said in the beginning, he was sick of it all.

"There he is now!" cried Mrs Hahn.

He saw the black-and-white cat pause under the fallen oak.

"Should I get my gun?" said Mr Hahn.

"No. It's his nature." He stamped his foot and hissed. The cat ran out of the yard. Where were the birds? They could be keeping an eye on the cat. Somewhere along the line they must have said the hell with it. He supposed there was a lesson in that for him. A man couldn't commiserate with life to the full extent of his instincts and opportunities. A man had to accept his God-given limitations.

He accompanied the Hahns around to the front of the house, and there they met a middle-aged woman coming up the walk. He didn't know her, but the Hahns did, and introduced her. Mrs Snyder.

"It's about civil defense," she said. Every occupant of every house was soon to be registered for the purposes of identification in case of an emergency. Each block would have its warden, and Mrs Snyder thought that he, since he lived on this property, which took up so much of the block . . .

"No."

"No?"

"No." He couldn't think of a job for which he was less suited, in view of his general outlook. He wouldn't be here anyway. Nor would this house, these trees.

While Mr and Mrs Hahn explained to Mrs Snyder that the place was to become a parking lot for the college, he stood by in silence. He had never heard it explained so well. His friends had been shocked at the idea of doing away with the old house and trees—and for a parking lot!—and although he appreciated their concern, there was nothing to be done, and after a time he was unable to sympathize with them. This they didn't readily understand. It was as if some venerable figure in the community, only known to them but near and dear to him, had been murdered, and he failed to show proper sorrow and anger. The Hahns, however, were explaining how it was, turning this way and that, pointing to this building and that, to sites already taken, to those to be taken soon or in time. For them the words "the state" and "expansion" seemed sufficient. And the Hahns weren't employed by the college and they weren't old grads. It was impossible to account in such an easy way for their enthusiasm. They were scheduled for eviction themselves, they said, in a few years.

When they were all through explaining, it must have been annoying to them to hear Mrs Snyder's comment. "Too bad," she said. She glanced up at the old red house and then across the street at the new dormitory going up. There had been a parking lot there for a few years, but before that another big old house and trees. The new dormitory, apricot bricks and aluminum windows, was in the same style as the new library, a style known to him and his wife as Blank. "Too bad," Mrs Snyder said again, with an uneasy look across the street, and then at him.

"There's no defense against that *either*," he said, and if Mrs Snyder understood what he meant, she didn't show it.

"Well," she said to Mr Hahn, "how about you?"

They left him then. He put the shovel away, and walked the boundaries of the yard for the last time that day, pausing twice to consider the house in the light of the moment. When he came to the grave, he stopped and looked around for a large stone. He took one from the mound where the hydrant was, the only place where the wild ginger grew, and set it on the grave, not as a marker but as an obstacle to the cat if it returned, as he imagined it would. It was getting dark in the yard, the night coming sooner there because of the great trees. Now the bats and owls would get to work, he thought, and went into the doomed house.

BILL

IN JANUARY, JOE, who had the habit of gambling with himself, made it two to one against his getting a curate that year. Then, early in May, the Archbishop came out to see the new rectory and, in the office area, which was in the basement but surprisingly bright and airy, paused before the doors "PASTOR" and "ASSISTANT" and said, "You're mighty sure of yourself, Father."

"I can dream, can't I, Your Excellency?"

The subject didn't come up again during the visit, and the Archbishop declined Joe's offer of a drink, which may or may not have been significant—hard to say how much the Arch knew about a man—but after he'd departed Joe made it seven to five, trusting his instinct.

Two weeks later, on the eve of the annual shape-up, trusting his instinct again though he'd heard nothing, Joe made it even money.

The next morning, the Chancery (Toohey) phoned to say that Joe had a curate: "Letter follows."

"Wait a minute. Who?"

"He'll be in touch with you." And Toohey hung up.

Maybe it hadn't been decided who would be sent out to Joe's (Church of SS. Francis and Clare, Inglenook), but probably it had, and Toohey just didn't want to say because Joe had asked. That was how Toohey, too long at the Chancery, played the game. Joe didn't think anymore about it then.

He grabbed a scratch pad, rushed upstairs to the room, now bare, that would be occupied by his curate (who?), and made a list, which was his response to problems, temporal and spiritual, that required thought.

That afternoon, he visited a number of furniture stores in Inglenook, in Silverstream, the next suburb, and in the city. "Just looking," he said to clerks. After a couple of hours, he had a pretty good idea of the market, but he was unable to act, and then he had to suspend operations in order to beat the rush-hour traffic home.

Afterward, though, he discovered what was wrong. It was his list. Programmed without reference to the *relative* importance of the items on it, his list, instead of helping, had hindered him, had caused him to mess around looking at lamps, rugs, and ashtrays. It hadn't told him that everything in the room would be determined, dictated, by the bed. Why bed? Because the room was a *bed*room. Find the bed, the right bed, and the rest would follow. He knew where he was now, and he was glad that time had run out that afternoon. Toward the last, he had been suffering from shopper's fatigue, or he wouldn't have considered that knotty-pine suite, with its horseshoe brands and leather thongs, simply because it had a clean, masculine look that bedroom furniture on the whole seemed to lack.

That evening, he sat down in the quiet of his study, in his Barcalounger chair, with some brochures and a drink, and made another list. This one was different and should have been easy for him—with office equipment he really knew where

he was, and probably no priest in the diocese knew so well—
but for that very reason he couldn't bring himself to furnish
the curate's office as other pastors would have done, as, in fact,
he had planned to do. Why spoil a fine office by installing inferior, economy-type equipment? Why not move the pastor's
desk and typewriter, both recent purchases, into the curate's
office? Why not get the pastor one of those laminated mahogany desks, maybe Model DK 100, sleek and contemporary
but warm and friendly as only wood can be? (The pastor was
tired of his unfriendly metal desk and his orthopedic chair.)
Why not get the pastor a typewriter with different type? (What,
again? Yes, because he was tired of that phony script.) But keep
the couch and chairs in the pastor's office, and let the new
chairs—two or three, and no couch—go straight into the curate's office.

The next morning, he drove to the city with the traffic, and
swiftly negotiated the items on his office list, including a desk,
Model DK 100, and a typewriter with different type, called
"editorial," and said to be used by newscasters.

"Always a pleasure to do business with you, Father," the
clerk said.

The scene then changed to the fifth floor of a large department store, which Joe had visited the day before, and there life
got difficult again. What had brought him back was a four-
poster bed with pineapple finials. The clerk came on a little
too strong.

"The double bed's making a big comeback, Father."

"That so?"

"What I'd have, if I had the choice."

"Yes, well." Joe liked the bed, especially the pineapples,
but he just couldn't see the curate (who?) in it. Get it for himself, then, and give the curate the pastor's bed—*it* was a single.
And then what? The pastor's bed, of unfriendly metal and
painted like a car, hospital gray, would dictate nothing about

the other things for the room. Besides, it wouldn't be fair to the curate, would it?

"Lot of bed for the money, Father."

"Too much bed."

The clerk then brought out some brochures and binders with colored tabs. So Joe sat down with him on a bamboo chaise longue, and, passing the literature back and forth between them, they went to work on Joe's problem. They discovered that Joe could order the traditional type of bed in a single, in several models—cannonballs, spears, spools (Jenny Lind)—but not pineapples, which, it seemed, had been discontinued by the maker. "But I wonder about that, Father. Tell you what. With your permission, I'll call North Carolina."

Joe let him go ahead, after more discussion, mostly about air freight, but when the clerk returned to the chaise longue he was shaking his head. North Carolina had gone to lunch. North Carolina would call back, though, in an hour or so, after checking the warehouse. "You wouldn't take cannonballs or spears, Father? Or Jenny Lind?"

"Not Jenny Lind."

"You like cannonballs, Father?"

"Yes, but I prefer the other."

"Pineapples."

Since nothing could be done about the other items on his list until he found out about the bed—or beds, for he had decided to order two beds, singles, with matching chests, plus box springs and mattresses, eight pieces in all—Joe went home to await developments.

At six minutes to three, the phone rang. "St Francis," Joe said.

"Earl, Father."

"*Earl?*"

"At the store, Father."

"Oh, hello, Earl."

Earl said that North Carolina *could* supply, and would air-freight to the customer's own address. So beds and chests would arrive in a couple of days, Friday at the outside, and box springs and mattresses, these from stock, would be on the store's Thursday delivery to Inglenook.

"O.K., Father?"

"O.K., Earl."

Joe didn't try to do anymore that day.

The next morning, he took delivery of the office equipment (which Mrs P.—Mrs Pelissier—the housekeeper, must have noticed), and so he got a late start on his shopping. He began where he'd left off the day before. Earl, spotting him among the lamps, came over to say hello. When he saw Joe's list, he recommended the store's interior-decorating department—"Mrs Fox, if she's not out on a job." With Joe's permission, Earl went to a phone, and Mrs Fox soon appeared among the lamps. Slightly embarrassed, Joe told her what he thought—that the room ought to be planned around the bed, since it was a *bed*-room. Mrs Fox smacked her lips and shrieked (to Earl), "*He* doesn't need *me*!"

As a matter of fact, Mrs Fox proved very helpful—steered Joe from department to department, protected him from clerks, took him into stockrooms and onto a freight elevator, and remembered curtains and bedspreads (Joe bought two), which weren't on his list but were definitely needed. Finally, Mrs Fox had the easy chair and other things brought down to the parking lot and put into his car. These could have gone out on the Thursday delivery, but Joe wanted to see how the room would look even without the big stuff—the bed, the chest, the student's table, and the revolving bookcase. Mrs Fox felt the same way. Twice in the store she'd expressed a desire to see the room, and he'd managed to change the subject, and then she did it again, in the parking lot—was *dying* to see the room, she shrieked, just as he was driving away. He just smiled. What else could he do? He couldn't have Mrs Fox coming out there.

In some ways, things were moving too fast. He still hadn't told Mrs P. that he was getting a curate—hadn't because he was afraid if he did, she'd ask, as he had, "Who?" Who, indeed? He still didn't know, and the fact that he didn't would, if admitted, make him look foolish in Mrs P.'s eyes. It would also put the Church—administrationwise—in a poor light.

That evening, after Mrs P. had gone home, Joe unloaded the car, which he'd run into the garage because the easy chair was clearly visible in the trunk. It took him four trips to get all his purchases up to the room. Then, using a kitchen chair, listening to the ball game and drinking beer, he put up the curtain rods. (The janitor, if asked to, would wonder why, and if told, would tell Mrs P., who would ask, "Who?") When Joe had the curtains up, tiebacks and all, he took a much needed bath, changed, and made himself a gin-and-tonic. He carried it into the room, dark now—he had been waiting for this moment— and turned on the lamps he'd bought. O.K.—and when the student's table came, the student's lamp, now on the little bedside table, would look even better. He had chosen one with a yellow shade, rather than green, so the room would appear cheerful, and it certainly did. He tried the easy chair, the matching footstool, the gin-and-tonic. O.K. He sat there for some time, one foot going to sleep on the rose-and-blue hooked rug while he wondered why—why he hadn't heard anything from the curate.

The next day, Thursday, he gave Mrs P. the afternoon off, saying he planned to eat out that evening, and so she wasn't present when the box springs, mattresses, student's table and revolving bookcase came, at twenty after four—the hottest time of day. He had a lot of trouble with the mattresses—really a job for two strong men, one to pull on the mattress, one to hold on to the carton—and had to drink two bottles of beer to restore his body salts. He took a much needed bath, changed, and, feeling too tired to go out, made himself some ham sandwiches and a gin-and-tonic. He used a whole lime—it was his salad—and ate in his study while watching the news: people starving in Asia and Mississippi. He went without dessert. Suddenly, he jumped up and got busy around the place, did the dishes—dish—and locked the church. When darkness came, he was back where he'd been the night before—in the room, in the chair, with a glass, wondering why he hadn't heard anything from the curate.

It was customary for the newly ordained men to take a few days off to visit and shake down their friends and relatives. Ordinations, though, had been held on Saturday. It was now Thursday, almost Friday, and still no word. What to do? He had called people at the seminary, hoping to learn the curate's name and perhaps something of his character, just in the course of conversation. ("Understand you're getting So-and-So, Joe.") But it hadn't happened—everybody he asked to speak to (the entire faculty, it seemed) had left for vacationland. He had then called the diocesan paper and, with pencil ready, asked for a complete rundown on the new appointments, but the list hadn't come over from the Chancery yet. ("They can be pretty slow over there, Father." "Toohey, you mean?" "Monsignor's pretty busy, Father, and we don't push him on a thing like this —it's not what we call hard news.")

So, really, there was nothing to do, short of calling the Chancery. Early in the week, it might have been done—that was when Joe made his mistake—but it was out of the question now. He didn't want to expose the curate to censure and run the risk of turning him against his pastor, and he also didn't want the Chancery to know what the situation was at SS Francis and Clare's, one of the best-run parishes in the diocese, though it certainly wasn't his fault. It was the curate's fault, it was Toohey's fault. "Letter follows." If called on that,

Toohey would say, "Didn't say when. Busy here," and hang up. That was how Toohey played the game. Once, when Joe had called for help and said he'd die if he didn't get away for a couple of weeks, Toohey had said, "Die," and hung up. Rough. If the Church ever got straightened out administrationwise, Toohey and his kind would have to go, but that was one of those long-term objectives. In the meantime, Joe and his kind would have to soldier on, and Joe would. It was hard, though, after years of waiting for a curate, after finally getting one, not to be able to mention it. While shopping, Joe had run into two pastors who would have been interested to hear of his good fortune, and one had even raised the subject of curates, had said that he was getting a *change*, "Thank God!" Joe hadn't thought much about it then—the "Thank God!" part—but now he did, and, swallowing the weak last inch of his drink, came face to face with the ice.

What, he thought—what if the curate, the unknown curate, *wasn't* one of the newly ordained men? What if he was one of those bad-news guys? A young man with five or six parishes behind him? Or a man as old as himself, or older, a retread, a problem priest? Or a goldbrick who figured, since he was paid by the month, he wouldn't report until the first, Sunday? Or a slob who wouldn't take care of the room? These were sobering thoughts to Joe. He got up and made another drink.

The next morning, when he returned from a trip to the dump, where he personally disposed of his empties, Mrs P. met him at the door. "Somebody who says he's your assistant—"

"Yes, yes. Where is he?"

"Phoned. Said he'd be here tomorrow."

"*Tomorrow?*" But he didn't want Mrs P. to get the idea that he was disappointed, or that he didn't know what was going on. "Good. Did he say what time?"

"He just asked about confessions."

"So he'll be here in time for confessions. Good."

"Said he was calling from Whipple."

"*Whipple?*"

"Said he was down there buying a car."

Joe nodded, as though he regarded Whipple, which he'd driven through once or twice, as an excellent place to buy a car. He was waiting for Mrs P. to continue.

"That's all *I* know," she said, and shot off to the kitchen. Hurt. Not his fault. Toohey's fault. Curate's fault. Not telling her about the curate was bad, but doing it as he would have had to would have been worse. Better she think less of him than know the truth—and think less of the Church. He took the sins of curates and administrators upon him.

That afternoon, he waited until four o'clock before he got on the phone to Earl. "Say, what is this? I thought you said Friday at the outside."

"Oh, oh," said Earl, and didn't have to be told who was calling, or about what. He said he'd put a tracer on the order, and promised to call back right away, which he did. "Hey, Father, guess what? The order's at our warehouse. North Carolina goofed."

"That so?" said Joe, but he wasn't interested in Earl's analysis of North Carolina's failure to ship to customer's own address, and cut in on it. He described his bed situation, as he hadn't before for Earl, in depth. He was going to be short a bed—no, not that night but the next, when his assistant would be there, and also a monk of advanced age who helped out on weekends and slept in the guest room. No, the bed in the guest room, to answer Earl's question, was a single—actually, a cot. Yes, Joe could put his assistant on the box spring and mattress, but wouldn't like to do it, and didn't see why he should. He'd been promised delivery by Friday at the outside. He didn't care if Inglenook *was* in Monday and Thursday territory. In the end, he was promised delivery the next day, Saturday.

"O.K., Father?"

"O.K., Earl."

The next afternoon, a panel truck, scarred and bearing no name, pulled up in front of the rectory at seven minutes after four. Joe didn't know what to make of it. He stayed inside the rectory until the driver and his helper unloaded a carton, then rushed out, and was about to ask them to unload at the back door and save themselves a few steps when a word on the carton stopped him. "Hold everything!" And it wasn't, as he'd hoped, simply a matter of a word on a carton. Oh, no. On investigation, the beds proved to be as described on their cartons —cannonballs. "Hold everything. I have to call the store."

On the way to the telephone, passing Father Otto, the monk of advanced age, who was another who hadn't been told about the curate, and now appeared curious to know what was happening in the street, Joe wished that monks were forbidden to wear their habits away from the monastery. Flowing robes, Joe felt, had a bad effect on his parishioners, made him, in his cassock, look second-best in their eyes, and also reminded non-Catholics of the Reformation.

"Say, what is this?" he said, on the phone.

"Oh, oh," said Earl when he learned what had happened. "North Carolina goofed."

"Now, *look*," said Joe, and really opened up on Earl and the store. "I don't like the way you people do business," he said, pausing to breathe.

"Correct me if I'm wrong, Father, but didn't you say you liked cannonballs?"

"Better than Jenny Lind, I said. But that's not the point. I prefer the other, and that's what I said. You know what 'prefer' means, don't you?"

"Pineapples."

"You've got me over a barrel, Earl."

In the end, despite what he'd indicated earlier, Joe said he'd take delivery. "But we're through," he told Earl, and hung up.

He returned to the street where, parked behind the panel truck, there was now a new VW beetle, and there, it seemed, standing by the opened cartons with Father Otto, the driver, and his helper, was Joe's curate—big and young, obviously one of the newly ordained men. Seeing Joe, he left the others and came smiling toward him.

"Where you been?" Joe said—like an old pastor, he thought.

The curate stopped smiling. "Whipple."

Joe put it another way. "Why didn't you give me a call?"

"I did."

"Before yesterday?"

"I did. Don't know how many times I called. You were never in."

"Didn't know what to think," Joe said, ignoring the curate's point like an old pastor, and, looking away, wished that the beetle—light brown, or dark yellow, sort of a caramel—was another color, and also that it wasn't parked where it was, adding to the confusion. (The driver's helper was showing Father Otto how his dolly worked.) "Could've left your name with the housekeeper."

"I kept thinking I'd get you if I called again. You were never in."

Joe moved toward the street, saying, "Yes, well, I've been out a lot lately. Could've left your name, Father."

"I did, Father. Yesterday."

"Yes, well." Standing by the little car, viewing the books and luggage inside, Joe wished that he could start over, that he hadn't started off as he had. He had meant to welcome the curate. It wasn't his fault that he hadn't—look at the days and nights of needless anxiety, and look what time it was now—but still he wanted to make up for it. "Better drive your little car around to the back, Father, and unload," he said. "The housekeeper'll show you the room. Won't ask you to hear confessions this afternoon." And, having opened the door of the little car for the curate, he closed it for him, saying, through the window, "See you later, Father."

When he straightened up, he saw that Big Mouth, a neighbor and a parishioner, had arrived to inspect the cartons, heard him questioning Father Otto, saw, too, that Mrs P. had decided to sweep the front walk and was working that way. Joe called to her.

"I've bought a few things—besides the bed and chest here— for the curate's room," he told her, so she wouldn't be too surprised when she saw them. Then he gave her the key to the room, saying, perhaps needlessly, that she'd find it locked, and that the box springs, mattresses, and bedspreads would be found within. The other bed—the one that should and would have been his but for the interest shown in it by Father Otto and Big Mouth—the other bed and chest, he told Mrs P., should go into the guest room. "Fold up the cot and put it somewhere. Get the curate to help you—he's not hearing this afternoon."

Turning then to the little group around the cartons, he saw that his instructions to Mrs P. had been overheard and understood. The little group—held together by the question "Would he take delivery?"—was breaking up. He thanked the driver and his helper for waiting, nodded to Big Mouth, said "Coming?" to Father Otto, since it was now time for confessions, and walked toward the church. He took the sins of curates and administrators and North Carolina upon him. He gave another his bed.

That evening, after confessions, and after Father Otto had retired to the new bed in the guest room, Joe and the curate sat on in the pastor's study. Joe, doing most of the talking, had had less than usual, the curate more, it seemed—he was yawning. "Used to be," Joe was saying, "we all drove black cars. I still do." Joe, while he didn't want to hurt the curate's feelings, just couldn't understand why a priest, even a young priest today, able to buy a new car should pick one the color of the curate's. "Maybe it's not important."

"Think I'll turn in, Father."

Joe hated to go to bed, and changed the subject slightly. "How's the room? O.K.?"

"O.K."

Joe had been expecting a bit more. Had he hurt the curate's feelings? "It's not important, what I was saying."

The curate smiled. "My uncle's the dealer in Whipple. He gave me a good deal on the car, but that was part of it—the color."

"I see." Joe tried not to appear as interested as he suddenly was. "What's he call his place—Whipple Volkswagen? I know a lot of 'em do. That's what they call it here—Inglenook Volkswagen."

"He calls it by his own name."

"I see. And this is your father's brother?"

"My mother's."

"I see."

"Think I'll turn in now, Father."

"Yeah. Maybe we should. Sunday's always a tough day."

The next morning, with Joe watching from the sacristy, and later from the rear of the church, the curate said his first Mass in the parish. He was slow, of course, but he wasn't fancy, and he didn't fall down. His sermon was standard, marred only by his gestures (once or twice he looked like a bad job of dubbing), and he read the announcements well. He neglected to introduce himself to the congregation, but that might be done the following week in the parish bulletin.

The day began to go wrong, though, when, after his second Mass, the curate mentioned an invitation he had to dine out with a classmate. "Well, all right," Joe said, writing off the afternoon but not the evening.

He still hadn't written off the evening, entirely, at eighteen after eleven. The door of the pastor's study was open, and the pastor was clearly visible in his Barcalounger chair, having a nightcap, but the curate went straight to his room, and could soon be heard running a bath.

So Joe, despite the change from a week ago, had spent Sunday as usual—the afternoon with the papers, TV, a nap, and Father Otto (until it was time for his bus), and the evening alone. Most of it. At seven-thirty, he'd had a surprise visit from Earl, his wife, and two of their children.

The next morning, Joe laid an unimportant letter on the curate's metal desk. "Answer this, will you? I've made some notes on the margin so you'll know what to say. Keep it brief. Sign *your* name—Assistant Pastor. But let me have a look at it before you seal it." And that, he thought, is that.

"Does it have to be *typed*?"

"What d'ya mean?"

"Can't *type* it."

"What d'ya mean?"

"Can't *type*."

Joe just stood there in a distressed state. "Can't type," he said. "You mean at the sem you did everything in longhand? Term papers and everything?"

The curate, who seemed to think that too much was being made of his disability, nodded.

"Hard to believe," Joe said. "Why, you must've been the only guy in your class not to use a typewriter."

"There was one other guy."

Joe was somewhat relieved—at least the gambler in him was—to know that he hadn't been quite as unlucky as he'd supposed. "But you must've heard guys all around you using typewriters. Didn't you ever wonder why?"

"I never owned a typewriter. Never saw the need." The curate sounded proud, like somebody who brushes his teeth with table salt. "I write a good, clear hand."

Joe snorted. "*I* write a good, clear hand. But I don't do my parish correspondence by hand. And I hope *you* won't when you're a pastor."

"The hell with it, then."

Joe, who had been walking around in a distressed state, stopped and looked at the curate, but the curate—pretty clever —wouldn't look back. He was getting out a cigarette. Joe shook his head, and walked around shaking it. "Father, Father," he said.

"Father, hell," said the curate, emitting smoke. "You should've put in for a stenographer, not a priest."

Joe stopped, stood still, and sniffed. "Great," he said, nodding his head. "Sounds great, Father. But what does it *mean*? Does it mean you expect me to do the lion's share of the donkey work around here? While you're out saving souls? Or sitting up in your room? Does it mean when you're a pastor you'll expect your curate to do what you never had to do? I hope not, Father. Because, you know, Father, when you're a pastor it may be years before you have a curate. You may never have one, Father. You may end up in a one-horse parish. Lots of guys do. You won't be able to afford a secretary, or public stenographers, and you won't care to trust your correspondence to nuns, to parishioners. You'll never be your own man. You'll always be an embarrassment to yourself and others. Let's face it, Father. Today, a man who can't use a typewriter is as ill-equipped for parish life as a man who can't drive a car. Go ahead. Laugh. Sneer. But it's true. You don't want to be like Toohey, do you? *He* can't type, and he's set this diocese back a hundred years. He writes 'No can do' on everything and returns it to the sender. For official business he uses scratch paper put out by the Universal Portland Cement Company."

Depressed by the thought of Toohey and annoyed by the curate's cool, if that was what it was, Joe retired to his office. He
sat down at his new desk and made a list. Presently, he appeared in the doorway between the offices, wearing his hat.
"And, Father," he continued, "when you're a pastor, what if
you get a curate like yourself? Think it over. I have to go out
now. Mind the store."

Joe drove to the city and bought a typing course consisting
of a manual and phonograph records, and he also bought the
bed—it was still there—the double, with pineapples. He was
told that if he ever wished to order a matching chest or dresser
there would be no trouble at all, and that the bed, along with
box spring and mattress, would be on the Thursday delivery to
Inglenook.

"O.K., Father?"

"O.K., Earl."

And that afternoon Joe, in his office, had a phone call from
Mrs Fox, She just wondered if everything was O.K., she said—
as if she didn't know. She was still dying to see the room.
"What's it *like*!" Joe said he thought the room had turned out
pretty well, thanked Mrs Fox for helping him, and also for calling, and hung up.

Immediately, the phone rang again. "St Francis," Joe said.

"Bill there?"

"*Bill?*"

"For *me*?" said the curate, who had been typing away, or,
anyway, typing.

Joe tried to look right through the wall. (The door between
the offices was open, but the angle was wrong.)"Take it over
there," he said, and switched the call.

There were no further developments that day.

None the next day.

And none the next.

No more phone calls for the curate, and no mail addressed

to him, and nothing in the diocesan paper, and no word from Toohey. And Mrs P. with her "he" and "him" was no help, nor was the janitor with his "young Father," and Father Otto wouldn't be there until Saturday. But in one way or another, sooner or later, perhaps in time for the next parish bulletin, though the odds were now against that, Joe hoped to learn Bill's last name.

FOLKS

SOME TIME LATER when Jean and I had both gotten married and our husbands had been brought into our very close relationship, we disclosed our early experiences one night. When our husbands first heard our story, they were not only shocked but disbelieving. However, they believed readily when Jean went over and sat on my husband's lap while I beckoned her husband into the other room. Since then we have swapped regularly and have recently added two more couples. We are all very close friends so have no special rules. All four couples met recently in a big cabin in the mountains and it worked so successfully that we plan to try it for a full week next summer. *

---

*From *Mr*, Vol. 4, No. 6, whose editors say: "Any assumption that we, because we have had the courage to present a factual and unemotional report, therefore sympathize with the points of view described is a complete misreading of our purpose."

Dear Lloyd and Jean:

I am doing my Xmas letters, and Les says not to forget you folks, and so here I come. It's almost a year since you moved away, and all I can say is we sure do miss you both. I wish you could see our tree. Les got it from the same guy down at the plant. We added more lights and now have 128. The whole block agreed not to have roof displays this year. Lloyd's bad fall last year had a lot to do with this decision. Only Bensons held out. They would. They have a new Snow White but the same old dwarfs. He came to Les about using ours, said since we wouldn't be needing them this year. Of course Les had to turn him down. We were all worried about the couple that moved into your house, since he is an electrician, but they promised they wouldn't have a roof display. Now it looks like they won't even have a tree. She works, I guess. Both of them nice-looking, but Les thinks they don't get along. They sure keep to themselves.

Say, we were sorry not to see you at Rocky Ridge last summer, but didn't expect you when you didn't write. I remember Lloyd said he might have to take his vacation at a different time. Was that it? Well, after two days of pouring rain, we decided to drive up to Yellowstone. Just the two of us. Some drive, but this new wagon we have can really eat up the road. Came back through the Black Hills. They needed rain. I suppose you got the cards.

Say, the big tube burned out about ten days ago. Didn't you say it was almost practically new? The serviceman (Red) tried to tell me it came with the set. Did you ever find the warranty papers? Les wanted to wait until we could afford color, but I didn't think it would be fair to him, with the Bowl games coming up, and so we now have a new picture tube. How many channels where you are now?

Les is giving me a gift certificate that I may apply on a dryer. It is now definite we are getting natural gas in the spring. Do you have it there? He is getting an outboard motor from me. He says what should we do with that old kicker you forgot and left in our garage. Be glad to send it to you. Or if you want us to try and sell it for you, we will. Just let us know. By the way, what do you think we should do about the power mower? If you want to keep it, that's O.K. with us. Or if you want to send it to us, that's O.K., too. In that case, we would forward you your share in it ($44). Maybe you could let us know your decision when you write about the old outboard motor? Lloyd, will you get Jean to write? Les says he's never heard of people like you folks for not writing, and I agree. Ha. Ha.

Hey, don't get us wrong about the mower. If you want us to have it, we will forward you your share ($44) right away, but we don't expect you to send it back unless you want to. Les says you might be smart to hold on to it, and not have to go to the trouble and expense of sending it back. Whatever you decide to do is O.K.

Les is talking about bed and so I'll close with a Merry Xmas and a Happy New Year. Hope our card arrived safely. Yours hasn't come as yet. As always.

Les and Lil

P.S. Les just called about the freight charges in case you decide to send it back. $5 or $6. You don't have to crate it. We don't want to tell you what to do, but it looks like you'd be smart to just forward our share ($44). We used Bensons' last summer, but we hated to ask for it, and the grass got so long each time. Don't want to go through that again and would appreciate hearing from you soon so we can make our plans for the coming year. Les says if you want to send it back we'll split the freight with you—and of course forward you your full share ($44).

KEYSTONE

AT HIS DESK in the Chancery, the brownstone mansion that was also his residence, John Dullinger, Bishop of Ostergothenburg (Minnesota), was hard at work on a pastoral letter, this one to be read from the pulpits of the diocese in some five weeks. The Bishop was about to mention the keystone of authority, as he did so often in his pastoral letters, that stone without which . . . when Monsignor Holstein, Vicar-General of the diocese and rector of the Cathedral, a lanky man in his late sixties, arrived with the Minneapolis *Tribune* and a paper bag. "*Wie geht's?*" said Monsignor Holstein, and deposited the bag on the desk.

The Bishop peeked into the bag, said "Oh," and, with a nod, thanked Monsignor Holstein for his kindness—for the fine new appointment book. It was that time of year again.

"I hear Scuza's worse, John," said Monsignor Holstein.

The Bishop had heard this, too, but assumed that Monsignor Holstein had later word. New Pilsen, where Father Scuza lay dying, was Monsignor Holstein's hometown.

"A bad month, John."

The Bishop sighed. He figured to lose a couple of men every December, and had already lost one that year.

"Another foreign movie coming to the Orpheum, but I can't find out much about it—only that it's Italian," said Monsignor Holstein.

The Bishop sighed.

Monsignor Holstein, who had rolled up the Minneapolis *Tribune*, whacked himself across the hand with it, but did not sit down. On mornings when there was clear and present danger in the diocese—a dance for ninth-graders scheduled for the Eagles' Hall, *Martin Luther* coming to the Orpheum—Monsignor Holstein sat down and beat himself about his black shoes and white socks with the Minneapolis *Tribune*, while the Bishop, a stocky man, opened and shut his mouth like a fish, and said, "Brrr-jorrk-brrrr." On such mornings, by the time the Bishop got the paper it was in poor shape, and so was he. But this wasn't going to be one of those mornings. Monsignor Holstein was about to depart.

"Like me to take that over to the printer?" he asked, looking down at the pastoral letter.

"Not finished."

When Monsignor Holstein was halfway to the door, he saw that he had the paper in his hand, and came back to deliver it. "Like me to wait a few minutes?"

"*No.*" There was more to writing a pastoral letter than getting it to the printer—a lot more than Monsignor Holstein would ever know. He'd never make a bishop.

"Hello, Tootsie," said Monsignor Holstein when he opened the door, addressing the housekeeper's kitten, whose name was not Tootsie but Tessie—and the Bishop wished the man would remember that. "*Raus*, Tootsie!"

"It's all right," said the Bishop, and the kitten came over Monsignor Holstein's shoe, kicking up her heels.

While waiting for the kitten to come and sit on his lap—Monsignor Holstein had upset Tessie—the Bishop checked the helpful data in the new appointment book, as was his custom each year. He was sorry to see that the approximate transit time from New York to Minneapolis by air was still given as seven hours, which took no account of jet travel, and that among the cities with population over fifty thousand there were more places than ever that he hadn't heard of, most of them in California, and that Fargo, North Dakota, which he regarded as his hometown, though he'd been brought up on a farm near there, was still not listed. Perhaps next year. He saw that young Kennedy was now among the Presidents—the youngest ever, except Theodore Roosevelt, to hold that high office—but that Alaska and Hawaii were not among the states. Otherwise—postage rates, stains and how to remove them, points of Constitutional law, weights and measures, weather wisdom, and so on—everything was the same as in the previous edition, including nicknames of the states and the state flowers (Alaska and Hawaii missing). Then, as was his custom, the Bishop examined his conscience:

GOOD RULES FOR BUSINESSMEN

Don't worry, don't overbuy; don't go security.
Keep your vitality up; keep insured; keep sober; keep cool.
Stick to chosen pursuits, but not to chosen methods.
Be content with small beginnings and develop them.
Be wary of dealing with unsuccessful men.
Be cautious, but when a bargain is made stick to it.
Keep down expenses, but don't be stingy.
Make friends, but not favorites.
Don't take new risks to retrieve old losses.
Stop a bad account at once.

> Make plans ahead, but don't make them in cast iron.
> Don't tell what you are to do until you have done it.

To the extent that these rules could be made to apply to him—and all of them could, to an extent—the Bishop was doing pretty well, he thought. Presently, with the cat on his lap, he took a call from the editor of the diocesan weekly, Father Rapp, who said that Monsignor Holstein had just left, after giving him an argument over the spelling of "godlessness." "I told him we never capitalize it," Father Rapp said. " 'Then you better begin,' he told me."

"Don't capitalize it," said the Bishop, and returned to the pastoral letter.

Father Gau, the Chancellor, who had put through the call, entered the office, saying, "I thought I'd better let him talk to you."

"Took care of it."

"Is that ready to go over, Your Excellency?"

The Bishop looked down at the pastoral letter. "No—and what's the big hurry?"

"No hurry, Your Excellency." Father Gau smiled in that nice way he had. "I guess I just wanted to read it."

Three days later, the episcopal Cadillac went to New Pilsen for Father Scuza's funeral. Father Gau was at the wheel, the Bishop and Monsignor Holstein in the back seat, where there was some talk, on the Vicar-General's part, of possible successors to the deceased. The Bishop was careful not to commit himself. St John Nepomuk's, where Father Scuza had been pastor, was one of the most important parishes in the diocese, and the Bishop intended to take more of a hand in such appointments. Every pastor in Ostergothenburg, where there were three churches besides the Cathedral, was one of Monsignor Holstein's men.

After the funeral, on the way back to Ostergothenburg, Monsignor Holstein raised the matter again. "We were down in the church basement, and Leo"—who was Monsignor Holstein's choice for pastor of St John Nepomuk's—"says why not heat the rectory from the church? Run a pipe underground, and convert the rectory from hot water to steam. Not a bad idea."

The Bishop said nothing.

"I was worried about the radiators in the rectory, but Leo says they're sound. Just have to watch your joints when you go to steam. And switch from oil to gas, Leo says. That's one thing Leo understands—heating."

The Bishop liked Leo well enough. Leo might easily have had the job in days past, but he was one of Monsignor Holstein's men.

"House needs a lot of work," said Monsignor Holstein. "As usual, curates don't give a damn. Saw their rooms—nails in the walls and woodwork, and so on. Whoever goes there will have plenty to do. I'd say Leo's your man, John."

The Bishop said nothing.

As if he'd settled that matter, Monsignor Holstein moved on to the next one. How did the Bishop feel about relocating the big cross in the cemetery so that it would be visible from the new highway? "John, wouldn't it be fine if, next summer, people driving north on their vacations could see the cross?" Then, not mentioning the argument he'd had with Father Rapp, although Father Rapp was present now, riding up in front with Father Gau, Monsignor Holstein got onto the spelling of "godlessness." He said he could see how the word, under special circumstances, might not be capitalized. A heathen of no faith at all—and there were many such in ancient Rome, by all accounts—might be said to be godless as well as Godless. "But, of course, when we use the word, we don't mean anything like that, do we? I don't know whether I make myself clear or not."

Father Gau and Father Rapp, no longer conversing, seemed

to be listening for the Bishop's response. It was the Bishop, after all, who had said, "Don't capitalize it." Later, the Bishop had checked the dictionary and found himself right, but as he saw it now the dictionary was wrong. He said nothing.

Father Gau glanced around and, smiling, said, "How would you spell 'atheism,' Monsignor? With a capital 'T'?"

By tradition in the diocese of Ostergothenburg, whoever became chancellor had to be a good, safe driver. Always before, with his long confirmation trips in mind, the Bishop had taken a young man a few years out of the seminary—a practice that might have been criticized more if the diocese hadn't enjoyed the services of a very able, though aging, bishop and a strong vicar-general. For a number of years, Monsignor Holstein had had a lot to say about who should be chancellor, but Father Gau had been the Bishop's own choice for the job. He had come to it at the ripe old age of forty, after years spent entirely in rural parishes, ultimately as pastor in Grasshopper Lake, a little place that hadn't been much in the news until he went there —until, to be more exact, Father Rapp, a classmate of Father Gau's, took over as editor (and photographer) of the diocesan paper.

In May, on a confirmation trip to Grasshopper Lake, the Bishop had had a chance to see some of the wayside shrines he'd been reading about (and seen pictures of). They weren't as close to the road as he would have liked them, but Minnesota wasn't Austria, and the highway department had to have its clearance. The figurines in the shrines were perhaps too much alike, as if from the same hand or mold, and the crosses had been cut from plywood. But, garnished with the honest flowers of the field, as they were in May, these shrines—these outward manifestations of the simple faith of simple people in a wide and wicked world—were a very pretty sight to the Bishop. When he'd pulled up at the church in Grasshopper Lake, little chil-

dren had suddenly appeared and, grouping themselves around
his car, raised their trained voices in song, pure song. The
Bishop had never heard the like. "First time I ever heard angels
singing, and in German at that!" he told the congregation before beginning what turned out to be a good, long sermon.

Late in August, returning from a trip that had taken him to
the northern border of the diocese, the Bishop had paused at
Grasshopper Lake. It was the day of the parish's harvest festi-
val. Such occasions still had meaning in the Ostergothenburg
diocese, the Bishop believed, and he did all he could to encour-
age them, only asking that they be brought to a close by sundown, that there be no dancing, and that pastors keep an eye
on the beer stand. Father Gau was doing this when the Bishop
arrived, and was *not* tending bar, which was something the
Bishop didn't want to see, as he'd said time and again. Together
they had strolled among the people, the Bishop smiling upon
the pies and cakes and upon the women who had baked them,
and occasionally giving his hand to a man for shaking. To the
grownups he'd say, "You earned this. You worked hard all
year," and to the children, "Give us a song!" And, since he was
still a long way from home, he had kept moving, in time with
the little *Ach-du-lieber-Augustin* band that played in the
shade of a big tree, until he was almost back to his car—in
which his chancellor of the moment sat listening to the Game
of the Day. After asking whether Father Gau's driver's license
was in good order, and hearing that it was, the Bishop had said,
"Like to live in Ostergothenburg, Father?"

"I'm happy here, Your Excellency."

"I can see that."

"What parish, Your Excellency?"

"I'm looking for a new chancellor."

"Gee," Father Gau had said. "Gee, Your Excellency."

In September, Father Gau had moved into the Cathedral
rectory. He handled the routine work at the Chancery, drove

the Bishop's car, heard confessions at the Cathedral on Saturdays, and said two Masses there on Sundays. He also organized a children's choir—this at the earnest request of the Bishop. All went well. Then, with the Bishop's consent, Father Gau formed a men's chorus, and there was trouble. Mr McKee, the director of the Cathedral choir, a mixed group, said that if male members of the choir wanted to get together on purely social occasions and sing "Dry Bones," that was one thing, but if they were going to sing sacred music, that was something else. The men's chorus would be a choir, and a choir couldn't serve two directors, said Mr McKee and Monsignor Holstein backed him up. Father Gau took no part in the controversy. In fact, he offered to resign as director of the men's chorus, or to disband it, or to turn it over to Mr McKee—and the children's choir as well, if that would help any. The men of the chorus wouldn't have this, nor would the mothers of the children. The Bishop said nothing—wouldn't discuss the matter with anybody, not even Monsignor Holstein. In the end, in a surprise move, Mr McKee resigned. And so Father Gau, who already had enough to do, was obliged to assume the direction of the choir. But what the Bishop had feared, an all-out choir war, hadn't happened, and for this he was grateful to all concerned.

Then, a week before Christmas, soon after Father Scuza's funeral, the men of the chorus put on bright tights and sweatshirts and, thus attired, went caroling through the streets of downtown Ostergothenburg. The Ostergothenburg *Times*, whose editor Father Gau had already got to know better than the Bishop ever had (the Bishop didn't like the man's politics), printed a very nice story about the minstrels in their colorful medieval garb. The Bishop had just finished reading the story when in came Monsignor Holstein, who said he'd spotted the men in Hokey's, the town's leading department store, and complained bitterly that they had been singing pagan-inspired drinking songs. The Bishop listened to him but said nothing, and Monsignor Holstein went away. Did it matter to Monsignor Holstein that the minstrels were important men in the community, that they thought they were engaged in a good work, that the *Times* thought so? Monsignor Holstein had just plunged in, as was his habit—a very bad habit. Monsignor Holstein was a rash man, an unsuccessful man, and even when he was right, as he sometimes was, there was something wrong— something wrong about the *way* he was right. However, the Bishop did feel that jolly songs shouldn't be performed under his auspices during Advent, which, as Monsignor Holstein had said, was a penitential season second only to Lent, and so Father Gau was asked to see that such songs were dropped from the minstrels' repertoire, the Bishop citing "Jingle Bells," and another that, to quote Monsignor Holstein, went "Ho, ho, ho, the wind doth blow!" When Father Gau heard these words from the Bishop's lips, he smiled, and then the Bishop, too, smiled. Until then, he had been worried that Father Gau might think that the Vicar-General was running the diocese. Father Gau, though, had made a joke out of the incident—and, to a certain extent, out of Monsignor Holstein.

In January, after Monsignor Holstein left town—he was appointed pastor of St John Nepomuk's, in New Pilsen—the Bishop and Father Gau were often seen together in the evening, in the main dining room of the Hotel Webb. The food was good and plentiful at the Webb. The tables weren't placed too close together, there was light enough to eat by, and there was music. In fact, the organist, a nice-looking middle-aged woman who didn't use too much make-up, was a Cathedral parishioner.

These evenings at the Webb, topped off with Benedictine and Dutch Masters, were great occasions for Father Gau (who called himself a country boy), and this was a good part of the Bishop's pleasure in them, although he also did most of the talking. He spoke of his youth "in and around Fargo," of his years of study at home and abroad, of his ordination at the hands of a cardinal in Rome. Back and forth in time he journeyed, accompanied by Father Gau, who now and then asked a question. One evening, the Bishop spoke of the curious role the number two had played in his career: curate in two places, pastor in two, chaplain to the Catholic Foresters for two terms, fourth Bishop of Ostergothenburg (and four is the square of two), and consecrated on his forty-second birthday, on the second day of the second month. "In 1932."

"Gee."

On another evening, the Bishop said, "I couldn't have been more surprised if I'd landed St Paul or Milwaukee, or more pleased." The Ostergothenburg diocese might well be what it was sometimes called, "the biggest little diocese in the world," for you really couldn't count Europe and South America. There might be dioceses to compare with it in the French part of Canada, but had the faithful in those dioceses been completely exposed to the temptations of a high standard of living? Ostergothenburg, and all the roads around it, blazed with invitations to drink, dine, dance, bowl, borrow money, have the car washed, and so on, but let the diocese stage a rally of some kind at the ballpark and there wouldn't be much doing anywhere else. Oh, of course, if you looked for Ostergothenburg on the map, or judged it by any of the usual rules of thumb —population, bank debits, new construction—you might not think it was much of a place. It had no scheduled air service and no television station and it had lost its franchise in organized baseball. But if you looked at the *diocese*—well, pastors in Minneapolis and St Paul, who might compare their situations very favorably with those of bishops in barren sees to the north and west, knew they weren't in it with Dullinger. Catholics outnumbered non-Catholics by better than three to one in the diocese. The Bishop had a hundred thousand souls under his care.

"We're well *over* the hundred thousand mark, Your Excellency."

"When I first came here, we were under seventy thousand."

"Gee."

Another man arriving in such a diocese, with no previous experience as a bishop and only forty-two years old, might have chosen to leave well enough alone. This the Bishop had not done. He had twice voted for F.D.R., had backed the New Deal in all its alphabetical manifestations, and, in general, had tried to do what the government was already doing for the common man, only spiritually. "My words were widely quoted. I was referred to as 'the farmer Bishop.' Some thought it sounded disrespectful. I didn't."

"I don't."

But then had come the war and prosperity. The Bishop went out as before and spoke to gatherings, not so large as before but interested. After the war, to combat the changed times—changed for the worse—the Bishop had reached into the faculty of the seminary for Monsignor (then Father) Holstein.

"We were all sorry to see him go," said Father Gau, who had been a seminarian then.

"A good man, in his way."

Monsignor Holstein had done well with public events of a devotional nature—field Masses, "living rosaries," pilgrimages, and processions. And he had stamped out the practice of embellishing the cars of honeymooners with crude sentiments. But in too many ways he had failed. There had been no change at the Orpheum, and at the normal school some smart alecks who hadn't been organized before—before Monsignor Holstein —now made themselves heard on the slightest provocation. When the second Kinsey report had come out, Monsignor Holstein had played right into their hands, telling the *Times*, "Only an old priest with years of experience in the confessional should write such a book, and he wouldn't." This, though true, had looked silly in print.

The Bishop was glad that the troublesome postwar, or Holstein, period was over. Father Gau had been stationed at some distance from the front during this period, and might have been interested in a firsthand account of the fighting, but he seemed to understand that the Bishop didn't care to talk about it.

Father Gau was very understanding. The organist in the main dining room at the Webb did not forget the Bishop's one request—for "Trees"—and night after night played it, sometimes at great length, which was all right, but when she took to rendering it as a solemn fanfare to mark his arrivals and departures, the Bishop wasn't sure he cared for it, but he said nothing. After a while, the organist abandoned the practice, and Father Gau, when questioned by the Bishop, admitted that he'd asked her to do so.

During the day, too, on trips and at the Chancery, Father Gau saw to it that the Bishop's will was done—sometimes before the Bishop knew what his will was. "Just say yes or no, Your Excellency," Father Gau would say, offering a solution to a problem the Bishop might not have been aware of, or to one he'd regarded as tolerable.

One such problem had to do with the regulations for fasting, which, of all the regulations of the diocese, were the ones of most concern to the laity. Monsignor Holstein, trying to make these regulations perfectly clear and binding wherever possible, had gone too deeply into the various claims for exemption—youth, old age, poor health, pregnancy; "But if you *can* fast, so much the better!"—and had shown an obsessive preoccupation with "gravy and meat juices," the abuses of which were subtle and many. The regulations had been "clarified" until they were in need of codification and took a good half-hour in the reading. Father Gau, with the Bishop's permission, let the wind out of them, and took up the slack with the magic words "If you have any questions, see your pastor."

Father Gau suggested other changes. "You know what, Your Excellency? People don't *know* you." This couldn't be helped, the Bishop felt, but he was interested, and after listening to Father Gau, and seeing that the greater good of the diocese was involved (something he hadn't always been sure about when listening to Monsignor Holstein), the Bishop did promise to be seen more in public. He attended a Bosses' Night banquet given by the local Jaycees, going as Father Gau's guest and giving a talk on "My Boyhood in and Around Fargo," which turned out very well. He kicked off the Red Cross campaign, which hadn't had direct support from the diocese before, and won the approval of non-Catholics, who, economically and ecumenically, were not to be sneezed at, as Father Gau pointed out. The Bishop was even seen at concerts at the two Catholic colleges, which, in recent years, he had visited only when necessary, for commencement exercises, and had departed from as early as he possibly could, as soon as he'd said all he had to say against the sin of intellectual pride. The Bishop really got around. On some nights, returning home, he fell asleep in the car and had to be roused, and it was all he could do to get into his pajamas. But he often retired with a sense of satisfaction he hadn't experienced since his New Deal days.

In his pastoral letters he became more and more humane, urging the faithful to drive carefully, to buy a poppy, to set their clocks ahead for daylight-saving time. Formerly it had been his custom to visit the orphanage once a year, at Christmastime, with six bushels of oranges. He hadn't gone oftener because it always made him feel bad—and mad. Now, at Father Gau's suggestion, he went every month, and found it easier. "They wait for you, Your Excellency," said Father Gau, and he was right.

There were other changes. For some years, the Bishop had had his eye on a certain large family, had noted the new arrivals in the birth column of the *Times*, and had inquired of the family's pastor whether there was any improvement otherwise. (The head of the family was an alcoholic, his wife a chain smoker.) There was no improvement until Father Gau, fighting fire with fire, found the father a job in the brewery. Miraculously, the man's drinking and the woman's smoking fell off to nothing. "There's your model family, Your Excellency," said Father Gau, and the family's pastor agreed. So the Bishop dropped in on the family one Sunday afternoon with a gallon of ice cream, and was photographed with the parents and their fourteen children for the diocesan paper.

And there were other changes. In June, Father Gau, who had been acting rector of the Cathedral, became rector in fact, and a domestic prelate.

"Gee," said Monsignor Gau after the colorful ceremony—at which the choir had performed under the direction of Mr McKee, whose reappointment had been one of the first official acts of the new rector. "Gee, Your Excellency."

"Just call me 'Bishop.' "

The next day, a scorcher, it was business as usual for the Bishop and Monsignor Gau at the Chancery. In the afternoon they drove out to the cemetery, where the big cross was to be relocated so that it would be visible from the new highway across the river—the Bishop had noticed many out-of-state cars in town during the past week. He had hoped to escape the heat by coming out to the cemetery, but the place just *looked* cool. He walked along the edge of the low bluff, below which ran the river, until he found a spot he liked, and Monsignor Gau marked it with a brick. Then the Bishop gazed around the cemetery with an eye to the future. "I give it ten years."

"If that," said Monsignor Gau.

The Bishop shot a glance at the adjoining property, a small wilderness belonging to the Ostergothenburg Gun Club.

"It's a thought," said Monsignor Gau.

But that evening at the Webb, which was comfortably cool, Monsignor Gau said he doubted if any land at all could be had from the Gun Club, and also if purchasers of cemetery lots would care to be any closer to the activities of the Gun Club. As for buying the Gun Club lock, stock, and barrel (to answer the Bishop's question), even if that could be done, it would be a very unpopular solution. The center of population had shifted north since the war, people following wealth and the river as closely as they could, and now, all along the river, right up to the cemetery and continuing on the other side of the Gun Club, there were these large estate-type houses, while back from the river the prairie was filling up with smaller but still very nice houses. "The Gun Club's holding the line against us, as some people see it, and they'd take us to court if we could get the Gun Club to sell—*if*."

"I had a chance to buy that property long before it was the Gun Club's, and I wish I had," said the Bishop.

"Things go on there at night," said Monsignor Gau.

"What kind of things?"

Monsignor Gau didn't seem to know how to put it. "Shenanigans," he said.

The Bishop just looked at him.

"Cars drive in and park," Monsignor Gau explained. "In fact, there have even been trespassers in the cemetery."

The Bishop sighed. He had heard that such things happened, but not in Ostergothenburg. A high wall? A night watchman? He thought of the cost to the diocese, and sighed again.

"Bishop, don't say yes or no to this right away," said Monsignor Gau. Proceeding slowly, with great caution—as well he might, if the Bishop understood him—Monsignor Gau offered a solution to the problem. For the sake of the town and the diocese, for the sake of the living and the dead, said Monsignor Gau, the Bishop should *move* the cemetery.

"No, no."

"Frankly, I don't see what else we can do, Bishop," said Monsignor Gau.

"Wait a few years," said the Bishop, finally.

"I just thought now, rather than in a few years or ten years from now, might be better, all things considered."

Monsignor Gau, it seemed, hadn't given any thought to the possibility that the Bishop might not be around in ten years. This was comforting, in a way, but it also forced the Bishop to recognize, as he hadn't before, clearly, that it had been his intention to leave the problem of the cemetery to his successor, and, seeing this as a defect in himself, he took another look at Monsignor Gau's solution. No, all the Bishop liked about it was being able to thwart the desires of trespassers. That was all. That, however, appealed to him strongly. "Where?"

"I was thinking of the old airport—high, level ground, good visibility from the road. Hilly, secluded cemeteries were all right in the past."

The Bishop just looked at Monsignor Gau.

"Think of the mower, Bishop."

When the Bishop noticed where they were in the conversation, he didn't want to be there. "The cemetery's consecrated ground," he said.

"Yes," said Monsignor Gau—and did not (which was wise) point out to the Bishop that consecrated ground could be deconsecrated and put to other use in case of necessity. Instead, he spoke of the capacity crowds on Sundays in all four churches in Ostergothenburg, and of the parking problem he had at the Cathedral, which he could do nothing about because of his downtown location. "Oh, I'm not at all *enthusiastic* about moving the cemetery." (The Bishop hadn't realized that they were coming back to that, and sighed.) "Still, if it has to be done, it has to be done."

The Bishop agreed with that statement, in principle, but gave no indication that he did.

"Bishop, don't say yes or no to this right away," said Monsignor Gau, and, having offered his solution to the problem of the cemetery, now offered his solution to his solution: on the consecrated ground, once the mortal remains of the dead had been removed to another location, the Bishop should raise a great church and make *it* his cathedral.

The Bishop said nothing.

"Don't say yes or no right away, Bishop."

No more was said on the subject that evening.

The next morning, at the Chancery, Monsignor Gau entered the Bishop's office saying, "Oh, Bishop, about relocating the cross in the cemetery . . ."

"Better hold off on that. Yes," the Bishop said.

That very day, the Bishop called on Mumm, of Mumm and Muldoon, lawyers for the diocese, and went into the legal aspects of moving the cemetery. It wasn't an easy interview, for Mumm, a man as old as the Bishop, kept coming back to all the paperwork there'd be, as if that were reason enough to abandon the idea. But since the diocese owned the cemetery land, and the graves were only held under lease, subject to removal in case of necessity, there was nothing to stop the Bishop from doing what he had in mind. "Legally," said the old lawyer sadly.

At the Webb that evening, Monsignor Gau, who was working with Muldoon of Mumm and Muldoon, said that Muldoon, whose hobby was real estate, had learned that the old airport could be purchased for only a bit more than the going price for farmland in the area. "Dirt cheap, Bishop. But renting those big earth-moving machines is something else again. We'll need 'em at the old cemetery."

"There'll be a lot of paperwork," the Bishop said, preferring to think of that part of the operation. "And, of course, I'll have to get in touch with Rome."

This he did the next day—entirely on his own, because of a slight difference of opinion with Monsignor Gau over the means to be employed. The Bishop had been going to write to the Apostolic Delegate in Washington, but learned (from Monsignor Gau) that the Apostolic Delegate was in Rome. "Better cable," said Monsignor Gau.

"No, it might give the wrong impression," said the Bishop, who had never, so far as he knew, given Rome that impression.

"To save time," said Monsignor Gau.

"No," said the Bishop, and did not cable.

In his letter, however, he did request that a reply, if favorable, be cabled to him, in view of all that had to be done and the earliness and severity of winter in Minnesota.

After ten days, the reply came. The Bishop let Monsignor Gau read it.

"We're in business, Bishop," said Monsignor Gau. "You *asked* them to cable?"

"To save time," said the Bishop, and their relationship, which had gone off a few degrees, was back to normal.

Things moved quickly then. Letters to the nearest living relatives of those buried in the cemetery and to those, like Mumm, who had contracted for space were drawn up by Muldoon and Monsignor Gau, approved by the Bishop, and dispatched by registered mail. After two weeks, the paperwork was well in hand. During the first week, Muldoon and Monsignor Gau purchased the old airport for the diocese, and the following week it was measured for fencing—galvanized chain link eleven feet high and, as a further discouragement to trespassers, an eighteen-inch overhang of barbed wire. "That should make it as hard to get in as to get out," said the Bishop.

Next, Monsignor Gau and Muldoon, who had been seeing a

lot of "the boys at the Gun Club," came to the Bishop and proposed an agreement under which the diocese, soon to have
more room than it would need for a new cathedral and perhaps
a school later, and the Gun Club, soon to transfer its activities
to a location farther up the river, would, for the sake of getting
the best price, sell off two contiguous parcels of land as though
they were one, as indeed they would appear to be when cleared
and leveled, this tract to be restricted to high-class residences
only and to be known as Cathedral Heights, with thorough-
fares to be known as Cathedral Parkway, Dullinger Road, and
Gun Club Memorial Lane. This agreement—over his protests
against having a street named after him—was approved by the
Bishop. So it went through June, July, and August.

And then, with September and cooler weather, came the
hard part for the Bishop, although people who stopped him in
the street would never have guessed it. Under his steady gaze,
the question that was uppermost in their minds changed from
"How could he?" to "How would he?" The Bishop didn't say
that he had responsibilities that the ordinary person was neither able to face up to nor equipped to carry out, but he let this
be seen. "What has to be done has to be done," he said, "and
will be done with all due regard and reverence." And so it was
done, in September.

Trucks and earth-movers rolled into the old cemetery, and
devout young men from the seminary did the close work by
hand. The Bishop was present during most of the first morning
to make sure that all went well. Thereafter, he dropped by for a
few minutes whenever he could. The Bishop also visited the
old airport, now consecrated ground, where clergy in surplices,
as well as undertakers and seminarians, were on duty from
morning till night. Everything had been thought of (Monsignor
Gau, with his clipboard, was everywhere), and the operation
proceeded on schedule. After twenty-two days, it was all over,
and there was a long editorial in the *Times*.

The Bishop was praised for what he'd done for his town and his diocese, and would do. It didn't stop there. On the street and at the Webb, the Bishop began to see people who had been avoiding him, among them old Mumm, who said, simply, "I got to hand it to you."

And the clergy, too. Men who had stayed away from the Chancery all summer came in again, and some of them, perhaps mindful of the assessments to be levied for the new cathedral, talked up the next parish as they never had before and belittled their own. Some of the Bishop's callers found him not in but at the site of the new cathedral. As long as he had them there, he thought it well to put them in the picture. Pointing to one of the big yellow machines, he'd say, "That one's costing us over two hundred dollars a day. I don't know where it's all coming from, do you, Father?"

On the good days in October and November, the Bishop spent many happy hours at "the job," as it was called. Had bishops in the Middle Ages been so occupied, they might have saved a few years on cathedrals centuries in the building, he thought, for it seemed to him that the men accomplished more when he was around. Some of them he knew from other jobs, and called by name, and others he got to know. One day, he took aside a young workman who was to be married the following morning and spoke to him on the purpose of sex in God's plan, and was so pleased by the response that he gave the young man the rest of the day off and also a cigar, which, since it was a good one, he advised him to save for his honeymoon. Others he spoke to on the purpose of work—a curse, yes, but also a means of sanctification—and cited the splendid example of St Joseph, a carpenter, the patron of workmen, or workingmen. (The Bishop preferred those words to "worker.") To give additional substance to his remarks, the Bishop spoke of the manual labor he had performed in the years when, home from the seminary for the summer, he'd driven an ice wagon and worked on a threshing crew, and also, though briefly, as a section hand on the Great Northern. "Between Barnesville and Moorhead—until I was overcome by the heat."

By December, the foundation had been poured, the structural steel was in place, and the walls were rising—so slowly, though, that it didn't pay the Bishop to visit the job daily. The men he knew were gone. A few masons drew $4.05 an hour. The Bishop was reluctant to interrupt them. Inside, the air smelled and tasted of oil. Outside, the ground was frozen. By the end of December, the architects—Frank and Frank, of Minneapolis—and the contractors—Beck Brothers, of Ostergothenburg—were feuding.

The Beck brothers (there were four of them) said that Frank and Frank, also brothers, were making too many changes in the plans. If Beck Brothers had known this was going to happen, they wouldn't have bid on the job, they said. They hadn't really wanted it. The plans called for a church such as Beck Brothers had never built before, or seen. "Too goddam modern," they said.

None of this reached the Bishop directly, and almost all of it he discounted, having dealt with contractors for many years, but one evening at the Webb, early in February, he mentioned the part that did bother him.

"Frank and Frank are modern, all right, but they're not *too* modern," Monsignor Gau explained. "Contemporary" was the word for them. They believed in beautiful but simple structures, less expensive, but more impressive structures, and churches were their specialty. They'd done churches in such places as Milwaukee, Dallas, and Fargo, not to mention St Paul and Minneapolis. "They're tops—and so, locally, are Beck Brothers," said Monsignor Gau.

"Yes, I know," said the Bishop.

"I can tell you what the trouble is, but you can't do anything about it."

"No?"

"Frank and Frank are from Minneapolis, if you know what I mean."

The Bishop did. More than once, he'd heard the contractors refer to the architects as dudes.

The feuding continued into April. In April, the Bishop was planning to fly to Rome.

By then, the cathedral was beginning to look like something—a chasuble, said the architects; a coffin, said the contractors. It looked like neither, the Bishop thought, and it never would unless you viewed it from above, from an airplane. The Bishop thought that the little model of the cathedral in the contractors' shack could be blamed for much of the trouble—it *did* look like a chasuble or a coffin—and so, on his last visit to the job, before leaving for Rome, he carried it off and locked it in the trunk of the car.

That evening, in the main dining room of the Webb, which he wouldn't see again for perhaps a month, the Bishop got a pleasant surprise, for there, not too close to the organ, having a drink, and soon to break bread together, it seemed, were the two architects and the four contractors. Monsignor Gau was also there, but the Bishop had expected him.

"Well, well," said the Bishop, joining the party. He sat at one end of the table, Monsignor Gau at the other. On the Bishop's right sat an architect, on his left a contractor, and on Monsignor Gau's right and left there was one of each. The seating arrangements had been worked out by Monsignor Gau, the Bishop felt, but how had Frank and Frank and Beck Brothers been brought together?

Presently, this question was answered for the Bishop—and for the Beck brothers, too, to judge by their faces. An architectural journal of excellent repute and wide circulation was planning an article on the new cathedral. If it followed the usual pattern of such articles, said one of the Franks, there would be photographs of the new cathedral and of those intimately associated with the job. "All of us here."

"Why me?" said Monsignor Gau, with a surprised look that didn't fool the Bishop, for obviously Monsignor Gau had heard the good news earlier, had talked it over with Frank and Frank, and on the strength of it had arranged the evening.

"You're rector of the Cathedral—that's why," said the Bishop. "But why me?"

"It's your church," said Monsignor Gau. This was true. In fact, without the Bishop it wouldn't be a cathedral.

The evening now went better. The Beck brothers, who were rather shy men away from their work, opened up as they hadn't before. Frank and Frank said that the food at the Webb surpassed anything Minneapolis could offer and, a little later on, that they wished there were contractors like Beck Brothers in Minneapolis. At that point, the Bishop called for a round of Danish beer, a new thing at the Webb, and they drank a toast to the job.

The Bishop, trying to hold the attention of those at his end of the table, said that they might be interested to know that he had at one time given some thought to building the cathedral out of fieldstone. Yes, plain, ordinary, everyday stones, just as they came from the hand of God and were collected by farmers from their fields. The true and special character of the diocese and its people might be expressed in a cathedral of fieldstones. Monsignor Gau, however, had more or less discouraged the idea, saying that he doubted if fieldstones would look good in a structure of such size, or if fieldstones would hold together as well as, say, bricks. The Bishop had had nothing against bricks, but for a cathedral he preferred stone—good, honest stone. Yes, he was happy with the gray stone that had been chosen. He had wanted a rough finish, yes, until he had learned that this would be too hard to clean, and now he was happy with the smooth. For some reason, perhaps because of his romantic ideas about cathedral-building, he was sorry that the walls wouldn't be solid stone—that the stone slabs, which were being anchored to the steel structure, were only two inches thick. Yes, he'd have reason to be sorry if the walls of the cathedral *were* solid stone—no air space, no insulation. He knew how buildings were constructed now, and wouldn't have it any other way. He wasn't complaining. Yes, he knew that they were doing things with stone that had never been done before, using it as if it were plywood, saving time, labor, and stone, and he was happy. He wasn't complaining. Why should he? He was getting everything he'd ever wanted in a cathedral. It would be ideal for processions—wide aisles, assembly space, space to maneuver in. He was getting landscaped parking lots. He *wasn't* getting as high a structure as he'd wanted at first, but, as Monsignor Gau had pointed out to him, the site would do a lot for the cathedral. From across the river, from the new highway, it wouldn't look anything like Mont-Saint-Michel—another idea the Bishop had had in the very beginning and recognized as crazy even then. In short, he was getting a fine contemporary building with a distinct Romanesque flavor. He was getting real arches. "Oh, I've entirely given up the idea of fieldstones. I wouldn't want 'em now if I could have 'em. But from what I know now, I think it might have been possible."

"Anything's possible, if you're talking about the facing," said the architect on the Bishop's right. "What counts in a building, be it skyscraper or cathedral, is the steel. That's *all* that holds it together."

"Oh, it's *safe*," said the contractor on the Bishop's left. He must have seen that the Bishop could use a little reassurance on that point. "It'll be good for fifty, seventy-five—maybe a hundred—years."

The architect nodded.

Driving up to the job on his return from Rome (where, except for the Holy Father, nobody had seemed very glad to see him), the Bishop was pleased to note how much had been accomplished in his absence. But then, getting out of the car, coming closer and looking up at the arches, none of which had been completed when he last saw the cathedral, he couldn't believe his eyes. Going inside, he found, of course, that what was true of one arch was true of all—those over the windows, those along the aisles, the one over the baptistery, and, worst of all, the one over the sanctuary. In the middle of every arch there were *two* stones—*where the keystone should have been there was just a crack.*

Had any of the responsible parties been with him then— Monsignor Gau, Frank *or* Frank, or any of the Becks—the Bishop wouldn't have been able to conceal his dismay. He decided to say nothing. In the evening, he consulted the complete set of plans in Monsignor Gau's office—and wished that he hadn't relied so much on just the floor plans, for the plans he was looking at did show how the stone would be set. But they didn't say why.

The next day, at the job, the Bishop approached a workman and said in an offhand manner, "No keystones in the arches."

The workman said that keystones weren't necessary in *these* arches—that steel was all that counted in a building nowadays. From another workman whom he questioned in the same manner the Bishop received much the same reply, and again did not pursue the matter. The following day, an intelligent-looking truck driver, the father of seven, told the Bishop that keystones in the arches would have clashed with the architects' overall plan. The Bishop nodded, hoping to hear more, but did not. The next day, the Bishop spoke to one of the Becks about cathedral-building in the Middle Ages, saying in an offhand manner, "I suppose keystones in those arches would've clashed with the architects' overall plan," and was told that you didn't

see keystones much anymore. Then for two days the Bishop
was out of town, but on his return he tried one of the architects, saying, "You don't see keystones much anymore." You
did, he was told. You still saw them, and more often than not,
if not always, they were ornamental. Out of honesty to their
materials and, in the case of the new cathedral, out of a desire
to give a light and airy feeling to what was, after all, a very
heavy structure, Frank and Frank had rejected keystones. It
hadn't been easy to give what was, after all, a very heavy, *hori-
zontal* structure, and a rather low one at that, a *vertical* feeling. That was what the cracks did, and what keystones, apart
from being obsolete, would not have done.

That was early in May—a very wet month, as it turned out.
At the job, there were signs of erosion and subsidence, and the
ground was quickly sodded. Fortunately, the hairline cracks
that appeared here and there in the fabric of the structure, and
that had to be expected, did not widen.

At the Chancery, there were also signs of erosion and subsidence in the Bishop's relations with Monsignor Gau, but here
the hairline cracks (which, perhaps, had been present before)
did widen. The work of the diocese went on, of course, but
there was much less dining out than there had been. The
Bishop didn't enjoy being with Father Rapp, and Muldoon
and the others, who seemed to appear regularly at the Webb
at Monsignor Gau's invitation, and who, though they gave
the Bishop all the attention he could stand, still had a way of
excluding him from the conversation. On confirmation trips,
more often than not, the Bishop was driven by a curate—the
Bishop had given Monsignor Gau a third one for Christmas.
Much as Monsignor Gau enjoyed being with the Bishop, driving him and attending him, he could seldom manage it that
spring. "Chancellor" was no longer a synonym for "chauffeur"
in the Ostergothenburg diocese. Monsignor Gau was chancellor in the proper sense of the word, as well as rector of the

Cathedral, building inspector for the diocese at the job, and troubleshooter there and everywhere—no man in the diocese below the rank of bishop had ever been so honored, trusted, and burdened with responsibility. Monsignor Gau also ran the newly created Diocesan Procurement Office.

The D.P.O. stocked, or took orders for, practically everything a Catholic institution required—school and office supplies, sporting goods, playground equipment, sacramental wines. It was saving money for the priests, nuns, and people of the diocese, but it also made demands on Monsignor Gau's time and energy. He had to spend long hours with his catalogues and clipboard in the basement of the high school, and he had to go out of town on buying trips. There had been one or two too many of these, it seemed to the Bishop, who hadn't anticipated any when he authorized the D.P.O., which, though, was unquestionably a success.

However, when the Bishop had approved the sale of sweatshirts bearing his coat of arms to seminarians and clergy, he hadn't anticipated seeing one of these articles, as he did in the middle of June, in front of Hokey's department store, on the person of a well-developed young lady. Immediately, he stepped into the lobby of the Webb, phoned Monsignor Gau, and asked that the stock of sweatshirts be checked. "No more, when those are gone," he said, after he'd got the count.

"Gee," said Monsignor Gau, but he sought no explanation, and the Bishop offered none.

By June, that was how it was with them. During the previous winter, at Monsignor Gau's suggestion, the Bishop had become a columnist in the diocesan paper, dealing with events at home and abroad, and more than holding his own, according to Monsignor Gau, Father Rapp, and others. In June, he gave up his column. "No more," he said, again in a way that didn't invite questions. That wasn't all. For over a year, at Monsignor Gau's suggestion, letters of congratulation had been going out

to Catholics in the diocese who had done something worthy
of the Bishop's attention—an honor defined with great latitude
by Monsignor Gau—and then, in June, the Bishop ended the
practice. "No more," he said.

The Bishop was sorry that he couldn't think of better ways
to assert himself in his relations with Monsignor Gau, and was
quite prepared for the consequences. Total obscurity held no
fears for him at the moment—not that that would ever be
his fate. He just didn't want it thought that he wasn't running
the diocese. Or was it already too late—again—for any but the
strongest proof? If it was, did he wish to give such proof—
again? Monsignor Gau was a very popular man with the people, as well as a very successful one. Monsignor Holstein hadn't
been either. And the Bishop was older now.

The Bishop had never felt so out of it as he did late in July, at
the dedication of the new cathedral. For many months, Monsignor Gau had been busy with the arrangements—not only
bishops from nearby sees were asked to attend but also several
archbishops, whose acquaintance, it seemed, Monsignor Gau
had made, or almost made, on his buying trips. Two archbishops actually showed up for the dedication, as did an unimportant and indigent Italian cardinal, an added starter, who had
more or less invited himself. This, apart from the expense of
flying the man in, round trip and first class, from Syracuse
(N.Y.), where he had relatives, was unfortunate. He talked a lot
of nonsense about rice, having been informed somewhere that
this was a major crop in Minnesota, as it was in his part of
Italy, and nobody had the nerve to tell him that the only rice in
Minnesota grew wild and was harvested by a few Indians.

At the dedication itself, this Prince of the Church played
with his handkerchief and closed his eyes during the sermon
—which might have been shorter, in view of the oppressive
heat, and would have been if the Bishop's train of thought

hadn't eluded him twice. Both times, he covered up nicely by reviewing what he'd been saying earlier, once shot ahead on the intended line and once on another just as good. Trying to appeal to everybody present—clergy, nuns, and laity, Catholics and non-Catholics, and even children—he spoke of the splendid progress made by the Church and the country in his own lifetime, reckoning it in terms of Popes and Presidents, a number of whom he'd met or seen and come away from with varying impressions, which he did his best to describe, ranging back and forth between Popes and Presidents, pinpointing the great events and legislation associated with each and, whenever possible, bringing in the diocese. Such an effort would have taxed a much younger man on a cool day. As it was, with the temperature in the nineties, the humidity high, and the robes of his office heavy on him, the Bishop left the pulpit in a weakened condition.

The tour planned for the visiting prelates—first, the seminary and then lunch under the trees unless it rained, then the new cemetery, then the high school, and then back to the cathedral for lemonade and a look at the residential quarters— went on without the Bishop. Monsignor Gau led the tour. The Bishop spent the afternoon in seclusion, trying to recover. Monsignor Gau phoned. "No, it's just the heat," said the Bishop, and wouldn't have a doctor or an air-conditioner. In the evening, it was Monsignor Gau who presided over the banquet at the Webb.

The Bishop stayed home with the housekeeper's cat. He found it too warm for the cat and the paper, but not before he read that His Eminence (as the *Times* called the wandering cardinal in one place) had landed in "the country of Columbus" with the hope of seeing Niagara Falls and what he could of the frontier, and that he was delighted with Ostergothenburg, which was not unlike Brisbane, with the new cathedral, which was not unlike St Peter's, with the local clergy and laity, whose good sense and piety were not unlike what he'd been led to expect, and with the Orpheum for exhibiting an Italian film during his visit.

In a black mood, the Bishop wondered whether he shouldn't do away with the D.P.O. Later on, when it must have been about time for cigars at the banquet, and for Monsignor Gau to rise and say once again that though he greatly enjoyed city life, he was a country boy and would be proud and happy to be a rural pastor again, the Bishop wondered whether that shouldn't be arranged. At another point in the evening, thinking he might read awhile, the Bishop went into his office for a book but then forgot why he was there, and stood for some time before a chart on the wall. The chart, which was in the form of a cross, had been made by an artistic nun at Monsignor Holstein's instigation, and showed the spiritual plan of the diocese: bishop at the top of the tree, vicar-general below him, then chancellor, and then to the right, on the right branch, clergy in general, and to the left, on the left branch, nuns, or religious, as they were designated on the chart, and, finally, down the middle, on the trunk of the tree, the laity. The Bishop hadn't really looked at the cross for years, and now saw it as he never had before. What struck him was the favored position of one officer of the diocese. He hadn't noticed it before, or it hadn't meant anything to him before, but the chancellor occupied the very heart of the cross. It seemed to the Bishop that the chart, in that respect, gave a distorted view of the spiritual plan of the diocese. He thought of taking it down. But he didn't. He went back to his bedroom and got into his pajamas.

It rained sometime in the night, and cooled off, and the next day the Bishop was almost himself again.

One night about a month later, in a black mood—it had come to his attention during the day that the senior members of the model family had gone back to their old ways—he was standing before the chart again, and again it seemed to him that it gave a distorted view of the spiritual plan of the diocese. He tried one of the thumbtacks, then another. When he had the chart down, he carried it around for a while, not knowing what to do with it. He didn't care to throw it away. He thought of burning it—respectfully burning it, as one would an old, outdated, or perhaps defective flag. In the end, he rolled it up gently, carried it out to the garage, and put it in the trunk of the car with the little model of the new cathedral.

The next morning, he noticed that the cross was still there, in outline, on the wall, and that same morning he received word that he was getting an auxiliary—something he certainly hadn't asked for and didn't want—and that the man chosen for the job was Monsignor, or Bishop-elect, Gau.

ONE OF THEM

SIMPSON, A CONVERT, had been well treated in the seminary, given a corner bed in the dormitory, then a corner room with two windows, deferred to in class and out, and invariably he (and two Koreans) had been among those chosen to meet visiting speakers. In fact, Simpson may have been too well treated in the seminary, in view of what was to follow, namely, going out into the world, into parishwork.

The parish, Trinity, was in a still good area of apartment houses and residential hotels. The church (no school) was built of crumbly gray stone in the form of a cross but a cross carrying a load on one shoulder—this was the rectory attached. The pastor was said to be something of a hermit, a man of few words.

Simpson took this into consideration the afternoon he reported for duty, and when the door of the rectory at last opened to his knocking, and the pastor, whom he hadn't met before but had seen in processions, a spare, gray Irish type, just looked at him, Simpson did his best to display an uncritical nature and a genuine concern by smiling and frowning at the same time.

"Doorbell out of order, Father?"

The pastor nodded, just perceptibly.

Simpson nodded back—a curate was supposed to model himself on his pastor—and seeing no need to introduce himself, his suitcases having already done that better than he could, without words, he entered the dim hallway. There he placed his suitcases longwise against the wall so nobody would fall over them, using his head (the pastor would be glad to see), and then he faced the office.

But the pastor was making for the stairs.

Simpson swooped down on his suitcases, thinking, Yes, of course, he was to be shown his quarters first, after which they'd come down to the office for a little talk, or maybe the pastor would brief him while showing him around—Simpson saw them up in the choir loft, down in the boiler room.

The pastor opened a door in the upstairs hallway, stepped back, and *spoke.* "Room."

Simpson nodded, entered, and placed his suitcases longwise against the wall, again making a good job of it. "Nice room," he said, and noticed that he was alone. Hearing a little noise in the distance like a door closing, he foolishly went and looked out into the empty hallway. He left his door open in case the pastor was coming back.

This seemed less and less likely as the afternoon wore on, and after unpacking, and reading his office, Simpson closed his door and tried his bed. He was there when he heard a knock, just one. Nobody at his door, but footsteps on the stairs, going down. He put on his collar and coat, found the bathroom, and hurried downstairs where he soon found the dining room.

The pastor, seated at the table, greeted him with a nod and introduced him ("Father uh Simpson") to the elderly housekeeper, a small wiry individual ("Uh Miss Burke").

"*Miz,*" she said.

The pastor bowed his head in silent grace, as Simpson

did then, and while they ate—hashed brown potatoes, scorched green beans, ground meat of some kind—Ms Burke set the table with things that should have been on it earlier (such as a napkin for Simpson), then appeared at intervals with a loaf of sandwich bread under her arm, put out some (the pastor ate a lot of bread), and disappeared into the kitchen, talking to herself.

"Still sore," said the pastor, silent until then. "Sat where you're sitting. Beeman."

"Father Beeman?" Father Beeman was Simpson's predecessor in the curate's job, an older man, an ex-pastor with, it was said, personality problems.

"Know him, do you?"

"No, but I know what he looks like. I've seen him in processions. Big man."

The pastor nodded. "Threw stuff. Threw his food on the floor."

Simpson nodded.

The pastor shook his head. "At Holy Sepulchre parish now."

"One of my classmates—Potter—*he's* at Holy Sepulchre."

There was no response from the pastor, and no more conversation.

Ms Burke came in with dessert—sliced canned peaches and cardboard Fig Newtons—and began to remove things from the table.

Simpson thanked her with a nod, almost a bow, when the meal was over, caught up with the pastor in the hallway, and got into step. "Ms Burke's been with you for some time, Father?"

The pastor nodded, just perceptibly. "Take the eight o'clock Mass, Father. Weekdays."

"Eight o'clock." Simpson repeated it to minimize the chance of error. "Weekdays."

"See about Sundays later."

"Right." It was Simpson's impression that briefing had begun and would continue in the office, which they were approaching, but the pastor kept going, and at the head of the stairs it was Simpson's impression that the man was about to leave him.

"G'night."

"*Father*"—it came out sounding desperate—"I've been wondering about things."

The pastor, on the point of entering the room at the head of the stairs, looked embarrassed. "Uh. Convert, aren't you?"

"No, no. I mean—yes." Simpson had answered the question in order to get back to the assumption underlying it—it was understandable—that he, as a convert, might be shaky in his faith. "No, no, Father, I was just wondering about things—you know, like what time I say Mass." And, quickly, lest that be misunderstood: "Eight o'clock. Weekdays."

"See about Sundays later."

Simpson sort of nodded. "The rest can wait, Father?"

The pastor nodded, just perceptibly, opened the door but not much, and in a crabwise manner that aroused and thwarted Simpson's curiosity, entered the room at the head of the stairs.

The next morning Simpson said the eight o'clock Mass and had breakfast (learned from Ms Burke that he got Wednesday afternoons off), went upstairs and brushed his teeth, but after that he didn't know what to do. Ms Burke had made his bed. On the chance that he'd find his orders for the day in the office, he went downstairs and checked it. No, nothing for him. Acting then on information from Ms Burke, and again using the door he'd discovered, the door between the rectory and the church, he entered the sacristy, and was there when the pastor came in to vest for Mass, there with the idea of bringing himself to the man's attention, and also of being useful, but was told when he attempted to help with the alb, "Not necessary, Father." So he returned to the rectory and, because the pastor could have dropped something off there on his way to

Mass, rechecked the office. No, nothing. He then went up to his room and sat down with his breviary, leaving his door open, though, because he was (he thought) on duty. But nobody called at the rectory, or at least nobody knocked, during this period. When he heard footsteps—another reason for leaving his door open—he got up and left his room, again with the idea of bringing himself to the man's attention. He met the pastor at the head of the stairs, was nodded at in passing, nodded back, and went down and checked the office. Nothing.

He wanted to retire to his room and settle down with a good book, but thought it wouldn't look or, perhaps, be right if he did. So he kept coming and going between his room, the office, and the church (with which he was familiarizing himself), and took a side trip down to the boiler room. In this fashion, moving about, looking for the action, he got through the morning.

In the afternoon—lunch, conversationally, wasn't up to dinner the evening before—there were a number of developments:

1. Simpson dealt with several parishioners in the office, with all satisfactorily, he thought, though not to the satisfaction of one, who unfortunately couldn't be helped (marriage case).
2. The pastor emerged from the room at the head of the stairs and left the rectory carrying a brown canvas suitcase such as students once used to mail laundry home.
3. Simpson visited the kitchen for the first time and learned from Ms Burke, who was having coffee with a middle-aged man to whom Simpson wasn't introduced, that laundry was not sent out, was done right there, and that the pastor used the brown canvas suitcase "to carry his goddam envelopes"—"Oh," said Simpson, and swiftly departed, under the impression that Ms Burke had been referring to collection envelopes, actually the contents thereof, and that the pastor had gone to the bank.

4. The pastor returned to the rectory with the brown canvas suitcase (but it was apparently no lighter) and entered the room at the head of the stairs.

5. Simpson discovered that the man he came upon (praying?) in the choir loft was the same man he'd seen earlier in the kitchen, and that this man was the janitor—who said he hadn't introduced himself in the kitchen because he and Father Beeman, a real man whose guts Ms Burke, a holy terrier, hated, had been very close. "I didn't want her to get any ideas about *us*, Father."

Those were the developments that afternoon, some good, some not so good, and one puzzling to Simpson but probably none of his business (the brown canvas suitcase).

That evening, when Simpson came to the table, there was a bad development, a pamphlet—*The Marks of the True Faith*—by his plate.

"Uh. Might interest you."

"Yes, well, *yes*. Thanks."

The silence that set in then—to which Simpson contributed handsomely, rather than try to explain his words of the evening before, his "*Father*, I've been wondering about things," to which words he attributed the pamphlet—lasted until they rose from the table.

"Uh."

"Oh."

Simpson had almost gone off without the pamphlet!

At the head of the stairs, the pastor, silent since alluding to the pamphlet, said, "G'night."

"Father, I've been wondering"—he'd stepped out for tobacco that afternoon, and rather than knock had entered the rectory through the church—"shouldn't I have a key to the front door?"

"Uh. See about it," said the pastor, and entered the room at the head of the stairs in a crabwise manner, the door closing after him.

Simpson waited a few moments there, just in case the door opened and a hand came out with a key, which didn't happen, and so, treading softly, he went down the hallway to his room, his thoughts turning from the key to the pamphlet, which, after brushing his teeth and filling his pipe, he read at one sitting and found excellent.

After a few days, with the pastor keeping to the room at the head of the stairs, Simpson accepted the odd fact that he was on his own at Trinity, stopped looking for the action, and sometimes settled down with a good book—was reading *Enthusiasm: A Chapter in the History of Religion: With Special Reference to the XVII and XVIII Centuries*, by Monsignor Knox (a convert), and shook his head at the hysteria in the Church then, as he did at the hysteria in the Church now, thinking, *Plus ça change* the more it's the same, as he did after trying another position in the hard swivel chair.

The office, where he now had a few of his books and his rubber-tire ashtray, and where he now hung his biretta and stole, he was gradually making his own.

The pastor had looked in once to say, "Smoke a pipe, do you?" and twice to say, "Need that light on, do you?" And one afternoon, when Simpson was doing his best to describe the quality of life after death to a curious parishioner, the pastor came all the way in (for a paper clip) and left the door open on his departure—a mistake, Simpson realized then, for him to be alone with a member of the opposite sex (whatever her age) with the door closed, and he didn't let it happen again.

Simpson learned from his mistakes.

Instead of going up to the door of the room at the head of the stairs to announce the arrival of a salesman—had received no response at all the second time he did that—he now dealt with such callers himself in a courteous, businesslike manner, and never bought anything.

He was the same with parishioners if the matter was one on which the Church's position was still clear and negative—some people seemed to think there were now two or more schools of thought about everything. Unlike some newly ordained men, and here perhaps he showed the pastor's influence, he didn't try to say too much. He just tried to do all he could for people, but not *more* than he could (which a visiting speaker at the seminary had called the great temptation to the priest today), and in pursuing that limited objective he had his first (and, he hoped, last) confrontation with the pastor, the man suddenly on the stairs, whispering down:

"*What's this? What's this?*"

"Bell."

"*Bell?*"

"Bell. Man fixing it."

"*What?*"

"Bell."

"*Man fixing it?*"

"Is, yes."

"*Called man?*"

"Did, yes."

"*Get estimate?*"

"Sort of."

"*How much?*"

"Not much."

"*How much, Father?*"

"Not much, Father."

There, the pastor retiring to the room at the head of the stairs, the matter had ended, with Simpson, who, after all, had called man, paying him (not much) and keeping the receipt in case he was ever asked for it.

Relations between Simpson and the pastor were the same

as before the confrontation, and this was to the pastor's credit, but as before there was room for improvement—a sort of gap, like the Grand Canyon, that had so far defeated all efforts to fill it. Simpson, on his first Sunday at Trinity, had praised the pastor's sermon, saying he hadn't heard the like since he didn't know when (hadn't wanted to say since coming into the Church), and the man had just nodded, just perceptibly—not a good sign, Simpson knew now. Taking a chance, Simpson had asked the pastor where he got his hair cut, and the man had said, "Anywhere." Taking another chance, Simpson had complimented the pastor on his white teeth, and the man had said, "Don't smoke."

But Simpson was still hoping to fill the gap, still looking around for common ground, and, not finding any, he created some by visiting the zoo (one of the pastor's few outside interests, according to John, the janitor) and came to the table that evening full of it.

"Father, I didn't know they let those big turtles run around loose."

"Tortoises, Father. Harmless."

"Tortoises. But people shouldn't write stuff on their shells."

"Do it here, in the pews."

That had been it for the zoo.

On his next afternoon off, Simpson visited the Museum of Natural History (one of the pastor's few outside interests, according to John) and came to the table that evening full of it.

"Father, how about that big moose by the front door!"

"Elk, Father. *Megaceros Hibernicus.*"

"Elk. Those crazy antlers! Wouldn't want to run into him!"

"Extinct."

That had been it for the Museum of Natural History.

Maybe, if Simpson had had some doubts or difficulties of a spiritual nature, and these had been brought to the pastor's attention, they would have filled the gap, but Simpson didn't have any such doubts or difficulties, and there was little or no audible response from the pastor—a noise like "Umm," or a nod—when Simpson tried to discuss the merits of the pamphlets he continued to find by his plate.

Oh, they were excellent pre-conciliar works, and maybe the pastor would have done as much for any young man fresh from the seminary in times like these ... but the fact that *Simpson* was receiving such attention, and the fact that *Simpson* was still without a key to the front door—these facts when taken together—did sort of suggest that *Simpson* wasn't trusted, and that troubled him.

Three times he'd raised the matter of a key, and three times he'd been told, "Uh. See about it."

One evening—well into his fourth week at Trinity—he raised the matter again, indirectly, but urgently:

"Father, what if, like tonight, I'm out with my classmates and I come in late—after nine, I mean—and the church is *locked*?"

" 'M up till 'leven or so. Just knock. Uh. Ring."

So Simpson, a few minutes before eleven that night, rang.

He was determined not to complain. He thought there was too much of that going on these days among the clergy, of all people. He would not, he thought, be happier in another parish, neither in the suburbs nor the slums, for he was not, though fresh from the seminary, one of those who expect to change the world by going out into it. For him the disadvantages in his situation were outweighed by the advantages. At Trinity he could feel that he was still in the church of his choice, with divine worship and the cure of souls still being conducted along traditional lines—no guitars, tom-toms, sensitivity sessions, speaking in tongues—and at Trinity he could also feel that he, though newly ordained and a convert, though keyless and considered a suitable case for pamphlets, was the man in charge.

Simpson had visitors one afternoon, Mother and Aunt Edith, and began by showing them the church, which, he could see, disappointed them.

"Yes, it's quite nice," said Mother.

"Why, yes," said Aunt Edith.

"Actually," said Simpson, "it's quite ugly. But it serves its divine purpose, and *that's* the main thing." He felt tough, had sounded the rude Roman note (GIVE ME SOULS!), and had hit a nerve or two, he knew.

"Well, if you say so, dear," said Mother.

"Hell, yes," said Aunt Edith.

Simpson moved toward the sacristy—had taken the visitors into the sanctuary for a close-up view of the main altar—but stopped, hearing a noise from the body of the church, the emptiness of which he'd been regretting for the sake of the visitors (non-Catholics), and saw the middle door of the spare confessional, the door to the priest's compartment, open, and John appear, then disappear into the vestibule.

"Just the janitor," said Simpson.

"Thank *God*," said Aunt Edith.

"Why," said Mother, "he was in there all the time. Did *you* know he was in there, dear?"

"Didn't, no."

"He goes in there to pray, dear?"

"No, he just *goes* in there—to sleep, I think. Maintenance could be better."

"But should he *do* that, dear? In *there*?"

"Oh, what the hell," said Aunt Edith.

"He really shouldn't, no, but we're not rigid in the Church," said Simpson. He took the visitors through the sacristy, his usual route into the rectory, and, since this was their wish, back to the kitchen, where they met Ms Burke, who could be heard talking to herself again after they left.

"Actually," said Simpson, "she's all right."

He took the visitors into the office ("my headquarters"), where they admired the secondhand *Catholic Encyclopedia* (Unrevised Version) he'd purchased with gift money from the family, and two hard-to-find works by Cardinal Newman (a convert). At Mother's request, he sat for a moment at the desk. "Now I'll know how you look, dear." Aunt Edith tried on his biretta. Then, thinking that later, when they were leaving, would be soon enough to knock at the door of the room at the head of the stairs, he took them to his room, where they inspected his closet, pulled out his dresser drawers, and had the pleasure of seeing and hearing him on the phone with a misinformed but docile parishioner. And then who should walk in (the door was open, though the pastor's open-door policy might not apply in this case) but Ms Burke with a loaded tray!

Overwhelmed by this womanly display, ashamed of himself for having underestimated Ms Burke, and thinking it would be a nice gesture anyway, Simpson invited her to sit down, and when Aunt Edith insisted, she did. So Simpson hurried off for another cup, hoping for the best.

When he returned, they didn't seem to notice—they were talking—and since he was the host, he poured, delivered the cream and sugar, the cardboard Fig Newtons, and was shocked to hear Aunt Edith say, sweetly, "*Homemade?*" but she got away with it.

"Pooh," said Ms Burke. "I just keep 'em in a plastic bag with a clothespin on it."

"And warm before serving?" said Mother.

"I did *these.*"

Simpson tried one of the Fig Newtons, and they *were* slightly better this way. "Umm," he said. Otherwise he contributed nothing to the conversation, just listened along, nodding or shaking his head—detergents did strange things. But after a bit he began to stiffen and was soon rigid. Hearing that "your boy" was easy to cook for, *not* like Father Beeman

("That big *Beer*man!"), who had thrown his food on the floor, rolled in at all hours, and pounded on walls, and that "your boy" kept his room very clean for a man, and certainly for a priest (Ms Burke here sniffing in the direction of the room at the head of the stairs), "your boy" regretted that praise for him should be so much at the expense of others. And was afraid that admonishment from him would aggravate what might otherwise pass off as tittle-tattle. To think, he thought, that the pastor had once said to him, speaking of Ms Burke, who was carrying on with herself in the kitchen at the time: "Uh. Very loyal."

Very loyal to tell the visitors—outsiders, non-Catholics—that the pastor was a pack rat, and wouldn't let her into the room at the head of the stairs to clean? That the pastor was a skinflint, and kept the Christmas ham in the trunk of his car, bringing it out for meals? That the pastor would do anything for a buck, and addressed envelopes for an insurance company in his spare time?

"Tried to get *me* to do it, but I *wouldn't*," said Ms Burke.

"Why *should* you?" said Aunt Edith. "You've got *enough* to do."

Simpson stood up, and moved toward the door.

Mother asked, "You didn't know about the envelopes, dear?"

"Didn't, no."

"*He* thought they were *laundry*!" said Ms Burke, and smilingly explained how Simpson had made that mistake. "That's how much *he* knew!"

Simpson—who had been suspicious of the brown canvas suitcase from the start and had since seen it too often in transit for it to be going to and from the bank—shut the door, and while this did not have the desired effect, there is some justice in the world and Aunt Edith, overstimulated, spilled her coffee.

Simpson smilingly scrubbed it into the carpet with his feet, making nothing of it, the good host.

Ms Burke, concerned about a few drops on Aunt Edith's dress, scurried off to her room for her spot remover.

The visitors went down the hallway to the bathroom for plain cold water.

When Ms Burke returned from her room, which was adjacent to Simpson's but accessible only by the stairway off the kitchen, she was panting and, not seeing the visitors, gasped: "Gone!"

"No, no," said Simpson.

They regrouped in his room, and after some talk of stains (what it came down to was, no stain should be allowed to *set*, which Simpson planned to use as an argument for frequent confession), the entire company—Ms Burke saying, "Pooh, I'll clean up in here later"—moved out, and went down the hallway three abreast, one behind, that one thinking, Some other time, as he passed the door of the room at the head of the stairs. But when he opened the front door to let the visitors out, there, about to use his key, was the pastor.

"Uh," he said.

"Uh," said Simpson, and made the introductions.

The visitors were happy to see the pastor, and so was Simpson—to see him there, to think he'd been out, probably at the hospital (one of his few outside interests), while Ms Burke was assassinating his character with the door open. The pastor was doing as well as could be expected, responding with little nods, and noises like "Umm," to the compliments on his church, rectory, housekeeper, until—suddenly, if you didn't know the man—he made for the stairs.

"Oh, *good-bye*!" cried Aunt Edith.

"Why, *yes*," said Mother.

The pastor, on the stairs, stopped and turned. " 'M takin' a trip next week."

This was news to Simpson.

"Oh, *where*?" said Aunt Edith.

"Winnipeg."

"Oh, *why*?" said Aunt Edith.

"Catholic Wildlife Conference."

"Oh," said Aunt Edith.

"While you're away," said Mother, "will . . . will *Father*, here, be in charge?"

The pastor, before turning and continuing up the stairs, nodded, just perceptibly.

Simpson was glad to see his authority confirmed, but wished the signal had been a little stronger, for the sake of the visitors, who then left.

Ms Burke said, "Think they'll come again?"

"It's possible," said Simpson.

"When?"

"Oh, I couldn't say when."

"Soon?"

"Oh, I wouldn't say soon."

"You ask 'em this time?"

"Why, yes, of course."

"Ask 'em again."

"Uh. See about it."

The next evening, while brushing his teeth, Simpson noticed that there had been a blessed event among the towels in the bathroom, twins, two little pink ones.

"Father," said Simpson, coming to dessert, and remembering how he'd phrased the question before ("Father, how long will you be gone?") rephrased it, "will you be gone long?"

"Not long," said the pastor, as before.

"Father," said Simpson when he'd eaten his peaches, "while you're away, if I have to go out at night—hospital or something —and the church is locked, I can knock or ring, I know, but I'd hate to disturb Ms Burke, if you know what I mean, Father?"

The pastor nodded, as if he did know, but bowed his head in silent grace.

So did Simpson then, and, when they rose from the table, did not forget the pamphlet by his plate. "So I should knock or ring, Father?"

"Ring," said the pastor.

A little later that evening, after the pastor and John departed for the airport, John to drive the car back, Simpson stepped out to do some shopping. When he returned, the front door, which he'd left unlocked, was locked (Ms Burke), and so, rather than ring, he went through the church. He was carrying a brown paper bag and a six-pack of beer for which he'd spurned a bag because his generation, he understood from the media, was perhaps most admired for its lack of hypocrisy. He reached his room (unseen by Ms Burke, he believed), opened the potato chips, some of which he shook into a dish after first removing the paper clips and dusting it with his elbow, and then opened the cheese dip, this marked down but still not cheap, probably because it came in an attractive wooden bowl suitable for entertaining. Simpson was entertaining two of his classmates, Potter and Schmidt, that evening. He had brought up his rubber-tire ashtray earlier.

When Schmidt arrived with a surprise guest, a Father Philippe, an older man who belonged to a small order recently expelled from one of the developing countries, Simpson hoped to hear something of the Foreign Missions (little discussed these days), but Father Philippe's English was poor, and Potter made the usual remarks about Rice Christians and Spiritual Colonialism, and dominated the conversation.

So Simpson heard more about the developments taking place in the Church, notably in Holland, which he'd heard so much about from Potter and other activists in the seminary, and then more about the developments taking place at Holy Sepulchre, Potter's parish, "exciting" being Potter's word for these developments, "depressing" being Simpson's.

"Look, Simp," Potter said, "we have to do all we can to extend our outreach—to use a term widely used in the Protestant
churches." Women were now allowed to take up the collection
at Holy Sepulchre, and strobe lights had been ordered for the
sanctuary ("We have to think of the kids"), and Potter and his
pastor, who was under Potter's influence, were hoping to get
Holy Sepulchre changed to Holy Resting Place as less off-
putting to the churchless. Potter and his pastor were also hoping that it would soon be possible for people to fulfill their obligation to attend Sunday Mass not only, as now, on Saturday
but also on Friday or *Thursday*, a better day, since so many
people took off for the lake, or started drinking, right after
work on Friday. Potter and his pastor were making an effort to
keep the confessional doors—the doors to the priest's compartment—open when the confessionals were not in use, to show
the people, to bring home to them the idea, that God
("Jahweh" to Potter) was not within but on the altar.

"Wow," said Schmidt, who was under Potter's influence.

"No, no," said Simpson. He assured Father Philippe that
keeping the confessional doors open was not a local custom, nor
was it a growing one, as Potter would have allowed a stranger
to believe (all in the day's work for the enthusiast), and for this
Simpson was frowned on by his classmates.

Potter produced a copy of the Holy Sepulchre parish bulletin, the entire contents being just one word spread over four
pages, a letter to a page, LOVE.

"Wow," said Schmidt.

"To think we've come to this," said Simpson, shaking his
head, but, thinking the "we" might be resented by his classmates, cradle Catholics, he said to Father Philippe, "I'm a convert, Father."

"Simp, you should do something about your triumphal-
ism," said Schmidt.

"Simp and Lefty," said Potter, and likened Simpson to

Father Beeman: *he* had called the LOVE issue a waste of recycled paper but a step in the right direction (*he* wanted no bulletin at all), and *he* was almost certainly the one who kept shutting the confessional doors. "A real cross, that guy, and I'm afraid he knows your pastor's away."

"So?" said Simpson.

"He said he might drop by tonight."

"Oh?" said Simpson—he'd been worried enough before, about the beer running out.

"He might not come," said Schmidt, but he was a Teilhardian optimist.

Father Beeman came, appeared at Simpson's door with John, who was carrying a bag of ice cubes, and was himself carrying a brown paper bag that obviously concealed a bottle. "Surprise," he said.

"No, you're expected, Father. In fact, I was just going out for beer."

"Beer?" said Father Beeman. "Missionary?" he said, when introduced to Father Philippe. "Why aren't you in Holland?" He held up a hand for silence, cupped an ear to hear what Potter, who was ignoring him, was saying to Schmidt, commented "I got your old outreach," and handed Simpson the bottle.

Simpson had to go down to the kitchen for glasses (he had invited John to stay), and while down there heard the light in the back stairway snap on from above (Ms Burke), but he did not have to go out for beer. No, as Simpson saw it, those so inclined could simply switch to the bottle when the beer was gone.

And that was what happened, the evening then turning into more of a party, without, however, coalescing—there were still two conversations.

Simpson was in the one with Father Philippe, John, and Father Beeman, who controlled it, not by doing all the talking as Potter had done earlier, but by changing the subject frequently, giving others a chance to be heard briefly. Father Beeman also kept a tap on the other conversation, and occasionally issued a *monitum* ("It's always been a hotbed of heresy, Holland") or posed a question ("What's so relevant about saying Mass in a barn in Belgium?"). Father Beeman also served as bartender to the entire room, a good thing, since Simpson wouldn't have known how much to put in. Father Beeman and his bottle added a lot to the evening, and made it go as it hadn't before. He appeared to be interested in Simpson.

Yes, for when Potter moved down to the floor, into the lotus position, and, at his request, Simpson, who had been sitting on the bed, moved into the vacant chair, which put him with Schmidt in easy range of Potter's voice, he found that he was still regarded as one of Father Beeman's claque (by Father Beeman), and had to attend to two monologues that seemed to be on a collision course.

Father Beeman said, "I don't blame the young clergy for what's happened to the Church, even the screwballs and phonies."

Potter said, "Just because the Protestants do it, is *that* what's wrong with hymn-singing? Next to a married clergy, I'd say *that's* what we need most."

Father Beeman said, "I blame the older men, pastors like the one where I am now—no hair on his head, just sideburns, and those industrial glasses that make *any* man look like an insect."

Potter, wearing such glasses, said, with some difficulty, gulping, "You're the one . . . Lefty . . . shuts those doors." And stood up, with some difficulty.

Father Beeman, looking belligerent and (Simpson thought) guilty, said, "*What* doors?" And stood up.

"Uh," said Simpson, and was wondering what he, as host, should do, and was also recalling what a visiting speaker at the seminary had said, that the greater incidence of fist fights between members of the clergy since Vatican II was yet another sign of the times, and perhaps of the end, when . . .

Father Philippe stood up, and, going over to the wall and standing with his back to everybody, began to disrobe . . . collar, coat, dickey . . . then turned, and displaying his T-shirt, the blue and gold seal of a university thereon, cried, "*Voilà! Souvenir de Notre-Dame!*"

Ms Burke could be heard pounding on the wall!

"She *still* do that?" roared Father Beeman, and went to the wall and pounded back.

"Uh," said Simpson.

Ms Burke could be heard again.

"*Listen* to her!" whispered Father Beeman, but did not pound back. "Don't let her push you around, Simpson. See that man there?" (Yes, Simpson saw John.) "She *runs* that man. *And* the pastor. But she didn't run *me*. So don't let her run *you*, Simpson. Be like me."

Simpson sort of nodded.

When Potter, who had left the room when the pounding began, returned, he looked pale and said, "I think it was that cheese dip, Simp."

"Nothing wrong with that cheese dip," said Father Beeman.

Simpson saw Potter, Schmidt, and Father Philippe down to the front door, and returned to his room, wondering why Father Beeman and John were staying, and, again, why they had come.

The answers to those questions were not immediately forthcoming, and Simpson soon forgot those questions, for he heard some very interesting things from Father Beeman and (until he fell asleep) John. *That* the insurance company the pastor addressed envelopes for was Catholic owned and oriented, which Simpson was glad to hear, though he still felt uneasy about such employment for a parish priest and could only accept, in principle, Father Beeman's argument that the pastor was a priest-worker. *That* John had another job, as a night watchman in a warehouse ("Security," he said), which in a rash moment he'd boasted of to Ms Burke, and now lived in fear that she'd inform the pastor, Father Beeman doubting this ("Suits her better this way"). *That* Ms Burke, who received a prewar salary like John, never cashed her checks, and this, quite apart from its salutary effect on the pastor, Simpson considered a meritorious practice, even after Father Beeman discounted it ("Hell, she owns a four-hundred-acre farm"). *That* Father Beeman believed the pastor's fine sermons to be the product of reading rather than living, to be thought out, perhaps even written out, before delivery, which struck Simpson as a very Roman view of preaching. *That* the pastor had been active in the so-called streetcar apostolate, this terminated when buses replaced streetcars, buses not having any windowsills to speak of, or the kind of seats on which literature could safely be left—which started Simpson thinking . . .

"Father," he said, taking a chance, "when you were here, did the pastor ever—how shall I put it?—put pamphlets by your plate?"

"At first."

Good news for Simpson!

Father Beeman frowned at Simpson (who had been smiling at him). "But I never felt he was trying to straighten me out—and I came here under a cloud."

"Oh?" But Simpson was only interested in hearing about the pamphlets. " 'At first,' you say?"

"Not at the end. I left here under a cloud."

"Oh?"

"Trouble was, he kept his door open at night—he still do that?"

"Oh, no."

"Well, he did when I was here. I used to come up the stairs

in the dark—so as not to disturb him—carrying my shoes. Never made it. 'Is that you, Father?' That's what he'd say. Night after night. One night, I'm sorry to say, I let him have it—threw a shoe."

"*Oh?*" Simpson was shocked, but tried not to show it.

"It didn't hit him."

"Oh."

Father Beeman rattled his glass. "*So,*" he said, "I wouldn't worry about the pamphlets if I were you. I can see how you might. But don't. You've got what it takes, Simpson. Or what it did. *You* would've made it through the seminary in the old days—*un*like your classmates who were here tonight and wouldn't have lasted a week. Hell, I wouldn't be afraid to introduce *you* to *my* classmates."

This was high praise to one who'd wished for years at the seminary, and for weeks at his first parish, not to be an object of special concern, neither of charity nor of suspicion, to his dear brothers in Christ, but simply to be one of them, and that praise, coming as it did from one who, whatever his faults, and we all have our faults, was certainly one of them, made Simpson blush.

"I've had *very* good reports on you, Simpson."

Simpson said that several parishioners had mentioned Father Beeman to him ("*How?*"), oh, favorably ("*Who?*"), and supplied a couple of names, after which while John slept on, they sat on, finishing the bottle and discussing the Church, as many must have been doing at that hour in rectories.

"Well, Simpson. Say, what's your first name anyway? Heard those clowns calling you Simp. Didn't care for it."

"Fitch," said Simpson.

Father Beeman brought his glass, empty except for ice, down from his mouth with a clunk.

"It's a family name," said Simpson.

"Well, Simpson, I was sorry for you tonight—her acting up

like that in front of everybody. Still, it happened to me when I was here, if that's any consolation to you."

Simpson sort of nodded.

"Don't let her run you. That's the main thing. Don't let her get anything on you. That's the main thing. But *if* she does don't let her run you."

Simpson sort of shook his head.

"Well, Simpson." Father Beeman glanced at his watch, became interested in the back of his hand, tasted it, dried it on his sleeve, and got up, saying, "Nothing wrong with that cheese dip." He woke John (who had to go to his other job and for whom he'd been watching the time), and then he handed Simpson a key, saying, "Carried it away."

Good news for Simpson!

The evening, though dull at first with Potter doing all the talking, and bad at one point with Ms Burke acting up like that, had certainly ended well, Simpson was thinking, as they went down the hallway, when Father Beeman stopped and said:

"The thing is, Simpson, I never got my shoe back."

Hearing this, and seeing where they'd stopped in the hallway, Simpson was shocked, but tried not to show it, and quickly made his position clear. "Afraid you'll have to see the pastor, Father."

Father Beeman said, "Should've said something at the time —the next day, or the day after. But you know how these things are, Simpson—the longer they go on, the worse they get. We weren't talking at all—not that that was much of a change. You know how he is. Was going to say something the day I left, but thought, No, why embarrass him, why embarrass us both?"

"Afraid you'll have to see the pastor, Father."

Father Beeman said, "Look, Simpson, how'd you like to have one shoe, and know where its mate is, and not be able to lay your hands on it?"

"Afraid you'll have to see the pastor, Father."

"Look, Simpson. It's *my* shoe. Come on, John. Help me hunt."

John did.

Simpson walked up and down the hallway, and having had his first look into the room at the head of the stairs—an indoor dump—and hearing Father Beeman tell John the shoe wasn't where it should be (*"Going by the flight pattern"*), he began to hope that it wouldn't be found, which would be best for all concerned.

"How about that? He must've picked it up!"

Father Beeman came forth with the shoe, looking pleased with himself, and under the impression that Simpson wished to shake his hand

Simpson gave him back the key.

"Look, Simpson, this is *your* key."

Simpson casually put his hands behind him and held them there.

"Wouldn't want to say where you got it?"

"In the circumstances, no."

"O.K., Simpson." And Father Beeman gave the key to John.

"Put the shoe back, Father," Simpson said, "I'm in charge here now."

"Look, Simpson, *this* is *my* shoe. Good shoe, too. Bostonian. Hell, it'll never be missed in *there*. Even if he misses it, which he won't, he'll just think it's lost. You won't have to say I was here."

Simpson, remembering the pounding, shook his head. "No," he said.

The pastor and Simpson ate their hashed brown potatoes, scorched green beans, and ground meat of some kind, and Ms Burke set the table with things that should have been on it earlier, then appeared at intervals with a loaf of sandwich bread under her arm, put out some (the pastor and Simpson ate a lot of bread), and disappeared into the kitchen, talking to herself—a typical meal, nothing unusual about it, except the collection of airline condiments and comestibles at the pastor's place. The pastor had come to the table straight from the airport, and Simpson, though he'd come to the table after the pastor that evening, doubted that there had been time for Ms Burke to report what had happened at the rectory while the pastor was away, not long, not quite forty-eight hours.

"What was your trip like, Father?"

"Turbulence."

"Oh?" And Simpson thought of the turbulence at the rectory during the pastor's brief absence. The worst thing, in a way, was that one of Simpson's guests, probably Potter, had used the little pink towels in the bathroom. These Simpson, before retiring that night, had noticed in the bathtub, had smoothed out, folded, and hung up where they belonged, but in the morning, waking with what he could only assume was a hangover, he had found them gone. Alluding to them at breakfast—"Uh. One of my guests . . ."—he had received no response from Ms Burke; and then he had, a bitter one. "I know *who* was here, and I know *why*." "*I*," Simpson had replied, and had been going to say *I tried*, but the thought of his failure to protect the pastor's interest had silenced him. Ms Burke hadn't spoken to Simpson since then, and he hadn't spoken to her. His idea was not to let her intimidate him, not to let her run him. What he had lost with Ms Burke in the way of respect, he had gained in camaraderie with John, who—overly solicitous about Simpson's "head," comparing it with his own, and with some heads he'd had in the past (in some of which Father Beeman had figured), and spending more time in the combination chair-coatrack-umbrella stand just outside the office, and less time in the spare confessional—had become a nuisance by the end of that day, a long day. Simpson had gone to bed early, and was planning to do so again. There could be something in what John said, that the second day after could be worse than the first. "Air turbulence, Father?"

The pastor nodded. He was eating his dessert.

So Simpson picked up his fork.

Ms Burke came into the dining room. "What!" she cried, breaking her great silence where Simpson was concerned. "Eatin' peaches with a fork?"

"No spoon," said Simpson, breaking his great silence where Ms Burke was concerned.

"No *spoon*?"

"No spoon."

"Look on the floor!"

"Looked." To be sure of his ground, Simpson looked again.

Ms Burke, who had been looking on the floor, gave up and went to the sideboard, again rebuking Simpson. "Eatin' peaches with a fork! You see that, Father?"

"Use spoon," said the pastor.

"Don't have one," said Simpson.

Ms Burke popped one down on the table, sort of sleight of hand. "*There!*"

"Thanks," said Simpson.

"Pooh!" said Ms Burke.

"Uh," said the pastor.

Simpson finished dessert, said silent grace, and left the table with the pastor. They drove down the hallway at their usual clip, and were making for the stairs, Simpson thought, when the man suddenly turned out of his lane, saying "Uh." Simpson followed him into the office and, a moment later, thought *this* was how he'd imagined it on his first day at Trinity, the pastor at the desk, himself in the parishioner's chair—and wished he'd emptied his rubber-tire ashtray.

"Talk," the pastor said, still looking at the ashtray.

"*I*," said Simpson.

"Women," the pastor said—evidently had meant that he would, and not that Simpson should, talk—"still great force for good in the world, Father. Be worse place, much worse, without 'em. Our Blessed Mother was one." (Simpson nodded, though the pastor wasn't looking at him.) "Have to watch ourselves, Father. As men. More. As priests. Get careless. Get coarse. Live like bears. Use spoon, Father. Peaches. No spoon, ask for one. Father"—the pastor was looking at Simpson— "don't use guest towels."

"I," said Simpson, and was going to say *didn't*, but didn't.

"In future," the pastor said, mildly.

"I," said Simpson. "Won't."

The pastor nodded. He rose from the desk.

And Simpson rose swiftly and gladly and guiltily from the parishioner's chair.

The pastor handed Simpson a key. "It turned up."

"Oh, thanks, Father."

"Visit hospital, Father?"

"Did, yes. Twice. Everybody's fine."

They left the office then, and made for the stairs, the pastor's step quickening—Simpson's, too—at the sound of Ms Burke's voice in the distance (rebuking John), but Simpson was grateful to Ms Burke for not telling the pastor more than she had, and wondered how he could reward her.

While brushing his teeth, Simpson noticed that the little pink towels were back.

MOONSHOT

A PLAY IN THREE ACTS

MOON BUILDINGS—*Jack Green, a North American Aviation scientist, said moon explorers might be able to construct buildings with pumice dust, a hard, powdery substance that may exist around volcanic craters on the moon. In a report for a meeting in Washington, D.C., of the American Astronautical Society, Green said it might be possible to shape the dust into blocks. These could be held together by a "waterless cement," obtained from sulphur, which is also believed to exist on the moon.*—Minneapolis Morning Tribune, January 17, 1962.

CAST

TOM BROWN, a young scientist.

HUB HICKMAN, his friend, a young astronaut.

SENATOR HODGKINS, chairman, Senate Committee on Oceans, Rivers, Lakes, Harbors, and Space.

SENATOR WOODROW, his friend, a member of the Committee.

SENATOR MELLER, a member of the Committee, of another party.

NANCY, Senator Hodgkins's pretty daughter and secretary.

SOPHIE, Senator Woodrow's pretty daughter and secretary.

SERGEANT AT ARMS, PRESS, TELEVISION, and RADIO PEOPLE, LOBBYISTS, SPIES, STUDENTS OF GOVERNMENT, CHAPERONES and SCHOOLCHILDREN, and OTHERS.

ACT ONE

Time: Now

Place: A crowded hearing room, Washington, D.C.

HODGKINS (*continuing*): You a friend of Jack Green?

TOM: No, sir.

HODGKINS: But you know him, don't you?

TOM: No, sir. I don't.

HODGKINS: Don't tell me you haven't heard of him.

TOM: I won't say I haven't heard of him, sir.

HODGKINS: I thought not.

MELLER (*coming to*): Not so fast, Senator. Who's Jack Green?

WOODROW: A North American Aviation scientist.

HODGKINS: And these are *his* ideas that this fella's putting forward. What's your name again?

TOM: Brown, sir. Tom.

MELLER: You're a young scientist?

TOM: Yes, I am, sir.

MELLER: Employed by?

TOM: Self-employed, sir.

MELLER: And your friend also?

TOM: Yes, sir. He's a young astronaut.

HUB (*rising*): Glad to make your acquaintance, sir.

MELLER: Glad to make *your* acquaintance, young man. I'm always glad to meet a young astronaut. Now these ideas, Tom—are they yours or somebody else's?

TOM: I wouldn't claim them as my own, sir. I doubt that any-body would. It's been known for a long time in this country —and in others, unfortunately—that moon explorers might be able to construct buildings with pumice dust.

HODGKINS (*rapping table*): Quiet! You people will please re-member that you're here as guests of the Committee.

MELLER: What is this pumice dust, anyway?

TOM: It's a hard, powdery substance that may exist around vol-canic craters on the moon.

MELLER: I'm not sure I understand.

TOM: It's believed that it might be possible to shape the dust —or p.d., as it's called—into blocks.

MELLER: Blocks?

TOM: Blocks, sir. These could be held together by a "waterless cement"—not to put too fine a point on it—obtained from sulphur.

MELLER: Sulphur?

TOM: Yes, sir. Sulphur also is believed to exist on the moon.

HODGKINS: I'm surprised you didn't know this, Senator.

WOODROW: I'm not.

MELLER: This isn't my only committee, gentlemen.

HODGKINS: This isn't *my* only committee.

WOODROW: Or mine.

HODGKINS: Nancy, see that the Senator gets copies of a report for a meeting in Washington, D.C., of the American Astro-nautical Society.

NANCY: Oh, all right.

WOODROW: Sophie, will *you* see that the Senator gets copies?

SOPHIE: Why do I have to do everything? Oh, all right.

MELLER: Thank you.

HODGKINS (*looking toward door*): Who're all those people? Never mind. I thought they were coming in here. Well, Brown, we'd like to be of service to you, of course, but, as you know, this Administration is dedicated to economy as well as security, and we need every penny we have for projects under way—for *regular* agencies of the government. If there was anything really new in your approach, or if you'd actually made the trip to the moon and back, it might be different.

ACT TWO

Time: Later
Place: The Moon
HUB: Any luck, Tom?
TOM: It's easy enough to get the dust shaped into a block, but as soon as you turn your back something happens to it.
HUB: We're using too thin a mixture, you think?
TOM: Too thin, or too rich, or conditions aren't right—or something! It won't hold. How you comin'?
HUB: Well, this one worked up better than the last. The question is will it hold any better. Nope.
TOM: One more try, to use up what we've got on hand here, and then I'm turning in. We've had a long day, Hub.
HUB: You can say that again.
TOM: Round up some more p.d. and sulphur, so we can get an early start tomorrow. Go ahead, Hub. I'll clean up here.
HUB: Thanks, Tom. You're a brick.
TOM: That last batch of sulphur seemed to have more to it.
HUB: There's plenty more where that came from. (*Goes off.*)
TOM: Don't go too far away, Hub. It's getting dark.

ACT THREE

Time: Later
Place: A crowded hearing room, Washington, D.C.
HODGKINS: Brown? Who's he? How'd he get scheduled?
WOODROW: I'm sure I don't know.

MELLER: Don't look at me.

HODGKINS: Brown, if you're Brown, who scheduled you?

TOM: I'd rather not say at this time, sir. When you hear all we have to say, sir, I think you'll understand.

HODGKINS: *We? Who's we?*

TOM: My friend and I.

WOODROW: Is your friend present?

HUB: Yes, sir. Hickman, sir. Hub.

HODGKINS: Who scheduled *you?*

HUB: We've just returned from the moon, sir.

HODGKINS (*rapping the table*): Quiet! You people will please remember that you're here as guests of the Committee.

MELLER: *Tom* Brown?

TOM: Yes, sir.

MELLER: Is it true, Tom, that you've just returned from the moon?

TOM: Yes, sir. Actually, we've been back about a week.

HODGKINS (*rapping the table*): Now see here—*quiet!*

HUB: We wanted your committee to be the first to know, sir.

CYNICAL REPORTER: They came to the right place.

TOM: We would've come sooner, sir, but couldn't get past your administrative assistants.

HUB: And legislative assistants, sir.

HODGKINS: I'm always available.

WOODROW: Me, too.

MELLER: Just the two of you made the trip, Tom?

TOM: Yes, sir. There wasn't room for more, what with all the gear. It's just a little two-seater, Hub's heap. Supercharged, of course.

WOODROW: What kind of cock-and-bull story is this?

MELLER: My witness, Senator. And how was it on the moon, Tom?

TOM: About as expected, sir. Dusty. Airless, and therefore soundless, but we used sign language, and later lip reading.

Hot during most of the day and cold at night. No rain to speak of while we were there, no moonquakes, and only an occasional meteor hit—none very close to us, fortunately.

HUB: Don't you believe it, Senator. Tom had one near miss.

TOM: I'd say the hardest thing about it was the duration of the days and nights—each day, each night lasting two weeks. This made for a long workday, to say nothing of the time spent in the—pardon the expression—sack. But our bodies soon got used to it. Our thoughts were often of home.

HUB: You can say that again.

TOM: And of course it took a while to get used to the buoyancy. I weighed thirty-two and a half pounds, but had the full use of my strength, and a corresponding bulge on matter, which made our work a lot easier than it would have been otherwise.

MELLER: What was your work, Tom?

TOM: Constructing buildings, sir, with pumice dust. We had a devil of a time at first. Couldn't get the p.d., as it's called, to mix properly with the stickum—this obtained from sulphur, which is abundant on the moon, though in varying strengths, so that you have to know what you're doing. We ran quality tests constantly. Once we got the hang of it, we were all right.

MELLER: Did you construct a building?

TOM: Two, sir. Oh, nothing like this one, but good and solid and not too small at that.

HUB: About the size of a bank.

TOM: But for the buoyancy factor, these buildings might have taken the two of us years to complete.

HODGKINS: Who scheduled you two birds?

WOODROW: I've had enough of this.

MELLER: Not so fast, gentlemen. Any signs of other life, Tom?

TOM: If you don't mind, sir, I'd like to reply to the other Senator. We took the precaution to document our trip, fully expecting to be treated as we have been by some here today, though (*to Meller*) not by you, sir. Photographs of the buildings, samples of the soil, if you can call it that, p.d., sulphur, and so on—actually very little else.

HODGKINS (*rapping*): Quiet!

TOM: Now, sir, to your question. Yes, as you *might* expect if you keep up with the developments in the interstellar field, there were signs of other life on the moon.

HODGKINS (*rapping*): Here! Here! Order! Order!

MELLER: Pray continue, Tom.

TOM: With your kind permission, sir. Signs of other life, yes, and more than signs!

HODGKINS (*rapping*): Sergeant, do your duty. Order! Order! Order!

MELLER: You mean *they* are there?

TOM: Yes, sir.

MELLER: You saw them, Tom?

TOM: Yes, sir, and so did Hub.

HUB: Yes, sir.

TOM: In great numbers, sir. In very great numbers. They did not see us, but we saw them.

MELLER: What were they doing, Tom?

TOM: Why, constructing buildings with pumice dust, sir.

MELLER: How many buildings would you say they have?

TOM: Well, sir, when we left they had the beginnings of only one. Doubtless they ran into the same trouble we did at first, but, like us, they overcame that trouble. How many buildings they have now—with *their* program—I could not say. If I could, sir, I would not care to say in such a public place as this.

CYNICAL REPORTER: Well, I'll be darned!

HODGKINS (*seeing a man trying to slink out*): Stop that man!

SERGEANT AT ARMS: Oh, no, you don't!

MAN: Чёрт возьми! ["Devil take it!"]

HODGKINS (*seeing another man trying to slink out*): Stop *that* man!

SERGEANT AT ARMS: Oh, no, you don't!

MAN: 怎么办? ["What's to be done?"]

HODGKINS: Lock the doors! Lock the doors!

MELLER (*presently*): Well, gentlemen? What do you say now?

HODGKINS: My hat's off to you, young man.

TOM: Thank you, sir.

HODGKINS: And to you, too, young man.

HUB: Thank you, sir.

WOODROW: Same here to both of you.

MELLER: You see, Tom and Hub, they really aren't so bad. Whatever our party differences, we never fail to close ranks when threatened from without. What we have to do now is get that little machine of yours into production.

HODGKINS: And put a million men on the moon constructing buildings with pumice dust.

WOODROW: Two million.

MELLER: Three.

HODGKINS: I still don't know who scheduled you young men.

TOM: You haven't heard *all* we have to say, sir.

HUB: What Tom means, sir, is that he'd like your daughter's hand in marriage.

TOM (*to Senator Woodrow*): And what Hub means, sir, is that he'd like *your* daughter's hand in marriage.

HODGKINS: You mean it was Nancy who scheduled you, Tom?

TOM: Yes, sir.

WOODROW: And it was Sophie who scheduled you, Hub?

HUB: Yes, sir.

HODGKINS: Well, in that case, I don't see why not.

WOODROW: I'll go along with that.

CYNICAL REPORTER: Let me out of here!

THE TIME TO plant grass seed is in the winter, the man in the next parish had told Joe: just mix it in with the snow and let nature do the rest. So Joe had done that—had believed a priest who rode a scooter and put ice cubes in his beer—and, toward the end of April, had ordered sod. When he discovered that leftover sod couldn't be returned for credit, he'd had it laid down alongside the church, over the flower beds—things like petunias—and now, on a warm Sunday, he could walk in what shade there was during the last Mass, read his breviary, and keep an eye on the parking lot. *"The story is told..."* And when the church windows were open, as they were now, he could catch the sermon. He had heard his curate, Bill, earlier, and now he was hearing the old monk who helped out on weekends, Father Otto. *"In like manner, my good people, one part of the camel's corpus was followed by another (indeed, it could not be otherwise) until, at last, the rough beast was inside the tent, and the merchant, poor man, with all his good*

intentions, was out in the raging desert storm, or simoom.
How. Like. Sin. That. Is."

While Father Otto took it from there, Joe moved out of range,
out into the sun. Crossing the parking lot, he paused before a
little pile of cigarette butts in the gravel, thought of inspecting
the ashtrays of the nearest cars, thought again, and moved on
toward his new rectory, thinking, As this church is the house
of God, my good people, so this parking lot is—forget it. "You're
good people," he called to a young couple. "Good and late." No
response. People who'd once been able to take and even enjoy a
little friendly needling from their pastor, like the customers in
a night club where an insulting waiter is part of the show, were
restless and crabby nowadays. They wanted their "rights," expected a priest to act like a minister, to say things like "So nice
to see you" and "So glad you could make it," and still they
emptied their ashtrays in his parking lot. Entering the rectory
by the back door, he washed his hands at the kitchen sink,
then slipped into his illustrated apron, wearing it inside out
over his cassock so the funny stuff was hidden, and set about
making Father Otto's breakfast.

When Bill, on his way over to church to help Father Otto
with Communion, passed through the kitchen, Joe looked up
from the breadboard, from sawing an orange, and said, "This
isn't for me"—just as he had a few weeks back, anxious then to
explain his continuing presence in the kitchen to Bill. (It had
been Bill's first Sunday at the rectory.) "This isn't for me"
had since become something of a family joke, the thing to
say when making another nightcap, when not declining dessert, which showed what a good guy Joe was, for he had a
slight eating problem, unfortunately, and also a slight drinking
problem.

As Bill went out the back door, Joe intoned, "*The story is
told* ..." Father Otto's sermons had become something of a
family joke, too. There should be others in time.

Fifteen minutes later, Father Otto passed through the kitchen, and breakfast—or brunch, as he sometimes called it with a chuckle—was served in the dining room. Joe and Bill ate in the kitchen on Sunday, the housekeeper's day off, but Joe felt that Father Otto deserved better, as a man of the old school *and* as hard-to-get weekend help. After serving him, Joe sank down at the other end of the table with a cup of coffee. What he really wanted was a cold beer. "How's everything at the monastery, Father?"

"About the same," said Father Otto, and helped himself to the strawberry preserves. He praised the brand, Smucker's. He said he preferred strawberry to red raspberry, and red to black raspberry, as a rule, and didn't care for the monastery stuff, as the nuns skimped on the natural ingredients. "And make too much plum."

"That so?" said Joe. He'd heard it all before. As a rule, he didn't sit with Father Otto at breakfast.

"My, but those were fine berries," said Father Otto, referring, as he had before, to some strawberries no longer grown at the monastery. "Small, yes, but with a most delicate flavor. And then Brother, he went and dug 'em out."

"Brother Gardener?" said Joe, as if in some doubt.

Father Otto, carried away by anger, could only reply by nodding.

"More toast, Father?"

"All right." Father Otto helped himself to more preserves. He kept getting ahead of himself—always more preserves than toast.

Joe produced another slice from the kitchen, and also the coffeepot. "Warm that up for you?"

"All right." But first Father Otto drained his cup. "You make good coffee here."

Joe poured, sat down again, considering what he had to say. (On his last trip to the kitchen, he had removed his apron as a hint to Father Otto that the dining room was closing.) "Father, I was thinking"—and Joe had been thinking, for the past month, ever since Bill moved in—"you *could* go back on the one-thirty bus."

Father Otto, who ordinarily returned to the monastery on the six-thirty bus, gazed away, masticating, sheeplike. He seemed to be saying that there ought to be a reason for such a drastic and sudden change in his routine.

"Know you want to get back as soon as possible," Joe said. Monks, he'd often been told (by monks), are never very happy away from their monastery. Between them and their real estate, there is a body-and-soul relationship, a strange bond. Monks are the homeowners, the solid citizens, of the ecclesiastical establishment. Other varieties of religious, and even secular priests like Joe—although he'd built a school, a convent, and now a rectory—are hoboes by comparison. That was certainly the impression you got if you spent any time with monks. So, really, what Joe was suggesting—that Father Otto return to his monastery a few hours earlier than usual—wasn't so bad, was it? "Of course, it's up to you, Father."

Father Otto folded his napkin, though it was headed for the laundry, and then he rolled it. He seemed to be looking for his napkin ring, and then he seemed to remember it was at the monastery. "All right," he said.

Bill barged in, saying, "That was Potter on the phone. Looks like there'll be one more, Father."

Seeing that he had no choice, Joe informed Father Otto that a couple of Bill's friends—classmates—were coming to dinner, and that Mrs Pelissier, the housekeeper, would report at three. "She's been having car trouble," he added, hoping, he guessed, to change the subject, but it was no good.

"Who else is coming?" Father Otto said to Bill.

"Name's Conklin. Classmate. Ex-classmate."

Joe didn't like the sound of it. "Dropout?"

Bill observed a moment of silence. "None of us knew why Conk left. I don't think *Conk* did—at the time."

"That's often the case, Bill. It's nothing to be ashamed of," said Father Otto, looking at Joe.

"Who said it was?" Joe inquired, and then continued with Bill. "So now he's married. Right?"

"No. Not exactly."

Joe waited for clarification.

"I guess he thinks about it," Bill said.

Father Otto nodded. "We all do."

"That so?" said Joe.

Father Otto nodded. "It's nothing to be ashamed of."

"That so?" said Joe.

"Is it all right, then?" Bill said.

Joe looked at Bill intently. "Is *what* all right?"

"For Conk to come? He's a pretty lonely guy."

Father Otto was nodding away, apparently giving *his* permission.

"It's your party," Joe said, and rose from the table in an energetic manner, as a hint to Father Otto. "I'd ask you to stay for it, Father. Or Bill would—it's his party. But we plan to sit down—or stand up, it's buffet—around five. You'd have to eat and run." And somebody—Joe—would have to drive Father Otto to the bus.

"But stay if you like," Bill said.

"All right," said Father Otto.

Joe and Father Otto were watching the Twins game and drinking beer in the pastor's study when Bill brought in his friends and introduced them. The heavy one wearing a collar, which showed that he, or his pastor, was still holding the line, was Hennessy. The exhibitionist in the faded Brahms T-shirt was Potter. And the other one, the one with the mustache, a nasty affair, was Conklin.

"What's the score?" Bill asked, as if he cared.

"Four to one," Joe said.

"Twins?"

"No."

Potter and Conklin moved off to case the bookshelves, and Father Otto joined them, but Hennessy stood by, attending to the conversation.

"What inning?" Bill asked.

"Seventh."

"Who's pitching?"

Joe took a step toward the television set.

"Leave it on," Bill said. "We're going to my room for a drink."

Bill and his friends then departed, Hennessy murmuring, "See you later."

"Fine young men," said Father Otto.

"Uh-huh," Joe said. "Split a bottle, Father?"

"All right."

Joe carried the empties into the kitchen. "Everything O.K. in here?" he said to Mrs P., and opened the refrigerator—always an embarrassing act for him, even when alone. He had cut down on snacking, though, had suffered less from "night hunger" since Bill moved in.

"Sure you want to eat in the study, Father?"

"It's Bill's party," Joe said, although he felt as Mrs P. did about eating in the study.

"He's lucky he's got you for a pastor, Father."

"Oh, I don't know," Joe said, but didn't argue the point. He returned to the study and poured half of the beer—more than half—into Father Otto's glass. "Hey. How'd that man get on second?"

Father Otto observed the television screen closely and nodded, as if to say yes, Joe was right, there was a man on second.

"The official scorer has ruled it a single and an error, not a double," said the announcer.

"Who made the error?" Joe said, more to the announcer than to Father Otto.

"According to our records, that's the first error Tony's made this season," said the announcer.

Father Otto got up and, as was his habit from time to time, left the room.

After a bit, Joe went to see if anything was wrong, but Father Otto, who used the lavatory off the guest room, wasn't there. Then, listening in the hallway, Joe heard the old monk's voice among the others in Bill's room, and returned to the study. Sitting there alone, finishing off Father Otto's beer, Joe asked himself, What's wrong with this picture? Nothing, really, he told himself. The curate was entertaining in his room so as not to interfere with the game, the visiting priest was a fair-weather fan, if that, and so, really, nothing was wrong—it meant nothing, nothing personal that the pastor sat alone. He didn't like it, though.

One of the best things about the priesthood, Joe had been told in the seminary, is other priests—"priestly fellowship." The words had sounded corny at the time, but Joe had believed in the idea behind them and he still did. For years, though, he hadn't had room in his life for those who should now be his intimates—two of his classmates had died, and others seemed equally remote. Pursuing his building program as he had, he had been forced to associate almost exclusively with the laity, and now, at forty-four, he found he wanted more from life. And for some reason he wasn't finding as much priestly fellowship as he'd hoped to find where he kept looking for it—under his own roof.

Despite the age gap, Joe had tried hard with Father Otto. In the beginning, there had been pro football games (spoiled by Father Otto's totally uninformed comments and rather amused attitude), drives into the countryside to see the autumn foliage

("You should see it at the monastery"), visits to new churches of all denominations, since Joe would have to build a new church someday (visits discontinued because Father Otto wasn't, as he put it, terribly interested in new churches, or, for that matter, old ones, and disliked the bucket seats in Joe's car). Now, as a rule, they spent Sunday afternoon at home, in the pastor's study, sent out for seafood dinners, which Father Otto seemed to look forward to, and watched television, which the monk didn't have in his cell in the monastery. This was all right when there was something on, by which Joe meant major sports, not water-skiing, and also things like *Meet the Press* and *Face the Nation*, but Father Otto wasn't so discriminating—he enjoyed quiz programs and government propaganda. At such times, Joe would go downstairs to his office to read, or slip into his bedroom for a nap. All in all, not an ideal situation.

With Bill, Joe had tried harder, since so much more was at stake—the pastor-curate relationship. It had begun badly. Bill, reporting for duty on his first day, a Saturday, had barely made it in time for afternoon confessions, had dined out the next day without giving sufficient notice, had come in late that night, and had to be summoned to the office area the next morning. (Evidently, he'd thought that a priest just sat around in his room waiting for something to turn up.) And he'd been ordained without even a hunt-and-peck command of typing—a great blow to Joe, who'd said that a man who couldn't type was as ill-equipped for modern parish life as a man who couldn't drive, and Bill had laughed. A very bad time in the relationship.

Joe was still carrying the work load he had carried before, doing all the parish accounts and correspondence and trying to find jobs that Bill could do—quite a job itself. The future looked better, though, with Bill going ahead in his typing, using the text and records provided by Joe and his own phonograph, which, at first, at the end of each day, he'd lugged up to his room to play folk and protest songs on but now, thank God, left in his office. Bill was sweating it out now, yes, but so was Joe, and really Bill couldn't complain. It wasn't all business in the office area. With the connecting door open, they could carry on conversations desk to desk, and if the flow was rather more one way than the other, that was because there was so much that Bill didn't know about procedure and policy, about the local community, about the world in general. Here, too, Joe tried to help Bill, working from a dozen or so periodicals that crossed his desk, passing them on with some articles marked "Read" or "Skip." It was all right if Bill read the recommended matter during office hours as long as his typing and filing didn't suffer. Sometimes, too, Joe would drop in on Bill and smoke a baby cigar with him (wanted to get Bill off cigarettes), and two or three times a week, an hour before closing time, Joe would put on his hat and say, in the gruff voice he affected when he was about to be more than ordinarily decent, "Knock it off." Bill would then cover his typewriter (Joe was strict about that), and they'd go off in Joe's car, the radio playing for Bill. They had visited a number of rectories on business that could've been handled by telephone simply because Joe liked being seen with his curate. At least once a week, after what might have started out as a routine stop at the hospital or the garage (Joe's car was a lemon), they'd dined out in style, and gone on to box seats at the stadium. They had attended a half-dozen games before Joe really accepted the fact that Bill wasn't terribly interested in baseball. At Bill's suggestion, they had taken in a couple of lousy foreign movies. But mostly they spent their evenings at home, in the pastor's study, pastor in his chair, his Barcalounger, feet up, curate in attendance, with cigars and drinks (served from the bathroom, where the liquor was kept in the same drawer with the shoe polish and thus kept in its place), TV if wanted, and good talk.

Well, fairly good talk.

Little interest was shown when Joe spoke of the remarkable personalities who had flourished at the seminary during his era, and likewise when Bill spoke of his recent trials there—of piddling causes that already sounded like ancient history. Bill could say the usual things about the late Pope John, and about the present Pope, but he couldn't discuss Frank Sinatra ("the Guv'nor") or Senator Dirksen, and he hadn't even heard of people like Fishbait Miller and Nancy Dickerson. Large, fertile areas of conversation—Capitol Hill, show business, sports—had therefore been abandoned. But what made the likeliest subjects impossible—the difference between Joe and Bill—was what kept them going when they got onto religion.

Bill talked up the changes in the liturgy, the vernacular, lay participation, ecumenism, and so on, and Joe didn't. Bill claimed that religion had hit bottom in our time and had no place to go but up, and Joe questioned both statements. Bill said that religion (though not perhaps as we know it) was the coming thing, and that the clergy (though not perhaps as we know them) were the coming men. "Fuzzy thinking, Pollyanna stuff," said Joe, and advised Bill to stop reading Teilhard de Chardin and other unpronounceables. So Bill was inclined to be bullish, and Joe bearish, about the future.

As for the present, the immediate present, Joe could understand how Bill might be unhappy in his work, considering the satisfactions there were, or were said to be, in the priesthood, which, unfortunately, was not what it was cracked up to be in the seminary and not what *you* chose to make it. If Bill had expectd to labor in certain parts of the vineyard, and not in others—in the slums, and not in the suburbs—he should have said so years ago and saved the diocese the expense of educating him. And if Bill felt, as he said, thwarted and useless where he was—well, that was exactly how men in slum parishes felt. The truth was Bill had got what he wanted—a tough assignment—without the romantic props that went with a slum parish: bums, pigeons, and so on. Naturally, after living in the rarefied atmosphere of the seminary, Bill was finding it hard to adjust to reality. A slight case of the bends. That was all. Or was it?

Sometimes, late at night, Joe would call Bill an apostolic snob—accuse him of looking down his nose at the parishioners just because they weren't derelicts or great sinners—and sometimes, late at night, Joe would call Bill a dreamer. In that connection, Joe had noticed that Bill had a faraway look in his eyes, and that Bill had a head like a violin. Dreamers hadn't been so common in the Church back when he'd been one himself, hadn't constituted a working majority then, Joe was saying one night, when a picture of Rudolf Hess appeared on television and Joe noticed that Hess had a head like a violin. Joe was beginning to develop his thesis, saying the fact that Hess had flown to Scotland in the hope of stopping the war, a war that still had years to run, certainly proved that he was a dreamer, when Bill interrupted: "The fact that you've got a head like a banjo, Father—what's *that* prove?" Well, Joe had tried not to show it, had smiled, but he had been hurt—a very bad moment in the relationship.

On the whole, though, they were getting along. There were nights, yes, when Bill had to be called more than once before he came out of his room, before he left off strumming his Spanish guitar, listening to FM, or talking to his friends on the phone. There were nights, too, when Bill returned to his room earlier than Joe would have liked, when Joe had maybe had one too many . . . The truth was these weren't the nights that Joe had looked forward to during his years as a pastor without a curate, and during his years as a curate with a pastor who avoided him . . . and still they weren't bad nights, by rectory standards these days. There had been some fairly good talk— arguments, really, ending sometimes with one man making a final point outside the other man's door, or, after they'd both gone to bed, over the phone. "Bill? Joe." And there had been moments, a few, when the manifest differences of age, position, and opinion between pastor and curate had just disappeared, when Joe and Bill had entered that rather exalted and somewhat relaxed state, induced in part perhaps by drink, that Joe recognized as priestly fellowship.

At one such moment, feeling content but wondering if he couldn't do better, Joe had invited Bill to have a friend or two in for a meal sometime.

"Should I call the others, Father?" said Mrs P., sounding apprehensive, for the others were getting kind of loud in Bill's room.

"I'll do it," Joe said, but when he saw himself knocking at Bill's door, looking in on a scene he'd been more or less excluded from, he phoned over. "*Bill!*" Either Bill or Father Otto should've answered the phone—possibly Hennessy or Potter, but *not* Conklin.

They arrived in the study like conventioneers, some carrying glasses, and immediately formed a circle that did not include Joe. He came between them, mentioning Father Otto's bus, and bumped them over to the food. Then he went and stood at the other end of the table, by the wine—ready to pour, hoping to get into conversation with someone. Father Otto was first in line. "Just like the monastery," Joe said, referring to the nice display of food on Father Otto's plate.

"Yes," said Father Otto, who'd been saying (to Hennessy) that some days were somewhat better than others to visit the monastery if one intended to eat there. "We have a cafeteria now."

"Wine, Father?"

"What kind is it?"

Joe, speaking through his nose, named the wine.

"On second thought, no," said Father Otto, and moved off

with his plate, which he carefully held in both hands but in a sloping manner.

Hennessy was next, and he also refused wine. But he complimented Joe on his building program, calling the new rectory "a crackerjack," which suggested to Joe that the works of Father Finn—*Tom Playfair, Claude Lightfoot,* and the rest—were still being read and might have figured in Hennessy's vocation, as they had in his own.

"You should see the office area," Joe said to Hennessy. "Maybe, if there's time later, I could take you around the plant."

"Oh, *no!*" said Conklin, next in line, and then turned to Potter to see if he'd heard, but Potter was talking to Bill, and Hennessy ("Maybe later, Father") was moving off, and so Conklin, after more or less insulting Joe, had to face him alone.

"Wine, Mr Conklin?"

"*Sí, señor.*"

It went with the mustache, Joe guessed, wondering whether a priest should be addressed as "*señor,*" whether "*reverendissimo*" or something wouldn't be more like it, whether, in fact, Conklin had meant to pay him back for the "mister." At the seminary, as Conklin would know, there were still a few reverend fathers who made much of "mister," hissing it, using it to draw the line between miserable you and glorious them. That hadn't been Joe's intention. What *was* Conklin now, and what was he ever likely to be, but "mister"? It didn't pay for someone in Conklin's position to be too sensitive, Joe thought.

And listened to Potter, who was saying (to Bill) that he'd had a raw egg on his steak tartare in München and enjoyed it. "'*Mit Ei,*' they call it there."

"You can enjoy it *here,*" Joe said. "Mrs Pelissier!" he cried, not pronouncing the housekeeper's name as he usually did, but giving it everything it had, which was plenty, in French.

Joe and everybody (except Father Otto) urged Potter to have a raw egg on his steak tartare, as in München—*Mit Ei! Mit Ei!* But Potter wouldn't do it, although Mrs P. produced a dozen nice fresh ones, entering the study in triumph, leaving it in sorrow. Joe almost had one himself, for her sake. Potter came out of it badly.

Joe was hoping the Barcalounger would clear when he set forth with glass and plate, but Conklin was in it, and it didn't, and so he went and sat near Hennessy and Father Otto. "Never cared for buffet," he told them, and got no response. (Hennessy was saying that the monastic life was beyond one of his modest spiritual means, Father Otto that one never knew until one tried.) Joe tried the other conversation. (Potter was building up the laity, at the expense of the clergy, as was the practice of the clergy these days.) "Some of your best friends must be laymen," Joe said, and was alarmed to see Potter taking him seriously: that was the trouble with the men of Bill's generation—not too bright and in love with themselves, they made you want to hit them. "But what about the ones who empty their ashtrays in your parking lot?"

Potter smiled—*now* he thought Joe was kidding.

"Not much you can do," Conklin said. "Judah took possession of the hill country, but he couldn't drive out the inhabitants of the plain, because they had chariots of iron."

"That so?" said Joe, thinking, What *is* this? He tried his wine. "Not bad," he said to Potter and Bill (who still had their drinks from Bill's room), but he didn't get through to them. Potter was a talker.

"What kind is it?" said Father Otto.

Joe, speaking through his nose, named the wine.

"Grape," said Conklin, coming back from the table with the bottle from which only he and Joe had partaken so far, and sitting down with it, in the Barcalounger. "Anybody else?"

"No, thanks," Joe said, and was silent for some time—until

he heard Conklin refer to Beans McQueen as Beans. "You a friend of Father McQueen's?"

"They taught this course together, at the Institute," Bill said. "Scripture for the Laity."

"That so?" said Joe.

And the talk went on as before, on two fronts, without Joe, leaving him free to go over to the table for the other bottle of wine. Hennessy wasn't having any, but Father Otto was. "Grape, you say?" Joe served Father Otto, and also himself, and left the bottle on the coffee table in front of him, but beyond his reach—not that wine, unfortified wine, was really alcoholic, not that *he* was. He just had to watch himself. He wasn't a wine drinker, but could see how he might have been one in another time and place—one of those wise old abbés, his mouth a-pucker with *Grand Cru*, his tongue tasting like steak, solving life's problems by calling people "my son."

Potter was telling Bill and Conklin that the clergy should cast off their medieval trappings, immerse themselves in the profane everyday world, and thus reveal its sacred character.

"That why you're immersed in that shirt?" said Joe, but Potter just smiled and went on as before. It was odd the way Bill looked up to Potter, odder still the way they both looked up to Conklin—as *what*, a layman? It was a crazy world. Father Otto was telling Hennessy that the monastery should employ trained lay personnel in key positions, replace the kitchen, if not the laundry, nuns, and also certain brothers. "So Brother Gardener has to go?" said Joe.

Father Otto turned on Joe. "*You*," he said, speaking with deliberation, as if the wine, and whatever he'd had in Bill's room, and the beer before that, had suddenly gone to his head. "*You. Covered. Up. Those. Flowers.*"

"Flowers?" said Joe, and listened to the silence in the study. For the first time since the party began, he felt that others were interested in what he might have to say. "Things like petunias," he said, and started to tell them about the leftover sod. At once he saw that they already knew about it, that it was later than he'd thought, that he was not to escape the pastor's fate, was already being discussed in his own rectory and therefore in others by curates and visiting priests, those natural allies. "Didn't realize you felt that way about petunias, Father. Strawberries, yes."

"Humph," said Father Otto.

"Excuse me," Joe said, feeling that everybody was against him, and went over to the table, where he had work to do. He had to fire up the chafing dish, pour the juice from the pitted Bing cherries into the top pan, or blazer, place it directly over the flame, bring the juice to a boil, thicken with $1/2$ tsp. of arrowroot dissolved in a little cold water, but Potter was telling the others that family life was in such tough shape today because Our Lord had been a bachelor, and so, carrying a dead match to the ashtray, Joe appeared among them again, saying, "We used to ask a lot of silly questions in the sem. Would Our Lord be a smoker, drive a late-model car, and so on. Kid stuff—nobody got hurt. But I wonder about some of the stuff I hear today."

"People living normal lives can't identify with Our Lord," Potter said. "Or with *us*—because of the celibacy barrier."

"That so?" said Joe. "And where you *don't* have that barrier? I mean how well do *we* identify with Our Lord?" Joe put the question to Bill and Hennessy, too, with his eyes, passed over Conklin, tried but failed with Father Otto, who was spearing kernels of corn with his fork, making a clicking noise on his plate—rather annoying, since it broke what otherwise would have been an impressive silence.

"He's got you, Pot," said Conklin, and then to Joe: "We may be closer than I thought."

Joe, not seeing why Conklin's last words should cause Bill and Potter to look so sad, continued, "And when you consider we work at it full time, unlike the laity—well, it makes you wonder, doesn't it?"

"It did me," said Conklin

Bill sighed, and Potter held out his glass to Conklin for wine—a highball glass with ice in it. Joe said nothing about a proper glass, afraid that Potter (who'd said earlier that he longed for the day when he'd be able to say Mass with a beer mug, a coffee cup, a small flower vase of simple design, because such things were cheap and honest and made, like us, of clay) would refuse a proper glass and, furthermore, would say *why*. In that way, Potter could easily evade the issue he'd raised, the celibacy issue, as he had the egg. Potter was tricky, had to be watched, but Joe was doing that—and then Father Otto had to butt in.

"There's been a lot of talk in the community about family life, but whatever the future holds for you fellas, I think it's safe to say our status, or situation—some would say our lot— won't change. When you get right down to it, a monastery's no place for a family man."

"I'll buy that," said Joe.

"Oh, well," said Father Otto. "The community's family enough for me."

And that, Joe thought, is why you're here.

"When you get right down to it," said Conklin (to Father Otto), "a monastery's no place for *you*. Priests weren't meant to be monks, and monks weren't meant to be priests—and *weren't* in the Age of Faith."

"We all know that," Joe said—Conklin sounded just like an ex-seminarian, or an educated layman.

"Times change," said Father Otto.

"Status-seeking," said Conklin.

Joe gave Bill a look for grinning, and to make it absolutely clear where his sympathies lay, as between Conklin and Father Otto, who appeared to be slightly wounded, Joe fetched the bottle. "Father?"

"All right," said Father Otto.

Joe filled the monk's glass, also his own, and went back to the table, with Potter's voice following him. "Why put such a premium on celibacy—on sex, really? Think of the problems it creates."

"Think of the problems it *doesn't* create," said Joe, and while Potter and the others were thinking of those problems (Joe hoped), he poured the juice from the pitted Bing cherries into the top pan, or blazer. That done, he appeared among them again, saying, "The premium isn't on sex. It isn't on celibacy. It's on efficiency and sanctity."

"Oh, *no!*" said Conklin.

"Oh, *yes,*" said Joe. "Even if we don't hear much about that aspect of the priesthood today." And, having given them more food for thought, Joe left them again, for he still had work to do, but before he reached the table the impressive silence his words had produced was cruelly violated.

"Father, how can we make sanctity as attractive as sex to the common man?"

Joe had put that question to a Discalced Carmelite before an S.R.O. audience at the seminary during the war years, and Joe could hear it yet, that famous question, and had to expect to hear it yet from certain men—Potter's permissive pastor was one—of that era, but *not*, Joe thought, from somebody like Conklin, and showed it.

"Got to talkin' . . . in Bill's room," Father Otto said, apologetically, and paused to watch his plate (which he'd been holding in a sloping manner) start down his outstretched leg, jump, and land on the floor, right side up. Once, twice, he nodded, as if to say no harm done, but his head hung down, finally, in an uncompleted nod.

Joe sprang into action. Others, nearer to Father Otto, had already sprung. But it was Joe who removed the fork (in the circumstances, a dangerous instrument) from Father Otto's hand and thrust it at Potter, who hesitated to take it by the greasy end, and it was Joe who deftly kicked the plate aside and told Bill to pick it up, and Joe who instructed Hennessy and Conklin, instead of foolishly trying to firm him up, to lay the monk out on the couch. Joe then changed his mind about that, in view of the sepulchral effect it might have on the party. "Bedroom! Bedroom!" he cried. "Not mine! Not mine!" Conklin and Hennessy, frog-marching Father Otto this way and that, didn't seem to know what they were doing. Then Joe saw what the trouble was. It was Conklin. Why, when there were plenty of clergy present, when the person in distress was himself one of them, why should a layman be playing such an important part? "Here, let *me*," Joe said, shouldering in, but the layman wouldn't let go. Joe ended up with Hennessy's portion of Father Otto. And so, borne up by Joe and Conklin, the helpless monk was removed from the scene.

When Joe got back from the guest room, he found that the juice, which he had yet to thicken with 1/2 tsp. of arrowroot dissolved in a little cold water, had already thickened, having been kept at, rather than brought to, a boil. Until then, he had hoped to serve cherries jubilee for dessert and to do the job himself, so Mrs P. wouldn't have to be present, but now he didn't know. The juice had definitely lost its liquidity, was hardening or charring at the edges of the top pan, or blazer. To go ahead now, with or without the arrowroot, might be a mistake. So, playing it safe, he blew out the flame, dished up the cherries as they were, room temperature and rather dry without their juice, and served them swiftly, with spoons. He said nothing, and nothing was said.

The conversation died when Joe sat down with his dish and spoon. He had tuned in earlier, though, while serving, and was curious to know why Hennessy thought that Conklin shouldn't go on teaching at the Institute. "If he's reasonably competent, and if Beans wants him back—well, why not?"

said Joe, feeling broad-minded. (Hennessy, too, had that effect on him.) No response. "O.K. I'll put it another way. What if he shaved off his mustache?"

Potter and Bill shuffled their feet and protested, but Joe ignored them. "Why not?" he asked, speaking directly to Conklin.

"You talkin' about the mustache or the Institute?"

"Both."

Potter and Bill protested again.

"It's a fair question," said Conklin. "About the Institute. You better tell him, Bill."

Joe looked at Bill. "Well?"

"Conk's lost his faith," Bill said.

"That so?" said Joe. He was sorry to hear it, of course, and felt that more was expected of him, but he also felt that condolences weren't in order, since some people regarded the loss of their faith as a step forward, and since he didn't want to sound like he was rolling in the stuff himself. He now saw why Conklin had been invited, saw why so much was being made of him by Potter and Bill, saw what was really going on. It was an old-fashioned spiritual snipe hunt, such as they'd all read about, with Potter and Bill, if not Hennessy, happy to be participating, and also, it seemed, the snipe. That was the odd part.

"Conk just doesn't take God for granted—unlike some of us in the Church," Potter said, apparently to Joe. "That's been our trouble all along. Atheism and faith—true faith—have that in common. They don't take God for granted."

Joe looked cross-eyed at Hennessy.

"But Conk's not an atheist," Bill said to Joe. "Are you, Conk?"

Conklin smiled. "No, but I'm working on it."

Joe wanted to hit him.

"That's what I like about Conk," Potter said, grimly. "He's honest."

Bill nodded, grimly.

Joe sniffed. "What I don't get," he said to Conklin, "is why you want to go on teaching at the Institute if you've lost your faith. Just want to keep your hand in, or what?"

"Don't blame *Conk*," Potter said

"*Conk* wants to quit," Bill said.

"He should," Joe said, and gave him an encouraging nod.

"*No!*" cried Potter, and stood up. "What matters in teaching is a man's competence, not his private beliefs, or lack of same. And that applies to things like Scripture and theology, if they're teachable, and *I* say they are. By agnostics, infidels, and apostates, you say? *Yes!* I say. And, thank God, some of our better institutions agree!" Potter sat down.

Bill stood up. "But how many of our *seminaries*, Pot? How can we go on calling theology the Queen of Sciences?" Bill sat down.

"How about Beans?" said Joe, without getting up. Joe was pretty sure that Beans didn't need Conklin, was just doing an ex-seminarian a favor, letting him keep his hand in, and maybe hoping for a delayed vocation. "*He* know about this? No? Better tell him, then, so he can find somebody else, if necessary."

Potter and Bill both stood up, both preaching, and Potter, of course, prevailed, but he was repeating himself.

"Look," said Joe. "The Institute isn't one of our better institutions." Even as an adventure in adult education, which was all it claimed to be, it probably didn't rate too high. "And it wouldn't be one of our better institutions if you guys pulled this off."

"It'd be a start," said Potter, sitting down.

"It'd be a stunt," said Joe, getting up. Going to the door, he took the tray from Mrs P., but on his return, with his mind on the trouble there could be over Conklin at the Institute— factions, resolutions, resignations, and so on—he overran the coffee table, jarring it and cracking his shin. In some pain, he backed up and put down the tray, saying, "I worry about you guys." Pouring and handing around coffee, sloshing it, he spoke to them as he sometimes did to Bill alone, late at night.

HOME TRUTHS

He said that he, at their age, had dearly wanted to be a saint, had trained for it—plenty of prayer and fasting, no smoking, no booze ("Actually, I didn't drink anything but beer then"), and had worn a hair shirt for a short period. At their age, *he* had worked out on himself, not on other people, and that was the difference between the men of his generation and theirs. One of the differences. "You guys even *want* to be saints? I doubt it. You're too busy with your public relations."

CHANGING STANDARDS

There might be worlds to be won, souls to be harvested, and so on, but not with stunts and gimmicks. He had been rather pessimistic about the various attempts to improve the Church's image, and he had been right. Vocations, conversions, communions, confessions, contributions, general attendance, all down. And why not? "We used to stand out in the crowd. We had quality control. We were the higher-priced spread. No more. Now if somebody drops the ball somebody else throws it into the stands, and that's how we clear the bases. Tell the man in the next parish that you fornicated a hundred and thirty-six times since your last confession, which was one month ago, and he says, 'Did you think ill of your fellow-man?' It's a crazy world."

STRANDED

There had always been a shortage of goodness in the world, and evil and ignorance were still facts of life, but where was the old intelligence? He had begun to wonder, as he never had before, about the doctrine of free will. People, he feared, might not be able to exercise free will anymore, owing to the decline in human intelligence. How else explain the state of the country, and the world, today? "We don't, maybe we *can't*, make the right moves—like those poor whales you read about. We're stranded."

HUMAN NATURE

The Church was irrelevant today, not concerned enough with the everyday problems of war, poverty, segregation, and so on, people said, but such talk was itself irrelevant, was really a criticism of human nature. Sell what you have and follow me, Our Lord had told the rich young man—who had then gone away sad. That was human nature for you, and it hadn't changed. Let him take it who can, Our Lord had said of celibacy—and few could take it, then or now. "And that applies to heroic sacrifice of all kinds. Let's face it."

BRUEGEL THE ELDER

People, most people, lay *and* clerical, just weren't up to much. Liturgists, of course, were trying to capitalize on that fact, introducing new forms of worship, reviving old ones, and so on, but an easy way would never be found to make gold out of lead. Otherwise the saints and martyrs would have lived as they had, and died, in vain. All this talk of community, communicating, and so on—it was just whistling in the dark. "Life's not a cook-out by Bruegel the Elder and people know it."

TOO FAR?

Sure it was a time of crisis, upheaval, and so on, but a man could still do his job. The greatest job in the world, divinely instituted and so on, was that of the priest, and yet it was still a job—a marrying, burying, sacrificing job, plus whatever good could be done on the side. It was *not* a crusade. Turn it into one, as some guys were trying to do, and you asked too much of it, of yourself, and of ordinary people, invited nervous breakdowns all around. Trying to do too much was something the Church had always avoided, at least until recently. At the Council, the so-called conservatives—a persecuted minority group if ever there was one—had only been afraid of going too far too soon, of throwing the baby out with the bathwater. "And rightly so."

FLYING SAUCERS

The Church couldn't respond to all the demands of the moment or she'd go the way of those numerous sects that owed their brief existence to such demands. People had to realize that what they wanted might not be what they needed, and if they couldn't—well, they couldn't. Religion was a weak force today, owing to the decline of human intelligence. It was now easy to see how the Church, though she'd endure to the end, as promised by Our Lord, would become a mere remnant of herself. In the meantime, though, the priest had to get on with his job, *such as it was*. As for feeling thwarted and useless, he knew that feeling, but he also knew what it meant. It meant that he was in touch with reality, and that was something these days. Frequently reported, of course, like flying saucers, were parishes where priests and people were doing great things together. "But I've never seen one myself, if it's any consolation to you guys," Joe said, and paused.

Did the impressive silence mean that they were now seeing themselves and their situations in a new light, in the clear north light of reality? Bill, *finally*? Potter? Even Conklin? Joe hoped so, in all cases. On the whole, he was satisfied with the response. The bathwater bit hadn't gone down very well (groans from Potter, "Oh, *no!*" from Conklin), and there had been other interruptions, but Joe had kept going, had boxed on, opening cuts, closing eyes, and everybody, including Conklin, looked better to him now.

He wanted Hennessy and Potter to come out again, and not just to visit Bill, and not just to discuss their problems with him (Joe), though that would be all right. He wanted them to come out whenever they felt like it, whenever they needed a lift, a little priestly fellowship. Actually, there might be more for them with him, and more for him with them, than with Bill—who, to tell the truth, wasn't much fun. It could happen, first Hennessy and Potter coming, then coming with others, and these in turn with others. There would be nights, perhaps, when Bill wouldn't leave his room. "Where's Bill?" "Oh, he's listening to FM." Joe's rectory could become a hangout for the younger clergy, a place where they'd always be sure of a drink, a cigar, and if he put a table in the living room, never used now, a cue. Pastors at first critical ("Stay the hell away from there!") would sing his praises ("He sure straightened out that kid of mine"). Time marching on, Hennessy seldom seen, a bishop somewhere, first of the old crowd to make it, but the others still around, pastors now with curates of their own—tired, wiser men, the age gap narrowing between them and their old mentor, not so old, really, and in excellent health, eating and drinking less. A few missing, yes, the others, though, still coming out to Joe's—in a crazy world, an asylum of sanity—for priestly fellowship, among them, perhaps, Father Conklin, old Conk, a pretty lonely guy for a while there, until he started coming out, shaved off his mustache, found his lost faith, the road back, second spring, and so on.

"So what's the answer?" said Potter. "Watch the Twins?"

"Those bores," said Conklin.

Hennessy reproved them with a look, and spoke with his future authority. "What's the answer, Father?"

Eying Father Otto's glass on the coffee table, Joe said, "A few monks saved civilization once. Could be the answer again. Principle's sound. You'd have to work out the details. Wouldn't have to be monks. Could happen right here." Joe reached for Father Otto's glass, the last of the wine, and swirled it clockwise, counterclockwise, clockwise, denying himself before downing it. "Wanna see how Father is," he said then. "Be right back." At the door, as he was about to leave them, he turned and said, "How can we make sanctity as attractive as sex? Answer I got was 'Just have to keep trying.' Not much of an answer. Nobody remembers it—just the question. Guess it's the answer to all these questions. Be right back."

Father Otto's eyes opened when Joe approached the bed. "Get you anything, Father?" Joe asked.

"All right."

"Aspirin?"

"All right."

Joe administered aspirin and water to Father Otto, flipped his pillow, eased him down. "Want your shoes off?"

"Is the party over?"

"Not yet."

"Then why is everybody leaving?" said Father Otto, his eyes closing.

"Not yet," Joe said patiently, but when he returned to the study he saw that he was wrong.

Hennessy—he was the only one there—said, "How is he?"

"All right," Joe said.

Led by voices to a window on the street side, gazing down, he saw Bill, Potter, and Conklin talking to a young woman—older than they were, though—in a convertible.

"Conklin had to leave," Hennessy said.

Joe came away from the window. "So I see."

"Want to thank you, Father."

"It was Bill's party."

"All the same." Hennessy seemed to know what it was like to be a pastor. "Oh, and I should thank the housekeeper."

"Good idea." Joe saw Hennessy, who'd go far, off to the kitchen, and returned to the window. Below, the young woman moved over on the seat and the mustache took the wheel. Potter and Bill then fell all over themselves saying good-bye, making it look hard to do. And the convertible drove away. Then, to Joe's surprise—he had meant to say something about coming out again, soon—Hennessy appeared below, having, it seemed, left the rectory by the back door. Without a word or sign to Potter and Bill, who stood together, Hennessy got into the driver's seat of the black sedan at the curb. Potter and Bill then parted, rather solemnly, Joe thought, and Potter got into the *back* seat of the black sedan. It drove away. And a few moments later Bill entered the study.

"Who was that?" Joe asked.

"His mistress."

Joe stared at Bill. "Say that again."

Bill said it again.

"*That* what he calls her? How d'ya know *that*?"

"He told us."

"He did, huh?" Joe was thinking if he had a mistress he wouldn't tell everybody.

"He's honest about it, Father. You have to give him credit for that."

"I do, huh?"

Father Otto came in, looking much the same.

"You missed your bus," Joe said, and then to Bill, "Why don't they get married?"

"Complications."

"Like what?"

"She's already married."

Joe sniffed. "Great."

"Her husband won't give her a divorce. *He's* still a Catholic."

"Say that again."

Bill said it again.

Joe turned away. "And you wanna get back to your monastery—right?"

"How?" said Father Otto.

"I'll drive you."

"Eighty miles?" said Bill. "Can't he stay overnight?"

"He wants to get back to his monastery. I need the air. Well, what d'ya say, Father?"

"All right," said Father Otto.

FAREWELL

IN JULY, about a month before he was to retire, the Bishop of Ostergothenburg (Minnesota), through a clerical error, received a letter from the Chancery, his own office, asking the clergy of the diocese to contribute—pastors twenty dollars, assistants ten dollars—toward buying him a car.

The Bishop was unhappy about the letter. Why set a goal that might not be attained? Why be so explicit about the nature of the proposed farewell gift? Wouldn't men driving old clunks be put off? Why not just say "gift," or "suitable gift"? And, since he'd still be there, living upstairs in the brownstone mansion that was also the Chancery office, why say farewell? Arguing with the letter in this fashion, and wondering about the response to it, and hearing nothing, the Bishop spent his last days on the throne in a state of apprehension.

The day before he retired—he'd still heard nothing—he gave the girl in the office his set of keys to the aging black Cadillac that belonged to the diocese and was what he'd driven when he drove, which had been seldom.

The day after he retired (he'd still heard nothing), he went out and bought himself a car, a Mercedes—a gray one, as there wasn't a black one in stock. When his successor, Bishop Gau, saw it, he said, "Bishop, *we* were giving you a car. The clergy. I sent out a letter. I was just waiting until I heard from everybody."

"You should live so long," said the Bishop, embarrassed, certain that the response had been disappointing, if only because of the tone of the letter.

But when presented with what Bishop Gau smilingly called "the loot," which included a check from him for a hundred dollars and one from his chum Father Rapp for fifty dollars, the Bishop reckoned that it was only a few hundred less than it might have been ideally, and that the clergy—they were a good bunch, by and large—*did* appreciate him.

In the following days, weeks, months—he was still at it in October—he wrote and thanked the contributors but returned their contributions, saying the money could be put to better use. Quite a job, writing a hundred and sixty-eight letters by hand, personalizing each without showing partiality and without repeating himself, except in promising to remember each man at the altar, asking to be so remembered himself, and signing his name, "✝ John Dullinger," or, in a few instances, simply, "✝ John."

Early in October, when all the contributors had been taken care of (except Bishop Gau and Father Rapp) and the weather was still fine, he got out the Mercedes and drove forty-six miles to see a church under construction, the last of many he'd laid cornerstones for—his administration, so rich in achievements, will be remembered not least for its churches (Ostergothenburg *Times*). He was home safely, before dark, very pleased with the car's performance. He took two more trips. He was planning another—in October, with the trees a riot of color, the diocese was at its best. But then it rained and froze hard, and was winter.

At that point his retirement really began.

He still said the eight o'clock Mass at what was now the ex-cathedral (the new one was inconvenient), had breakfast at the rectory there, and lunch at home—prepared by the cleaning woman, though, since his housekeeper had retired. But between the time he got back in the morning and the time he left for his evening meal at the Hotel Webb, there was now a bad eight-hour period that hadn't been there before. He read, tried to watch TV, or just sat, sometimes wishing he had an absorbing hobby or a scholarly mind. (But how many bishops did, nowa-days?) If a car drove into the parking lot below, he went to the window to see who it was (too often only Bishop Gau or Father Rapp), then returned to his chair, to *Who's Who in the Mid-west*, which interested him more than *Who's Who in America* (he was in both), or to the *Times*, or the diocesan paper, which he read these days with more care and less satisfaction: there was a difference between reading and being the news.

Still, he didn't exactly envy Bishop Gau, with things as they were in the country and the Church, and becoming more so every day, though the diocese was still in pretty good shape, still heavily rural and Catholic. Bishop Gau was better suited to the times, more tolerant of the chumps coming out of the seminary, and of the older, suddenly unstable men, than the Bishop had been—running into one of them dressed in civvies, he'd say, "What's the matter, Father? Drunk, or ashamed of the priesthood?"

He could easily get carried away, which was bad even when the cause was good, and for this weakness he'd sometimes paid. Carried away, he'd written checks for a couple of hard-up dioceses behind the Iron Curtain whose bishops he'd met in Rome and liked, entertaining them and others at the Grand, where he always stayed, and then, returning home, had been humiliated by his pussyfooting consultors—thereafter all such checks had to be countersigned by the Auxiliary (as he was then). Bishop Gau, who had risen swiftly, helped by the Bishop at first, by himself and Rome later, understood finance, both high and low, better than the Bishop ever had. Bishop Gau and Father Rapp were now driving fast new Fords, identical silver ones, and the aging black Cadillac had vanished, presumably in a three-for-two deal. Bishop Gau handled such matters very well. Most matters, in fact. But he hadn't handled the Bishop's farewell gift very well.

The Bishop had been compelled, in the circumstances, to invest in an expensive car for which he had little use and then to take another loss by returning the contributions, the loot. That word, as he interpreted it, had left him no choice. But many who'd had their contributions returned to them would mention that awesome little fact, and that was where the Bishop had them, those two, Bishop Gau and Father Rapp, for he still had their checks. He often wondered what they must be thinking, and enjoyed the prospect of their hearing of his philanthropy from other contributors—a growing number. That was about all the Bishop had going for him these days.

His evening meal at the Hotel Webb had become more important to him these days, not that his appetite had increased. No, he just liked it at the Webb, where he'd always liked it, *more*: the good food there and the lighting (not dim), the tables and chairs (no booths), the background music, and, in December, the tasteful decorations and the big tree—a real one, green (un-whitewashed) and grown in the diocese. When people, other diners, paused at his table to pay their respects —they still did—he appreciated it more than he had in the past, and he wasn't so wary of those in the selling line, or of the clergy. And when told how sorry people were that he was retired he was happy to hear it, even when it reflected on his successor, as it sometimes did, at which times he praised his successor, or acted as if he hadn't heard.

That was how he acted one evening early in December when Monsignor Holstein—once rector of the Cathedral, Vicar-General of the diocese, and the Bishop's right-hand man, now only pastor of St John Nepomuk's, New Pilsen—said, "*Wie geht's*? You're sorely missed these days, John."

The Bishop invited Monsignor Holstein to sit down, which he did, in his white socks, saying, "Like old times, John."

Again the Bishop acted as if he hadn't heard, for, while agreeing it was like old times—the two of them together again at the Webb at the corner table, where they'd so often gone into the problems of the diocese and planned the campaigns— he was also regretting his later treatment of Monsignor Holstein, who had taken it so well at the time and recently had contributed his full pastor's share toward the farewell gift. Not vindictive, a good man in his way, Monsignor Holstein, but an idealist. Life had certainly been less difficult for the Bishop and others, including, unfortunately, the humanists at the normal school and the management of the Orpheum, after the man left town. Never content to leave well enough alone, always after the Bishop to do something—always something—Monsignor Holstein might have risen even higher, or stayed where he was, but for that weakness. And it came out again that evening at the Webb, with the cigars, when he spoke of this woman, a Mrs Nagel, in the country who thought she'd seen an apparition of Our Lady in a tree on several likely occasions. Always something, yes.

Oh, the Bishop agreed that it would take something sensational to get people thinking along more spiritual lines these days, and that this *could* be it, and, if so, that it would be a great thing for the diocese. But this woman's pastor, a reliable man, and this woman's husband, also reliable, a school-bus driver—they weren't too sympathetic, the Bishop understood, and that, while not unheard of in such cases ("Those closest to the scene are often the last to believe, John"), settled it for the Bishop. "See the Auxiliary," he said—he still thought of Bishop Gau as the Auxiliary—and let it stand.

"Saw him this afternoon, John."

Yes, the Bishop from his window had watched Monsignor Holstein arrive at the Chancery that afternoon. "What'd he say?"

"Can't give credence to this woman. Too many fakes."

Yes, but if the Bishop were to visit this woman mightn't *he* give credence to her? Monsignor Holstein seemed to think not. A slap in the face, wasn't it? Yes, but wasn't that what being retired was? So far, there had been—and, yes, there would be—fewer Christmas cards for him this year. It was the office that mattered, and nowhere more than in the Church—which otherwise would be just another institution and the gates of Hell would prevail against it. "The Auxiliary's right."

"John, what if he's wrong?"

"*He'd* still be right." The Bishop knew what he meant. "*He's* the Bishop now."

Monsignor Holstein said, "History hasn't been kind to the hierarchy in these cases, John."

Late that night, on his knees in his pajamas in the hallway, the Bishop pushed two envelopes under the door of the Chancery office, each envelope containing a Christmas card and a check, each check annotated some months earlier (in case he died unexpectedly): "Much obliged but can be put to better use, † J. D." And then he went to bed again, and this time he slept.

Traveling north the next afternoon in the Mercedes, he had no trouble until, a mile past Fahrenheit, turning off U.S. 52, he was fiercely honked at by a truck. He activated his turn signal to make amends, and drove, flashing and drumming, down a crushed-rock road a half-mile or so, coming then to a white farmhouse with an orange school bus in the driveway and, parked behind the bus, a car, the color of which was reassuring. With his signal still flashing, right, he turned in, left, and came to rest behind the black car.

Monsignor Holstein materialized alongside the Mercedes— so it seemed to the Bishop, who'd been having trouble again with his seat belt. They went around to the back of the house, Monsignor Holstein saying the front door wasn't used in cold weather, the Bishop assessing the Nagel property, noting the windbreak of blue spruce, the only sizable trees, though there were many seedlings.

Lest Mrs Nagel, perhaps put up to it by Monsignor Holstein, attempt to kiss the episcopal ring, which was a practice best confined to the clergy these days, the Bishop kept his gloves on—a needless precaution. Mrs Nagel was more concerned with Monsignor Holstein and his glasses, which had misted over in the warm kitchen, and which she polished with a linen towel while he stood blindly by, the Bishop enjoying the scene as one who, though older, wore glasses only for reading. In Mrs Nagel, who was blond, fairly young, fifty or so, he thought he saw the perky, useful, down-to-earth type of woman, a type he associated with hospital nuns and airline stewardesses, and liked, but he wondered that he didn't see something else in *her*.

"Now, shoo!" she said when she'd finished with the glasses, and returned to the cake she was frosting.

So the Bishop and Monsignor Holstein, both smiling—both firm believers in the supremacy of women in certain areas— left the kitchen and passed through the dining room, where, as in the kitchen, there were numerous plants, and on into the living room, where there were many more. Yes, all kinds of green, growing things (some, in tubs, were immense), and so thick that the Bishop, settling down on the settee, and

Monsignor Holstein, over by the TV, which was crawling with vines, had to look through a gap in order to see each other face to face.

"What'd I tell you, John?"

"What?"

"She's a real homemaker."

"Yes." Yes, that was in Mrs Nagel's favor, from the human standpoint. But when the Bishop thought of spiritual phenomena (of which he had no firsthand experience) he thought of way-out types. And that Mrs Nagel wasn't one of them, that she wasn't, according to Monsignor Holstein, unusually devout —only went to Mass on Sundays and holy days of obligation, to confession once a month—that she was to all appearances just a good, average Catholic, and not some kind of nut, was not in her favor, in the Bishop's view. That, though, was what was so wonderful about this case, according to Monsignor Holstein, who, though—in interpreting it as he did, as a sign from Heaven that the traditional precepts and practices of the Church were still O.K.—might have a vested interest, the Bishop feared. Monsignor Holstein, like many pastors in recent years, had been under considerable pressure from curates, parishioners, and media, all crying change, change, change. The Bishop had been under similar pressure but could be more objective now, being retired, and the truth was he couldn't see this woman, though he'd liked her in the kitchen, as one specially chosen by Heaven.

No, and when she came into the living room and sat where he could see her, beside him on the settee, he still couldn't see her in that role. Nor could he while, over coffee and cake, they listened to her story, which was on tape because she'd had so many visitors and dreaded repeating it. ("The Little Flower felt the same way," said Monsignor Holstein.) The Bishop resented that—the Little Flower, after all, was a canonized saint of many years' standing—and after he'd heard the tape, which he also resented, believing an exception should have been made in his case, he was silent.

"Bishop, you're free to ask questions," said Monsignor Holstein, whom the Bishop, since moving over on the settee for Mrs Nagel, could no longer see.

"Oh, am I?" said the Bishop tartly, pausing to let the words sink into the greenery where Monsignor Holstein was, and then he addressed himself to Mrs Nagel. "This branch"—this branch that had disturbed her sleep and that she'd been about to cut off one morning when the apparition first appeared to her in that very tree, the figure of a woman all in blue, smiling but shaking her head—"has it stopped brushing against the house?"

"Oh, no. Not when the wind blows hard from the north."

The Bishop had known as much from Monsignor Holstein, but was checking, testing. "Still brushes against the house?"

"Oh, yes, when the wind blows hard from the north. But I don't mind it *now*."

"No miracles yet," Monsignor Holstein said, from his concealed position, "and none are claimed."

There were footsteps overhead. The Bishop said, "What does your husband say, Mrs Nagel?"

"Oh, Mart never did mind it. His hearing's not so good."

There were footsteps on the stairs. The Bishop said, "I meant, what does he say about . . . all this?"

Mrs Nagel laughed—an honest laugh, the Bishop thought, nothing bitter about it. "Oh, Mart just thinks I'm seeing things."

Monsignor Holstein said, "Those closest to the scene are often the last to believe."

"Mart just doesn't like all the visitors," said Mrs Nagel. "Oh, he's very good. But there've been so many visitors—*busloads*—and we just don't have, you know, the facilities."

The back door slammed.

"Mart has to go for the kids," said Mrs Nagel.

The Bishop, with an effort, got to his feet, saying, "Shouldn't we move our cars, Monsignor?"

"It's all right," said Mrs Nagel.

"Ground's frozen," said Monsignor Holstein.

The Bishop moved over to the side window and peeked through the foliage there. He saw the bus go by on the lawn, traveling fast.

"Mart's late," said Mrs Nagel.

The Bishop, who'd been wondering why Mr Nagel hadn't come in to meet him, sat down, saying, "On these occasions" —so far there had been five occasions, all feast days of Our Lady, counting Christmas as one—"*she*, whoever she is, never says *who* she is?"

"No."

"And you've never asked?"

"No, I *know*."

The Bishop was silent for a moment, weighing the claims of faith against the demands of prudence, which had been his job for thirty years but hadn't got any easier. "And the message— it's always the same?"

"Yes."

"And you understand it?"

"Oh, yes."

"When did she tell you not to tell it to anybody else?"

"Oh, Father Barnett told me that."

The Bishop had known that, but again was checking, testing. "So he's the only one you've told it to?"

"And Mart. I told him before I told Father, but Father said that was all right. Just not to tell anybody else."

"You accept that from Father, do you?"

"*Oh, yes.*"

The Bishop had to smile. "Because he's your pastor and confessor?"

"Of course."

The Bishop had to smile again. "Even though he may not himself—believe?"

"Oh, yes." And Mrs Nagel, as she had earlier at the idea that she could be seeing things, laughed.

And that was exactly how a woman chosen by Heaven would and should respond to skeptics in this world, the Bishop believed, but what impressed him even more, what really moved him, was the way this woman deferred to her doubting pastor—to proper ecclesiastical authority.

What a wonderful world this would be if everybody did the same!

"I have no more questions, Monsignor," the Bishop said.

On the way home, alone in the Mercedes, the Bishop stopped at the rectory in Fahrenheit and rang the doorbell. "Is Father in?"

"In!" cried the housekeeper.

Father Barnett, in his late fifties, the kind of priest once taken for granted and now much prized, stable, was in his bedroom, in a wingback chair, with a pillow behind him. His first words to the Bishop were "Yesterday, Bishop, going for the alarm—I keep the clock there on the TV, out of reach, so I have to get up when it rings. Anyway, *phffft*. Slipped disk. What they *call* it, but *they don't know*. I've talked to 'em in Minneapolis. I've talked to 'em in St Paul. We had a couple of back men here from Rochester, up here fishing, and I talked to 'em. Waste of time. Some of 'em will admit it, some of 'em won't. Bishop, there are two parts of the human body we still know nothing about—the back and the head. Or next to nothing, I'd say, from talking to 'em. I've *stopped* talking to 'em, Bishop. Treat myself. A *firm* pillow, Bishop. *Not* soft. *Pressure's* what you want. Give your back support. Give your tissues a chance to heal. That's all you can do. And wait. I'll be all right in a few days, Bishop. I always am. Lucky I was able to treat it at once. Not like the last time. Was under the bed, straightening the boards—I have boards under my bed, Bishop—and couldn't make myself heard. Housekeeper out. Funny feeling, Bishop. Flat on your back, paralyzed, see your whole life pass before you, and so on. Sit down, Bishop. What brings *you* up here?"

"Mrs Nagel."

Father Barnett nodded.

"Monsignor Holstein was there."

Father Barnett nodded.

"Strange case."

Father Barnett nodded.

"Well, we can talk about it later, Father."

The Bishop (he hadn't sat down) stepped over to the phone, dialed the Chancery and spoke to the girl in the office, said he'd be in Fahrenheit for a few days ("Father Barnett's down with his back, nothing serious"), asked that the ex-cathedral and the Webb be notified, and hung up.

Father Barnett said, "This is mighty good of you, Bishop."

The Bishop nodded.

Then he went downstairs, and after speaking to the housekeeper he drove to the business district and made a few purchases, among them an alarm clock. He was recognized by clerks in stores, and by other shoppers, farmers and their wives who knew from his pastoral letters over the years that they were his favorite people, and when he was standing out in the street with the door of the Mercedes open, about to embark, he was honked at by a woman in a passing car with one of those musical horns—all of which was personally gratifying. But, more important, it showed that the Church was well regarded locally, and, *more* important, since there was nothing special about the town (except, maybe, its nearness to Mrs Nagel, whom one farmer's wife had mentioned), it showed that the diocese was still in good heart.

He pulled into the driveway when he returned to the rectory, and was sorry he had to leave the Mercedes out in the cold (only a one-car garage and Father Barnett's car was in it). Rather than ring the bell again, he entered the rectory by the back door, and, rather than wait until the day he departed, he presented the housekeeper with a box of chocolates then, along with a carton of eggs he said "somebody" had given him, rather than mention Mrs Nagel. With a breviary from Father Barnett, he went over to the church, where, after familiarizing himself with the light switches in the sacristy, he sat in a pew and read his office until the Angelus sounded automatically overhead, then stood. Returning to the rectory, again using the back door, he dined alone—not as well as he might have at the Webb but well enough.

On a tip from the housekeeper, he dropped in on a gathering of women in the church basement that evening, and a good thing he did, for word had got around that he was in residence, and there was a much larger turnout than usual, so he was told. At his insistence, the program proceeded as planned —a talk by one of the women on Christmas in Bethlehem— but when it was over he was again asked to speak. So he did —on Christmas in Rome, not very well. Leaving Rome, he traced his career in the Church, from curate to pastor to bishop, from North Dakota to Minnesota, to the diocese—incidentally, he said, the best place in the world to be at Christmastime, or any other time. For this he was warmly applauded, and should not have gone on to say that if the history of the human race had been different the first Christmas might have been cele- brated in more suitable surroundings, which had confused some of the women and offended the one who'd spoken earlier. Still, a very successful evening. Held in conversation (several women mentioned Mrs Nagel), he didn't get back to the rec- tory until ten.

He watched the news with Father Barnett. Then they had a drink, the able-bodied one going down to the kitchen for ice, and played cribbage—something the Bishop hadn't done since seminary. Father Barnett talked about his back and his parish, more about the former than about the latter, and didn't mention Mrs Nagel. After an hour, the Bishop retired to his room, out nineteen dollars and very tired, but lay awake in his new pajamas, listening to his new alarm clock, which had a loud tick.

The next morning, he saw that it had snowed on the Mercedes. After Mass, borrowing a broom from the housekeeper, he swept the car and part of the walk, working up an appetite. After breakfast, he looked in on Father Barnett, who asked about the attendance at Mass in his absence, as pastors will, and when given the count, which the Bishop knew from the housekeeper was three times the usual for a weekday, just nodded, as pastors will.

The Bishop made himself useful that morning—answered the phone, saw people (only two), and had a nice talk with the mailman, as well as with the man who delivered the fuel oil. In the afternoon, the Bishop called at the jail and admonished the no-good husband of a sad case he'd seen that morning (and written a check for), after which he called at the Chrysler garage, since there wasn't a Mercedes dealer in Fahrenheit, and arranged for the car to stay there, since it had again started to snow. He ordered snow tires for his rear wheels. Then he walked over to the Rexall store, where he exchanged his alarm clock for a travel model with a quiet tick, bought a combination snow brush and ice scraper for the Mercedes, and joined the proprietor at the soda fountain in a cup of coffee. He was soon having another with the local Lutheran minister—a pleasant, if somewhat intellectual, young man—who drove him back to the rectory.

That evening, seeing lights flashing in the church basement, he went over to investigate, and there were the Scouts!

He returned to the rectory too late for the news, after a nice talk with the Scoutmaster and an Eagle (a vocation?), but not too late for a drink and cribbage. He heard more about Father Barnett's back, and still nothing about Mrs Nagel, about whom he was now less inclined to ask. He did better at cribbage that night, losing eleven dollars, and went to bed less tired, though he'd had another busy day. For some time he lay awake, being pleased with his new clock, its quiet tick, and with himself, as he hadn't been for thirty years. It was good to be working as a parish priest again.

Three days later, the Bishop said good-bye to the housekeeper (with whom he'd had a nice talk) and to Father Barnett, who, now recovered, saw him to the front door, where (and this after repeatedly telling himself that he was retired, that it was none of his business now, that he wouldn't do this) the Bishop asked, "What about Mrs Nagel?"

Father Barnett replied, "She's a good person, Bishop. Of her sincerity I have no doubt. But there's this that leads me to believe—*not* to believe, Bishop. This so-called message. Since it was told to me in confession, I can't tell you what it is. But I can tell you this—that it's noncontroversial, nothing about praying for the conversion of Russia, China, or the U.S., and that I advised her to keep still about it (naturally, I didn't tell her this) because it wouldn't be believed, even by people who believe in the visions, and I was afraid she'd be hurt. Should've advised her to keep still about the visions—I know that now—but doubted at the time that I could make it stick. Should've tried. Should've imposed total silence, or none at all. I fell between two stools, Bishop, and I'm the one to blame. Not Mrs Nagel. She's a good person. Sincere. About all I can say, Bishop. There are two parts of the human body we still know nothing about."

After that, the Bishop left.

That evening, he dined at the Webb, said the eight o'clock

at the ex-cathedral the next morning, and resumed his routine at home. But the following night he was in the rectory at Gebhardt, near Fahrenheit, in response to a call for help (flu), and was there for five days, including a Sunday. The day he returned home, a call came from Glanville, in the western part of the diocese, word of his availability having spread among the clergy, and he was there for twelve days (two Sundays). While there, he had a call from Grasshopper Lake (flu again), whence he proceeded directly, not returning home. He spent the days of Christmas in Grasshopper Lake, and was very happy there, nightly entertaining members of the choir in the rectory—a grand bunch, for whom he kept the beer coming and had the piano tuned. From there he went on to Pumphrey, was there ten days, and so it was the middle of January when he got back home.

"Look," Bishop Gau said, "you don't have to go on livery-horsing"—what the monks at the college, who helped out in parishes on weekends, called it—but then he spoke of the situation at Buell (with a mission at Kuhl), where the pastor, one of the few priests in the diocese not ordained by the Bishop, and one of the few noncontributors to his farewell gift, was AWOL. Bishop Gau said he thought that Father (soon to be Monsignor) Rapp, even though it was the height of the bowling season, should go to Buell temporarily, to still the waters. The Bishop, believing he'd be better in such a delicate situation— more experience and more, though he was retired, clout—said he'd go, gassed up, and went.

In Buell and Kuhl, he disposed of the amateurish posters (Peace, Joy, Love, and so on) in the churches, got the women to scrub the floors and pews, the men to wax and polish them, participating in these activities himself. He visited all the parishioners in their homes, spoke here and there, honoring all invitations, and, in general, did what he could (threw big parties in both places) to make the people forget their late pastor, except, of course, in their prayers. Owing to the special circumstances, he also said Mass daily in Kuhl, which meant driving twenty-eight miles over an unimproved road before breakfast, through ice and snow, for which, though, the Mercedes was equipped.

When, after a month, he left Buell, the car had ice on its roof (unheated garage), frozen glunk under its fenders, salt on its tires, was looking older and grayer, but was still a great performer. The Bishop couldn't say as much for himself. After a bad night at home, he checked into the hospital (flu). When he came out ten days later, he was still in demand—two calls the first day—but had to say no, he wasn't himself yet, he was convalescing.

During this period, one afternoon about three, he saw Father Barnett arrive at the Chancery and a few minutes later, in his black car, Monsignor Holstein and Mrs Nagel.

I may be called upon, he thought, and put on his shoes, collar, and coat. Then he hovered about, waiting for the phone to ring, until he began to feel foolish doing this. So he sat down with *Who's Who in the Midwest*.

After a bit, though, the phone did ring.

The Auxiliary. "Bishop, I didn't know you'd visited Mrs Nagel."

Not a question, and so why say anything?

"Bishop, if I'd known"—as he should have known; that was the implication beneath the apologetic tone—"I would've called you earlier."

Again, not a question.

"I just now found out, Bishop."

Not a question.

"Bishop, if you're not too busy up there, could you come down?"

"Be glad to," said the Bishop, and hurried down.

Entering the big inner office, once his own, he stopped at the first chair, expecting to be directed to another, one near the desk, but he wasn't, and so sat down, as the others did then—Bishop Gau at the desk, to his right Monsignor Rapp, and facing them Mrs Nagel, Monsignor Holstein, Father Barnett.

"Mrs Nagel, I appreciate it, the way you've answered my questions, especially now I know you were visited by the Bishop, here. I'm sorry I didn't know that before," said Bishop Gau (the Bishop, *in petto*, replying, *O.K., O.K.*). "And I'm sorry I had to ask you to tell your story again, but thought I should hear it live. I can understand, though, why you decided to cut a tape. Just as I can understand your husband's feelings about visitors. I don't like to say it, Mrs Nagel, but it's possible, even for one in my position, to see too much of people. I'm sure the Bishop, here, will vouch for that."

The Bishop wasn't sure he would, but nodded to be helpful, wondering what the hell was wrong—*something* was, from the sound of it.

"Mrs Nagel, I want this understood. A thing like this can take years, even centuries, to check out, and then what? Win or lose, it's still a matter of faith. Anyway, whatever I've said, or might say, is in no way a judgment—official, personal, or any other kind—on you or your experiences. Is that understood, Mrs Nagel?"

"Sure."

"Good. Now, about your purpose in coming here today. While considering this, while *you* have my sympathy, Mrs Nagel, I must also consider what, in my opinion, is best for all concerned. And then, of course, I can only advise, not command. Now, what I advise, Mrs Nagel, is what your pastor, here, has already advised. Namely, silence. You've done very well so far."

"I know. But I don't like it this way, and I never did," Mrs Nagel said, giving the Bishop the impression that she had said this earlier, before he came in. "Why *shouldn't* I tell people the message?"

The Bishop thought he heard somebody (Monsignor Holstein?) moan.

"People wouldn't believe you, Mrs Nagel," said Father Barnett, sounding, the Bishop thought, *too* calm.

"*Some* people don't believe me now."

"More wouldn't," said Father Barnett. "Many more."

"I wouldn't mind. I don't mind now."

The Bishop distinctly heard Monsignor Holstein moan.

Bishop Gau said, "Mrs Nagel, I have to consider what, in my opinion, is best for all concerned, including you. And I advise silence. Not only about the message but about everything concerning your experiences. Silence, Mrs Nagel."

"But *why*?"

"My *dear* Mrs Nagel," said Monsignor Holstein, and then held his jaw, which he had been holding previously.

Monsignor Rapp cleared his throat in such a way as to attract attention. "Mrs Nagel, you haven't told anybody else the message—except your husband and us here?"

Us here?

"No, I haven't. But I think I should. I really think I should."

What's the message?

Bishop Gau said, "All right. Then I advise you to go ahead, Mrs Nagel. Tell people of your experiences, and tell them the message, too."

"You're not advising *that*!" Monsignor Holstein was very upset.

"If silence is impossible, yes, I am," said Bishop Gau.

"Why not?" said Mrs Nagel. "It's the truth, after all."

"No, *silence*!" cried Monsignor Holstein.

"No, the truth," said Bishop Gau. "It's the next-best thing. She can't go on like this. And we can't."

What's the message?

"You," said Monsignor Holstein, "*you* told me it was non-controversial."

"I meant," replied Father Barnett, "in the political sense."

What's the message?

" 'KEEP MINNESOTA GREEN'!" cried Monsignor Holstein, very upset. "What about the *rest* of the country? Or, for that matter, the *world*?"

Bishop Gau, swiftly rising from the desk, called upon the Bishop with a look and a nod, and stood with bowed head.

The Bishop, rising with an effort, responded with a prayer.

Mrs Nagel did reveal the message to visitors, and consequently Mr Nagel was less troubled by them, but life went on as before for the clergy concerned. Monsignor Holstein was very upset in April to hear that one of his ex-curates and one of the nuns from his parish school, whose union he had opposed, were being divorced in California, and in August Father Barnett was down with his back again. This took the Bishop to Fahrenheit again—quite a homecoming! He had continued with his livery-horsing, wasn't often seen at the Webb, and had put plenty of mileage on the Mercedes. He would have put on more if one day early in October, when the diocese was at its best and he was driving along U.S. 52, enjoying the scenery, he hadn't been sideswiped by a truck. He was in the hospital for a while, doing fairly well for a man of his age, he understood, until he took a turn for the worse.

PHARISEES

And he spake this parable unto certain which trusted in themselves that they were righteous, and despised others:

Two men went up into the temple to pray; the one a Pharisee, and the other a publican.

The Pharisee stood and prayed thus with himself, God, I thank thee, that I am not as other men are, extortioners, unjust, adulterers, or even as this publican.

I fast twice in the week, I give tithes of all that I possess.

And the publican, standing afar off, would not lift up so much as his eyes unto heaven, but smote upon his breast, saying, God be merciful to me a sinner.

—LUKE 18:9–13

TAKING A HARD-BOILED egg from the bowl on the bar, the publican—if he could be called that, for the joint was in his wife's name and he was now retired from his job as tax collector—squeezed it, trying to break the shell in his grip, and failed. So he held the egg down on the bar, rolled it back and forth, and in this manner broke the shell, which he removed. He sprinkled salt on the small end of the egg, and was eating this when a customer entered the joint.

"I see you're eating an egg," said the customer, an elderly Pharisee in a dark suit of conservative cut.

"I'm on this new diet," said the publican.

"What new diet is this, Walt?"

"It's this new cholesterol diet."

"Oh, yes. I've been hearing about it."

"In cholesterol, which I prefer to take in the form of eggs, I get all the things my body needs—animal fats, blood, nerve tissue, bile, to name but a few."

"Sounds good, Walt. Small brandy, please."

The publican was pouring a small brandy when a young thief entered the joint with a gun, saying, "This is a holdup."

While the holdup was in progress, another customer, an unfrocked Pharisee now engaged in community work, entered the joint, saying, "Hi, fellas. Hey, what's happening?"

"Watch it," said the young thief.

The ex-Pharisee then spoke to the young thief in a nice way, telling him that he could jeopardize his future in the community by such conduct, if, that is, he persisted in it.

"Maybe you're right," said the young thief sheepishly.

"I don't say I'm right. I don't say you're wrong," said the ex-Pharisee. "I try not to make value judgments. All I ask is that you think again. In the meantime, what'll you have, fella?"

"Just a beer."

"Two beers, Walt."

After serving them, the publican picked up the egg, which was eroding on the bar.

The Pharisee said, "Saw you this morning, Walt, unless my eyes deceived me."

"No, I was there. I was standing afar off."

"Walt, how is it I never see your wife there?"

"She's pretty busy."

"We're all pretty busy, Walt, but we can still find a few hours a day for the things that matter most."

"Such as?" said the ex-Pharisee.

"*We* were talking," said the Pharisee. "Walt and I."

"About what?" said the ex-Pharisee.

The publican leaned over the bar and, with a mouthful of egg, whispered, "Religion."

"Oh, *that*," said the ex-Pharisee.

A young woman, a dish, entered the joint rattling a can of coins. She approached the Pharisee with it.

"What's it for?" he asked.

"People."

The Pharisee shook his head. "I give tithes of all that I possess," he said.

"Oh, sure," said the dish, and rattled the can at the publican.

"My wife takes care of all that. She's off today."

"Oh, sure," said the dish.

"Hey, don't forget us," said the ex-Pharisee—who then folded a dollar and slipped it into the can.

The dish rattled the can at the young thief.

"We give at home," he said.

The ex-Pharisee slipped the young thief a five, which *he*, having seen how it was done, folded and slipped into the can, saying, "Now I see."

Watching the dish leave, the publican squeezed an egg, then rolled it on the bar, removed the shell, and salted the small end. "Want one?" he said to the Pharisee.

"Not today, Walt. Small brandy, please."

"Hey, what's happening?" said the ex-Pharisee. Going out into the entryway, where the dish was being attacked by rapists, he said, "Hi, fellas," and after apologizing for the young ex-thief, who had attacked one of the rapists from behind, he spoke to them all in a nice way, telling them that they could jeopardize their future in the community by such conduct, if, that is, they persisted in it. Not surprisingly, they all agreed.

The ex-Pharisee, the young ex-thief, the dish, and the six ex-rapists then repaired to the bar where they sat in a row, but could see each other in the mirror, all talking about poetry, music, drama, and better recreational facilities.

"Tired?" said the ex-Pharisee.

"A little," said the dish.

The young ex-thief said he'd be glad to go out with the can in her place, and offered to turn his gun over to her, the ex-Pharisee, or the ex-rapists, if that would make him more acceptable in her eyes, but that was not required of him, and he came back shortly with a full can.

"Don't thank me," he told the grateful dish. "Thank *him*."

The ex-Pharisee said, "You did it your way, fella."

The publican squeezed another egg, rolled it on the bar, removed the shell, salted the small end, and pointed it at the Pharisee invitingly.

"Not today, Walt. You see, I fast twice in the week, and this is one of my days."

"Big deal," said the ex-Pharisee. "I don't fast, and I don't give tithes, and I don't go to temple, and I thank God (if there is one) I'm not like the hypocrites that do!"

"And so say all of us," said one of the ex-rapists.

TINKERS

NOT COUNTING TEDDY bears and the like, they were seven—two teenage girls, two boys, seven and nine, a girl of five, Mama, and Daddy—and after eight days over land and sea, Daddy had a great desire to be out of the public eye. So when they landed in Cobh, though they'd intended to stay overnight there or in Cork, he phoned the hotel in Ballydoo, near Dublin, and was happy to hear that it would be all right to arrive that evening, a day earlier than planned. At Dublin, the train, to their surprise, became the boat train to Dun Laoghaire, and, since Ballydoo lay in that direction, they stayed on it—Daddy was happy to be saving a bit on taxi fares. At Dun Laoghaire, he was happy not to have to take ship again, and to find a taxi big enough (he'd been thinking they'd need two) to accommodate them and their luggage. Things, it seemed to him—after the hotel in St Paul, the heat in Chicago, the train trip to New York (who ever heard of washing your hair on a train?), the Empire State Building, Gimbel's, Schrafft's, Hammacher Schlemmer's (for compasses), and six days at sea—were looking up.

Except for overcrowding in the taxi, there was no difficulty until they reached their destination, almost. On the road, caught just in time by the taxi's headlights, there was a noisy gathering of some kind, around a two-tone horse.

"*Tinkers,*" the driver said with contempt, and proceeded slowly, half off the narrow pavement, while the tinkers and the horse, hoofs clonking, surged about in the dark.

"*Jem, don't sell that harse!*"

"*'M sellin' the bugger!*"

"Daddy," said the younger boy, who was sitting on Daddy's lap with Kitty, his stuffed cat, on his lap. "What's *wrong*?"

"Nothing's wrong. The man who owns the horse—his friend doesn't want him to sell it. That's all."

"Beebee'll buy it," said the older boy, who was sitting with Beebee, his teddy bear, on his lap, between Daddy and the driver, and gurgled at the thought of Beebee's wealth.

"Give it a rest," Daddy said.

Beebee, a millionaire (hotels, railroads, shipping, timber), had thrown his weight around on this trip—rather, had had it thrown around for him. When they checked into the hotel in New York, not a bad hotel, Daddy had been told, "Beebee usually stays at the Waldorf," and when they found their cabins on the ship, "Beebee usually goes First Class," and in the dining room on the first night, "Beebee usually drinks champagne"— and the wine steward, obviously a foreigner with ideas about American parents and children, had to be told no, that was not an order. Mama and Daddy were getting a little older, and had suffered a little more on this trip.

It was not their first one to Ireland. They had gone there for a year when the teenagers were small, again when the boys were smaller, and—the last time—the youngest child had been born there. Each time, they had rented a house in Ballydoo, and were hoping to do so again. And this time they wouldn't have to settle for what was immediately available, would be able to look around for a while, because they would be staying on as sole tenants of the hotel after it closed for the winter and the proprietors, Major and Mrs Maroon, went to London. This arrangement, initiated by Irish friends, had been concluded by correspondence, and since the rent would be reasonable, and Mama and Daddy could not recall a small hotel facing the harbor, they were anxious to see it. When they did, they recalled it (*them*, rather, these Victorian terrace houses, externally two, now internally one), now the—though it, or they, looked eastward to the sea—Westward Ho Hotel.

Without too much ado, Mrs Maroon, a fiftyish outdoors type, received and registered them as guests, which they'd be for two weeks before coming into their tenancy, and after they were shown their rooms and given tea in the lounge (in the presence of two other guests, women such as one sees in lounges in the British Isles, one reading a book, one knitting), Major Maroon, portly in a double-breasted blue serge jacket with one of its brass buttons, a top one, missing, so that the five remaining looked like the Big Dipper, appeared and proposed billiards—to the boys.

"Oh, I don't know about *that*," Daddy said, rising, and, with visions of cues plowing up green pastures of cloth, accompanied the boys and Major Maroon, who smelled of stout, to what he called the Smoking Room and Library, which smelled of dog.

Billiards proved to be a form of skittles, the little table to be coin-operated. Major Maroon financed the first game, Daddy the second, after which he, having looked through the Library, a bookcase containing incunabula of the paperback revolution (Jeeves, Raffles) and Aer Lingus schedules for the previous summer but one (Take One), said it was past bedtime. "Ah, the lads'll like it here," said Major Maroon, and showed them where they'd find the cues.

Later that night, when the children were, it was to be

J. F. POWERS

hoped, asleep in their rooms, and Mama and Daddy were having a duty-free drink in theirs (no bar at the Westward Ho), Daddy mentioned the little coin-operated table.

Mama said severely, "It's something we'll have to watch."

And Daddy resented this—that she'd not only taken his point and given it back to him as her own, which was one of her conversational tricks, but that she had turned it against him in the process. He was touchy on this subject, the subject of thrift. He had been profligate in the past, yes, though badly handicapped by lack of wherewithal to be profligate with. But he had learned plenty from Mama in the years since their marriage, and while he still had plenty to learn about thrift, he did think it was time she forgot the past and saw him, if not as her equal, *as he was today*. He hadn't used shaving cream or lotion in years, and he hardly ever changed a blade. He always bought, *if* he bought, the economy size, and didn't take the manufacturer's word for it—had learned from Mama to weigh price against ounces. He saved string, wrapping paper, claret corks, and the parts of broken things that might come in handy, though many never did—pipestems, for instance. He kept the family in combs he found in the street and washed—how many fathers, not professional scavengers, did that? He had paid for only three deck chairs on the ship coming over. In Ireland, he always smoked pensioners' plug. In short, he was probably America's thriftiest living author. Yes, but—this was where he pooped out as a paterfamilias—he could not provide his loved ones with a lasting home. He had subjected them to too many moves, some presented as trips abroad, but still moves. And this one, at the other end, before they left, had been the worst to date.

The big old house they'd occupied as tenants had been sold, and the new owners, Mr and Mrs Stout, who planned to turn it into a barracks with bunk beds for college students, as they'd done with other big old houses in the neighborhood, had been underfoot constantly in the last thirty days—asking if it would be all right to have a few trees cut down; the front sidewalk taken up; the yard paved for parking; a notice posted at the college inviting students, possible occupants of the bunk beds, to drop around; and more, much more. It had been hard not to go along with all these requests, even though Mama and Daddy were free, legally, to reject them and were up to their ears in packing, for the Stouts were very pleasant people and were motivated, it seemed, by charity in their dirty work. "Golly, where will those poor kids park their cars?" Mama and Daddy had felt guilty about rejecting the paving project, even when the trees came crashing down. The Stouts had been too much.

Fifteen years earlier, when Mama and Daddy had begun their career as tenants and travelers, when they'd surrendered their house in the woods, the first and last place they'd owned, to the faceless men of the highway department for a service road, and a few years later, when they'd surrendered the beautiful old place, the oldest house in town, to the faceless men of the department of education for a parking lot (now occupied by a faceless building), there had been acrimony, arguments about the nature of progress, between usurpers and usurpees. This time, no. The Stouts, such pleasant people, had been too much. Mama and Daddy were still talking and, in the case of Mama, still dreaming about this move.

That night, at the Westward Ho, she suddenly said, "You know who *they* are?"

"Who *who* are?"

"The Maroons."

"How d'ya mean? Who *are* they?"

"The Stouts."

"Oh, now, I wouldn't say that."

The hotel closed for the winter on schedule, but for some reason the Maroons were still there a week later. Mama and

Daddy then heard from the youngest child, to whom Mrs Maroon had confided, that London might not agree with Happy. (This was the *genius loci* of the Smoking Room and Library, a hairy terrier that looked like Ireland on the map when in motion, a very mixed-up dog, to judge by the way—ways, rather—it relieved itself.) So Mama and Daddy spoke up, and two days later the proprietors checked out.

Life in the hotel was then homier for the tenants in one respect than it had been in any house to date, in that they had a pet, but otherwise was much the same for them there as anywhere else they'd settled for a time. The children—the teenagers attending school in Dublin, the younger ones in Ballydoo —had their new friends (the older boy often entertaining his at billiards: it had occurred to Daddy but evidently not to Major Maroon that it would be a good idea to leave the tenants with the key to the little coin-operated table). Mama, of course, had her shopping, cooking (in a kitchen caked with grease), and her house- or hotel-keeping. Daddy had his "office," a small room in the uninhabited part of the hotel, where he read the *Irish Times* and the *Daily Telegraph*, listened to the BBC, and did his writing.

He was between books, preparing to strike out in a genre new to him. What he had in mind was a light-hearted play, later to be a musical and a movie, about a family of campers, possibly Germans, who, on arriving in Ireland and wishing to do it right, would hire one of those colorful horse-drawn caravans but make the mistake of pulling into a bivouac of tinkers for the night. There would be singing, dancing, drinking, and fighting around the campfire, a nice clash of lifestyles (*these*, in the end, would be exchanged!) with plenty of love interest along the way—German boy, tinker girl, or vice versa, maybe several of each for more love interest. He couldn't overdo it, since he was writing for the theatre, but there *were* problems. He knew nothing about tinkers or Germans or, they might be, French, and if he got them acting and talking right, would they, particularly the tinkers, be intelligible to an American audience? Would this audience—as it must—immediately grasp what the Germans, French, or, they might be, Japanese would not; namely, that the tinkers were not proper campers like themselves? He was afraid he'd have to do the whole damn thing in basic American first, then do a vivid translation, thoughts of which, since he was still in several minds as to the campers' nationality (*Wunderbar! C'est magnifique! Banzai!*) turned his stomach slightly. He had once read that nobody ever wrote a best seller, however bad, without believing in it, but he doubted this, and even if it was true, he doubted that it was true of a smash-hit play, however bad. And what had struck him as a good idea for one ("This one will run and run") continued to do so.

But he wasn't getting on with it. Hoping to see or hear something he could use, perhaps another line of tinkerese to go with those he had ("A few coppers, sor," and, "I'll pray for you, m'lord"), he would take the train into Dublin, visit the junky auction rooms on the Quays, the secondhand bookshops, just wander around—too bad, what was happening to Dublin's fair city—and come home tired, with a few small purchases, always pastry from Bewley's, cherry buns, shortbread, barmbrack (at Halloween), or fruitcake (as Christmas approached).

This they'd have that evening in the lounge, some with tea, some with cocoa and wearing their pajamas—a nice family scene, yes, but one of those present was an impostor, Daddy would think, considering his responsibilities and how he'd shot the day. On some evenings, while Mama was reading aloud from Captain Marryat, one of the few clothbound authors in the Library, Daddy would have a new chapter from Beebee's family history to read, which was then in the writing and remarkable in one respect: the Beebee of the period (eighteenth century) had had a wife, children, and business associates with names like Kitty, Pussy, Toydy, Lion, Bear, Dragon, and Owl, whose present-day descendants were in precisely the same relationship to the present-day Beebee!

Stability, Daddy would think.

On some evenings, when the younger children were in bed and he was saying good night to them (another nice family scene) he would hear something to his credit, that the little girl liked living so close to the sea, the boys so close to the trains—sea and trains thanks to him, he'd think then, though the railway was now owned by Beebee, he understood. He was wary of Beebee. The millionaire had such a poor opinion of the Westward Ho that he wouldn't buy it, he said—when Beebee spoke, it was through the older boy, dryly, rather like Mama's father—but Beebee wasn't in such good shape himself. He was worn smooth in places, and had a new nose (thanks to Mama) of different material, which he was sensitive about, withdrawing from the conversation if it was mentioned, as he did when frivolous remarks were made about his extreme wealth. "Well, good night, Millions," Daddy would say—and might be told that Beebee (though present) was somewhere in the Indian Ocean, aboard *Butterscotch*, his yacht, on a trip around the world, and on his return would be buying new motorbikes for Lion and Bear, who, being teenagers, had crashed theirs. "On the yacht?" "They're not with Beebee now. They radioed him about it." "What'd Beebee say?" " 'Crazy kids. Just have to buy 'em new ones.' " The older boy would gurgle, and Daddy would shake his head in wonder at Beebee's magnanimity. "Lion and Bear— they're back at the ranch?" "Um." "That's the one in Colorado?" "Partly." "It's a big ranch." "Um."

Daddy would then retire to the same room he and Mama had occupied on the first night, where they now had two relatively easy chairs and special lighting—they now sat by two brass table lamps that he'd picked up at an auction, instead of under the traditional bulb suspended from the ceiling—and there, with the radio and the electric fire playing between them, with their reading matter and drinks, they'd spend the long evening.

By the middle of December, they were talking more about their problem. They had looked at a couple of houses that were too small, and one just not what they'd come to Ireland to live in (a thirties-period "villa" of poured concrete spattered with gravel—the agent had called it "pebbledash"), and one very nice place, "small Georgian," with a saint's well on the grounds, but unfurnished and rather remote *and*, it then came out, not for rent, the agent having presumed that they, as Americans, might buy it. That was all they'd done about their problem by the middle of December.

They weren't worried yet. They had the hotel, if need be, through January, and felt secure there, so secure that on some evenings they were inclined—at least Daddy was—to feel sorry for their homeowning friends in America. He wouldn't, he'd tell Mama, want to be Joe out there in the country, with the highway, perhaps, to be rerouted through his living room; or Fred by the river, with the threat of floods every spring (the American Forces Network, Europe, reporting six-foot drifts in the Midwest); or Dick in town, with that big frame house to paint every five years and those big old trees that, probably now heavy with snow and ice, might *not* fall away from the house if they fell.

One evening, after doing a spot of plumbing—Ireland, the land of welcomes, is also the land of running toilets—he told Mama that hard though it was to go through life making repairs in other people's houses and hotels, knowing that whatever you did you'd probably be doing again somewhere else, it was better than making repairs in your own home, knowing that THIS IS IT, that the repairs might well outlast you, or the dissolution of your household. This was one of the consolations of vagrancy that he hadn't heard about until he heard it from his own lips, and he liked it very much. Mama took exception to it.

One evening he told her that he'd heard a man on the BBC, on *Woman's Hour*, say that mobile families were superior families—and she took exception to it. He hadn't been listening carefully until it was too late, so couldn't give her the details, only remembered that mobile families were more . . . couldn't remember exactly what, only that they were superior, that the man, who was the spokesman for some association or group that had carried out a survey and issued a report, had said that mobile families were more . . .

"*More mobile?*"

One of her conversational tricks.

One morning, about a week before Christmas, they had a letter from Mrs Maroon. She thanked them for sending on the mail, said that cabbages were very dear in London, and asked to be remembered, as her husband did, to the children and Happy. In a postscript, she said not to send on the mail for the time being, as she and her husband would be at the hotel shortly.

Mama and Daddy then had a lengthy discussion about "shortly," about whether it only meant *soon* or could conceivably mean *briefly*.

That evening, the Maroons returned.

Happy was glad to see them, and others were, too. "How long you staying?" the older boy asked them right away— a good question, but lost in the excitement. "*Daddy* calls Happy *Slap!*" the youngest child informed them, and Mama quickly offered them tea.

With the proprietors in residence again, the hotel wasn't what it had been for the tenants—their relationship to the dog, for instance, wasn't the same. No, even though proprietors and tenants went their own way, ate at opposite ends of the dining room, and in the evening at different times (like first and second sittings at sea, parents with small children at the first), it wasn't the same. And again, as before the proprietors left for London, there was a certain amount of overlap and flap in the kitchen. (Mama had once expected to have her very own.) Daddy was in trouble, too. After two days, he moved from the part of the hotel now occupied by the proprietors—lest his typing disturb them, his playing the radio during working hours scandalize them—to the part occupied by the tenants.

The next morning, in his new office, listening to *Music While You Work* on the BBC and reading the *Irish Times* before getting to grips with the light-hearted play (in which the campers were now Americans), he came upon an item of professional interest to him: "County councils and urban district councils throughout Ireland are awaiting the publication of a report prepared by the Government Commission on Itineracy." Shouldn't that be Itinerancy? "It is expected that the report will contain several broad proposals for integrating itinerants into the normal life of the community. Their presence has often caused friction, particularly in Limerick and Dublin suburbs, where residents claim that they indulge in fighting and leave a large amount of litter." Yes, he'd seen some of it, and while the women, babes in arms, begged in the streets, the men, as somebody had said in a letter to the *Irish Times*, drank and played cards in a ditch. "During the winter, the tinkers usually camp at sites in these suburbs, or at sites in provincial towns, but some caravans stay on the road all the year round." Nothing new here, nothing for him. "There are six main tinker tribes." Oh? "The Stokeses, Joyces, MacDonaghs, Wards" . . . now, *wait* a minute . . . "and Redmonds."

So the odds against him were greater than he'd thought.

He took the next train into Dublin, left the *Irish Times* on it, and gave the first tinker woman he met a coin, wanting and not wanting to know her name.

On the Quays, he found some secondhand paperbacks for

the younger children, and was tempted by a copper-and-brass ship's lamp, not a reproduction and not too big, to be auctioned that afternoon ("about half-four," he was told). He bought a French paring knife for Mama in a restaurant-supply place—he liked doing business in such places.

He then had a pot of tea and two cherry buns at the nearest Bewley's, selected a fruitcake, and, to pass the time until half-four, just wandered around, window-shopping and making a few small purchases: a couple of ornaments for their Christmas tree, which was now up in the lounge and rather bare; a tool, with a cloven end and an attractive hardwood handle, to remove carpet tacks and also suitable for upholstery work, should the need arise for him to do either; some brass screws that might come in handy and were, in any case, nice to have; a hardcover notebook (they did these very well in the British Isles) such as he already had several of, with inviting cream paper that he couldn't bring himself to violate; more soft-lead (3B) pencils.

For some time, he stood looking in a seedsman's window. Quite an idea, he thought, having a section of a real tree there so one could see the various kinds of branches, the various kinds of saws required to get at them, saws shown cutting into them, and one, an ordinary carpenter's saw, shown cutting into a sign, just a plank, that asked the question "WHY NOT HAVE THE SAW FOR THE JOB?" Since on the property one might own someday there would be many trees, wood being the fuel of the future, and one would spend so much time up on an extension ladder (shown) doing surgery, and might otherwise fall and kill oneself, and with no insurance and six dependents, why not—except for the expense—have the saw for the job? (Beebee would.)

On the way back to the Quays, he booked two seats to a coming play, and because the tickets hadn't been printed yet, and would be posted to him, he was asked to give his name and address (was suddenly sensitive about the former), and was told when he asked for a receipt, "Ah, that's all right." This he accepted, after a moment, remembering where he was (Ireland) and an attendant at this same theatre one night not undertaking to tap him on the shoulder when the time would come to leave (early, to catch the last train) but giving him his watch to hold. And also remembering the fruit huckster at the Curragh on Derby Day, short of change so early in the afternoon and on whose wares they'd lunched to economize, telling him to come back and pay later. And the bellboy at the old hotel in Dublin on their first visit to Ireland who, after making several trips up to their room to call them to the phone in the lobby (they were running an ad for a house), had politely declined to be tipped further for such service, which had continued. "Ah, that's all right." That was the beauty of, and the trouble with, Ireland.

He was early for the ship's lamp, and thought the prices made by the lots before it rather low, but saw right away that this was not going to be the case with the lot he wanted—a familiar feeling at auctions. He came into the bidding at the first pause, and after the figure he'd had in mind had been passed, the maximum figure, which was subject to revision in the event, he was still in it. And money talks! He arranged to take the ship's lamp with him, rather than come back for it the next day, saying he lived "down the country" and had to catch a train.

He returned to Ballydoo tired, took the short cut from the station, and entered the hotel by the rear, expecting to find Mama in the kitchen, but didn't. He assumed that something was taking too long in the oven. He went upstairs, expecting to find her in their room having a glass of stout by the electric fire, and perhaps reading the *Daily Telegraph*, but found her lying on the bed, face down, in the cold and dark.

"What's *wrong*?"

"Look in the lounge."

"What d'ya mean?"

"*Look in the lounge.*"

He threw a blanket over her, and hurried downstairs.

The younger children were in the lounge, as he'd expected they would be, with the Christmas tree turned on, but somebody else was there, too: a woman—he'd seen her there before, three months before—knitting.

So Daddy, right away, got on the phone, and during the second sitting (there wasn't a first one), with the help of the local taximan, who also did light hauling, they moved themselves and their effects, including groceries and Christmas tree, out of the hotel and into a house down the road. The agent was there, waiting for them with a temporary lease, which was signed by flashlight—the only hitch (a blow to Mama) was that the electricity was off in the house. But the agent had already called the Electricity Supply Board, and the teenagers, who had been dispatched to the shop that kept open, were soon back with a bundle of turf and a dozen candles. And a candle, as Daddy pointed out, gives a surprising amount of light for a candle. There was coal in the shed, enough for two or three days, also kindling, and the kitchen range only smoked at first. They had their meal of baked beans and scrambled eggs by candlelight in the kitchen. Then they had their dessert—the fruitcake from Bewley's—by firelight in the parlor, some with tea, some with cocoa and wearing their pajamas, and talking about the ship's lamp, which there hadn't been time to examine until then.

Mama explained its red and green windows and its internal parts—apparently all there except for the wick. Daddy was interested in the manufacturer's name and address (Telford, Grier & Mackay, Ltd., 16 Carrick St., Glasgow), almost invisible from polishing. He pointed out that copper and brass (and silver) looked better when slightly tarnished, better still when seen, as now, by firelight. No, he didn't know where the ship's lamp's *ship* was (the younger boy wanted to know), probably it *wasn't*, and no, didn't know what he was going to do with the ship's lamp. Just liked it, just liked looking at it, he said, and, seeing that that wasn't enough, said he might put it over the front door of the house they might have in America someday. They wouldn't have to worry about it, he said—these old ship's lamps were made to be out in all kinds of weather.

"Will we get to keep it, Daddy?" said the younger boy.

"Yes, of course."

"Daddy, he means the house," said one of the teenagers.

"Oh."

"The house in America," said the younger boy. "Will we get to keep *it*?"

"Yes, of course—when we get it." And Daddy remembered the paperbacks—one of them, actually, and then the others—still in his coat. Taking a candle, he went to the cloakroom (good idea, having a cloakroom in a house), and while there, heard a knock at the front door—hoped it was the Electricity Supply Board. It was a man in blue, a gray-haired *garda*, who had believed the house to be vacant, he said, until he saw the wee light from the fireplace.

"We're waiting for the E.S.B."

"Ah. You and the family were at the hotel, sir."

"We were, yes."

"And now you're here."

"We are, yes."

"And will you be here long, sir?"

"Six months. Have a six-month lease. May be here longer. Probably not. It's hard to say. We never know."

"Ah, indeed. We never know. Good night, sir."

No, not the E.S.B., Daddy said, returning to the parlor, and gave the younger children the paperbacks, saying of one (*The Market: The Buying and Selling of Shares*, in which subject the older boy had shown an encouraging interest—Beebee's influence?), "If you have any questions, ask Millions." And noticed how quiet it was then, so quiet the turf could be heard burning, puffing.

"Beebee's gone," said the youngest child.

Daddy looked at the older boy.

"Sold Beebee."

"Now, *wait* a minute."

"A friend wanted to buy him. One of my friends."

It was painful to hear the pride in the boy's voice, in having friends, and Daddy knew what Mama was thinking, that this is what comes from being a mobile family. "*What* friend? What's his *name*? Where's he *live*? What *kind* of boy is he? Do *I* know him? It doesn't matter. You can't *sell* Beebee."

"I can always buy him back. That's part of the deal."

"*You can't sell Beebee.* Go get him. *Now.*"

"In the morning," Mama said.

"No, *now.*"

"He's got his pajamas on," Mama said.

"He can take 'em off."

Mama said nothing.

"O.K., *I'll* go."

So Daddy went, and at the friend's house, a cottage, did *not* say that the older boy missed his teddy bear, or that others did, but still told the truth. "Beebee was a gift from my mother"—his mother whose funeral he, in Ireland then, had been too broke to attend—"and I don't think she'd like it if he left us." The friend, his mother, his older sister, his two small brothers, they all seemed to understand. No trouble. Ten bob. And after a cup of tea, Daddy and Beebee—who looked the same, grumpy, stuffy, and still sure of himself—came home.

The electricity was on when they got there, the Christmas tree was going, and the younger children were in bed.

When Daddy put Beebee in with the older boy and said,

"Good night, Millions," there was a gurgle in the dark that made him wonder if he'd been taken.

"Where's the money?"

"Spent it."

"*What?* Already? All of it? On *what*?"

"Billiards."

Mama and Daddy had work to do, but were tired, and spent the evening in the parlor before the fire (it and the tree gave enough light to talk by), with their drinks. There hadn't been time until then for him to tell her what Mrs Maroon had said: that it hadn't originally been the plan to open the hotel for the Christmas season, that unforeseen requests for bookings (she had thanked him again for sending on the mail) and the dearness of things in London had combined to change the plan, and that she and her husband had hesitated to inform the tenants, for fear of upsetting them.

"We're well out of that," he said.

"Yes," she said.

They talked about the house, about the carved mahogany chimney piece, which, though, was spoiled by the glazed tiles (these reminding him of the Men's Room at the Union Station in Chicago), and about what they'd need in the way of equipment—different plugs for the brass lamps, for instance, for there were a number of types in use in Ireland and they had the wrong type for this house, which, though, had to be expected.

"The odds are three or four to one against you whenever you move," he said.

"Yes," she said.

He tuned in the American Forces Network, Europe, for the home news, and heard that there was a blizzard sweeping across the Midwest. Then "Mr Midnight" came on with his usual drivel about "music for night people, romance, and quiet listening . . . lonesome sounds of a metropolitan city after dark"

—and they discussed "metropolitan city," Mama saying that it was redundant, Daddy that he didn't like the sound of it but pointing out that it might not be redundant in certain circumstances, citing bishops who were metropolitans, whose seats, sees, or see cities, were rightly called metropolitan seats, sees, or cities. But Mama still took exception to it.

After that, they talked—he did—about their friends in America, about Joe and the highway, about Fred and the river, more about Dick and those big old trees that were probably heavy with snow and ice now, and about that big frame house that had to be painted every five years.

"That's one good thing about a house like this," he said. "Pebbledash."

"Yes," she said.

TITLES IN SERIES

For a list of titles, visit www.nyrb.com or write to:
Catalog Requests, NYRB, 435 Hudson Street, New York, NY 10014

MURRAY KEMPTON Part of Our Time: Some Ruins and Monuments of the Thirties
DAVID KIDD Peking Story
ROBERT KIRK The Secret Commonwealth of Elves, Fauns, and Fairies
ARUN KOLATKAR Jejuri
TÉTÉ-MICHEL KPOMASSIE An African in Greenland
GYULA KRÚDY Sunflower
PATRICK LEIGH FERMOR Between the Woods and the Water
PATRICK LEIGH FERMOR Mani: Travels in the Southern Peloponnese
PATRICK LEIGH FERMOR Roumeli: Travels in Northern Greece
PATRICK LEIGH FERMOR A Time of Gifts
PATRICK LEIGH FERMOR A Time to Keep Silence
D.B. WYNDHAM LEWIS AND CHARLES LEE (EDITORS) The Stuffed Owl:
An Anthology of Bad Verse
GEORG CHRISTOPH LICHTENBERG The Waste Books
H.P. LOVECRAFT AND OTHERS The Colour Out of Space
ROSE MACAULAY The Towers of Trebizond
NORMAN MAILER Miami and the Siege of Chicago
JANET MALCOLM In the Freud Archives
OSIP MANDELSTAM The Selected Poems of Osip Mandelstam
GUY DE MAUPASSANT Afloat
JAMES McCOURT Mawrdew Czgowchwz
HENRI MICHAUX Miserable Miracle
JESSICA MITFORD Hons and Rebels
NANCY MITFORD Madame de Pompadour
ALBERTO MORAVIA Boredom
ALBERTO MORAVIA Contempt
JAN MORRIS Conundrum
ÁLVARO MUTIS The Adventures and Misadventures of Maqroll
L.H. MYERS The Root and the Flower
DARCY O'BRIEN A Way of Life, Like Any Other
YURI OLESHA Envy
IONA AND PETER OPIE The Lore and Language of Schoolchildren
RUSSELL PAGE The Education of a Gardener
BORIS PASTERNAK, MARINA TSVETAYEVA, AND RAINER MARIA RILKE
Letters: Summer 1926
CESARE PAVESE The Moon and the Bonfires
CESARE PAVESE The Selected Works of Cesare Pavese
LUIGI PIRANDELLO The Late Mattia Pascal
ANDREY PLATONOV Soul and Other Stories
J.F. POWERS Morte d'Urban
J.F. POWERS The Stories of J. F. Powers
J.F. POWERS Wheat That Springeth Green
CHRISTOPHER PRIEST Inverted World
RAYMOND QUENEAU We Always Treat Women Too Well
RAYMOND QUENEAU Witch Grass
RAYMOND RADIGUET Count d'Orgel's Ball
JEAN RENOIR Renoir, My Father
GREGOR VON REZZORI Memoirs of an Anti-Semite
TIM ROBINSON Stones of Aran: Pilgrimage
FR. ROLFE Hadrian the Seventh
WILLIAM ROUGHEAD Classic Crimes
CONSTANCE ROURKE American Humor: A Study of the National Character